2) Nuns

3) Monastic and
religious life of women

THE NUNS

Marcelle Bernstein

THE NUNS

J. B. Lippincott Company
Philadelphia and New York

For Eric
AND OUR RED PAVILIONS

Copyright © 1976 by Marcelle Bernstein
First edition
Printed in the United States of America

Published by arrangement with Bantam Books, Inc.

U.S. Library of Congress Cataloging in Publication Data

Bernstein, Marcelle.
    The nuns.

    1. Nuns. 2. Monastic and religious life
of women. I. Title.
BX4210.B377   271'.9   76–14794
ISBN–0–397–01135–0

Contents

Acknowledgments

It would be impossible to thank individually all the nuns and sisters in so many countries who, by their cooperation, made this book possible. They will know who I mean and, I hope, realize how grateful I am. But there are some I must single out.

First, Sister Morag Michael of the community of Saint Mary the Virgin. As the first sister I ever met, her tremendous enthusiasm for the religious life really caught my imagination. I owe a great debt to Father Gilbert Volery, secretary to the Conference of Major Religious Superiors, who gave so freely of his time and knowledge. Sister Honor Basset of the Society of the Sacred Heart and Mother Mary Joseph of the Vocation Sisters were sources of invaluable guidance. Sister Margaret Moran of the Good Shepherd sisters, Sister Madeleine of the Augustinian Sisters of Meaux, Sister Eileen Gielty of the Institute of the Sisters of Notre Dame of Namur, and Mother Joanna of the Deaconess Community of Saint Andrew gave much advice. David Miles Board and the Catholic Information Office did everything they could.

My special thanks for all the kindness shown to me by the many nuns I visited in Europe and America, particularly Sister Marie-Marthe of the Holy Child Convent in Neuilly and Sister Maria Lorenzina Guidetti of the Daughters of Saint Paul. The Maryknoll Sisters in New York, Sister Liz Thoman in Los Angeles, and Sister Pearl McGivney in the Coachella Valley all showed more hospitality than I can ever repay. I would like to acknowledge the help of the Catholic Central Library, and of the British Museum for access to their private pornography files—a curious experience. Finally, and most deeply, I thank Mother Michael and the Carmelites of Llandovery for showing me what the religious life can be.

Introduction

My first contact with nuns was a revelation.

I had gone to visit the Community of Saint Mary the Virgin in Wantage, Berkshire, for a magazine article I was writing. I knew what nuns would be like: I had a vivid picture in my mind's eye, acquired from books and films. At worst, I expected formidable strictness and the stuffy aura of sanctity; at best, sweet, unworldly women encased in black and white, hands folded in prayer, living in a convent out of *The Sound of Music*.

What I found could not have been more different. Here were chatty, intellectual women perfectly prepared to discuss not only their reasons for entering but the difficulties they encountered, not only what it meant to sacrifice much emotional and all sexual satisfaction but where they bought their underwear (in bulk from Marks and Spencers).

I left wanting to know much more. Surprisingly, most books on the subject seemed intended for the knowledgeable insider; they were

13

written by academics and theologians, or by nuns for other nuns, or by ex-nuns seeking to justify themselves. None of them answered my questions. I decided that the best way to learn what I wanted to know was to write a book myself.

My qualifications for such a task were, to say the least, unlikely. I could hardly have had a less Christian background; I am a Jew. I am in no sense a religious person; neither, I confess, did I have much sympathy for such a way of life. Celibacy, which more than any other single factor sets the nun apart from most other women, may be regarded by Christians as understandable, justifiable, even desirable, but Jews are likely to see it as a form of sterility and view it with disfavor.

On the other hand, as a journalist I was used to submerging my own opinions. I could be objective, because I had no ax to grind. I also was genuinely interested for two reasons: because of my husband, nominally at least a Christian, and my growing fascination. Fanaticism is a compelling force, and there is no doubt that nuns are, in our terms, fanatics. "No one is going to be a successful nun," one novice mistress told me, "unless she's touched with fire."

So I embarked on *The Nuns*. At that time there were a million of them. (In addition to those women in Roman Catholic orders, there are a few Protestant sisters; some are included here, but I have concentrated on the Catholic majority.) In precise religious terms, those in active orders—teaching, perhaps, or nursing—are sisters. Only those in contemplative communities, forever enclosed, are, strictly speaking, nuns. But "nun" is generally held to mean both.

Deciding which orders to cover in detail and which to mention briefly posed a major problem. In America alone in 1975 there were 359 different orders, and convents beyond number. The Sisters of Mercy, largest of orders worldwide, had almost two hundred convents just in Ireland, not to mention schools, colleges, hospitals, and homes. Ultimately, the choice had to be haphazard. Some orders—the Carmelites and Cistercians, for example—I found particularly intriguing, the Carmelites because of the character of their extraordinary Spanish founder, the Cistercians because of their extreme asceticism. Some I liked for their unexpected work, such as the French Sisters of Marie Joseph, who nurse in prisons; others were chosen because they are in some way experimental, like the Deaconess Community of Saint Andrew, which has sisters in the only permanent mixed-sex religious community in Britain. Then there were communities which had undergone extraordinary change, in particular the Immaculate Heart Sisters in California, all of whom have been officially "reduced" to lay people. Finally, there were individuals who stood out from the rest, women attracting attention because of what they were saying or doing.

Nuns at this moment are in an unprecedented position, caught between two worlds. Many still cling to the rules and standards of the Middle Ages, unable to wash their clothes in anything but soda, encouraged to scourge themselves with whips, sleeping fully dressed upon pallets of straw and rising at night to pray for a world they will never see again.

For others there has been a revolution; they are moving out of their medieval chrysalis into the modern world. These nuns are among the most highly trained professional women in the West: doctors and economists, scientists and policewomen. There are nuns working on factory floors, staffing ghetto schools, and running homes for unmarried mothers. Nuns nurse alcoholics and lepers, drug addicts, and the destitute of city slums. They are to be found as missionaries in the most remote corners of the world: in the mountains of Peru and the forests of the Amazon, in the deserts of Australia, and in the Arctic wastes of Canada. They are politically aware and active on issues as diverse as the rights of Jews in Russia and the equality of women.

This process of modernization was brought about partly by increased awareness and a growing sense of responsibility among the nuns themselves, and partly by the need for change pressed upon them by the Second Vatican Council, the great meeting of bishops in Rome in 1965. Yet desirable as this process may seem, there are those who question the need for it. Certainly it has brought nuns to a crisis point. Coming out of their enclosures, abandoning their habits, rethinking their rules—these changes have made many of these women question their relevance for the first time, and thousands have walked out of the convents. Others have left not because of uncertainty about new roles but out of disgust with a system which legally classes women with children and idiots. With eyes newly opened by their realization of the growing social importance of women, they find it totally un-

15

acceptable that the male hierarchy retains such power over matters which vitally concern them—even to denying them a voice. Women outnumber men in religion by more than two to one, but they are forced to remain a silent majority.

For four years I talked at length to more than five hundred nuns tackling work as diverse as helping handicapped children in France, picketing with farm workers on the Mexican border, publishing books in Italy, and working in the ghettos of Harlem and Chicago—where they still walk in pairs, but now for protection rather than from modesty. I met nuns nursing people dying of cancer; I listened as they advised pregnant schoolgirls and helped battered wives. I saw architects and artists, professors and poets, nuns who won the Croix de Guerre for their bravery during the German occupation of France and missionaries who survived prisoner-of-war conditions in the Philippines.

Throughout that time I was deeply moved and greatly impressed. For some of these women I now feel immense and lasting affection. If my ignorance about so much of their lives amused them, they did not let it show. They were painstaking in answering my questions and responded with an honesty and openness for which I had hardly dared hope. I was treated with unfailing kindness and hospitality. They let me use their cells. They drove me around. (Nuns, incidentally, are perhaps the world's worst drivers. They seem to have the touching belief that if they point the car in roughly the right direction, God will take care of everything else.) I shared silent meals on wooden tables in European refectories and warmed-up TV dinners in the apartments of liberated American sisters.

Out of all the nuns and sisters to whom I talked, only one or two older women clearly found me hard to take on religious grounds. "I don't think," one told me sharply, "that a Jew can really understand Christianity." So perhaps I should point out that I have not tried to do so. This book is not an attempt to justify or vilify, to "explain" Christianity or Catholicism, or to present a particular point of view.

The constant question in my mind was: Why should any woman choose to live the life of a nun? I believe I understand a little better now, although I still cannot totally comprehend; it is, I am reluctantly convinced, incomprehensible. It is a mystery of the human spirit that cannot be completely explained or understood.

I intended to make this book objective, but I think that finally it has become very personal: This is how I see the nuns I have met. What I really wanted to do was listen to what they said about all aspects of their lives and help give them the voice they still do not have. They discussed their work and their superiors, their relationships with the outside world, and their need for more freedom. I asked how they felt about the vows they had taken, whether they missed the company of men or regretted the children they would never bear.

"Nuns," declared an irate sister at a recent convention, "have remained a mystery for far too long." This book is an attempt to unravel that mystery.

*Now that you are sweetly dead to the world,
and the world dead in you, that is only a part
of the holocaust.*

—FRANCIS DE SALES

1

Inside the Enclosure

Turn left out of Llandovery station and walk along the wet Welsh road up into the hills until, on the right, there is a long winding drive with a one-room lodge spouting smoke at the gate. A great round sign reads *Llan Carmel*. It used to read CARMELITE MONASTERY, but the Welsh Nationalists started painting over it at night.

The heavy piece of wood on which the words are written was once inside the monastery. It used to be the "turn," the revolving cupboard which was the only communication the nuns had with the outside world. Two extern sisters, who lived outside and could never enter, would put provisions and letters on it and the nuns within would swing it around; it was so designed that they never even saw each other's faces.

The turn has gone now—but only just. Life here continues as it always has, and as it is lived in every Carmelite monastery in Europe.

The Carmelites are one of the oldest orders, following the rule of life as it was laid down by Teresa of Ávila in sixteenth-century Spain. Together with the Cistercians, Benedictines, and Poor Clares, they are among the grandes dames, the aristocrats of the religious world. The Carmelite life is contemplative and penitential; the Divine Office—the Catholic church's official prayer—is recited daily, and enclosure is complete and constant. The way the nuns look and the way they live has not changed in a thousand years. This is the way most people imagine all nuns and convents to be.

This particular Carmel is a solid foursquare house standing high on its thirteen acres of ground surrounded by a ramble of rhododendrons, looking out across a gentle triple-rivered valley that caused one of the nuns to nickname it "Llanduckery." It is the last of three foundations made in Wales in the 1930s by Mother Mary of Jesus, the French-born prioress who first brought the Carmelites to London in 1878 and established thirty-three monasteries in Britain. Bishop Vaughan invited the Carmelites to Wales—scarcely a Catholic stronghold—and on October 15, 1934, he performed the enclosure ceremony in the open in a deluge of rain that cost him a week in bed afterward. Then, as was the Carmelite custom, the local population was invited inside to visit before the enclosure door was shut forever.

Today, a visitor arriving at the house across the gravelly driveway rings a bell and enters the hallway. The only furniture is a dark wooden dresser which contains Christmas cards for sale, even in May, and little notes designed and printed by the nuns, with bluebells on them—*May your prayers ascend to God this happy day and draw upon you the blessings of heaven*—and a large printed card: PLEASE WOULD ANY KIND CALLER POST THESE LETTERS. THANK YOU! At the end of the hall a heavy door is set with a massive lock and key and a panel which slides back to reveal a wire grille painted gray. Sister Rosalie, the turn sister, opens the panel cautiously when the bell is rung; only her pretty round face is visible through the crack. She directs all visitors to the parlor, on the right of the hall, whether they are family members, priest, or friends. No one may enter the enclosure except, in emergencies, the doctor, though the Holy See does permit exceptions in the case of cardinals, bishops, and reigning heads of state.

The parlor is a small room, with a comfortable chair and an

upright one, a table with a little bunch of blue flowers, clearly gathered by a child, and an electric fire. The end of the room is partitioned off by a low wall. Beyond this, another upright chair is for the nun. This fitment is all that is now left at Llandovery of the formidable double grilles of Carmel. The nuns still keep, as perhaps they always will, the sturdy outer enclosure door with its massive double keys. But the grille itself used to consist of an iron grid fitted with spikes several inches long, then a wooden screen of heavy slats, and, finally, black shutters which could be closed and locked. These not only reached from floor to ceiling but were hung with black veiling—as were the nuns who went to the grille, even to see their parents. In addition, each nun had to be accompanied by two other sisters. The mother prioress is delighted the grille has gone. "We took it for granted, but it was medieval. It didn't mean anything."

Many visitors come, to this parlor, not only relatives and other religious, and students on their summer vacations, but men and women who over the years, through their visits, have built up close friendships with the enclosed. And there are "souls," as the nuns calls them: women who need a day or two away from demanding families, people in all kinds of distress. They come in such numbers that the nuns tell you they are "very booked up in the summer," and they recently built a bungalow to accommodate their guests.

That they come in the numbers they do is a tribute to Mother Michael, the mother prioress, a woman of marvelous warmth and wisdom. Fifty years a professed Carmelite, she had her golden jubilee in 1971. Like so many nuns, she looks years younger than her seventy-odd years, her face comfortable and benign beneath the soft headdress. She is a woman of considerable intellectual power, who in her youth corresponded with Jung about her dreams. It is undoubtedly her personality, her deep quiet voice, and her energy which hold the community so firmly together.

A Carmelite prioress is elected by the community every three years and can be reelected only once. After that the father general of the order in Rome must be approached for permission to elect her yet again; it is done only when qualities of leadership are outstanding. Mother Michael's religious career has been by any standard extraordinary; she has been prioress almost continuously since 1938.

It is under Mother Michael's guidance that the Llandovery Car-

21

melites have begun, in accordance with the obligations put upon religious by the Second Vatican Council, to renew and revitalize Carmel. They have, for example, relaxed their rules sufficiently to allow a nun out into the world briefly—perhaps when a close relative is ill and there is no one else to nurse. But these women have chosen to follow that chilling decree of Pope Boniface VIII in 1298, "We command by this present constitution, whose validity is eternal and can never be questioned, that all nuns, collectively and individually, present and to come, of whatsoever order of religion, in whatever part of the world they may be, shall henceforth remain in their monasteries in perpetual enclosure."

Perpetual enclosure. The words ring heavy with drama and denial, as well they might; any woman who cuts herself off from her family and forfeits her freedom has made a complete sacrifice. And yet the nuns of Llandovery go into great giggles at the idea that they are in any way heroic. For them, this choice was as inevitable and irresistible and undeniable as a great love affair, only their love is not for any man. One nun, over eighty now and nearly blind, says of her entry into Carmel, "It was wonderful to give up everything to God."

For Carmel is, above all things, a giving of the self to God. As Mother Michael says, "People who think that we're wasting our time and ought to be doing good in the world have not recognized that God has his needs." She acknowledges, however, the perils of Carmel's physical and mental isolation from the world. "The danger for enclosed nuns is to become an island, used to being on your own. It's terribly important to remember that we're not."

Just behind the enclosure door lies a small white-washed courtyard. Carefully tended, with daffodils and the blue stars of forget-me-nots round a central rockery, it has a Spanish air. Around three sides of it the house stretches, providing shelter under which, in bad weather, the nuns move from office to office, their feet in great big Wellingtons, their habits tucked up into their belts to reveal heavy tweed underskirts, their headdresses topped by plastic pixie hoods.

The interior resembles any large and underfurnished English country house, remarkable chiefly for its abundance of religious statues—like the Saint Joseph dear to the Carmelites, standing as a protection to the home. In a long stone-flagged corridor a sign reads, PLEASE NO

SPEAKING IN THIS PASSAGE. THE CELLAR STEPS FOR A QUICK WORD, FOR LONGER SPEECH THE LAMP OFFICE OR THE COMMUNITY ROOM. This corridor leads to the heart of the community, the chapel, where the nuns gather for prayer seven times a day—matins and lauds, prime, terce, sext, none, vespers, and compline—in the pattern of homage which has continued unbroken in religious houses since the sixth century.

The day begins when the nuns rise just after five o'clock to go to an hour of silent prayer and meditation in choir. They enter through the antechoir, with its polished wooden floors and little pots of garden flowers offered before a carved figure of Our Lady of Walsingham. The chapel is modernized, with big windows and reading lights which the nuns switch on in the predawn darkness. Their side of the chapel is cool and empty, with rows of seats down the sides and high-backed chairs at the head for the mother prioress and the mother subprioress. A wide-meshed grille divides the nuns' choir from the public side of the chapel, which is used by visitors to the monastery and the local Catholic population. This grille has a square opening in it, through which the nuns are given Communion by the priest and through which they reach to light the great Paschal candle in its brass and copper holder, made for them by a Caldey Island monk. Just to the right is a relic cupboard covered in damask, containing what they believe to be a piece of the true cross and slivers of bone from various saints; tiny portraits of Saint Teresa and Saint John of the Cross are enclosed inside crucifixes.

This chapel is the hub of their lives. Aromatic from the incense and pine branches with which the walls are decorated, hushed except for the slip of sandaled feet on wood, the only music the high and unaccompanied voices of the nuns, it is simple and austere, as functional as a workroom. And that is, in fact, very much its nature. The nuns make formal and measured prayer, but they are as matter of fact about it as women in a kitchen.

These nuns of Carmel can themselves do nothing for the world but pray; in prayer they believe they become instruments through which strength can flow. It is a contract with God which brings down love into the world. "It is a very mysterious thing."

The purpose and aim of the enclosed life of prayer is perfectly defined by Mother Michael: "A few should have their lives centered on God, on worship." A woman who wants to live so, leaving everything else to search for God, must have sufficient mental and physical health to withstand so arduous an existence. "Many people," explains Mother Michael, "long for this kind of life yet psychologically may be unfitted for it. Enclosure is very strict, and if they weren't really suited everything would go wrong." Even when there were a million women in religious life, there were only about sixty thousand contemplatives—the 6 percent return on capital, they have been called, which God reserves to himself. And so, to these women, prayer comes as easily as breathing. Mother Mary of Jesus, the nineteenth-century French prioress and founder, would ask for anything on which she needed guidance or help: for the best way of altering a building, for the removal of obstacles, that the Carmels be supported, that some tiny salad plants might thrive. No nun of Carmel ever asks for proof of the efficacy of her prayer. They are praying for the world and are quite certain they are helping. Proof is unnecessary. "We don't need it. We know."

After that first silent hour in choir, the nuns breakfast in refectory. The refectory is a new extension of the old house, a wide, modern room with wooden floors. Six long tables are set with benches. Before each place there is bread in a polyethylene bag, basic cutlery, and a napkin. There is a pat of butter on a plate, a handleless cup called a godet, and a platter. At one end of the room there is a hot plate. Before the mother prioress's place is a little bell, which she rings for the meal—tea and the crusty brown bread they bake weekly—to commence. Until religious orders of women were ordered to undertake revitalization in 1965, the only hot drink they ever tasted was sugared water. As one sister remembers, "My first cup of tea sent me into *raptures*."

Subprioress Mother Imelda is the cook. In her early thirties, she is one of the youngest sisters, serious and shy. Until three years ago, she had never cooked at all; in those days she would start dinner at 9:30 A.M.—in case anything went wrong. Now she is highly organized in her huge high-ceilinged kitchen, with rows of cereal laid out ready for the next meal in brown earthenware bowls. These days she orders from Llandovery by telephone, and food is delivered in bulk. But the nuns provide for themselves as much as possible. In the larder there are

24

two bins full of preserved eggs laid by the monastery hens at the rate of forty a day. Fruit and vegetables grown in the kitchen garden are stored in the freezer. "I don't know how we managed without it. We wouldn't have such a luxury, but a sister had a legacy." Working in silence, everyone in turn helps prepare the vegetables for the day. At the end of the meal, washing up is communal. One nun wrapped in a huge oilcloth apron stands on a box to reach the high sink, with its teak washing-up bowl, while another dries and puts away.

Fifteen minutes is allowed for breakfast, before matins at seven. Then the nuns do odd chores and make their beds until lauds at eight, followed by mass and terce, for which the priest from the village has dressed in one of the handmade vestments which hang, glowing with the subdued colors of stained glass, in the sacristy. Then, just after nine o'clock, the nuns begin work.

To "live a life of prayer" sounds easy. It conjures up a vision of calm and candlelight, of slow hours in silent gardens, hands clasped in tranquillity, minds bent on the spiritual. Hard on the knees, perhaps, but scarcely arduous. Such imaginings could not be further from the truth. All the Carmelite nuns have the lined, stubby hands of good workers, which is exactly what they are. "People think," comments one nun about certain aspirants, "that they're going to sit and pray. Well, we haven't much time for that; we don't think much of that sort of prayer."

Much of their day is spent in hard physical labor, repetitive work deliberately chosen so that it can be done mechanically. For *what* they do, the exterior, is not important. They regard it merely as an outer shell. What matters is that their minds are free for God. So their work must not encourage them to worry and bustle, which is against the prayer life. Nonetheless, Teresa of Ávila herself laid down the rule that they must support themselves, not living on alms or eating the bread of the poor unearned.

Sister Antonia Maria of Jesus is one of several nuns who has as part of her work the making of altar breads. This work was picked for the community as being reasonably rewarding financially, something that can be done alone and simple enough to leave the mind free for contemplation.

In the stone-floored cooking office overlooking the little courtyard

25

stands the square cooking machine, which works rather on the principle of a giant waffle iron. It needs to be regularly greased with wax, collected from the monastery candles, to keep the surfaces smooth. The upper metal plate provides a number of designs. White flour and water are mixed by hand to a soft paste, and a dollop—it must be exactly the right amount, and practice, says Sister Antonia, makes perfect—is placed on the hot lower plate. Then the top plate is brought down by hand, pressing the two plates together, so that the dough oozes out. (It is rapidly trimmed with a knife and given to local farmers for pig food.) After a few minutes the machine is opened. Inside is an almost opaque sheet of altar bread, stamped on the back with the chosen design, perhaps a crucifix, incredibly smooth and perfect. At the end of the day, those sheets of bread to be kept, which by then have cooled, are taken on enormous trays down steep stone steps to the cellar, where they are stored on racks under cloths until they are taken up to a room on the first floor to be cut. In this room, tied to the pipes, hangs a rope ladder which is the community fire escape; the nuns occasionally practice shinning down it, which they rather enjoy.

The machine can stamp out four thousand breads a day, all fed through by hand. They are then packed into tins for the various religious retailers and individual churches who have ordered them; Anglicans insist that theirs have crucifixes, Catholics prefer a waffle finish. When there is a rush on, for Christmas or Easter, all the nuns sit around the table and help pack them, three hundred to a tin.

The work is done in silence. It is the profound quiet of enclosure that strikes the outsider most forcibly. Peace wraps itself around the monastery like a cloak, a contemplative silence which one Carmelite has called "the wordless understanding between two lovers." Except at mealtimes, when one of the nuns will read, or during the occasional hours of recreation, they rarely speak to each other. The only times when speech might be necessary would be for their work or in an emergency, such as illness or the breakdown of a piece of machinery. And special permission to speak can be asked of the mother prioress, if it might help one nun spiritually to talk to another. When they do talk, they are so articulate it is hard to realize how little "conversation" they have. "No one," says a particularly quiet woman with a wide smile, "enjoys talking so much as an enclosed nun."

26

Although most of the day is spent working, their tasks are well balanced and they do not feel they do too much at a stretch. Each day is broken up several times by the bell ringing high above the convent for prayer. Sister Antonia stops the exhausting altar-bread work after an hour—the heavy top plate is very tiring to raise and lower—and goes up to her old-fashioned sewing machine in the robe room on the first floor, where the bulky habits are stored. Each nun has two for summer and one for winter. Sister Antonia makes these for each nun, to a strict pattern set out under the rules of the order, in which it is specified that "before a new habit is given to a Sister, the Sister in charge of the Robe Room must ask permission to have it blessed by a priest." Every little detail must be observed, to the exact length of the points at the side of the habit.

The Carmelites wear a comfortable, monkish, dark-brown habit which reaches to the ground, and their hair is covered by a white band and a heavy black veil. It gives them a timeless look, like figures from a medieval manuscript, and they certainly need the warmth and comfort of the robes during cold winters. But the habits have none of the advantages of wash-and-wear synthetics, and even the relatively light summer habit must make gardening, for instance, singularly difficult. But as Sister Antonia points out, "It's only since we got not so terribly penitential that we have summer clothing. When I entered, everything was thick. I was clothed on June second, and it was a sweltering hot day."

There is a story the nuns tell with glee about two nuns and a postulant who entered at the time when the same heavy habit was worn winter and summer, regardless of the temperature. The postulant said she did not know if she would like wearing the same habit in all seasons. "Oh, that's all right, Sister," said one of the nuns. "Don't worry. In summer it's loose and cool, and in winter it's thick and warm." But the other nun said, "It's very penitential, our habit. In winter it's very drafty and in summer it's very hot." The nuns use this to demonstrate that what you get out of life depends on what you are looking for, but the fact is that the habit does look as if it could be something of a mixed blessing.

Originally, the only thing that changed from summer to winter was the bodice, which in cold weather was double wool, hand seamed. Each nun was given this and two separate long sleeves, which she had

27

to sew in. There is an underskirt of thick tweed with a hem which can be let down; the width of this must be exactly five inches. There is a big pocket at the front of the underskirt in which the nuns keep their enormous white handkerchiefs and any oddments they might need. Over it all goes the scapular, the sleeveless coat that slips over the head, covers the robe, and reaches the ground back and front. This is held to the robe with scapular pins, a sort of primitive safety pin. Sister Antonia makes these out of berries, which she collects in the garden and keeps in a tin till they harden. They are soaked in water and strung onto cords. The nuns wear a headdress, which they call a torque, wrapped around the head under the veil. When a girl is clothed as a postulant, the mother prioress will trim her hair to fit neatly under it.

Sister Antonia herself entered Carmel in 1954 when she was twenty-eight. A gentle woman with the melancholy dark eyes of her Italian ancestors, she found she had "great doubts" in those early days but felt strongly that life is short "like the grain of sand and the seashore. And it wasn't worth giving your love to that."

It is this attitude, more than any other, which distinguishes contemplatives. They believe that love of the world, of ease and comfort, does actually come between themselves and the love of God. God has called them to something which is, in Sister Antonia's words, "more pleasant—but less pleasing." He is calling them to himself. "You just know that God is there, that good things are prepared. So it's worth giving up the joys of the world; there's something more lasting at the end of this."

Like all other Carmelites, she knows well how unnoticed they are by the mass of the world outside. She folds the tunic she is stitching and pats it smooth. "We're doing little things. We're completely tucked away, forgotten, of no importance. Yet we're accomplishing a great missionary work by putting love into every little action."

Just down the corridor, Mother Michael is working in the prioress's office. There is a picture of the Good Shepherd on the door. On the desk is the typewriter with which she was presented on her golden jubilee and, next to it, the *Church Etymological Dictionary* and the *Anathemata* by David Jones. There is also a list of names. "We're all going to sign the Mary Whitehouse petition for public decency.

Though as we don't see television, we can't say we know about that from experience."

There is also a book on wood carving and another on anatomy for artists; Mother Michael is an accomplished artist and is now working on the headstone of her mother's grave. "I hoped very much to do a carving, but it's taken me three years to do a very small inscription." The grave is within the enclosure. A special dispensation from the bishop allowed this, for normally none but Carmelites lie here. Mother Michael's sister, Mildred, is at the Carmel at Falkirk in Scotland. "She was my novice at one time; she was a worldly little miss but she realized this was her call." When their mother died alone at ninety the rules had not been relaxed, and neither daughter was with her. "My mother wouldn't have wanted us to come to her. She would have felt we were breaking something. She'd given us to God—she didn't want to take us back."

Yet Mother Michael herself was at first reluctant to see her destiny in a convent. "I remember thinking, How ghastly to shut myself up with a lot of women for the rest of my life." She entered at twenty-one—the same age as another unwilling nun, Teresa of Ávila. Teresa was as flirtatious and romantic as it was possible for a wellborn and well-chaperoned Spanish girl to be in sixteenth-century Spain. She felt she should become a nun, yet the idea of religious life repelled her. Even so, she went into the Carmelite convent of the Incarnation in Ávila believing that if the cloister was purgatory there would be heaven at the end of it.

Mother Michael, who has been more than fifty years in Carmel, affirms that the life can be "terribly hard," and the natural things which are renounced and sacrificed and done without "can be a pull. After all, this is against our natural desires and longings. Naturally one wants to marry and have children. Naturally we want to have friends. Naturally we want to have a career." Even now, she finds that faith cannot be put into words. "It's alive and real, it's an assurance of truth." She knows that this life is the direct search for God. "And yet the paradoxical truth is that if you hadn't already found him, you wouldn't be searching for him."

Mother Michael, like all other nuns, knows God's silences. "When there's no response from God, that's hard. If you have a very positive

29

awareness of God's presence as love, you can stand anything. When you haven't got God—or anything else—things are pretty grim." It is a feeling to which contemplatives are perhaps more subject than those in active orders, for they cannot bury themselves for a while in outside work or in the problems of others. "You just feel hours of great despondence," explains Sister Antonia, "when you sense that he is not pleased. But you know that deep down nothing is going to pull you away from God." Mother Michael has, however, a piece of advice culled from Thomas Aquinas which she particularly treasures. "If you're in a stew there are four things to do: You can have a hot bath, talk to a friend, have a good cry, contemplate truth." And this, she feels, improves matters. "Even in bad times, God sends compensation. He'll send you a special friend, or you'll find the community is very fond of you."

The Llandovery community is clearly not only very fond of Mother Michael, it also relies on her. For the Carmelites, as for other contemplative orders, the personality of the superior is vitally important to the happiness of all. Because the community is small—it is laid down that there should always be twelve nuns and the prioress—and carefully regulated, there is no area in which her influence is not felt. For even the slightest thing—an aspirin to relieve a headache—the nuns will ask a "permission" from her before going to the well-stocked infirmary.

It is, though, with some relief that Mother Michael serves her final term. "I shall be enormously glad to be an ordinary member of the community, not to have to make decisions." The Llandovery Carmel comes under the authority of the bishop of the diocese, in their case Menevia, and under the laws written by the Carmelite fathers. "But now we're all being asked to say what we want, to change that." It would, she feels, be better to have government by the nuns themselves, which Teresa herself would surely have wanted, "though we ought to have regional authority of some kind." She feels that if everything were left to the individual Carmel prioresses, "you might get somebody too rigid. And left to each prioress, it might put too much strain on her."

It was in the early 1960s that Mother Michael first arrived at Llandovery, brought in from the main Welsh Carmel of Presteigne to revitalize a community literally dying on its feet, since the nuns were all elderly and there were no novices. There are several young nuns now; the turn sister, Sister Rosalie, is twenty-two, and the new novice, Sister Ann Patrice, is twenty-eight. There are a couple in their thirties and forties, but "four of us are in our seventies." Nor is it easy for the Carmelites to attract new entrants; Mother Michael has advertised twice in the Catholic press to no avail. "It's so much a special vocation that just asking people won't do."

Sister Mary of Carmel looks after the tunic office where the nightshirts are stored, woolen ones for winter and flannelette or cotton for summer. There are great piles of thick sheets ("I'm afraid they only get washed once a year") and more piles of long-sleeved, round-necked undergarments made out of scratchy, hopsacky material. "Ten years ago no one wore pants. For more than half my religious life I didn't have them."

Sister Mary is a vigorous woman with a strong face. When she was considering the religious life, she says, "I thought to myself, I'm a very active person. My attraction would be to action. But even in an active order, one can do so little, and there's so much to be achieved. It wasn't enough, somehow."

But Sister Mary has been very happy. Her one regret is that she did not see more of the world before entering, though she did manage to visit Rome three times. She does think that "going about might cheapen this life." It is not that she feels contaminated by the world, like Thomas à Kempis, but "I feel I've been given something else." Rather wistfully, she says it might be nice to go for a walk, but adds realistically, "Each day I pray for the grace and perseverance to continue. I'm signed on for a Carmelite, and that's the finish of it." And she closes the door of the linen cupboard firmly.

Somewhere in the distance a bell tolls for sext, and every nun immediately stops whatever she is doing to make her way to choir. This is in obedience to the rule that the work of God comes first; obedience is important to the Carmelites. Twenty minutes later, everyone troops to the refectory for dinner.

Meals are taken without speech, but from the wooden reading desk the reader for the week will first go through the rules for the month because, said Teresa, "without this foundation, everything will

31

go wrong." They are reading the Book of Daniel, which they think is "gorgeous," and then the refectory book. At the moment this is Cardinal Heenan's autobiography.

Carmelite meals used to be less heartening affairs than they are now. Mother Michael "can remember being given for dinner soup, then cold fish with oil and vinegar, then just a plate of cabbage. And that wasn't nearly enough for me. In those days you were trained to the kind of appetite that needed a lot of food at one go. But no luxuries, no meat." Teresa of Ávila, despite the poverty of her Carmels, saw no harm in enjoying food when she got the chance; when a comment was passed as she ate a juicy bird, she retorted, "There is a time for partridge and a time for penance." Though the Carmels still do not serve meat, fish appears once a week—perhaps baked—and eggs most days—in salad, with sardines, with rice in fritters, in custards. There is always, dinner and supper, Carmelite soup, absolutely delicious and made with anything left over from the day before. Today it is followed by cheese dreams, roast potatoes and sprouts, then junket and fresh fruitcake. In the evening there will be nutmeat noodles, carrots, then apricots and hot milk. For half the year, from the Feast of the Exaltation of the Holy Cross in September until Easter, they fast. This means taking a cold collation in the evenings, which might be plain gingerbread with cherry jam at six o'clock.

After dinner there is the washing-up and more peeling of vegetables. Then, for an hour, they are free to read until the bell for none, at two. They have a library in the monastery, well stocked under various sections: Classics, Language, Poetry, Church and Secular, Popes, Memoirs of Lay Women, Women Religious, General Lives of Saints, Spiritual, and General. There is a lot of Teresa of Ávila, and a study of Cardinal Newman over which Mother Michael enthuses, "Oh, he's one of my greatest friends in heaven. I'll go great walks with him when I get there, over hills and mountains." Thomas Aquinas is there, a review for religious called *Cistercian Studies*, but few periodicals; one thing Mother Michael "can't abide" is "religious literary trash." There is a healthy amount of fiction, including a well-read copy of *The Borrowers* and C. S. Lewis's Narnia books.

The nuns of Carmel are encouraged to read; when a prioress complained to Teresa that one of her nuns read too much, Teresa flashed back, "Better a bookworm than a fool." Even so, their sources of information are limited, mostly by choice. They used to take *The Times* but stopped because Mother Michael felt that "except for the big things, at a shilling a time it didn't seem worth all that money." They had a transistor radio at one time, but found they didn't care for the "tittle-tattle," so it disappeared. Not long afterward, in July 1971, the Holy See, through the Sacred Congregation for Religious and Secular Institutes, the body which ultimately governs the affairs of all religious orders, approved a new statute for the next ten years which emphasized their enclosure. One paragraph specifically stated that the radio must be used by the community only for "special occasions of a religious nature" and must be kept under lock and key.

Now they just take the Catholic newspaper *The Tablet*. Not that they believe any of the papers outright, "but it gives us a good sense of what is going on in the world." They rely on the housekeeper who runs their guest bungalow for a précis of world events. "And our relations tell us things. We have an ear for what is important, and if anything blew up we'd take a paper—when the Irish thing began, we took *The Times*." Despite the inadequacies of such a system, they really do seem to have some kind of special antennae. They asked with great concern, for instance, about a South American earthquake which had received only the scantiest of news coverage.

But the nuns of Carmel, it is true, are remote from the seamy aspects of life. "I don't take in all the happenings of the world," says one. "I know there are great tragedies and people suffering in a way we don't suffer in Carmel. We are kept safe from so much that is sordid." Even so, they do not feel remote. "We can help by loving people in God, having that tremendous compassion for people." They do believe that in this way they are closely in touch with the unhappiness in the world. Through their way of life, they believe they have a more intense sympathy and understanding, a closeness with people in concentration camps and displaced people in the Third World. "We're more intensely united with the people who suffer."

It is because of their consciousness of suffering that they are in Carmel. "That," says one seventy-year-old nun, "is just what we're here for." They know that love is needed—so they give love. And though they are religious living under vows, they do not see themselves as any different from people outside. "There's the thought that people in the world are sinners," says Sister Antonia, "and I'm helping; I'm a sinner with them, and what I experience in myself is part of their suffering." The nuns do what they can to offer practical help. On Fridays they do without milk and send off the money saved to various charities.

They have little enough to send. The huge old house and the attached grounds are all the property they own and are common possessions. They have no capital at all, and their income of around $7,000 a year comes mainly from the altar breads they make. They own the machinery needed to make the breads, and also such things as the mini-tractor for their market garden. Even so, says Mother Michael, "We only just manage. There's nothing to fall back on." She firmly believes, however, that they are given security. "Oh, yes. In Providence, of course, we're secure, knowing we'll always be provided for, not being alone with no one to care." The nuns do not give in to anxiety on questions of money, even though they could not quite live on what they earn. "He does make it up quite inexplicably. It's Divine Providence. We get something like a tax return, or a grant. Once someone sent us a check for one hundred pounds out of the blue. It just," adds Mother Michael contentedly, "keeps about right."

The depositrix, the accountant of the order, is Sister Mary of the Holy Child, short and round and bespectacled, who sits in her office and admits that bookkeeping is "not my cup of tea at all, but if you've got to do a thing, you've got to do it." Before her, great account books sit in forbidding piles: "Analysis of All Expenditure" and "Withan and Wells on Concessional Relief," a breakdown of the amount each nun is allowed free of tax. In the corner cupboard, there are the toys Sister Mary makes for Teresa's feast day, which she either gives away or sells, like the little cribs made out of foam. She also paints cards for children. "When I sit down and paint, I forget everything." Also in her cupboards are some of the linen supplies, such as neat piles of vests. Next door to her office is more evidence of thrift: a lavatory laboriously and economically papered by the nuns with sample squares of wallpaper cut from the pattern book.

Apart from the altar breads, there are other ways for the Carmelites to make money. Sister Theresa, for instance, has her own cottage industry going. On a sturdy table that she made herself, she operates a large knitting machine, making not only garments for the nuns but special orders for friends of the convent, like the blue and white cardigan she is currently working on for the dentist's wife. She is enormously proud of what she can produce, showing off the intricate patterns the machine will follow. And outside the wafer cutting room there is a beautiful old spinning wheel, which the nuns used in Presteigne for spinning the creamy undyed wool to knit their stockings and the long white cloaks they wear for mass. They will be using it again here soon, when they get the sheep they are planning to buy, and the prospect delights them. "The grease in the wool is terribly good for your hands."

They are going to keep the sheep in the garden, a plan of which the gardener, Sister Mary of Carmel, vastly approves. It was her idea, but the decision, as always, was made by the community. Some sisters objected at first, but eventually they came around. They are starting with a ewe, and she will be put in the brambly wood behind the kitchen garden after Sister Mary has hacked down the undergrowth with a billhook. Sister Mary is in charge of the thirteen-acre grounds, apart from the kitchen garden and the lawn ("Our Mother does the mowing with the automatic machine"). She keeps several hives of bees. She has the touch for them; at Presteigne she could produce 150 pounds of honey from one hive if the weather was good. And there are also sixty hens, who have to be fed, their eggs collected daily, and their houses cleaned. When they get broody, she puts them in a shed and feeds them well. And she wrings the necks of the old ones herself. "You hold them for a minute and they don't struggle. I was shown that by a butcher, and very thankful to know it."

In a quiet walk near the hen run, the nuns are about to build a hermitage, facing the flowering cherries. Flourishing a wicked-looking gooseberry pruner, Sister Mary says she has moved a baby azalea and a baby wisteria already to make way for it. The hermitage will actually be a hut with an asbestos roof, but Sister Mary is going to put withies of willow branches in the grooves tied with wire so it looks more countrified. She contemplates the prospect with satisfaction. "It's extremely nice, you know, how good the Lord is to us. We just wait and wait and eventually it comes." There is already one hermitage at the front of the monastery, a garden house with nothing but a table and a chair, a cross with a fresh piece of greenery behind it, a statuette and an icon. It looks out onto the rather weedy herbaceous borders: "We don't have time for them." The two hermitages are for the nuns when, one day in every month, they have a day of recollection: desert days, when they do no work and need attend no prayers except Divine Office. Even their meals can be taken in solitude, and they can read or think or pray as they wish. "It's a wonderful help to our life of prayer," says Sister Mary, "to have these surroundings. And those days are marvelous. It's one of our penances, you see—'Oh dear, that bell'—and you want to go on and finish the job."

Mother Michael particularly would love a chance to lead a more solitary life even than she does now. As a child she used to draw pictures of caves in a desert, with a hole in the roof for light "and a bird's nest outside so I could eat the eggs." This has been her great longing for years, though she fears that perhaps now she might be too old physically to support a solitary life. "But I should love it. Perhaps it will come in my extreme old age." Such longings are very much part of the pattern of Carmelite thinking. Teresa of Ávila was forty-three when she decided to found a convent where the rules of the Carmelites were to be more strictly observed than they were in the then rather lax and easy life-style of the Calced Carmelites. She would return to the primitive rule of Mount Carmel, the eremitical order founded on the mountain itself in 1209 when Albert, the Patriarch of Jerusalem, gave the rule to a group of hermits. Teresa's convent of the Reform was to be a return to that simplicity, that devotion to prayer. In 1562 she settled in the convent of Saint Joseph overlooking the plain and the mountains. Behind the great walls of the garden, there are still four tiny hermitages hidden. And the French prioress Mother Mary of Jesus would beg her beloved daughters, "For the love of God, live on the mountain, the love and eye of your prayer fixed upon God, not upon the news of the plain."

The Carmelites of the Reform were called the Discalced, "the barefooted," to differentiate them from the Calced (literally, "those of the boots"), who did not accept Teresa's reform. (Though as the Calced Carmelite prioress in Bolton today points out, "We're all discalced at night.") At first, Teresa's friars and their students went barefoot, even in the snow, though she herself forbade it. The nuns always wore alpargatas—sandals with leather tops and thickly plaited hemp soles which they made themselves. They still do, pinning and sewing the hemp, then washing and heating them two or three times until the shape and texture are right. They last for about a year and are worn with "choses," as they call the inner bootee of linen cut like a pair of moccasins and coming up the leg. Teresa's nuns did not wear stockings until she began to expand her order and was forced to travel. When Venerable Anne of Jesus inadvertently displayed a shapely leg while climbing into a mule cart and the driver passed an admiring comment, Teresa decided that was the last time anyone would see the legs or ankles of one of her daughters.

The alpargatas are not only extremely picturesque but very quiet. On the other hand, those who wear them stand a good chance not only of getting wet feet but also of developing severe foot trouble. Some older nuns have badly deformed toes from wearing them. But it is not inconvenience so much as cost which is causing this footwear gradually to give way to comfortable leather sandals. As Mother Michael dryly observes, "Old-fashioned poverty is so expensive to-day." All the originally prescribed materials the nuns use—their foot-wear, their mattresses, the habits which in Teresa's time were made out of the coarse wool used for horse blankets—were the poorest then available. "But to have them specially made for us costs a fortune and would be quite out of the question." The nuns themselves regret the change.

When Mother Imelda is not in choir or her kitchen, she is out in the kitchen garden, which is her special territory. Most of the nuns have a good sense of time, living as they do by the hours of the day, but she works so far away from the priory that she tends to forget herself; she does not always hear the bell for prayer the first time and has to dash back breathlessly. The kitchen garden is vital for the community, providing as it does all their vegetables and fruit throughout the year. In the greenhouses are over a hundred tomato plants, and in frames grow strawberries, peas and beans, cauliflowers, lettuce, and brussels sprouts. There are apple trees and gooseberry and black cur-rant bushes; in the distance the hunched figure of Mr. Davies is working on the cabbages. He has been gardener here for many years, living quietly in his lodge at the gates. He is a great source of information, although until Mother Michael arrived at Llandovery he was only allowed to talk to the nuns when strictly necessary, and then only if there were two of them; one alone could not address him. When Mother Michael went out to introduce herself, he backed away nervously and held up two fingers. He does some of the heavy work three days a week, but not all of it. Mother Imelda, slight as she is, does a large part. Wearing thick gloves, with her habit looped up with two hooks and a lackey—a strap to hold the hem of the scapular up above the inner skirt—she plows with the little tractor or pulls the truck heaped with manure.

Mother Imelda is one of those nuns who make their decision about a vocation young and stick to it; she has been quite sure since she was fifteen and first visited Presteigne. Restricted as she is in many ways, she has never felt frustrated within the regime. "I've chosen it freely. I could go freely if I still wanted to. There's a terrific fulfillment in this life; it's all for love."

Mother Imelda, like all the Carmelites, is insistent that leaving the world as they have is in no way a flight from it. They are concerned only that they do not become "a slave of the world," as they put it. And the world they envisage beyond the boundary of their stone walls is mysterious and enticing. Mother Imelda feels that "there are so many pleasures, and we could become enamored of them. Standing back from it, we can keep it in focus not only for ourselves but for other people."

The contemplative life may perhaps be a flight from the world in one sense; a woman in an active teaching order suggested that such a choice might be influenced by a woman's need for solitude and tranquillity, intensified by the stress of modern living. But they go to a life of such introspection that there is nothing in themselves from which they escape, no thought they do not examine, no desire they do not question. As Sister Antonia says, "You pray to God that he will reveal yourself to yourself." Mother Imelda knows that "if you didn't have a vocation, it wouldn't be possible. Looking at it, humanly speaking, we're denying all human values, all the things we have a right to, like a husband and children. But it's only occasionally, when my nieces visit, that I feel the want of children."

In the distance, the bell peals seven times for vespers at four thirty. Mother Imelda strips off her gardening gloves and rushes

38

back through the gardens to chapel and, later, supper. On some evenings, after the nuns have eaten, they can go to the recreation room for an hour. "The real, ancient, old-fashioned Carmelite custom at recreation," according to Mother Michael, "was sitting in two rows with a workbasket and only talking to your neighbor. And you always sat in the same place, year after year. Now we just try not to talk shop. Some people love talking about their friends and their childhood, which can be an awful bore. And we do not gossip. If we did, this could be a little hell."

The community room, on the second floor, is the social gathering place for the monastery. High and sunny, with again the polished wooden floors, it is almost bare: only a few chairs around the walls and a heavy wooden sideboard almost lost in the space. "We always try to buy secondhand and cheap things. We must try to avoid any kind of luxury." There is, however, a large, modern painting called "Easter Candles," and the focal point of the room is an enormous table-tennis table which Mother Michael acquired when she had permission to go to an auction for furniture and got it as part of a lot. It is so big the whole community can sit around it together. But usually they play table tennis at it—and occasionally football, which is harder to imagine. When there are feast days, they may have "extraordinary recreation," which can go on all day if they like, and then they might do Scottish folk dances, or the novice might do some Irish reels; Mother Imelda occasionally gives an impromptu ballet performance. They have a record player now, a recent present. Until it arrived they had no way of listening to music at all. The first record they played was religious, the psalms, and they now have a small collection ranging from *Your Hundred Best Tunes* to Chopin, from Gregorian chant to *My Fair Lady*, a particular favorite.

Most of all they enjoy the simplicity of making their own entertainment. The Carmelites delight in excuses for self-expression; Teresa herself played a drum and little Spanish pipes and made up verses. "We need all this," she told her daughters, "to make life livable." The Llandovery Carmelites sometimes mime scenes from the Bible, and recently they did the Resurrection with a tin bathtub for the tomb, Sister Antonia of the beautiful voice hidden away as an angel, and Mother Michael speaking Christ's words from the scullery.

If there are visitors, the nuns will hold a *noson lawen*, Welsh for "happy evening." This will not be in the community room—forbidden, as the interior of the monastery is, to visitors—but in a small sitting room on the ground floor, which has a waist-high wooden partition dividing it in two, half for the visitors, the other half for the nuns. They squeeze into the crowded space in their heavy brown robes and sit perched on tables and cupboards. Amid chatter, songbooks are handed out and the mother prioress is begged for a certain song—"Oh, let Sister Antonia sing!"—so she does, unaccompanied—"The falcon hath borne my love away"—her voice soaring through the falls and cadences, the words heartbreakingly poignant. And when she finishes, there is a remembering silence.

Then they sing together—"Whoops, we've gone a bit flat!"—Psalm 23, "The Lord Is My Shepherd," and then into "Morning Has Broken." They enjoy themselves enormously, particularly when Mother Michael does her justly famous recitation about the priest and the potato, with much wagging of an admonitory finger.

Each other's friendship is understandably important to these women, aware as they are of the problems and boredom of being in such close proximity all the time. "But that means we have so many opportunities of practicing love with the sisters, giving the same love and attention to those you don't like as to those you do." They regard the community as their family, and that is certainly how it feels; the Carmelites are rather like Victorian daughters spending their chaperoned days at home. But the feeling of family goes deeper than that. Mother Imelda states, quite simply, "God is my husband. That is how I think of him. Normally, your husband would do anything for you. Well, I feel that about God. I talk to him about my family, and I feel he really does care. He's so real to me, so alive. I know I've given some things up, yet I'm enclosed within a greater love."

Teresa of Ávila would have liked that. A formidable mixture of practicality and mysticism, with her raptures, her visions, and her careful advice, she did not separate heaven and earth. And John of the Cross, Juan de San Matias, her first friar, that persecuted scholar of whom she said, "Small in stature though he is, I believe he is great in the sight of God"—there is much in the Carmelites that comes from him. Acknowledged now as one of the greatest of religious poets, in his lifetime he was hounded by the Inquisition; on his death he was recognized a saint. (People tore off his fingernails and bit off his big toe for relics.) It was he who explained the melancholy that comes sometimes in religious life, in that famous phrase, "the dark night of the soul." And it was he, too, who said of the nuns of Carmel that they should be "like mirrors, shining lamps, glowing torches, brilliant stars." In his day, of course, the life of Carmel was more rigorous even than it is now. Yet wherever the Carmels are—America, Britain, France— with their long hard hours, their flashes of joy ("I never laughed so much in the world"), and their intense asceticism, they keep the flavor and atmosphere of Spain. They are wholly Spanish. Teresa and Carmel could have been forged by no other country.

"And yet, we don't have perhaps as penitential a life as some people think. You'd think it was much more austere." In some ways, though, there are the remnants of more extreme discomforts: On Friday, after compline, the nuns say the Miserere, a long psalm, standing with their arms stretched out in the shape of a crucifix. It is all that is left of the severe penances which continued until less than ten years ago. One elderly nun remembers "losing my head in my cell at the idea of taking the discipline for the first time. We used to have it together at five in the morning. You slipped your robe off your shoulders and beat yourself with a little whip with lots of straps; you had to do it to offer up suffering for Our Lord in the world. Other people suffered in prison, so why shouldn't we suffer? But I must say, you got awfully used to it."

The woman who is talking is Mother Gabriel of the Resurrection. Over eighty, with the garrulous frailty of the old, the thick lenses over her near-blind eyes not quite hiding their blue beauty, she still keeps much of the manner and vocabulary of the girl she was at the turn of the century. One of a family of fourteen, she remembers asking to be a nun when she was seven, so she could go and help the lepers. For her, Carmel was like going to heaven, "everything I'd always wanted and more."

It must be difficult to remain vividly aware of a world you will scarcely see again. The nuns of Carmel used to have two extern sisters who lived outside the enclosure, doing the shopping and other business, spending their days in a little sitting room outside the enclosure. Their only contact with the nuns was receiving a tray of food through

41

the turn three times a day. They wore long skirts, little capes, and squared-off black bonnets, prim as Victorian governesses. The extern sisters were women who entered Carmel without any educational qualifications, while the better-educated choir nuns not only brought a dowry but could follow and make music and read the Latin prayers. In 1965, in response to the Vatican's call for change, Mother Michael brought in the two extern sisters, Sister Maria and Sister Cecilia. Sister Maria, a neat, birdlike woman, says she could not believe it; she had wanted to enter fully for so long. "But I knew that if God wanted me, he would arrange it."

The only other Carmelite who has spent much time outside the enclosure is Mother Gabriel; since 1945 the only thing she has really wanted is to found a Carmel in Russia. There are about 780 Carmels in the world, with thirteen thousand nuns. Teresa of Ávila, who spent much of her life traveling around Spain in a springless mule cart in all weathers making foundations, saw the handful of nuns in the convent of Saint Joseph grow to seventeen monasteries for women and fourteen for men, the latter founded with Saint John of the Cross. Teresa was still traveling three weeks before her death.

So Mother Gabriel's wish is in the best Teresan tradition. She was, oddly enough, in Alaska with a woman friend on special permission when the friend suggested they visit Rome. Here she obtained permission from the Holy See to visit Russia for a year and try to get a group of nuns together there, so off she went as a tourist through Cooks, all paid for by the same woman friend. Filling out the form for her visa, she put "spinster." "Not only was I a spinster, but I could spin." She wore a long brown postulant's dress and coat, with a little brown cap, not to look too noticeably a nun.

In Russia, traveling alone, she tried to find convents, only to be told that such places did not exist. Nevertheless, she made her way to two, where she was received with much suspicion. "I told one superior I wanted to live in Russia as a hermit and asked if she would let me use one of their little white houses round the church. But she said the Kremlin would never agree." Eventually, traveling home by train, she was hauled off by uniformed men at a border village and put unceremoniously into the guards' van. She protested that she was nearly seventy. "I was surrounded by Polish officers, and I said, 'You should be ashamed of yourselves; you're Catholics.' Of course," she adds reflectively, "they were Communists. So then I said, 'Do you think I'm a spy?' 'Yes,' they said, 'you're just the kind.' " Tired and frightened, she was finally helped by an American doctor who was also stopped. "But you know," she says, "I'd like to have been sent off to a camp, actually. I love adventure."

While she is talking, the bell rings softly again, through the monastery, calling Carmelites to compline at eight, the last prayers before Great Silence falls on the house, not to be broken before the first prayers of the morning. The chapel is darkening, and the lamps of the nuns gleam in pools, while the altar light glows red.

After compline, the nuns retire for the night, walking along the stone corridor (lined with neat rows of alpargatas) that leads to the cells. The cells themselves are something of a feature, instigated—as so much else here has been—by Mother Michael. At Presteigne, it was she who had a chapel specially designed so that the nuns could build much of it themselves, economically, with only minimal aid from local workmen. Twelve of them, doing "gang labor" for two years, built the choir and even cast the windows in cement. But they found they could not manage the weight of the blocks of stone for the walls.

Many of the cells at Presteigne were also built by the nuns, after they had finished the chapel. ("Until then a lot of us had slept in henhouses.") For this job they used old railway sleeping cars and stuffed the walls, for warmth, with nylon stockings; when Mother Michael made a phone call she always asked, "Would you mind my asking what you do with your old nylon stockings?"—with the result that stockings arrived in bundles.

The cells at Llandovery were also acquired from the Welsh railways. They are old guards' vans, parked in a large square which is roofed in for shelter and minimal warmth. One was also used for transporting bananas: "It smelled terrific when we got it." The nuns have painted them all silver, now, and built little brick stairs up to the doorways. But the lavatories are as they were, and so are the signs reading CAUTION. DO NOT LEAN OUT OF THE WINDOW. The two bathrooms with their heating lamps were once used for transporting horses.

Inside, cardboard shutters have been fitted across the windows at the ends of the coaches to keep out the worst Welsh drafts. The walls are painted white, the floors bare. There is in each cell a black cross over a little bookshelf, a stool, and a picture of Saint Teresa. There's a stoup of holy water, a bit of palm from Palm Sunday, and a piece of hedge from the garden. The cells are surprisingly warm. Sister Mary says she felt some trepidation about coming to Llandovery because of her arthritis. "I thought we'd be shivering all winter, and sometimes it's certainly pretty cold, but the cells don't hold the damp. Compared to most Carmels, this is the warmest cell I've ever had. And you don't hear snores and snuffles from the sister next door." The only heat necessary is a small electric fire.

The beds are divans—school beds, really, with flock mattresses—but Mother Michael felt these were a bit fancy after the straw mattresses that the nuns would have made themselves in the old days, so they put their old horsehair mattresses on top, with their heavy sheets and blankets. Over each bed is a reading light; beside it, a table with an alarm clock and a Bible. Across some of the cells, a clothesline of string is slung with pegs. If there is a wastebasket it has probably been made from an old can. And each nun has a thermos in her cell for hot drinks during the cold weather. "It isn't," explains Mother Michael, "the emphasis now to do without."

Even so, they live under the glance of God in an austerity few can match, confining the body in order to free the spirit. And the core and secret of the contentment they undoubtedly possess is their certainty of happiness to come. They have given their lives and their love to the glory of God, and in return they will know that glory themselves. As Mother Michael points out, "The afterlife is forever. But this is only seventy or eighty years at most."

But she has a very positive approach to life. "You should look for what is good and happy. You mustn't waste this life, but make the fullest use of your gifts." Much of what she says is, in recollection, couched in religious clichés. But when she is actually speaking, it is all so wise and true, and said with such utter conviction, that she sweeps the listener along with her. Yet it would be hard for the nuns to bear, acknowledging man's physical end as they do, regularly and often, without a certainty such as Mother Michael's that the spirit will eventually inhabit an eternity which she sees as an endless sunny garden

44

where "everything one wants is going to be happiness. One will be young, and everything will be marvelous. I simply long to have long, long walks and never be tired. And we'll have innocent friendships. On earth they're tremendous but there there will be no limitations. Oh, jolly times.

"Look," she says, leaning forward. "You *must* believe in the afterworld. It's a great comfort, you see. Pray to know. It is a matter of faith, beyond anything we can argue and reason about. Beyond reason and yet reasonable, in that we can discuss it and show that there is more than can be known by the senses. And one of the greatest arguments for eternal life is that you can't do all the things you want to in life."

Mother Michael has the serene, fulfilled look associated with happy marriages, with many children and grandchildren. Nothing of the elderly spinster there. It all becomes clear when she says, speaking of her belief in the afterlife, "Nobody in love can believe it will end."

So the nuns of Carmel go about their lives and their days pass quietly, quietly. Their eyes are turned inward, searching for that deep inner place where God and the soul meet, and their hearts are turned to the sorrows of the world beyond their walled acres.

Up in the kitchen garden, just before you come to the cabbages, there is a barred gate, once the heavy outer grille that kept them from the world. The inner, finer grille is against the wall of their little Spanish courtyard. This metal screen, that once kept them from ever touching their mothers and fathers, or their sisters and brothers, is almost hidden now. Sister Mary is using it as a support for a perfumed mass of golden roses named Peace.

*If you are a foolish virgin—if indeed you are a
virgin—you need the community. If you are a
wise virgin, the community needs you.*

—BERNARD OF CLAIRVAUX

2

Why?

"Why on earth are you going into a convent?"

There must be very few young women entering religious communities in the twentieth century who have not been asked that question. It is the single most intriguing speculation about any nun. One American Poor Clare, who made her decision twenty years ago, says that everyone asked her why. "A priest said, 'Don't expect the world in general to understand your way of life. But if anything in life is true, the truth will stand.'"

It is of course the voice of God that takes women into religious life: a calling heard only in the heart, a need. But it is not enough to say they enter because they love God. Obviously they do—but so do other people, and most of them do not become nuns. The one statement that was made to me by almost every sister I talked to—and it was the only one they all made in common—was that this was not something they had decided for themselves.

46

The Belgian Jew who converted and felt that anything less was not giving enough, the slender American with honey-colored hair living in a slum apartment in Rio de Janeiro, the elegant actress who became the superior of an Anglican community—all of them felt what one put into words: "It is less a question of choosing than of being chosen. It is a very strong conviction—I wouldn't even call it a feeling—that this is the life to which one is called."

The religious life was described by Matthew as "a city set on a mountain." Canon law terms it "a state of perfection," because by living it under vows the nun is removing the main obstacles to holiness, withdrawing from all that is against the habit of virtue. So a woman who has a religious vocation must be prepared to give herself to God. But it is not only what she can give but what she can give up that matters. The less she has, the better she is. Like an English Channel swimmer, she will go farther that way. Pope Pius XII summed up the raison d'être of religious life when he said it is "intimately connected with the special purpose of the Church, namely, to lead all men to the acquisition of holiness. Though every Christian is bound to attempt to reach that sacred pinnacle, the religious proceeds on a path which is entirely her own and relies upon help of a higher nature." A daunting prospect. Saint Bernard simplified it when he told his monks of Clairvaux, more than eight hundred years ago, "Brothers, the whole object of our lives is to love and to make ourselves lovable."

Basically, a religious vocation is a mystery, and perhaps to none will it remain so deep as to those favored with it. They themselves find it fascinating; at least two orders of nuns run a series in their house magazines on the subject—"How I Came" and "My Call"—and the motives for entering are as different as the entrants. "The varieties of call," according to a superior who has seen many women choose convent life, "are like the stones of the sea." One woman, trying to explain it, says, "You hear it. You know it." Another adds, "It's not so different to other things, to getting married, for example. You know you must marry a man, that this is right for you, that you are called to be joined with him and bring new life into the world. It is the same for us."

It is material for headlines when young women in the news decide to enter convents—particularly since such people tend to go to the strictly enclosed contemplative orders. The most successful contemplatives, one mother superior says, are not those you would imagine, not

47

the introspective, reflective people. "You need an extrovert personality to cope with the life. The bubbly, tomboyish ones make the best contemplatives."

In 1973, a former prima ballerina of the Paris Opéra, twenty-seven-year-old Mireille Nègre, who had danced often with Nureyev, entered the Carmelite convent at Limoges as Sister Mireille. She took her pink tights with her, and one pair of dancing slippers. About the same time an Australian beauty queen, Christine Francis, announced that she was joining the Cistercian nuns and had a last fling in London nightclubs. The *News of the World* immediately—and erroneously—announced that she would rise at 3:30 A.M. and start her day with five hours of prayer, but no one actually thought that a vivacious twenty-three-year-old from Brisbane would take such a step; the Cistercians are the most austere of all religious orders. But in fact, seven months later, Miss Francis returned to London and went straight from Heathrow to take the habit as a novice at Holy Cross Abbey, Dorset.

"Fear and desire," according to Sister Marie Edmond of the Helpers of the Holy Souls, are nearly always the first signs of a vocation. She believes every woman, called at whatever age, invariably feels both. "The first contact with God is disturbing," the conflict natural; "every woman wants to be loved by a man, to bear children."

The experience of Sister Mary of Carmel mirrors this exactly. At convent school, she says, "I had a great idea of being married and having lots of children." She was asked back to the order for retreats after leaving school and finally made one "to get it off my chest." To her surprise, she suddenly realized how happy she felt. "And I had this ghastly feeling, only God can give it, so perhaps I ought to give it back." She really did not want to give up living in the country, "hunting and all that sort of thing." Finally, she told a priest she would like to be a Carmelite, and was accepted by the order, but asked to wait until she was twenty-one. "I was delighted. I thought, I shall be married long before that. But no, it was meant for me."

One deputy superior, Sister Morag Michael of the Anglican Community of Saint Mary the Virgin, confirms that in her experience many women struggle for years against the conviction that God wants them to enter a convent. "I know a lot of my sisters would say they had fought hard against choosing this life. I think the majority of us came very reluctantly. Comparatively few said, 'How marvelous,' because it does mean you are turning your back on a lot of things that honestly are very desirable and great fun. But there is a feeling that one must *try*, at least, and see."

Mother Joanna is superior of the Deaconess Community of Saint Andrew in Tavistock Square, Bayswater, London, an Anglican order founded by Elizabeth Ferard. She felt she should enter a convent but at that time was not even aware that Anglican orders existed. "I went to the vicar and hoped he would say, 'Oh, no, quite ridiculous, you're not the sort to be a nun.' He didn't. He suggested an order. The mother superior gave three dates to see her, and I chose the very last one. I felt the whole thing was too extreme, that I'd like a middle-of-the-road thing, a job and a nice flat. I didn't want to give up all these things. But I felt this compulsion."

A member of Mother Joanna's community, Sister Denzil, was a medical worker at Saint Thomas's Hospital, London. "I had this feeling when I was very young, and resisted it till I was thirty-eight. I was happy and fulfilled, and I knew that if I entered I wouldn't have marriage or children, which I should have loved to have at some point. But it seemed to me like God saying, 'Look, I'm sorry, but this is the way you must work.' I railed against it for years. At one convent where I was very unhappy, I don't know, looking back, why I didn't pack up and go. But you don't."

No one seems to mind admitting their reluctance to enter. Sister Mary Victoria belongs to the Franciscan Missionaries of the Divine Motherhood, a missionary group based in a country house near the south coast of England. She said that she was in her first job when she read the *Life and Letters* of Mother Janet Erskine Stuart, a Sacred Heart nun. "Every time I picked it up there was a vague uncomfortable feeling at the back of my mind. The ghastly truth dawned on me—perhaps I ought to be a nun, too." Another sister in the same order, Sister Mary Simon Stock, remembers "kneeling in church and listing mentally on one side all the reasons why I should become a nun, and I could think of only one reason why I should not—I didn't want to. And to me, that didn't sound like a very good reason."

"God," says an Episcopalian sister, more succinctly, "just picked me up by the scruff of the neck."

An American girl went to the clothing ceremony of a friend as a Poor Clare. "I thought, That's beautiful, but not for me." She laughs and looks a bit amazed at herself. "Five years later, I was back." She is not the only nun who found herself in a convent for the first time almost by accident. An Anglican novice of twenty-seven said, "I'd never been inside a convent or had anything to do with sisters till I went to college to read theology. At the end I wanted to do some work, but I didn't want to go home. A tutor suggested I go to a convent as a quiet workplace. I wrote to one, but they didn't have room. And I thought, I'll have to go to that awful place in Paddington." Two years later, she entered there.

Even those who are certain of their vocation can be put off by the formidable exterior presented by some orders, particularly the contemplative ones. A woman who is now a Carmelite abbess had long realized she was going to be a nun: "I never had love affairs or anything like that; I wasn't interested." So she went to a clothing ceremony at the Carmelite convent in Saint Charles Square in London's Notting Hill. "It was a foggy November night, the building was vast and dark, and I saw these two young girls in this gloomy hole and my heart sank lower and lower: I'd wanted something that was absolutely *it*."

Many women deliberately test themselves first before acknowledging their vocation. An Anglican sister says that, having read maths at Oxford, she decided to teach for two years. "I went to the worldliest, richest, most aristocratic school I could find to see if I was influenced away from the religious life." Sometimes this is done at the insistence of parents. One young woman, who had wanted to enter as a contemplative from the time she was fifteen, spent eight months in an income tax office first, because her family wanted her to make some contact with the world before leaving it. "I sat at an enormous desk and thought about the convent."

Another enclosed contemplative, Sister Antonia Maria of Jesus, left school to work in Swansea as an adding machine operator for the National Coal Board. Then she went to London as a receptionist in the busy Strand Palace Hotel, "and it was in London that my vocation developed." She felt a great longing for close living with God, but "I wanted God to decide for me. I didn't want to get my own will entangled." She returned to her family, went to mass daily, but said nothing, lest by doing so she commit herself. "I wanted to be free until the decision." She had already received information about the order's life, "which I found very forbidding," but there was nothing to draw her away from it. "I didn't have the attraction for the married life, or for having children; I never was attracted enough to boys. I needed some purpose in life." When, finally, she entered, "I was very thankful. It was a tremendous relief when my life was settled, a feeling of great security."

For most women who become nuns, the conviction that this is a choice they must make overrides their realization of loss. As Sister Morag Michael puts it, "It isn't that you don't want to get married, have a home or family, travel, or have an exciting career, or any of the things that seem so desirable in life. They are as desirable for us as for other women. It's only that somehow you know they've got to take second place."

Many superiors and novice mistresses say they prefer entrants who talk like this. The Carmelite prioress Mother Mary of Jesus wrote in her diary, "Today, someone was asking to come in. I had to refuse. It is often so, when they want to come in. It is not we who choose, but He." Not everyone would agree, however. Sister Madeleine, novice mistress of the French community of the Augustinian Sisters of Meaux, considers that since religious are "easy prey for superficial psychologizing, they prefer the explanation 'I have been called by God,' since it shifts the initiative of their choice."

There are some women to whom religious life comes so naturally that there is for them no question of hesitation. "Everything in my life," remembers a contemplative, "seemed to lead to this." To a Spanish superior, the desire for religious life came from "just knowing *this* was what God meant you to be."

Sister Marie of the order of Saint Mary the Virgin is in her early twenties, a round girl with a gentle country face. "I was working in an accountant's office in Swindon before I came here. What made me come was, I believe, God's call. When I went to my job I was quite distressed at what I saw. The permissiveness, the suffering, the lack of care of people for each other. And I said to myself, What can you do about this?" And an American nun: "I happen to feel that helping people recognize the importance of God in their daily lives is a full-time

51

task. I want to do it not only in my daily work but also in personal and social situations. I feel I can do that best as a single person—but in the company of other people who have the same goals. I could never do it alone."

It is rare that a woman will know exactly which order she wants from the very beginning of her desire to enter religious life, though it does happen. Carmelite Mother Imelda remembers the moment when it became clear that "God wanted me." A sister at her convent school was explaining that solemnly enforced enclosure had replaced deserts for the hermit. "I thought, This is for me, a life of total commitment." It was not that she just wanted to be a nun, she wanted to be in Carmel.

Often the attitude of the family is the major influence on a vocation. Many nuns have brothers and sisters in the habit—and this is true everywhere, not only in Catholic countries such as Ireland and Italy, where it is traditional for one or two members of a large family to enter the church for reasons both of faith and finance. It is, however, an odd coincidence that contemplatives in particular seem often to come from big families. Perhaps it has something to do with learning early to live as part of a group. Mother Imelda, for instance, left behind her a warm family life; she is one of seven boys and three girls, and it was "terribly hard" to leave them. Yet she feels she can still reach and help them through her prayers. Because they can make the journey to her monastery only twice a year, she is allowed to spend as much time as possible with them for perhaps a week, though this would be more restricted if they visited regularly. "I've cooked the dinner and popped in and out to my mother in the sitting room in the middle of it."

The influence of the mother, particularly, in encouraging vocations is acknowledged to be immense. At a recent meeting in London to discuss the subject of vocations, one of the tactics recommended to boost the diminishing numbers of entrants was that a mother should "encourage her little ones to play at being nuns and priests." An Episcopalian sister believes that "my mother's influence on my vocation was much stronger that either she or I realized. I resisted, but in the end I saw it was the most important thing there was." A missionary, Sister Marguerite of the White Sisters, felt "very aware that God was asking me. I remember saying to my mother when I was seven, 'I'm going to be a nun but I'll enjoy myself first, and then when I'm thirty-five I'll

52

go in.' My mother said, 'Oh, so you'll give what is left over of your life to God?' "

Another woman who entered young remembers a superior saying, about the contemplative vocation, "Some of the sisters in this convent are in their eighties, and if you ask them to look back on their lives, the only regret they have is that they didn't give themselves to God earlier. Youth is a thing you only have a very short time, and it's very precious. And if you can say, 'I gave that to God,' it becomes even more valuable." This woman, Eileen Gielty, is a member of the Institute of the Sisters of Notre Dame of Namur, an educational congregation founded in France at the beginning of the nineteenth century. She, too, entered because of her mother. "She was a very pious Irishwoman, and I knew that the greatest desire of her heart would be if one of us became a religious. But I had no urge whatsoever to satisfy this desire. I was a bit of a rebel. If my mother suggested I went to church, it would be enough for me to decide I wasn't going. In fact, when I really thought seriously of becoming a sister, I had to face this, that I was going to please my mother in spite of myself."

Eileen Gielty fully expected the thought to pass. "But then, when I was seventeen, I went to the ordination of three young men. They were in their early twenties, and they were giving their lives to God. It was just terrific. I wept and wept and wept. And I came home and told my mother that night. I said, 'I've been thinking about this for some time. I don't seen how I can escape it now.' "

At the other extreme, there are families who are horrified at the idea of their girl's taking the veil. A superior who regularly gives talks on vocations says, "Of course, we often find parents are not terribly anxious for their girls to become nuns. They prefer them to get married, and then there are always possibly grandchildren." A recent inquiry into the subject of vocations carried out in France showed that, while a son becoming a priest was acceptable, a daughter choosing to be a nun was a calamity. A few months later, a similar survey in Britain produced the same results.

Sometimes parents object only until the daughter convinces them of the validity of her choice. "My father was a convert and he was opposed because of my youth. They wanted me to make some contact with the world before leaving it. So I spent eight months in an office.

When I couldn't wait any longer, I wrote to my father—and he agreed." Many parents never accept their daughter's decision. A thirty-year-old novice had desperately wanted to enter for ten years before her parents would consent. "I told them I wanted to be a nun at sixteen. There was a terrible row and they thought I was mad. But really they thought three years at university would put paid to that. Mummy was very upset but prepared to try and understand. It was Daddy who still hasn't accepted it."

Many nuns meet such intense opposition from their families when they enter that relationships with them are completely broken off. Both an Anglican and a Catholic novice mistress agree that this is quite a common occurrence. "It happens with a lot of my novices," says the Catholic. "Their parents have never spoken to them since the day they entered."

Pat Drydyk is an American Franciscan, a calm and intelligent young woman. "I went through five years of struggling with my parents on this. My mother has not really talked to me for thirteen years. When I go home, she speaks briefly, but she doesn't ever write. She told me that if I entered I'd not be a daughter of hers." An Englishwoman from a Catholic family who has been a nun for thirty years admits that her mother never forgave her for becoming a nun. "As for my father, he never spoke to me again." For many women such reactions have caused terrible unhappiness, like the sister I met whose mother had died years before after a long illness. The sister had only just learned of it through a letter from a friend; everyone assumed she already knew.

Almost all orders have their own stories of families bitterly resenting the entrance of their daughters: the angry mother who broke her umbrella on the spikes of the parlor grating, the father who threatened to abduct his daughter by brute force on the day of her Clothing.

Parental opposition has been in part responsible for enclosure; convent walls were put up not to keep the nuns in but to keep intruders out. In the thirteenth century an Italian girl called Diana d'Andolo determined, against her family's wishes, to enter the community of Saint Dominic. Her brothers forcibly removed her from the convent of Augustinian canonesses to whom she had gone for protection, breaking her ribs in the process. She did eventually start a Dominican community at Bologna, and Saint Dominic afterward put stout walls and metal grilles around his nuns; he even, in times of danger, provided special guards.

One case of parental obstruction at the end of the last century was a *cause célèbre* which involved the pope, five cardinals, two papal nuncios, an auxiliary bishop, and a grand vicar, as well as the French ambassador to the Vatican and a premier English duke. Marie Ambaud, a twenty-two-year-old French girl, left her home secretly to enter Carmel in London. Her father, inspector general of customs, objected on the grounds that public opinion would henceforth be against him—anticlericalism was rife in France at that time. He turned up in London to offer the prioress large sums of money if his daughter could leave. Failing in this, he next contacted Cardinal Manning, then the pope. When newspapers took up his story and began to attack the church for detaining Marie in a foreign convent, the Holy See undertook an inquiry. Marie wrote to the pope, begging to be allowed to remain, but was told to stay temporarily in another convent to "demonstrate her freedom." The night before she was to leave, she developed heart trouble. ("It is," wrote the prioress, "the greatest grace of her life.") This caused more scandal. Her mother could not enter the enclosure to nurse her; her father declared he would have her out dead or alive, "and if she dies, so much the worse for you." He even visited the father of the prioress to protest. But Marie was finally allowed by the pope to be professed a Carmelite. She died not long afterward.

Often, girls educated at convent schools are influenced toward the religious life, though as one superior points out, "While I think a great number of girls come to a particular teaching order because of the nuns they were at school with, sometimes the nuns who taught them actually put them off that order." Another sister does not think the nuns at her convent school put the idea directly into her head. "Example was always a very important factor. They certainly did impress us as women who had all the gifts. Not in terms of looks—though some were very good-looking. But they weren't castoffs of society; they were intellectually very able, and they were good personalities. I can remember in my last year at school having a realization of what their lives were about. It wasn't just teaching and encouraging people to go as far as they could; there was something else behind it, and that's what really first attracted me."

According to the mother general of a small order, "I'd been obsessed with the idea of being a nun ever since I developed a crush on one at my convent school when I was seven. When I was quite small I thought it was the acme of perfection to be a Sister of Mercy giving out eggs to the poor. And now I'm doing it, you see."

For many sisters, an outside event influenced the decision. To Mother Joanna of the Deaconess Community of Saint Andrew, "It was the war that made me think what life was about. I came back to the truth of Christianity." For another, the turning point was highly emotional. "I never believed in anything. I hated scripture at school. When I was fifteen, the death of President Kennedy started a search for something. I entered here to get to know God."

In view of the efforts so many women make to enter, it is strange that one of the false impressions outsiders have of convents is that they represent for the inmates an escape, an evasion of responsibility, an easy way out if life does not offer the conventional happinesses of a husband, a career, children.

This is a myth one Episcopalian sister, a former physical-training instructor, demolishes. "So many people think this life is a rejection, an escape from the physical. But that's not part of the pattern. If you marry one man, you're rejecting thousands—but people don't see *that* as a rejection."

"Would a life in common," asks a French sister, "of obedience and poverty, make up for the lack of a husband, beauty, intelligence?" Nuns cannot simply be dismissed as women no one wanted. Even if charming and intelligent people do not deserve more credit for the strength of the emotions which drive them to give their lives to God, their sheer numbers must prove something. Only recently, Christianity had approximately a million nuns and sisters—and they cannot all have been suffering from worldly disappointments.

"I could have married," explains an Anglican. "I still think of the men I knew and loved. But I don't regret my step into the convent. I knew, somehow, that one man wasn't for me, that God's love for me was so strong that I had to respond to the whole world." The reason, according to Mother Claire Bernes, an Algerian-born Daughter of Charity of Saint Vincent de Paul who was awarded the Freedom of Israel for her work with children, is that "we don't join the church in order to be happy but to give to others. That is what we mean by love."

One Good Shepherd novice actually became engaged three months before entering. "I think I did it just to show I *could* have married." This, she admits, was partly for the benefit of her parents, who are deeply unhappy about her choice. "They feel it's a life against nature. They imagine I'm not going to have anything—no married life, no young family. They don't consider that I've had any fun, or that this life has any possibilities of happiness." For a long time, she was torn between feeling she should become a religious and her emotions for her boyfriend. But having made the decision to marry, "I found I couldn't go on with my engagement. I had at least to give this a try. He couldn't understand, but then it's not the kind of thing you can explain so easily."

Another myth about nuns is that they are driven into convents by unhappy love affairs. As one very pretty young Anglican of twenty-seven said rather tartly, "It's much more likely that she's driven in by no affairs at all." A fairly typical comment from a middle-aged Spanish sister is, "I never thought of marrying. I was always disappointed by my acquaintances. I did not find enough in them. And then the urge of God's command became stronger."

There must be a great many women in convents today who entered because they felt they could not marry for one reason or another, like the middle-aged sister who admitted, "My mother said, 'You haven't got many offers of marriage because we've got no money.' I was very young and I entered because I couldn't meet men very well. I'd have lost my soul and maybe done low things; I was all for the stage and dancing and ruin."

It is true that some girls, afraid of their own sexuality, can, by entering, avoid contact with men and at the same time ensure their own holiness. But someone who is incapable of good relationships with people in the world is going to be no better off inside a convent. She is not, after all, living a hermit's life but a community one.

Some women undoubtedly still do decide to enter for other than religious reasons: because they promised a parent they would do so, or to please a teaching sister they admired at school. Many are first attracted to the idea of religious life by what one nun calls the "rubbishy

57

romanticism" of films and novels. But as one nun-theologian points out, "If you enter for the wrong reasons, it's certainly possible to be a religious, but not possible to be a *happy* religious. To do that you have really to make a success of your life. I don't mean professionally, but personally. . . . You can, of course, delude yourself that you are carrying the cross," she adds wryly.

There was a time when thousands upon thousands of women totally unsuited for convent life nonetheless entered, not of their own free will but through compulsion. In the first days of religious life, when European kingdoms were small and kings many, it was in the interests of royal families that their daughters remain in convents in preference to contracting matrimonial alliances which might involve their relatives in political difficulties. Numerous princesses of ruling dynasties remained unmarried in their convents—one German duke sent all nine of his daughters—but since their dowries were given them, they were able to make their own foundations and rule over them alone; they were powerful women. Margaret, daughter of a medieval king in what is now Hungary, was promised to a convent in return for victory over her father's enemies; the ruins of the foundation he made for her still stand on the island between Buda and Pest. And a seventh-century king of Northumbria made a vow that the Christian religion should profit if God granted him victory. His daughter Aelflaed he then gave to the Abbess Hilda at Hartlepool when the child "had scarcely completed the age of one year, to be consecrated to God in perpetual virginity, besides bestowing on the Church twelve estates."

The convent was a useful place to put women who became politically inconvenient, and several of the dynamic Romanov women ended up in Russian communities. One was Sophia, sister of Peter the Great, who was said to have a man's brain and clarity of judgment and who was made regent when Peter was a child of ten. When he was seventeen, he had a trained army guarding his three palaces, and it was not long before Sophia was arrested and taken to a convent outside the walls of the Kremlin, where she lived as Sister Suzanna. No one from outside ever saw her again, and to ensure her silence Peter ordered hideously mutilated bodies to be hung outside her windows. Later, he dealt with his wife, Czarina Eudoxia, in the same way. This time he wanted a divorce, which the bishops told him was out of the question so long as she remained a laywoman. But a woman who entered a convent rendered her marriage void, an important political consideration for a husband who wished to remarry. So Peter had their son taken from Eudoxia and imprisoned her in a convent where, perforce, she became Sister Elena.

The convent was also a convenient way to dispose of widows, particularly royal ones who would otherwise have retained vast amounts of money and land. This practice goes right back to the earliest days of monasticism; in Arthurian legend, Guinevere took the veil at Almesbury on the death of Arthur and remained there until her death. Some royal women regarded such enforced cloistering to be as unthinkable as suttee. When, for example, Elisabeth Charlotte, Princess Palatine and Duchess of Orleans, came to France to marry Monsieur, the younger brother of Louis XIV, her marriage contract—drawn up by the French—stated that she had to choose between spending her widowhood at a convent of her choice or at her dowerhouse. "I am not," she commented, "such a fool as to shut myself up in a convent. That is not my way at all." And sure enough, after Monsieur's death the distraught Liselotte was heard to shriek at the top of her voice, "No convent for me, I'll go to no convent! Let no one speak to me of convents!"

There were other reasons, too, for placing a young woman in a convent. If a girl had borne an illegitimate child, or even tarnished her reputation, it hushed scandal. And the Duc de Saint-Simon, the great French memoir writer who lived at the court of Louis XIV, mentions that it was perfectly acceptable for an elder, less attractive daughter to be sent to a convent to increase the dowry and desirability of a younger child. He even refers to a convent's providing a practical solution to embarrassing situations. When the Duchess de Piney remarried, her new husband, with an eye on the inheritance, had the son by her first marriage ordained a priest and the daughter made a nun. After twenty years the daughter started to grumble publicly from her convent near Paris, and the pope made her a dispensation. She returned to court with a title.

For some, the convent was a place to hide illegitimate offspring. Cardinal Wolsey himself had an illegitimate daughter at the convent of Shaftesbury. Ex-mistresses, too, found their way there, though sometimes through their own choice. Two of the women involved with Louis XIV ended as nuns. Louise de la Vallière, his shy and gentle mistress, obtained pensions from him for her family and servants, begged the queen's forgiveness, and entered the Carmelite convent in Paris. The last years of her life were so edifying that there was a movement to have her canonized: thirty years of reparation after so few of love. Her successor, Madame de Montespan, whose grand passion with Louis lasted twelve years and produced seven children, did exactly the same, spending sixteen years in prayer and good work. Her penance, said society with great satisfaction, equaled La Vallière's.

Ironically enough, the only woman in Louis's life who had always wanted to enter a convent was denied the privilege: his wife. Marie-Thérèse, Infanta of Spain, must have been a most unhappy woman. Married young to a grossly unfaithful husband, it was said that her apartment was like a cloister. She received the habit of the Third Order of Saint Francis with "profound humility" and always signed herself *Soeur Thérèse* to indicate her devotion to religion. When she died at forty-five, her body was clothed in the habit of a Franciscan nun.

There were women who entered to expiate their own sins. The sister-in-law of the Marquis de Sade, Anne-Prospère de Launay, fell in love with him, and they fled to Italy. She entered a convent at twenty-seven and died there of smallpox nine years later. Some entered to expiate the sins of others. Princess Louise, daughter of Louis XV and Marie Leczinska of France, believed that only a princess of royal blood could atone for her father's sins, so she entered the monastery of Saint-Denis as Teresa of Saint Augustine.

Perhaps the most unlikely nun of all was Héloïse, the beautiful pupil of Peter Abelard, the philosopher and theologian. Their love affair, one of the most poignant ever, still lives through the letters they wrote each other. She bore him a son but would not marry lest she hinder his career. When her uncle, in vengeance, had Abelard castrated, the only future he could envisage was in a monastery, and he begged Héloïse to enter also. She ended her life an abbess but it was a sham, for to Abelard she wrote, "I have no God but you."

What concerns religious orders now is recognizing the true vocations. This is made all the more difficult because one woman may have not only good, adequate, and conscious motives for wishing to enter but also unrealized subconscious motives: minor inadequacies, even personality disorders.

A girl who wants to enter usually contacts a parish priest. He may advise her to contact a local order, or one to which she is particularly suited. He may advise her against the life; one woman was told by a priest that she had too affectionate a nature to become a nun and should marry. (She is now in her eighties, having been a completely fulfilled member of a strictly enclosed order since she was twenty.)

Alternatively, the girl might go to someone like Mother Mary Joseph, a short, imperious woman in her sixties with an awe-inspiring manner, who founded the Sisters of Our Lady of Good Counsel and Saint Paul of the Cross, better known as the Vocation Sisters, with headquarters in a manor house in Leicester. The main entrance hall is seventeenth century, and when one comments nervously on the atmosphere, she responds, "I hope that it is one of prayer."

Together with a companion, Mother Mary Joseph started the Vocation Sisters to guide girls into the most suitable orders. "Until 1939, there were no places like this where you could come and get information about orders. They were unknown, often to each other. Nuns didn't even know other nuns who lived down the road. In those days you just couldn't obtain information about an order unless you happened to know one, or unless a priest told you where to go. So we realized there was a need for a place where girls could go to be quiet, to think, to be away from any influence towards any particular order, to find out about religious life: what it meant, what it was, what the vows meant, and what kinds of orders there were."

Their early days were a struggle. They got together just enough money to buy a small house, spent their weekends on their knees scrubbing it, and collected leaflets of the various orders. "There were enough then to cover a card table. Now there are racks of them."

Many girls come across Mother Mary Joseph in the course of her work: speaking in a school, perhaps, or at vocations exhibitions at churches in different parts of the country. She tells them that the most important thing for a girl who wants to enter is that she must "want to give herself wholeheartedly to God to use in whatever way he wants.

You don't join to be a typist or a bookkeeper, or to nurse or teach, but to do exactly what is needed." Mother Mary Joseph finds that few girls know what form of religious life they want. "They don't feel called to marry or to remain single in the world, but they don't know if they want to teach or nurse, go to the missions, or be contemplatives." To advise them, she discovers their interests and talents. She explains the qualifications they will need and describes the life-styles of various convents. She lends them books and gives them pamphlets. Often they spend a few days with her to get the feel of community life.

As early as this, clever guidance will often discourage an obviously unsuitable or immature girl. For convents now are far more concerned with quality than with quantity. Much as they want and need entrants, they realize as never before the problems the wrong recruits can bring. "Do not," wrote a founder to a young superior, "receive too easily. It is much wiser to wait."

They do not want those who fall in the category one Belgian novice mistress dismissed as "pious girl guides." And they might even be chary of over-encouraging suitable applicants. One Sacred Heart sister remembers the woman who later became her superior urging her to go to college. "I wrote to her from Leeds, saying that I was happy and busy but there was a deep-down loneliness. She wrote back, 'This is perfectly normal at twenty-two—you haven't met the one you'll probably marry.' I was terribly indignant."

"Prospective entrants," says Sister Margaret Moran, who handles admissions for the Sisters of the Good Shepherd, "might be the girl who writes from school or a widow of fifty with a grown-up family." She gets twelve-year-olds writing in to say they are interested in becoming nuns. "I've got one girl at school who writes very philosophically, telling me she knows she has a very long time to go. I've told her if God wants her to be a nun he'll let her know, but in the meantime to be a good girl. She'll very likely be the kind of girl to come. I don't deliberately keep in touch, but I sent her the life of our foundress."

The American missionary order of Maryknoll Sisters, as the Foreign Mission Sisters of Saint Dominic is known, has two of the order running the admissions department to handle the fourteen hundred inquiries a year they get from eighth-graders alone. The Order sends them information about the work and the prayer life in the community.

Out of this number, many will continue writing for years; then some might start doing lay missionary work. Out of that fourteen hundred, perhaps half a dozen will enter.

Most contacts come through *Maryknoll*, the magazine produced by their brother community, the Maryknoll Fathers, which has a vast circulation. And the admissions sisters also go around the country doing promotions work for the community with films and tapes, although, as they are quick to point out, "We're not yet beating bushes for girls; we have all the work we can do keeping in contact with those who write in." Their job is to see that the girls get to know the community and vice versa. The sisters travel anywhere to meet prospective entrants: Philadelphia, Chicago, Saint Louis. "We write and say we'll be in the area. We find it better not to go to their houses, because sometimes they haven't told their families." The meetings take place in the parents' home only by invitation. Usually they are in hotel lobbies or the girl's apartment, a neutral place, not threatening to the girl." Alternatively, the interested applicants might follow the European pattern of spending a weekend at the convent. Given American distances, the English habit of asking the girls to tea is impractical.

At this stage, the applicant will usually go into the pre-entrance program—that means she is in regular touch with the order, which gives her an abbreviated rule of life to follow, as well as some reading and a certain amount of prayer.

When a Good Shepherd applicant has spent some time at one of the convents, and if both sides are happy with what they find, she will be asked to join the staff, perhaps of one of the schools the order runs for maladjusted girls. During that time—usually about nine months —she is invited to spend part of her holidays with them at the house of formation, as they now call the novitiate.

The orders themselves have a very clear idea of the entrants they want, and their perfect applicant varies, depending on many factors: the order's country of origin, its work, the ideals of the community. Teresa of Ávila asked of a hopeful novice merely, "Has she good sense?" but there would seem to be no place for such simplicity today. The constitutions of one new English community, the Sisters of Our Lady of Grace and Compassion, state that they look "for women of sixteen to forty with a spirit of generosity, common sense, reasonable health, stability and a desire to give themselves utterly and unconditionally to God. The ability to get on with others is, of course, essential."

The founder of the American Maryknoll Sisters declared that her ideal entrant would be "distinguished by Christlike charity, a limpid simplicity of soul, heroic generosity, selflessness, unswerving loyalty, prudent zeal, an orderly mind, gracious courtesy, an adaptable disposition, solid piety, and the saving grace of a sense of humor." And the Anglican sisters of Saint Mary the Virgin feel that "the best people we get are those who have been most active in life. And, of course, the most important test is whether you can stay put."

In order to be considered suitable, the entrant not only must be emotionally attracted—and attractive—to the order she chooses; there are a great many other qualifications which she must, in canon law, fulfill. (Though, to one superior who showed signs of being too exacting, a founder once wrote, "It is not my intention to receive only postulants descended from Jupiter.") In their constitutions, under the section on admission of subjects, every order stresses that a candidate must not be encumbered by any "impediment." The impediments make up a considerable list, though in some cases special dispensations may be made under particular circumstances. Some restrictions seem unlikely, but they have evolved over the years—and not without cause. Among those women who cannot be validly admitted to the novitiate are those who are still married or who "are liable for punishment on account of some grave crime of which they have been or could be accused." Also excluded are "any who are entering under the influence of violence, great fear, or fraud, or who are received by a Superior under the same influence." Anyone who is in debt "and unable to pay the same" cannot enter, nor can those "bound to provide support for their parents, grandparents, or for their own children." Many women who have a "late vocation" have been eager to enter for years but had to wait until their obligations in these directions were fulfilled.

Another prohibition for a prospective entrant is to have "abandoned Catholicism to join a non-Catholic or atheistic sect." Such people would need a dispensation from the Holy See before they could enter. The same applies to women belonging to an Eastern rite; they must obtain written permission from the congregation of the Eastern church. Nor does the Catholic church beam upon those who have been converted less than two years before they attempt to enter religious life—

although, again, the bishop of the province can grant a dispensation so they can enter.

There are now, and always have been, a great many superb women who have changed their religious beliefs and then entered convents. Many orders will not accept those who have been members of another congregation, whether as postulants, novices, or fully professed sisters. This can be overcome in special cases, and I met several sisters who had tried life in one order only to find they were not suited. Different orders vary enormously. Their charism, their spiritual personality, is peculiar to themselves, and a woman might be utterly miserable in one order and totally fulfilled in another, like the Immaculate Heart sister who died in California recently at the age of a hundred and one after eighty-one years in the convent; she had first been in two communities in England, both of whom told her she had no vocation. Sometimes the problem is physical; two women to whom I talked, one English and the other French, had entered contemplative orders and found their health would not stand up to the rigors of the system— the frugal meals, the broken hours of sleep, the manual work, and the cold. And sometimes the clash is mental, as one Italian woman found. The order she chose was too restrictive, not modern enough for her ideas and beliefs. "It wasn't something I could have known until I entered." She is now very much happier with a teaching order.

The difference between orders has been intensified now that the rigid superstructure of convent life has undergone the massive undermining of the years since 1965. A Good Shepherd novice mistress remembers one entrant who "was so obstinate, we thought she'd never fit into community life. But she came back, and back, and back. And now she has settled. But the type of life we lived before Vatican Two—she could never have fitted into that."

The age of the applicant is also considered. Before Vatican II, sixteen was considered a perfectly acceptable age for entrance—and it was not unknown for girls to enter earlier. Orders would specify that applicants were only acceptable between seventeen and twenty-five. But it is now generally considered that a girl who is not yet fifteen is ineligible, and those under sixteen can be received only if the mother general and the council consider it wise. They would make an exception, one superior said, in cases of "a very unhappy home, something like that."

There was, of course, yet another route to the convent, though it is now out of favor. A hundred and twenty years ago, many orders had attached to them boarding schools for girls from fourteen to sixteen who intended to enter. These young aspirants led strange lives, half in and half out of the convent, subject to many of the rules, observing silence at certain times, changing into the black dress and stockings of the postulant when they got back from school at four o'clock. This method of recruitment lapsed as educational standards changed and religious orders became more enlightened; they now prefer that their girls sow their wild oats before entering and come into religious life with no regrets.

The Anglican sisters of Saint Mary the Virgin do not encourage entrants under twenty-two and prefer those between twenty-five and thirty-five. As Sister Morag Michael puts it, "We're much happier if they've been out in the world, had boyfriends, and trained in something, so they know what life is about." And a superior at the Deaconess Community of Saint Andrew says, "I'm always pleased if they've had ordinary relationships with boyfriends and started a career going." Out of a group of novices I talked to in one convent—a group made up mainly of girls in their twenties, though one was over thirty—there was a laboratory technician, a teacher, a civil servant, a clerk, and a secretary, as well as one girl who had been working as a matron in an approved school.

There are strong arguments for not taking girls too young. As an Italian superior, Sister Maria Lorenzina Guidetti, explains, "It's not that life has a big secret. But it can be frustrating if a girl comes very young to the convent. Life, it seems so long." She feels, too, that "those who are all their lives in convent, they don't mature so well." Father Eamonn O'Doherty, an Irish priest and psychiatrist who has written a great deal about the recognition of vocations, believes that entering young was reasonable at the time when adolescence ended at about nineteen. But in these days of extended student life, he is certain that a girl does not have a clear "self-image," or a clear-cut idea of her personality, until she reaches her twenties.

There are, of course, those who still advocate entering young. As an elderly Sacred Heart sister says, "I do thank God so very much for my early vocation. I pretty well live with him now." And Sister Madeleine of the Augustinian Sisters of Meaux, comments, "I look askance at the eighteen-year-olds entering now—but I entered myself at eighteen. You're peculiarly receptive at that age. And I'm glad I stayed naïve. I didn't have time to become skeptical."

At the other end of the scale, there is an upper age limit of acceptance which, before Vatican II, was in many orders fixed at twenty-five. Today, several orders will not take those over forty-five without special permission from the mother general. On the other hand, Mother Alphonsa Lathrop, the daughter of Nathaniel Hawthorne, who founded her own nursing order, made her vows for life at fifty-four. And one Episcopalian house has two novices in their fifties.

The great bar to religious life used to be illegitimacy. Today few orders would refuse such a girl. Others, however, would still reject her—though making sure to justify it on more pragmatic grounds. As one novice mistress says, "She might well have an unstable family background."

The constitutions of most communities contain a phrase that asks that the entrant "have both the physical and mental capacity to understand and practice the spirit of the congregation." And a girl is asked to produce a recent medical certificate or have a physical examination just before joining. Inherited illness, particularly insanity, is something that bothers the communities a good deal. "We go into that really thoroughly. After all, our work is looking after lame ducks—we couldn't take in someone seeking refuge from the difficulties of life." Epilepsy, for instance, disbars a girl from entering.

There are, however, several orders which welcome those who are incapacitated. The Sisters of Jesus Crucified is one. They have a house in France, two in the United States, and eight more in Europe; they are even in Japan. The order began in 1930 when Suzanne Wrotnowska decided to make a genuine religious life possible for disabled women. While they cannot take anyone with nervous or mental illness, they accept all others who would be turned down by most congregations. They claim that poor physical health and handicaps should not be obstacles for someone wanting to live the religious life. Rather, they feel it logical that such women be accepted. They might even take someone with an illness as serious as terminal cancer, though this would be a risk. "It would all depend on the localization, the prognosis—and the person herself."

Few superiors would go so far as one Sister of Mercy who even

67

insists that among the qualifications for new entrants should be that they possess at least "middling good looks." Why? "Because you can't send people out visiting if they have huge birthmarks across their faces; they'd have to go to another community." Her argument for such discrimination was that "we're representing the community when we go out."

Some of the qualification may be financial. Until very recently it was not only customary but necessary for a girl to bring her dowry to the convent, as she would have brought it to her marriage. It was this that financed the convents and, in the case of those taking girls of good birth, brought them land as well.

It was not until World War I that this custom began to decline, and indeed in many orders it is still accepted as perfectly normal. The constitutions of an order founded in the 1950s read:

> No dowry is required but each one, if her means permit, should pro-
> vide for her support during the period of probation prior to the first
> profession. The amount is to be fixed at the General Chapter. This
> money must be returned in full should the aspirant return to the
> world. Also to be returned to her, if still remaining, are any other
> effects which she brought in with her and which must be carefully
> listed on her entry.

If the prospective sister is eligible for entry, she will then be asked to fill in an application form. Her family background, character, and conduct are carefully investigated. She used to have to provide written references of good conduct from the bishop of her birthplace and from the parish priests of all other places in which she had lived for more than a year since she was fourteen. This practice has just been dropped, but references from a priest who has known her for over two years are still required. An employer or a school might also be asked for references.

Until recently, aspirants were not screened psychologically at all. It was all done, says a superior, "in a very superficial way." In 1969, a priest speaking to a group of Anglican religious joked that religious life was the only profession left "in which it is not regarded as necessary to identify ink blobs in order to discover vocation." He would not say that now. In enlightened communities, the next step is "taking their psychologicals"; the girl is sent at the community's expense to see a clinical psychologist, usually making at least two visits.

Some European orders still prefer not to use these advanced screening techniques. "Psychiatrists with a list of questions," as one English novice mistress said scathingly; "*very* American." Such orders believe "there's a lot to be said for knowing people at a human level." So they invite sisters who know the girl, perhaps from college, to write a report on her. But any system can fail. As one sister who wrote such a report on a prospective candidate remembers, "I said this girl wasn't suitable or capable enough. She was highly strung and couldn't afford another failure in her life. Well, someone else wrote and strongly recommended her. So she was accepted. And she stayed one day."

The sisters responsible for the Maryknoll admissions say, "The main thing is to learn she's not pathological, to get to know her strengths and weaknesses. We need to know she's a normally sound, healthy girl, not entering for a refuge, not running away. We want to know how she relates to others, which is extremely important for this life. And she must also be mature enough to act independently."

Another American community, the Immaculate Heart of Mary, has a lengthy orientation program every summer. A girl interested in joining will be invited to attend three times in five years. They travel down to the Casa de Maria, an immense Spanish-style house on the California coast which was once the community's novitiate. The first three days take the form of a retreat. Then different members of the community, a number of them on the board of directors, will explain the ways of the group and its purpose. There are informal discussions and question-and-answer sessions. And, most important, there is time for the aspirants to get to know those who are in the community already.

Occasionally, superiors with an infallible eye for a vocation emerge. One such was Mother Barbara of the Sisters of the Most Holy Cross and Passion, an order founded to care for North Country mill girls in England. It was said of her that she had only to look at a new arrival to know if she would persevere. Gazing intently at the girl, she would say, "No need to unpack that child's trunk." She was, it is claimed, never wrong.

But those who are in favor of psychological tests, like Sister Madeleine of the Augustinian Sisters of Meaux, feel that "untangling people's motives is too complex a business to be done casually." She is well aware that an entrant with the very best of motives might also have problems which only a trained counselor could find; she might, for instance, have a compulsive need for order, a fear of marriage, or a desire for emotional or spiritual security amounting to arrested development. She might suffer from religious mania or neurotic timidity. Yet it is true that even negative-sounding reasons may nonetheless lead to genuine vocations. One woman, who would almost certainly have flunked stringent tests today, entered out of loneliness when her mother died thirty years ago. "I was eighteen and bitterly upset. I thought I might find happiness in a convent. And once the doors closed behind me I felt at peace; I knew I was in the right place."

In the United States, a number of clinical psychologists advertise in the religious press for community work. But in Europe there are perhaps only three or four such psychologists in each country, and they are used by everyone. Once a year in Britain, at Spode House, candidates from many communities are assessed by a group of experts. These assessments take the form of a day and a half of tests and depth interviews. Of course, these tests are not the final decisive factor. "I don't," says Sister Madeleine, "base my decision just on what they say."

The psychologists, while they cannot assure a novice mistress that a girl has a vocation, are expected to confirm that she is neither neurotic nor entering under some unhealthy compulsion. The prospective nuns themselves clearly appreciate the value of these tests. One said, "It made me feel they were really accepting me." But not all orders, even today, show this kind of restraint. One novice I met related with absolute horror what happened when she visited another order. "In half an hour they were handing me forms and telling me what day to come in."

In the past, convents would have received borderline cases, girls they thought might have a vocation but about whom they were uncertain. Not any more. Now a girl who on the surface seems to have all the qualifications and qualities for the religious life, and who desperately wants to enter, may not be found acceptable.

This report—abbreviated from a much more exhaustive document —was compiled on a girl who was anxious to join the Good Shepherd sisters:

> M.J. is a pleasant, open girl of 21. Her father works as a laborer, she is the eldest of a family of nine, left school and went to work in a factory for two years. After that, at 17, she tried her vocation at

another order but at the end of the first month was advised to leave as she was not considered mature enough. Before taking up nursing she worked as a cashier in a supermarket for 18 months. She has now completed two years of her training. Her intellectual ability is in the normal range. School-leaving age shows poor inclination for study, but should have passed her final examinations. Her interests are medical, the social services and clerical.

Personality test—good emotional balance, good self-confidence. Healthy ability to relate to others. Tends to be very austere in interpersonal relationships, has some leadership qualities but lacks self-discipline. During the interviews she is open and frank, a typical working-class girl who has still to make more use of her talents. Psychologically, there is no reason why she should not make a very good religious.

The entire report was presented to a council of eight sisters, under the guidance of the provincial superior who is in charge of all the houses in that particular province. (The novice mistress herself, who prepares the report, has no vote.) This girl was turned down, at which she was "quite relieved but a bit hurt." The order commented:

Her motivation for the religious life is centered on emotional feeling, sacrificial worship, and a seeking for self-fulfillment—that isn't terribly good. There are few signs of spiritual commitment, though the interviews provided an opportunity for her to think out the meaning of a vocation and the sort of behavior expected of a religious. But she must give evidence of ability to make a sustained effort: She gave up nursing; she couldn't discipline herself in a very demanding situation.

The novice mistress added that a few years ago, without the intensive detail available on this form and through the psychological tests, they would probably have accepted M.J. "And the problems would have shown up in the novitiate."

At this stage, orders will accept the girl as a postulant for a period. The idea is that each is on trial with the other, getting to know each other without any commitment on either side. If the girl decides to leave, she does so with no slur on her character; it is in no sense a failure, and she need not even explain why she is going. Some communities, like the Good Shepherd, would have the girl continue working at her job for at least six months during her postulancy. "We ask her to be in contact with a sister once a week for a chat to help with her reading. We ask her to be a good Christian." There are, too, more personal changes they ask the girl to make in her life. "We would ask her to give up dating, if she's got a boyfriend. Not her social life, but steady dating. We tell her, Look, it's not fair to lead a boy on to think she's available if she's not; she might break someone's heart for nothing. Oh, and we'd ask her to give up smoking and drinking."

Some orders stipulate three months of postulancy, but six is more usual, and recent Vatican decrees have extended it up to two years, because the concept of this period of testing has changed. The Augustinian Sisters of Meaux is one group which realizes that any girl needs "a long time of testing or preparation. For the first year or two, it should be quite clear they're not even novices. They're learning, getting to know us, our ideals and aims—and we can get to know them."

When all is said and done, the only way to test a vocation is to enter, and the only successful entrant is the one who stays. Because the varieties of call are so different, there is no norm against which they can be measured, no quick way to prove their validity.

Sister Louis Gabriel of the Congregation of Our Lady of Sion is an impressive woman. A German Jew by birth, she holds doctorates from German and American universities and is known again now by her worldly name, Dr. Charlotte Klein. Practical and highly intellectual, she is the last possible person to fantasize over a religious vocation. And yet, she says, "I certainly had the extremely strong experience that a call had come to me that was not manufactured by an exterior force but which was definitely, objectively, asking for a response outside myself." It is not as though she had been in any way actively seeking change. "I was completely happy, satisfied, and fulfilled. I had a job in the British Intelligence Service monitoring secret wireless stations. And when I finally said what I planned to do, the head of my department was amazed.

"There was nothing visionary about it. I wouldn't call it a mystical experience—I am against all such things. But I must say it was the definite perception of something outside me asking if I wanted this life. And the result, after all, after twenty years or so, has been for me wonderful beyond all expectation. It proves that this must have been a real experience."

We were told to emulate the angels—but the angels don't have bodies.

—A SACRED HEART SISTER

3

Initiation: Rites and Rituals

On the day of her Clothing, when a Benedictine novice makes her Simple Profession, she is a bride, a virgin crowned.

Dressed all in flowing white, veiled in gauze, and carrying flowers, she walks behind the monks and the priest into the abbey church to kneel there before the prelate conducting the ceremony. In the silence he turns to her.

"What do you ask?"

"The mercy of God and the grace of the holy habit."

"Do you ask it with your whole heart?"

"Yes, my lord, I do."

"God grant you perseverance, my daughter."

Then the choir sings "Veni creator spiritus," and two matrons of honor, young laywomen, take her hands and lead her forward.

"Oh God," prays the prelate, "who has called us from the vanity of this world to follow our vocation, keep thy handmaid, our sister, always modest, sincere, and peaceful."

Again the choir sings and the girl kneels before him as the two matrons take off her headdress and strip her of the veil. The bishop takes a pair of small silver scissors and cuts off a lock of her hair.

"She shall receive a blessing from the Lord, and mercy from God the savior."

She rises and leaves the sanctuary. In a small room she is helped off with her bridal clothes. She puts on heavy black shoes and thick stockings, dons a plain underslip, and sits on a low stool while the abbess quickly runs clippers over her head.

When the novice returns to the steps of the altar in a long black habit, cap, and wimple, she is almost unrecognizable as the bride of a moment before. The prelate hands her the leather girdle, which the matrons buckle around her waist. "May the Lord gird you with justice and purity, so that you may be worthy to approach the divine bridal chamber." Then the floor-length black scapular, the straight sleeveless garment, is passed over her head and settled around her shoulders. "Receive the yoke of the Lord and bear his burden which is sweet and light." Then she dons the white veil "in token of chastity and obedience. May it be to you a pledge of God's grace, enabling you to run the course of your probation without stumbling." A lighted candle is placed in her hand. "Grant her grace to persevere, so that with thy protection and help she may accomplish the desire thou has given her."

The girl kneels on the prie-dieu, the candle in a silver candlestick beside her, as the prelate speaks of the life she will lead, of the pleasures of the senses she is giving up forever, of the hard work and obedience that face her, of the silence and loneliness that will be hers "from now until death if all goes well."

She leans forward and kisses his hand to the music of the Te Deum, then rises and leaves the sanctuary. This time, she and her matrons walk before the prelate, the priest, and the monks. The chaplain carries the cross, and the parents and extern sisters complete the procession that winds now through the abbey grounds to the forecourt and through the front door, and so to the doors of the enclosure, where she knocks.

"Open to me the gates of justice," she calls softly.

From inside many voices answer. "This is the gate of the Lord; the just shall enter."

Then the door opens, and there stands the abbess, the great crook of the Benedictines in her hand, the entire community behind her. The clothed novice steps onto the threshold and kneels there. "This is my last resting-place forever," she sings, and as the final prayer is said she rises and kisses her parents.

The prelate takes her hand and gives her to the abbess. "We hereby entrust to you our sister and pray that, under the guidance of the Holy Rule and through obedience, she may deserve to obtain perfect union with God. May the peace of the Lord be always with you." Once more the novice is blessed. She passes over the threshold into the enclosure. And the doors are closed and locked.

This devastating ritual takes place not immediately upon the entrance of a girl to religious life but two years later, when she has advanced from the novitiate, has been accepted into the community, but still has not made her final binding Solemn Profession.

The first entry through that locked enclosure door was simpler but, for the girl herself, even more momentous. She was greeted at the door of the enclosure by the abbess and her councilors, who led her down the cloister to the church. She knelt with the abbess on the step facing the sanctuary, and the abbess presented her to her Lord for the first time. She genuflected at the burning lamp on the altar; then she was taken to the chapter house, where the whole community waited. Here, the new entrant was given her new name in religion, her old name having belonged to the old identity she had surrendered.

The novice mistress then took her ceremoniously around the community and each nun gave her the pax, the formal kiss of peace. She saw for the first time the women among whom she might live for the rest of her life. They were to be her family and her friends, and only for the rarest possible emergencies would she ever again leave them, even for a day.

Receiving a new name is one of the most traumatic acts of the novice's new life. The name may approximate her own, or it may not, but she is expected to emulate the qualities and virtues of her name-sake—though, as one sister given the name Humiliata remarked, she

75

never really thought she made it. Some orders allow the sisters to choose their own dedication, which might be Sister So-and-so of the Passion, the Precious Blood, the Resurrection, the Ascension, the Agony of Christ, the Peace of God, or perhaps the Divine Silence. Many orders actually add to the confusion by prefacing each name with "Mary." The Missionaries of the Divine Motherhood, for example, have Sister Mary Marcellinus, Sister Mary Inviolata, Sister Mary Pulcherima, Sister Mary Misericordiae, and Sister Mary Stigmata.

To an outsider, the process of going into a convent looks remarkably like being admitted to prison: the taking of the person's clothes, the removal of all personal items, the life in common, the assuming of a new identity—for the prisoner, a number; for the nun, the title "Sister." One woman vividly described how she hated the title, "the black nonentity of sisterhood." As a Jesuit priest comments, "This business of naming is said to be because it's a new way of life altogether. But frankly it's just a way of depersonalizing." That process is carried even further when many new nuns are given men's names, largely because the huge number of women in religion rapidly uses up the available well-known women's names. So there are Sister Mary Thomas à Becket and Sister John Bosco, Sister Anthony of Padua and Sister William Eugene, Sister Mary Cuthbert Mayne and Sister Mary Paul of Tarsus, while Sister Aelred is named after a Saxon bishop.

Current thinking, however, is moving away from the changing of names. "Freud," says one novice mistress, "is now listened to. We realize the past is important." The former Sister Godric, who has gratefully reverted to her baptismal name of Sister Maire, remarks, "Godric was a Saxon hermit, then a peddler and a merchant and a saint, and he ended up living in a forest near Durham. I found it hard to identify with him."

That first day provides a memory which no woman who has entered a convent ever forgets. They can all describe the journey to the door. "I remember my last taxi ride, puffing away madly on a last cigarette." A strictly enclosed nun, who entered over sixty years ago, recalls with a shudder how she felt. "It was very dark and there were four gaunt figures before me, draped in black. One put out her hand towards me, and it seemed to be enormous."

76

An American who entered the Poor Clare enclosed order was shown to her cell, with two holy pictures covered with cellophane and a straw mattress on the bed. "I thought of an early American bedroom. They left me there, telling me to learn where everything was quickly, because we didn't use electric light, though I was allowed to for the first day."

Margaret McConnell, who describes her convent life in the book *Open Then the Door,* admits that "what I had expected the inside of the convent to be like I cannot say. It is impossible to imagine a convent. It is not the building and not the nuns, but the strange worldless atmosphere that pervades the place."

Most entrants find the hardest thing to accept at first is the bareness, the simplicity, the fact that nowhere is there a single object which does not serve a purpose. "My parents' home was full of pictures," says an Italian girl, "and we had three cats. I just wanted something pretty to look at—not a statue, an ornament."

The period of postulancy is hard because it is a trial on both sides. It is what one novice mistress describes as a time "for the possible riding-on-the-crest-of-the-wave effect to subside, and the impact of daily reality to help that seep away, so they can discern our conviction with greater reality, and we can discern theirs."

In every order, there are funds of stories about the behavior of postulants, such as the one who arrived with an armful of magazines to get her through the time till she could decently leave or the prospective contemplative who had so little idea of the life that she turned up complete with her cosmetics. Postulants do leave in large numbers —which the orders fully expect. It might be because, once inside, they find that the life does not match up to their expectations. One girl assumed that, like Saint Catherine of Siena, the only nourishment she would need would be the communion wafer. When the rest of the community sat down to a large dinner, she left the house in painful disillusionment. Some women go in meaning to stay only briefly. "I eventually decided I would enter, though secretly I intended to stay only for the postulancy, thinking that after that I could with a clear conscience tell the Lord I had tried, and return to my own sweet life." This woman did remain, "maybe because for the first time in my life I was really happy."

The postulancy is a break with the past. Until a few years ago it was a harsh one. No journeys home were allowed, although parents could visit every third Sunday for a couple of hours. A postulant came under all the novitiate rules, such as the one decreeing that letters she wrote must be handed unsealed to the superior, and that letters she received would be handed to her with the envelope already slit. The girl was required to wear a uniform, though with a shorter dress than the full habit and with a small white veil instead of black.

The period of postulancy, however, has changed. During the early days of convent life, the postulant was shorn and should, in the words of an early Franciscan ruling, "leve the robis of the worlde." Today, in some communities, up to two years is spent half in and half out of the community, during which time the newcomer lives and dresses as she always has. In others, she will probably have the opportunity to live in several houses within the order, sharing different kinds of work. Enlightened novice mistresses now go to great lengths to determine that postulants are really suited.

Before the postulant can be admitted to the novitiate, she must ask formally if she may join the community. A vote may be taken among the members of any house where she has spent considerable time. On the basis of this, and their knowledge of her, the mother general and her council of sisters will formally decide whether or not to accept her. All orders mark this step with ceremony. The Benedictines clothe the new novice in a short version of the habit and a white veil. The Sisters of Our Lady of Grace and Compassion have a short initiation ceremony in church. There is an opening hymn, and then the postulant tells the superior, "Reverend Mother, I wish to become a novice in this congregation," to which the reply is "Thanks be to God. You are welcome to our family." She then makes her act of consecration, promising to dedicate herself to the Virgin Mary, and is formally received into the congregation and given her name in religion.

Until six years ago, the Good Shepherd order received its postulants with the full church ceremony complete with bridal dress. Now, after an eight-day preparation, the girls in their blue dresses enter the community room. The mother provincial—in a ceremony written hopefully for several postulants simultaneously—addresses them.

"Dear Sisters, what do you ask from us?"

They reply, "Drawn by God's merciful grace, we have come here to experience your way of life. We ask you to teach us to follow Christ the Good Shepherd, and to live in poverty, chastity, and obedience and zeal for the salvation of souls."

They ask to be allowed to learn the rule, and the mother provincial responds, "May our merciful God nourish you with his grace, and may Christ our divine teacher grant us his light." She then gives them a copy of the constitutions of the society.

The year of novitiate must, under canon law, be spent within the enclosure "devoted entirely to formation of character, study of the Constitutions, practice of prayer, instructions on the vows and virtues, and exercises suited to correcting defects, subduing passions, and acquiring virtues. Hence the novices are not to be applied to the study of letters, sciences, and arts; nor to be employed in the exterior works of the Institute." This is no longer strictly observed, particularly since the majority of young women will be taking some sort of higher education or professional training. But the purpose of the novitiate remains: to find, as Teresa of Ávila put it, "whether they are of the right temperament and have the other qualities for keeping our rule."

The novice mistress is the person with whom the new entrant has most contact. In the monastic orders, she is still "Mistress of Novices," and she should, in the words of Saint Benedict, be someone who "loves and is careful about the Divine Office, and is obedient, humble, and persevering." Until recently, many also seem to have been veritable martinets. It was the novice mistress who trained the novice in the ways of the convent, teaching her to join her hands in a special position, to walk on the balls of her feet, to observe silence. In so doing she was expected, if necessary, to "break the spirit"; this was not regarded as cruelty, since conformity was all.

Almost every nun I met had stories about her novice mistress's strictness. "She stood at the bottom of the stairs just before night prayers," remembers a German sister. "The novices, passing her, had to admit to any faults during the day and ask special permissions: 'I broke a glass.' 'I didn't finish my prayer at noon.' 'May I take a bath?'" As one Good Shepherd sister recalls, "My novice mistress was very cold—repelling, almost. She was very much the superior, and she felt it her job to turn out very humble and obedient souls." Obedience had to be, quite literally, blind. "It wasn't just teaching you what to do but the exact, precise way you always had to do it. You were taught to brush a corridor in a certain way, and woe betide you if you attempted improvements."

While it was undeniably destructive—"It was hardship at a psychological level, destroying me as a person. It took me years to get over it" —some women can look back and discover hard-earned benefits. Rita Hannon of La Sainte Union des Sacrés-Coeurs found "the discipline, as a background, meant I learned of the possibilities within me. I learned what I could endure. And that has remained with me. I feel now I could be jailed, or I could be free and sitting on a halfpenny, because of this experience."

The novice mistress is also responsible for explaining the intentions of the life. As Francis de Sales wrote to one of his sisters in 1690, "The victim must be consumed, you must strip your heart of self, cut back hard all the little shortcomings prompted by nature and by the world." This, he admitted, was no easy task; "it is not done in a day."

All the little shortcomings were cut back hard indeed. The following is part of the Carmelite *Manual for Novices on Mortification of the Exterior Senses*:

> Do not smell fragrant herbs, fruit or flowers etc. much less bring them into your cell, or keep them for their pleasant odour.
> When you eat or drink, think of something unsavoury in order to mortify the taste, especially if you take things agreeable to the palate.
> Sometimes mingle a little water or bitter flavouring with your food.
> At intervals put the body to some inconvenience, such as keeping one foot raised etc., in order that the discomfort of the body may impede the gratification of the taste or moderate it, that so each morsel may be dipped in the gall and vinegar of Jesus Crucified.

The role of the novice mistress has changed since that manual was published in the 1920s, and it is symbolic that many communities now prefer to call her "novice guardian" or "formation director." (Though perhaps her role has not changed that much: the sisters of one American order refer to their novitiate, Humility House, as "Humble Hut.") In most communities, she is at least thirty-five years old and professed

80

for not less than ten years; unlike the superior, she can be reelected as often as the community wishes.

The constitutions of one congregation, founded ten years ago, say that she must be "a model of obedience to her Superiors and very exact in the religious life. She should be charitable and prudent, motherly, just and firm, kind but not weak. She must be approachable, but not be afraid to humble the proud and correct the negligent and disobedient." She also must be knowledgeable about doctrine, scripture, and liturgy because she is also expected to instruct the novices in these subjects. "A very simple yet thorough knowledge of Christianity" is what one novice mistress defines as her aim. Another says, "We go according to what the girl can take in and what her interests are. Some are very interested in theology; others aren't. We teach scripture and how to read the Bible intelligently and read well in public. They're expected to know dogma before they come, though some don't."

It is accepted that a training period is needed for such a post, and there are now regular conferences and courses available. Today's novice mistress is aware of group dynamics and interpersonal relations; she worries lest she is not understanding enough. "I feel, Suppose I reprimand a novice because I'm in a bad temper? It would be dreadful; I'd be an obstacle in her path. I often pray for inspiration, that I may do what is most helpful for them."

Novice mistresses are very conscious of the responsibilities of their task. "It's quite a moment to see a person come in the door to enter, and know they've got to be transformed into a religious, the point of view they've got to get." Yet the role is not wholly one of encouragement. Sister Madeleine of the Augustinian Sisters of Meaux sees as part of her duty the job of exposing novices to the drawbacks of religious life as well as the advantages. She claims she is a devil's advocate. "If they take their vows after me, they make their choice in full, total conviction."

One of the first things the novice mistress teaches her pupils is the pattern of day. This usually begins around 5:00 A.M. with a knock on the door and a call from the sister ringing the handbell. The call varies from order to order. For some it is "May Mary's heart immaculate—" to which the response is "—be forever praised." Or it might be "Blessed be God," and the response, "Blessed be his holy name." The first gesture of the day might be to kiss the ground in monastic fashion, or perhaps to stand for a moment "religiously," before kneeling for prayer.

The hours of the novice's day used to be strictly divided. "We had to make a list accounting for what we did every half hour." This custom has not entirely died out. One novice was so closely watched that "in the dormitory and chapel someone used to come and check that you were meditating."

In the past, novices used to be separated from other members of the community in order that they should not be unduly influenced by them. This is now recognized as absurd, since the novice is there to learn about the community. But her day is still different from that of the established sister, because so much of her time is spent in study.

The most important thing for the novice to learn is the meaning of the vows and what it will cost her to live them. The only measure of loving, said Saint Bernard, is to love without measure. The purpose of the three vows of poverty, chastity, and obedience is to give the nun greater freedom to love, to achieve a kind of spiritual nudity by withdrawing her heart from this world. "Contentment," as one novice master described it, "is the absence of creature satisfactions." The reason for giving them up is not that they are bad but that the novice love God more than the best of the other satisfactions. So the vows are described as a sort of death, because they represent a complete break with the ways of the world and are felt in the body, heart, and mind as a death to things normally valued.

Vows did not exist at the beginning of religious life. The first religious, the desert fathers, lived without vows or a rule. It was only when communities developed that it became necessary to order the lives of the members more firmly—"to safeguard stability," as one priest puts it, "and strengthen the wavering will during time of weakness or stress."

Stability is particularly important to the contemplatives. The Benedictines, like some other orders, make their first vow of stability to the house so that, as Saint Benedict stated, "its members should have no need to go abroad, which can in no way be good for them." Their second vow is peculiar to themselves, the "conversion of manners," which teaches the opposite way of thinking to that in the world. Poverty is included; so is self-effacement, and listening rather than talking.

The religious state is a subjection of the individual, to be brought about by observing the vows. This is how the Anglican Deaconess Community of Saint Andrew defines them:

Poverty is "foregoing the right to personal ownership so as to live in simplicity and be more carefree in the service of God and people." Chastity is "living without the particular relationships of marriage and parenthood in order to be free to respond with warm yet unpossessive love wherever and whenever it is asked." And obedience is "giving up the right to determine one's own path so as to be available to be used by God in the way he wants."

Of the vows, the first, poverty, is something of a misnomer. The nun is to give up everything in order to identify with those who have little of their own. Yet, to most women, going into a convent means an end to financial worry and strain. Everything is provided for them— clothes and shoes, food and heat. In their old age, the community looks after them. Certainly they practice simplicity of life, but that is a very different thing from poverty.

Take the Poor Servants of the Mother of God; outsiders might well expect them to be just that. But visitors to their Somerset house would be rapidly disillusioned. The house stands amid beautiful grounds at the end of a long, winding drive. Inside, visitors are shown into a richly carpeted room with a magnificent conference-sized wooden table, a cocktail cabinet full of glasses, and a television set in the corner. Civilization has reason to be grateful for the superb buildings put up by some religious orders to house their nuns; that is, after all, to the glory of God. Rich carpets are harder to justify.

Sister Rita Hannon of La Sainte Union des Sacrés-Coeurs feels badly about nuns being "women of property. I wouldn't mind this if I could say that in the vast majority of cases we used our property generously. But the inspiring words of Christ about leaving all to follow him seem to have lost their appeal. It's disconcerting to think that, for many of us, these were the very liberating words which brought us into religious life."

Poverty means the absence of extravagance; it is not supposed to mean penury. Nuns are not expected to share their clothes, their teeth, or even their handkerchiefs, as in one lay community on the Canadian lakes which takes communal property a lot farther than any other religious community I encountered.

Mother Gabriel, mother general of the Sisters of Mercy convent in central London, says she estimates poverty by "what you could afford if you were a mother in a house with an ordinary family. We're supposed to be poor, not indigent." She feels it is a false economy to buy too cheaply, because "fairly good things, like good shoes, last much longer. And 'seeming to be poor' doesn't mean to be in rags.

But nuns are endeavoring, as the Sacred Heart sisters nicely put it, "to live a simple life, resisting the pressure of a consumer society." And of course, real and grinding poverty is no stranger to many nuns. As Teresa of Ávila said, when asked to make two foundations, "I had no means for making either but that was no disadvantage as I generally began with less than nothing." And in Toledo she wrote with mock despair that "we had not so much as a scrap of brushwood to broil a sardine on."

The Little Sisters of Jesus in Montreal live in the dock area. One woman who visited, planning to join them, said, "I asked them how they would heat their rooms during the subzero winter. They said they had no idea."

Nuns are charmingly unworldly about money when they do have it, like the superior who traveled across England with £400 tucked into her habit, secured with a safety pin. One of the touching characteristics of the poorer orders is their trust that money will be found. When the Little Sisters of the Poor wanted to open a house in Glasgow, they found one that seemed to be suitable and threw a statuette of Saint Joseph over the wall so he could take possession of it; sure enough, they later found the needed money. A member of the same order, Sister Emmanuel, wrote a letter to the French industrialist to whom she owed £500 for the building of a convent. She was dying and asked that she be released from half the debt. "From the chapter here, with God's help, the other half will be paid back at the rate of £50 a month. For that we are going to arrange with the Blessed Virgin and Saint Joseph to send you the amount in the first fortnight of every month."

The order of the Poor Clares must not have a fixed income but must live on alms. It has no endowments, no revenues of any sort.

84

"We just depend on Divine Providence and whatever we can earn with our hands to pay our way; we can never be self-supporting if we are to fulfill our life, our time of prayer, what our life is primarily about." Another Poor Clare superior adds, "When the bills come in, it's quite true that often I just don't know how I'm going to meet them. But I generally take them and show them to Our Lord and remind him of his promise. It is just as simple as that. And somehow, just before I'm due to be summonsed, the money comes in: sometimes it's just small amounts from the poor, or sometimes the occasional benefactor has come forward and taken over the bill for us."

All sorts of economies are practiced. It was said of a Franciscan for the Home Missions that, so keen was she on poverty, she used one toothbrush all her life. And the Oblates of the Eucharist, a French semicontemplative order at Sceaux, outside Paris, built their own first house after World War II. They were desperate for accommodations for their incurable patients, and in two years they had built a three-story building from their own plans, of dark-faced brick, complete even to electricity, which they installed themselves. Although an architect designed their cool white chapel, they built that, too.

One area where nuns do seem to economize is food, even in these days of nutrition and balanced diets. (It is said that this is far from true of male communities, whose members are reputed to eat vastly.) At one English house, the sisters ate in a gloomy basement lit by harsh neon. Twice, on the day I was there, the meal consisted of packaged fish fingers, great wedges of bread and margarine, canned fruit salad, and sponge cakes out of a packet. If these women treat their food with monastic disdain, the Daughters of Charity of Saint Vincent de Paul in Paris certainly do not. At their huge modern hospital in Neuilly, where they look after physically handicapped children, the sisters eat better than diners in many a restaurant: grapefruit or paté, followed by slices of beef, cauliflower au gratin, fresh green salad with vinaigrette dressing, then homemade fruitcake, an ample cheeseboard, and celery and fresh fruit—all this in a freshly painted dining room in the sisters' quarters above the hospital. Wine was served with the meal, and coffee afterward. It was a far cry from the contemplative order whose superior once told the sisters that the bell would be rung for dinner—if there was any.

The early founders of religious orders took their food very seriously. Saint Benedict, for instance, laid down that each day two kinds of "mete" should be provided, so that he who would not eat of one kind could partake of the other. And in 1400, a Barking convent's meticulous records mentioned twenty-two oxen, pigs and sheep, geese, fowl, and fish. At Saint Aldburgh's feast, every lady of the convent had half a goose, "also one hen or else a cock." At the other end of the culinary scale, the Poor Clares today eat soup, potatoes, and a meat substitute for their one full meal a day; for the other meals they make do with dry bread and coffee with, occasionally, butter for the postulants.

Much of the income of religious orders was originally brought by the novices. Today, if a novice brings a dowry, it may well be spent on some long and expensive training course. Plenty of orders still ask for dowries. The Sisters of the Holy Family of Louisiana, for instance, must have not only a dowry but a trousseau to dress them for three years, and a Benedictine choir nun brings a minimum of $1,500, but this is kept on deposit for her until her Solemn Profession.

On Solemn Profession, everything is given away. If a nun then decides to leave, she has no claim. "You can't," says one superior, "have people deciding to leave and claiming back this and that. It's impossible." Most orders now have organizations into which they pay funds for just such contingencies, because they feel responsible for those leaving, "but they have no absolute right to anything."

To earn a living, contemplative nuns in particular turn their hands to all sorts of things. In the fifteenth century, the nuns of Antwerp and Malines were famous for the lace collars and embroidered shirts they made for men of the aristocracy. Today it tends to be lavender sachets or cell models in polystyrene. They produce handbound books, like the Benedictines, on their own presses. They turn out Christmas cards, like those drawn for the American Immaculate Heart of Mary community by their former sister and famous artist, Sister Corita Kent. Members of another American order, the Sisters of the Cross, produce ceramic cruet sets and even ponchos. They also make "dressed infants of Prague" and bridal dolls.

Whatever they do, religious communities tend to find themselves in financial difficulties. These days, indigence is regarded by the public as evidence of inefficiency rather than holiness. "You can't live on the fringe of existence," says one superior. "For one thing, the state doesn't allow it." In Britain, the nuns are in an especially peculiar position. The orders that do charitable work with the poor, or teach, are actively proselytizing. They keep the income earned by their members tax-free; they are regarded as legal charities and enjoy relief from tax under the Income and Corporation Taxes Act of 1970. But the contemplatives, with their cottage industries, labor under the same massive burden of taxation as giant corporations. This absurd situation came about because in 1949 the law lords decided that, in this modern age, saying prayers could not be considered a charity. Religious orders, enclosed and established for "prayer and self-sanctification," are not charitable because they lack "the essential quality of public benefit," and because they are under vows of poverty, the income of contemplatives is treated as a common fund, so they are not even eligible for the full tax-free allowance that every other taxpayer gets.

In the past it was all too easy for a nun to have no idea of the value of money. If she needed a stamp or toothpaste, she asked for it. For a bus or train journey, the treasurer gave her a purse with the money and her ticket. If she taught at a local school, she was given a certain amount of money at the beginning of the week and had to give an exact accounting of it.

The years since Vatican II have changed this attitude. Now that nuns are moving out of their vast motherhouses, money is becoming real to them. One German sister says that, as housekeeper for a small group of sisters instead of one of a community of twenty, she really knows what poverty means. "I can't buy apples because they've gone up a penny a pound. It's the first time this vow has come home to me."

Today, a nun may be on a personal allowance, the amount to be decided by the community depending on her job—a teacher in a convent school may need very little, a nurse or university lecturer a larger amount. As one professional woman says, "You have to read the Gospel and see what demands are made of you. I can't go around with my books in a rucksack, so for me a briefcase is not a luxury but a necessity." The allowances may be quite small. The Holy Child sisters in Neuilly have had fifteen francs a month for the last two years for such things as special books or postage, and between three and four hundred francs a year for clothes, though this is not really enough.

Consequently, they are glad of relatives' hand-me-downs. Medical needs and books for study are paid for by the order. A Belgian Lady of Mary gets the equivalent of $5 a week for clothes, holidays, and the cost of attending retreats. Even such a small amount "makes for an individual's being very independent."

Most active communities have a common fund which is perhaps the combined salaries of their teachers. Out of this come the communal bills—heating, light, and food. Then they allot to each sister the equivalent of a small pension. And, of course, all religious communities are accustomed to make their needs known—like the order which puts notices in all visitors' rooms reading, *Our debt for the central heating is now £1,250. Will you help us to reduce this? May God reward you.*

Poverty remains the hardest vow for the people of developing countries to accept as part of the Christian religious life. Sister Alma, a black superior of the Little Sisters of Saint Francis in Africa, says the people see it as a contradiction. "These people hardly get the necessities of life, and they become very confused when they see the life the sisters lead. It looks artificial and seems hypocritical, an escape for girls from real poverty at home into that which is a made-up story, where sisters enjoy a high standard of living and security."

It is still true today that, of the three vows, obedience, like poverty, is considered in absolute theological terms. (Chastity, on the other hand, is passed over with what one sister calls, oddly, "euphemism and polite refrain.") The vow of obedience is said to be the very essence of religious life. It is the means whereby the nun's life is framed for her by the canon lawyers.

When she makes this vow, a religious binds herself under the authority of the superiors of her congregation in whom, as in God, she must have "great confidence." She undertakes to obey "all their lawful commands in everything which directly and indirectly governs the life and work of the congregation." Such commands are an expression of God's will which she must obey promptly, generously, and unquestioningly. "Grumbling or complaining are alien to the vow of obedience," says the rule. If a sister is changed from one house to another, or elected to an office, she may not refuse, though she may state her case to the superior in cases of special difficulty, knowing she will "humbly abide" by her decision. Sister Marissa of the Poor Servants of the Mother of God devoted years of her life to teaching subnormal girls in Brighton ("I was built into the place"). When she was asked to become superior at another house, she went without question. "If you're asked, you accept; you don't say no. That's not God's will. You'd never be happy again, having refused a work you were meant to do."

Obedience can bring special difficulties. It can, says one nun, "lead to exaltation of the rule, which encourages childishness and mediocrity." The community used to be thought of in terms of the hierarchical family, with the head absolutely and unquestioningly obeyed. Out of that idea came several convent practices, such as bobbing a curtsy whenever the superior appeared. No wonder the religious psychologists are pointing out that to attempt to mold young women into the pattern of their grandmothers is foolish. "A novice cannot be trained to passivity, docility, and subordination and still have a mature ideal," says one.

Of all the religious vows, obedience is today the hardest for a young well-educated woman to accept. She is, after all, used to freedom of thought and speech and to independence. But obedience is no longer practiced to bring about abdication of the will as a means of suppressing the individual. (Such things are not long gone, though; it was Teresa of Ávila who ordered a novice to plant a cucumber on its side in the ground without question, and one nun still in her forties remembers being told to sweep up the garden leaves in a high wind.)

Written into the constitutions these days is a clause stating that the authority of the superiors "should not be so exercised as to govern the most petty details of the lives of their subjects." It is no longer permissible for sisters to be "made to lose all sense of zeal and initiative over their work, nor be made to feel that they should be incapable of offering constructive criticism when it is required." In today's life, authority is thought of as a shared thing, as a responsibility. As one mother superior puts it, "It's just as much the concept of obedience, but it's thought out." Sister Margaret Moran, novice mistress of the Good Shepherd convent in Finchley, London, feels that "the whole concept of obedience, authority, and power is dying in women's orders. The great explosion is the fact that we are a group of adult women who have chosen to live in community for a certain purpose."

The time the girl spends in the novitiate is determined by how she gets along and by the custom of each order. It is usually not less than one year or more than three, and it can be terminated by either the novice herself or the mother general; no formal decision on her future in the community has been taken at this stage.

The novitiate ends with the profession of first vows. Sister Madeleine of the Augustinian Sisters of Meaux is adamant that "if someone isn't suitable, I won't let her make vows. But they must come to the decision for themselves; otherwise they'll feel rejected." It might take a girl as long as four years to realize the life is not for her, but Sister Madeleine does not worry. "I don't consider being a novice mistress is preparing future nuns but helping people find themselves, find their identity, position, and direction—inside or outside the order. Very often, I'm preparing future wives and mothers, and not nuns at all."

Before the first vows are taken, the novice is again considered by the mother general and her council, with the aid of reports from those with whom the woman has worked and lived. Among the Benedictines, not only is the novice examined on her understanding of the monastic life, the rule, prayer, vows, and liturgy—after which each nun and fellow novice gives her opinion about the novice's fitness for profession—but the whole community votes on whether or not she should be admitted to the community by putting either a black or a white ball secretly into a ballot box. If at least two thirds are in the novice's favor, the abbess may admit her to temporary vows. The only exception in any order would be a woman who was dangerously ill; she would be allowed to take her vows without a time limit so that she could benefit from their "spiritual advantages." If she recovered, she would make them in the usual way at the end of the novitiate.

A woman who is to be accepted then makes a retreat of a few days, although it used to last for three months—the time it took to sew the habit. Until recently, the retreat was preceded by a bishop's questioning. This was a practice known as "exploration of the free will," a lengthy examination by which the bishop hoped to judge whether or not the woman had a genuine vocation. As Eileen Gielty of Notre Dame of Namur remembers, "The bishop's questions were a laugh, really. They were within their rights to ask you all sorts of things, whether your parents had forced you into the convent, if you were properly fed, and whether you'd walk out if the superior gave you your freedom."

"Art thou free and unfettered by any bond of the church, or of wedlock; of vow or of excommunication?" asked the bishop of a girl who wished in the fifteenth century to join the nuns of the Bridgettine community. "I am truly free," she replied.

"Does not shame," he continued, "or perchance grief or worldly adversity urge thee to a religious profession, or perhaps the multitude of thy debts compel thee?"

And she answered, "Neither grief nor shame incites me to this, but a fervent love of Christ; and I have already paid all my debts according to my power."

The clothing of a novice is rarely carried out in public today; where this practice continues, it has become a private "family" affair. Dressing in bridal white with veils and bouquets has also to a large extent disappeared among major orders. "The bridal imagery," according to Sister Maria Boulding, a Benedictine of Stanbrook Abbey in Worcester, "is right in the Solemn Profession, which is the marriage ceremony—it belongs there. But this is only the engagement." Many of the Benedictine houses dropped the romantic ceremony described at the beginning of this chapter in the mid-1960s and replaced it with a far simpler service. Although they had given the habit at the beginning of the novitiate since the ninth century, they reverted to the original practice of giving it upon profession. Other orders see the abandoning of this custom not as lack of enthusiasm for a most touching rite but as acceptance of the harsh facts. "More and more sisters," explains a superior, "are leaving before taking final vows. We cannot, therefore, justify putting so much emotion and meaning into something so early in their religious life; we'd rather wait for the final profession." Mother Gabriel of the Sisters of Mercy was sorry to see the Clothing go. "I thought it was lovely, myself. The beautiful dresses and lace were made into vestments afterwards; there were orange blossoms and singing."

On the day of profession, those in the novitiate are allowed another half hour in bed after the six-o'clock bell. Margaret O'Connell, in her book on convent life, wrote:

> I lay and thought of the ordeal awaiting us. There was no greater hour on the earth, I was sure. How many worldly brides lay as we now lay? They awaited the hour of their dedication to a man who would die and pass and leave them only with a memory of passing pleasure. For us, when the final hour would come, we would all be gathered together in the land of Judgement.

Others have more prosaic memories. One twenty-four-year-old Sacred Heart sister was clothed on a freezing January day. "I wore this lovely white satin dress, and underneath a great big football shirt."

Each order has slight differences in the ceremonies. The Carmelites, for instance, have always had a tradition of wearing roses; their novices have white roses for the Clothing, a symbol of virginity they will wear again at the hour of their death. The Poor Clares bind their hair with a crown of thorns. Their novice walks to the superior, who stands with the bishop, and her hair is cut off ceremoniously and placed in a little rush basket on the table; then the superior helps her put on her bonnet. In other orders where the bishop performs the haircutting ceremony, the hair is braided first and cut off in public, and the superior trims the ends tidily later.

"God forbid that I should glory," recites the novice, "save in the Cross of Jesus Christ. By whom the world is created to me and I to the world."

The haircutting signifies self-effacement, but like so much else about the religious life there is not one simple reason for it. Cutting off the hair was a sign of mourning in many ancient societies—Egypt, Greece, and Rome—which both men and women practiced. The cropping of nuns and the tonsuring of monks seems, therefore, to have its roots in the idea that in entering religious life they are dying to the world. Another reason put forward was that a sister who could eradicate her sexuality stood a better chance of becoming holy, and so it became, says an American, "a point of virtue to make oneself unattractive, for attractiveness was sexual lure." For this reason mirrors were barred, curves were flattened, and heads were shaved—all in the name of virtue. There are orders where the hair is still cut short and the nuns accept it without demur, because "we haven't time for such

92

feminine vanities as looking after it." Some women still choose to keep their hair cropped for the sake of comfort beneath the headdress, but no one is now compelled to crop it "like a convict," as one woman remembers with a shudder. Many used to shave their heads completely: Dr. Charlotte Klein of Our Lady of Sion—who now has red-blond hair which she regularly sets on rollers—used to run a razor over her head every three or four weeks. The majority of women must have found this hard to accept. A young American sister recalls that her hair was tied back with a pink band and the next thing she knew it was all on the floor and her whole head was being shaved. "The terrible thing about it was the psychological effect, the feeling of how I looked with a bald head." Others regard it as a meaningful sacrifice. A nun of forty who used to keep her hair cropped says, "I can't tell you what immense spiritual joy it gave me, being in that condition. I'd done it for Him, and this gift of one's hair was something very special."

When First Profession is over, there are parties for the newly professed sisters, though they may be as simple as the large breakfast served by the Anglican Deaconess Community of Saint Andrew for one of their sisters; the many-tiered white-iced wedding cakes glowing with candles vanished with the wedding dresses. But some survivals of earlier times are still practiced at the first profession. In Italy, the Poor Clares have a skeleton which represents Sister Death; when the girl goes to change, the skeleton is supposed to move forward and embrace her. At least one Poor Clare house in Britain, too, had its own skeleton—until their bishop objected. A young Sacred Heart sister says that every week her laundry would appear on her bed neatly folded; starting the week after her profession, her brassieres were never returned to her.

Dressing in the habit is an elaborate business, with a short prayer to match each item. The veil is the most emotive garment. Particularly for contemplatives, it sums up the life they will know only from behind it. The original function of the veil—protecting the wearer against the evil eye and devils—has long been lost, and early in Christianity it became a sign of constancy. It signifies the nun's marriage with Christ, and her virginity. "Receive this veil," goes the profession of the Deaconess Community of Saint Andrew, "the token of purity and modesty . . . that thou mayest at last with the wise Virgins be ready to enter into the joyful marriage of the Lamb." The color of the veil also shows the wearer's religious status. In some communities a white veil is worn until Final Profession, when it is exchanged for a black one; other orders, like the Benedictines, give the black veil at the temporary or first profession.

Until the beginning of this century, a novice would leave the novitiate and immediately make her Final Profession. But in 1917 new legislation was introduced, and under the Code of Canon Law a period of temporary vows became part of the preparation for perpetual profession. It was a prudent move, the reason being that a woman needs time to live the life before committing herself to it totally. These vows are renewable each year, and the sister is free to reconsider her decision until she has taken her solemn and final vows, which might occur any time from three to nine years later. But the form a temporary commitment takes, and its intention, is exactly the same as that of the permanent vow for which it is an apprenticeship. Through these temporary vows in the presence of the community, she enters the religious state. Some orders make them for three years and renew for two; others renew yearly.

At the Anglican Deaconess Community of Saint Andrew in London, a young sister is taking her vows for the first time, for a year. The service is at eight in the morning, and before it she stands nervously outside the chapel with the novice mistress. When she enters, there is silence as she kneels before the chaplain. He hears her request to make her profession in the community, then asks, "Dost thou promise to remain in the holy estate of chastity?"

"God being my helper, I do so promise for a period of twelve months from this date."

"Dost thou promise to remain in a state of poverty?"

"God being my helper, I do so promise for a period of twelve months from this date."

She vows obedience in the same words; then her veil is blessed and handed to her, the cross is settled about her neck, and she is given the long cord for her habit, with the three knots marking the three vows.

Not everyone likes the idea of temporary vows. Superiors general and their councils can release a sister from temporary vows, but Rome must be approached before permanent vows can be waived. Some feel that because temporary vows are easier to dispense with than permanent vows, they are less serious. Others regard them as a holding back. One sister found that restriction to annual vows means that "I can neither say what I mean nor mean what I say"; another feels that "it's as if I want to get married and promise to be faithful forever, and I'm being told we can have an affair for a year and then think again."

Even so, in 1969, following a request made by many superiors, the Holy See issued an instruction, "Renovationis Causam," which allowed orders to make a different framework for the probationary period before Final Profession. Under this, a novice does not even have to make temporary vows but may make a promise to her congregation instead. Theologians define a vow as "a deliberate and free promise made to God of a possible and better good." It is made to worship God. But a promise is made to the congregation, to others, and breaking this promise is not regarded as against religion. For one thing, a person "in promises" is not a religious, as is one who has made temporary vows. There are many who see promises as a dangerous compromise, a sort of lower grade for candidates who cannot reach too high or come to a decision soon enough. "I do not feel at all drawn to exchanging triennial vows for promises," was the reaction of at least one superior. "I think if a would-be nun is not ready after six months' postulancy and two years' novitiate, she will never be ready." She is one of many women who feel that the whole system of temporary vows *or* promises is psychologically impossible. They argue that making a vow is a commitment, a consecration to God, and that by its nature it cannot be less than permanent. And they see a lack of generosity where they want radical statements and definite commitments.

There is, of course, an ever-increasing number who argue strongly for the temporary vow and promise system. They point out that the attitude toward entering religious life has changed, that more and more women leave convents at some stage of their training or even when fully professed, that this new system allows them to do so with more dignity, and that both the woman and the church are made to feel less a failure. At the most extreme, there are sisters who feel that even promises are too much, reflecting a trend which seems to be more widespread in the United States than in Europe. The attitude of U.S. sisters is in the main far more relaxed. They accept change more easily; they are accustomed to moving around an enormous country, and they are more open to tackling different work and ways of life. A typical American sister, a girl in her late twenties living in an apartment with a member of another community, says that so far as she is concerned she does not want to make perpetual profession. "There's just no way I would ever do that." She is due to do so under the constitutions of her order in another three years, but her superior has suggested that by that time there might be provision made by the Holy See under which she would be in some way exempted. She is not in any sense refusing to make perpetual profession because she feels she might want to move on to something else. She is a well-educated, highly intelligent, active woman with considerable drive and personality. "But if I were an ordinary woman, I guess I wouldn't get married either. It's just not the sort of finality I want in any relationship in my life."

The Anglican-Episcopalian church for a long time objected strenuously to "irrevocable vows" taken at times of great emotion. In 1885 it was decided that a promise for life should be made to the bishop—and therefore to a man—which would be dispensable. But by 1890 the fine distinction had disappeared, and it was made "in the presence" of the bishop.

Many young sisters are sure they want to dedicate their lives to God, but less sure they want to remain permanently in the same congregation. Honor Basset, superior of the Society of the Sacred Heart, feels that "thinking at the moment among the young says that if you make stable commitment in one place you're tying yourself up against the possibility that God might want you to move on." It fits in, she thinks, with the modern view of marriage. "It's the sort of thing we'd never have tolerated. We'd have said, If you're going to give your life to one man, that's all about it." She points out that, if a sister moves on after five or six years in one congregation, "it's a bit hard, since they've put all the money into their training."

Like the new marriage services which couples write for themselves, there is now a large section of sisters, particularly in the States, who write their own commitments. This one is a "Celebration of Promise," a renewal of annual vows, taken by a sister in the Midwest:

> God, Our Father, thank you for giving me your spirit (it's the real thing), and because I deeply feel your actions in my life I am moved today, in the presence of your people, to an ever deeper commitment to the task of search and service as outlined by the Congregation of the Humility of Mary.
>
> Guided by the Spirit and following the example of your Son, I promise to follow a life of simplicity in regard to material possessions, of openness to the Spirit of Truth as manifested by those with whom I live and work, and of celibate community where, together, we can accomplish in your work what one alone cannot.
>
> Because you have promised that what is asked in faith will be done in truth, I beg for myself and for all here present a deepening awareness of the power of your Spirit and a profound increase in the only real things: peace, joy, hope, love, celebration, and sunshine.

From about the fourth century, girls could make their profession as nuns when they were over twelve, and were given a veil of profession to wear. But they could not be solemnly consecrated by the bishop till they were twenty-five.

By the sixth century, no nun was allowed to be permanently bound by a vow till she was forty. Recently, however, final vows have been taken by very young women; several nuns I met took theirs in their early twenties. There is now a determined move to hold this off until at least twenty-five. Then, when it is felt a woman is ready for these perpetual vows, the mother general and her council once more discuss her, reviewing the person she has become and her role in the community. The Benedictines also require the community to vote on whether the junior should be fully admitted. The Solemn Profession at which she makes her vows for life—in one of the most ancient ceremonies of the Catholic church—comes perhaps five, perhaps nine years after her first entry.

The night before the ceremony, the Benedictine goes to the chapter house. There, before the community, she has to make her final choice between the cloister and the world. On one table is laid out the ring, the cowl and miter, the little silver crown of the virgin. On

97

another, neatly folded, are the clothes she wore when she first arrived at the monastery. In this ceremony of tacit profession, she must lay her hand on one table or the other.

If she chooses the cloister, next day she comes once more before the community in the abbey chapel. "Receive me, Lord, according to your promise and I shall live; and let me not be disappointed in my hope." The candle she carries is lit. "And now with all my heart I follow you: I fear you and I seek to see your face."

She stands before the prelate, who gives her the cowl, the habit of Saint Benedict, cautioning her to keep her vows "so that you may enjoy the company of God and his holy angels and of the saints who have worn this habit before you." The full black veil of a solemnly professed nun is pinned to her cap, and she is given the simple silver ring of the bride of Christ and the headband that is a token of her virginity.

"With this ring has my Lord Jesus Christ betrothed me; and as his bride he has adorned me with a crown."

She receives her breviary, sign of her right to begin the canonical hours and recite Divine Office. The chart of her vows is read out, she signs, and the abbess lays it upon the altar. Then the new nun goes with the community to choir, where she kneels in the center while the Collect of Thanksgiving is sung. The abbess takes her hand and with the mistress of ceremonies leads her to her stall. This stall, behind the chapel grille, is now hers by canonical right. She is an official representative before God of the church.

"Behold, that which I longed for already I see; that which I hoped for already I hold; I am united in heaven to him whom on earth I have loved with my whole heart."

After these ceremonies, the nun will keep silence for three days of retreat. Then she returns to community life, sitting in refectory for one meal on the right hand of the abbess, where her place at the high table is decorated with flowers. And when she retires to her cells that night, her bed will be strewn with little bunches of flowers from her sisters.

The most terrible and moving moment of the Final Profession has been removed by some orders: the moment at which the newly professed stretches prostrate on the ground while her sisters put over her the pall, the covering of the dead, and place a candle at each corner.

There she lies while the "Dies irae" is sung, as at a funeral, showing all who watch that she is dead to the world. "It was terrible for the parents," remembers a Good Shepherd sister, "and we stopped it because they got so upset." This order experimented for a time with the sister's coming up to the altar with hands outstretched. That, too, has been superseded, and current practice has the sister coming to the altar with her parents, holding among them the water, wine, and bread as a symbol of their offering.

But the words have changed little, and the Final Profession ceremony contains the most evocative religious prose. The blessing said over the finally professed sister of Our Lady of Grace and Compassion begs that "when you enter the chamber of the Bridegroom, you may carry a shining lamp in your hand and meet him with joy. May he find in you nothing disgraceful, nothing sordid, nothing dishonorable, but a snow-white soul and a clear and shining body."

And when the nun is finally professed and consecrated, the entire church turns to her. Now indeed is she sweetly dead to the world.

"Thy beauty now is all for the King's delight. He is thy Lord and God."

You can't sublimate it. You can't suppress it.
You simply have to damn well sacrifice it.
—AUGUSTINIAN SISTER OF MEAUX

4

A Celibate Life

The most important difference between nuns and other women, as groups, is that they choose lifelong chastity.

By her vow of chastity, the nun is consecrating her life more perfectly to God. She must abstain—and these words or very similar ones are used by every congregation—"from every act, internal or external, opposed to the virtue of chastity." She is advised to acquire this virtue through "fervent and persevering prayer" and to ensure its proper development by practicing constant mortification of her mind and feelings, particularly avoiding "exclusive and passionate friendships and observing a sensible modesty" in her appearance and behavior. But she must not be "coldly reserved, cheerless, and abrupt to others," for this would be failing in charity.

Behind chastity lies all the weight of ecclesiastical tradition. Yet in our society today, chastity and celibacy are considered neither desirable nor admirable. There is a feeling that the celibate is an aberration, a freak, someone with an emotional if not a physical impediment to normal pleasures, satisfactions, and happiness. A growing number of nuns echo this view. One American nun and theologian, for example, who feels that "the public thinks of celibacy as a negative thing—and the public is right," argues that "all this talk about celibacy freeing nuns to serve is just a rationalization. The choice not to marry is a personal one and has nothing to do with efficiency in the service of God."

Most religious would not agree, however. "The celibate," wrote a seventeenth-century Anglican, "like the fly in the heart of the apple, dwells in a perpetual sweetness, and is confined and dies in singularity." Virginity has been called a life of angels, the enamel of the soul. "A virgin," declared Saint Ambrose, "is purity's immolation, the victim of chastity."

In Christianity, virginity is seen as the consummation of love between God and the soul. The idea is that a woman, by foregoing any physical expression of sex, is achieving "spiritual motherhood" and thus belongs not to one family but to all. Virginity is seen as a positive thing: "a shining sword," one sister calls it. So a nun's chastity does not come merely from sexual continence. She is, in the words of one religious—a man—"in a condition of higher fruitfulness designed by God to give supernatural power to the world."

According to a Benedictine nun, Sister Maria Boulding, "Virginity is something important in the church, a special grace from God. To those to whom it is given it is pure grace." It is a virtue extolled by a church which believes—as Pope Pius said in 1954 in his Encyclical on Holy Virginity, still the official document on the subject—that "our bodily powers and passions darken the mind and weaken the will." It is considered to be more perfect than the state of marriage. Virginity, it has been said, is of gold, chastity of silver, and marriage of brass. The belief is that a consecrated woman is not important for what she can do in utilitarian terms—the schools where she can teach, the missions where she can work—but rather that because she *is* a consecrated woman, a living sacrifice, her every act is already sacred.

The vow of chastity is a solemn promise by which the nun clears the decks for action and her soul for union with God. It frees her, makes it possible for more than one person to have a claim on her love;

it is a means to an end. It is a reminder, too, that man is alone before God, and that in eternity there will be neither male nor female. She does not consider that through her vow of chastity she is depriving herself of a necessary human experience. "We're trying," explains an Episcopalian sister, "to be *more* human, not less." Another said it was like being separated from a marriage partner. "People wouldn't think you odd if you didn't enter into a relationship with another man while your husband was away, would they?"

At the same time, an American novice master says that the vow of chastity is negative if it "attempts to flee from the realities of sex and rigidly exclude the physical from thought and conduct." Sisters must be taught that they are dedicated to God's service as women, rather than as individual angels uneasily enclosed in a body. But that, of course, is exactly what they have been taught.

There is still much written and said about the vow of chastity that must worry a great many people. "The spirit abolishes the flesh in us," opines one theologian. "It is not celibacy that is the cause of nervous troubles," snaps an Italian master of novices, "but a lack of sense of total dedication." Yet many of the women I talked to candidly admitted what they feel as real losses. Sister Marie worked during her novitiate in a home for unmarried mothers and their babies—work at which many orders excel. "You do get times when you just long to have a baby in your arms; you could just sit back and feel distressed about it. And I do regret it, oh, yes, I regret not having babies. I would love to have married and brought up children. But there's no use. I'm here for a different reason." And Sister Morag Michael says, "When I see my sister happily married I think, How gorgeous. But there's something much deeper than human things. It's joy if you're meant to have them, and dust and ashes if you're not. And I'm as sure as I can be that I'm living as God wants me to."

"You feel," says an Italian nun, "that you've had a special call to God, and you mean to give your loving time to him, and so you can't give it to anyone else. It is a life of self-denial for that very reason; you are giving up the physical side of a profound love. I can't see what religious life is about if you don't have celibacy."

The fact that women in religious orders have given up sexual intercourse does not mean they necessarily lose the desire for it. "A celibate body," observes an American sister, "is still a feminine body." Such an admission could not have been made ten years ago. In respectable society, let alone in convents, women have never been allowed to acknowledge their sexual drive. Religious orders dealt—and indeed still deal—with the problem by refusing to admit it exists. Anything "physical" was to be avoided. Even crossing the legs was considered "unreligious"; one elderly nun said she had been very worried when the young and emancipated sisters in her order started doing so, in case they were breaking their vow of chastity.

The attitude that a nun has to "put to death one's natural inclinations" (in the words of one) is only slowly disappearing. Women are realizing that it is not possible to totally repress their sexuality—even though some still try. A twenty-seven-year-old Anglican sister describes such nuns as regarding their sex as something attached to themselves that they don't use, "like a spare tank of petrol on a car."

Male communities have been very little better than female ones in this respect. One sister remembers talking to a seminarian "who told me that when he found himself thinking about women, he visualized them just as a mass of blood and bone and muscle, so he couldn't be led on." This method of suppression is no more effective than that of Saint Benedict in hurling himself into a nettle bed, and about as enlightened as the Franciscan monks' belief that "woman is bitterer than death."

The suffering brought by total denial has always been regarded as valuable in itself. "The root and flower of virginity," as Saint Chrysostom wrote, "is a crucified life," and the pangs of celibacy are called the little crucifixion. One elderly sister volunteers that "it's not much to give up, when you make that comparison." Certainly sexual fulfillment is a trifling matter in that context, but surrendering it forever is nonetheless a real loss. Failure to acknowledge this has caused much unnecessary unhappiness for women in religious orders. Even today, the fact that chastity brings with it tensions and problems is often ignored; in 1975, Pope Paul VI called the celibacy and virginity of Catholic priests and nuns "happy and easy sacrifices."

"I still don't think anyone I've met in religious life," comments a young English sister, "admits there's a problem in suppressed sexuality." Others feel more strongly. "It's obscene the way we haven't talked about sex in an open fashion." Another points out that "we weren't given any education with regard to the facts of life. Some sisters entered when in their teens without knowing them, and they never came to grips with them in a realistic way. How could a girl with that background truly choose to be celibate?"

The young girl who went from school into the even more restricted and protective convent environment, who met men rarely and formally, if at all, and who had no chance to experience any attitudes or life-styles other than her own—this girl cannot have known what she was sacrificing. She did not choose sexual renunciation; it was a piously motivated manipulation. Anne Hyzy, an American Loretto sister in her late twenties, remembers that when she entered, not so long ago, "Things were still very much in the dark. Sex wasn't thought of as a bad thing—it simply wasn't thought of at all. Or if it was, not out loud." She says that "I read books that helped me to understand what was happening inside me. I turned to my friends, and being women we have the same experience; they helped me to understand myself in the area of sex. I've had feelings of jealousy, and envy, that I've had to learn to accept. But I know that has helped me to grow."

Many superiors of the orders, who are in a position to offer help and advice on the subject, are all too often unable to do so because they and their attitudes are those of an earlier generation. The superior general of one major order said firmly, "I don't think every woman wants to get married or in fact wants sex at all." She did admit, however, that whenever she had asked her own mother for information she was told she was too young, and she had still been too young when she entered religious life at seventeen. The superior of an Italian order told me that "discussing sexual matters with young women only makes them morbid," while another superior, a woman in her sixties, simply could not see any problem at all because "you never want what you've never had."

Sister Madeleine, an Augustinian sister, is one of the still rare novice mistresses prepared to discuss sexual matters in public lectures. "It's perfectly true that religious are alive, vibrating human beings—and the more they are, the better they'll be as nuns or monks; you don't want people impotent in their feelings, with no love to give to God." At the same time, she does believe that many religious grossly overrate the problem. "It's simply surprising how, especially if you're not trying to ignore or suppress when goes on in your body, the radiance of your own belief affects even that area. If you feel this fanaticism, if you're touched with fire, then it touches your whole being." She does, however, stress that "someone raving mad with sexual desire to the point where they have to masturbate has not got a vocation." Nor is she talking theoretically; she herself is in her early thirties and says, "I've had a spring evening or two. I've had that feeling, like having a toothache, a bit of an ache somewhere. Not to do with any particular person, just nameless and anonymous, and it comes for a little period.

"I can remember—let's see, was it before Rome or after?—lying awake and vibrating, and I thought, What's happening to me; am I losing my vocation? Then I realized the technique. You have to treat it like sleeplessness; if you lie there and worry about it, you'll never get to sleep. I said to a sister, 'Isn't it good, I haven't lost my femininity. I'm still normal.' And I felt, Let it come, let it go. I'm not going to get hung up about it, or masturbate to get relief."

Current feeling seems to be that the more experience a girl has before she chooses religious life, the better are her chances within it. "It's no use putting someone who's never faced up to the power of her own emotions into religious life," is the view of an Anglican novice mistress. And although nuns are celibate, they need not be virgins. "I'm sure," says a superior, "that girls who've had sexual experience might well think of becoming sisters and wonder whether this is possible. And of course the answer's yes; it's only a technical thing."

There are, however, some orders who do insist their entrants should be virgins. The Benedictines, for example, want the girl's assurance on this point before accepting her as a postulant. "We don't look her in the eye and say, 'Are you a virgin?' We tell her that here we have to be virgins, and then either we hear from her again or we don't. But we don't do it baldly, and if a promising girl comes along who seems to have a vocation but has lost her virginity—and some don't mind at all; they come right out and tell us without batting an eyelid—then we say, 'Well, we do insist on it here,' but give her the names and addresses of orders where it isn't so necessary." At the Solemn Profession, the new nun—who is referred to throughout the ceremony as "the virgin"—takes the three ancient vows of the Benedictines: stability, conversion of life, and obedience. The first binds her to the house, and the second includes the normal vows of poverty and chastity. Then there is the far older rite of the consecration of a virgin. "Do you," asks the prelate, "promise perpetual virginity?" And then, "Come, my chosen one," sings the choir, "and I will set my throne in you." The Benedictines very occasionally do accept a widow, in which case the Solemn Profession is changed accordingly. And in France a change has been made which is likely to infiltrate the order in other countries, by which the insistence on virginity has been dropped; the entrant is not expected to comment on the matter in any way, but at the time of profession she can choose whether she wishes to take the full ceremony, including the consecration of a virgin, or a simpler version—without giving any reason for her choice.

The loss of virginity does not prevent a woman's making a vow of chastity in most orders, because religious virginity can be either retained or recovered. "It begins," explains a French sister, "in the heart, and from there purifies the whole of one's being."

There is certainly no historical precedent for thinking that nuns have never had any sexual experience. Many of the early founders were married women who entered on the death of their husbands—and sometimes before. Hedwig, the patron saint of Silesia in southern Germany, was educated in a convent and married at thirteen to the duke of Poland and Croatia. She founded a nunnery at Trebnitz with part of her dowry, a convent of small houses around a church. She married to follow her parents' wishes rather than her own. "She hoped," says the account of her life, "to secure eternal life by giving birth to children, yet she wished also to please God by chastity, and with her husband's consent practiced self-restraint. Whenever she was aware that the duties of motherhood were beginning, she avoided her husband's proximity and firmly denied herself all intercourse until the time of her confinement." In this way the couple somehow produced three sons and three daughters, whereupon Hedwig "altogether embraced a life of chastity" —understandably perhaps, since the first child was born before she was fourteen.

Many married couples have separated in order to enter into religious life. Saint Bridget was a member of the fourteenth-century royal family of Sweden, and she went into the Bridgettine order she had founded once her seven children were grown; her husband became a

106

monk. Cornelia Connelly, from Philadelphia, and her husband, Pierce, a pastor, had a double vocation: In 1854 he was ordained a priest and she took a vow of perpetual chastity. Leaving their three small children in Pierce's care, Cornelia joined the new Society of the Holy Child Jesus. It led to some acrimony: Pierce gave up the priesthood and, through the Privy Council, claimed restitution of his conjugal rights.

One of the most touching of these double vocations was that of Brother Oswald and Sister Beatrice. In 1931, at the height of his career as a concert pianist, Alfredo Oswald entered the Jesuit order as a lay brother and his wife, Beatrice, joined the Carmelites. Several times a month he was allowed to visit the convent and talk to her through the grille, at which times she had special permission to lift her veil. In later years, she was allowed to visit him. In 1963—still man and wife in the eyes of the church—they celebrated their golden wedding anniversary. And in 1972 Sister Beatrice made her last trip to her husband, to attend his funeral in Washington, where he died at eighty-seven.

Only a few years ago, the social climate was such that a single woman choosing a convent would probably be sexually inexperienced. Now the chances are that in the West—with the possible exception of strongly Catholic countries such as Italy, Spain, and Ireland—a girl entering late in her twenties will have had some sexual encounters, even if she has not actually had intercourse. Certainly, the majority of young sisters I talked to had had boyfriends, often regular ones, or had actually been engaged, and several admitted to "heavy petting."

But as yet the difference such experience makes to these women has not been fully realized by the convents. When I asked the elderly superior general of one order whether the more sophisticated and knowledgeable young women now entering had greater problems with the vow of celibacy, she replied, "I don't think we have these problems if we're frightfully busy and extrovert. And anyway," she added, after a moment's reflection, "we wouldn't keep someone here if they were oversexed; we wouldn't have eccentrics."

But "constant and torturing sexual desire in a religious," feels one American novice mistress, "is not necessarily an indication of an 'oversexed' person but of an inability to relate sex to the finality of love."

People who enter religious life know what they are undertaking;

they accept celibacy—as everything else—freely, not under compulsion. These are the church's terms. And the majority of women do genuinely believe that it is more than mere physical continence. "It is in the soul first," says a Spanish sister, "and passes to the body."

Yet the gray cult of virginity did not begin with Christianity. It is a relic of older, more primitive religions, stemming from a time when men believed in many strange dark gods. An untouched virgin has been held to possess supernatural powers in every culture we can trace: the daughters of peasants dancing with unbound hair through the fields at dead of night to ensure the next year's crop; the virgins of Vesta in Rome, guardians of the sacred fire, who for thirty years vowed themselves to chastity and were whipped to death or walled up alive if they fell. In Thebes and Syria, in Babylon and Greece, priestesses had to remain virgins. The Incas of Peru had their sun brides, fifteen hundred of them, incarcerated in the convent at Cuzco. From them, the emperor chose his queen, but if any other broke her vow of chastity she was killed. The belief behind the insistence on virginity was that sexual intercourse was unclean and defiling, and many regarded the overpowering emotion of sexual desire as inspired by devils.

None of this, of course, would have been consciously in the mind of Saint Paul when he advocated the single in preference to the married state. He believed that time was short; there was no point in transitory obligations when the Second Coming was at hand. But for more than two centuries after Christ there was no such thing as an order of virgins. Indeed, anyone taking a vow of celibacy was warned to keep it secret. Tertullian wrote that, rather than boast of her virginity, the celibate maid should "lie in some sense to men, that God alone should be shown the truth." The Bishop of Carthage, however, urged the local virgins—some of whom were wealthy women—not to wear their jewelry, because they ought not only to be virgins but be seen and understood to be so "by the conspicuous plainness of [their] attire."

None of these virgins were held by any canonically binding vow, nor did they undergo any kind of service. The bishops were specifically told by Hippolytus to perform no ceremonies because "it is with her heart alone she become a virgin." It was not until the fourth century that these women were living together in organized groups.

It started in Egypt. In Asia Minor the increasing numbers of orders of virgins began to receive solemn consecration by the bishop. For a long time, though, it was possible for virgins to live individually, quite often in their parents' homes. Others, anchoresses, lived in small houses near the churches, attended by a couple of servants but otherwise alone. They were contemplatives under the solemn promise of obedience, chastity, and stability of abode. The *Ancrene Riwle* is an early-thirteenth-century guidebook for the lives of three of these women, living in communicating cells with two maids and a kitchen boy to look after them. They were warned to watch the senses, "the five guardians of the heart," to have small windows covered with two sets of curtains, through which they must "not peep out too much or use enticing looks and behaviour." They had visitors, though, both men and women, who came to them for their advice or teachings. Mother Julian of Norwich was such a woman—"a simple creature unlettyrde," she called herself—but while she was "a recluse atte Norwyche" she was famous as a spiritual counselor, and her *Revelations of Divine Love* shows her to have been a woman both of deep faith and great intellect.

But as the orders became established these women began to disappear, until eventually they were no longer recognized in the law of the church and finally were prohibited. Virgins, "the choice portion of the flock of Christ," required more protection than their vow of chastity afforded, to keep them from "crafty and insidious violation." By the end of the thirteenth century, the contemplative nun was safely in her cloister, hedged about by laws, under a strict regime, vowed not only to chastity but to total poverty and full obedience.

With the Reformation, standards of morality changed. The Protestant reformers—Luther, Bullinger—opposed the Church of Rome and all the monastic principles. Celibacy, they declared, was odious, and the vow of chastity not only foolish and presumptuous but contradictory to spiritual teaching. They condemned the unmarried equally—the priest, the monk, and the nun—and threw in the professed wanton for good measure. A woman, they declared, was to be a wife and mother or she was nothing. Celibacy was a thing of evil. Virginity and continence were equated with impotence and sterility. Clerical celibacy too was rejected, largely because the reformers disapproved of the Roman church clergy who, though marriage after ordination was invalid, were not averse to taking concubines instead. Despite that, the Archbishop

109

of Canterbury, head of the Church of England, has at various times been either celibate or married, according to the feeling of the age. Currently, he is married.

There must be occasions when the nun's celibacy is a genuine inspiration. In 1948, Agnes Newton Keith returned to America from Kuching, where she had been held in a Japanese prisoner-of-war camp. In a book called *Three Came Home*, she wrote of the experience of being exiled with hundreds of other women without their husbands. Among them was a community of Catholic nuns.

> We secular women, living with our own sex, had already tested ourselves and found ourselves wanting. We could not get on without men, their stimulation, comfort, companionship. But the Sisters were different; they were complete. They were wedded to Christ and the Church, and for the first time it became credible to me that they were Holy Brides. We wives had put our minds and hearts on our husbands, which is what a good marriage is; and we were without them, and lost. The Sisters had put their minds and hearts on God alone, and they had Him; and only they were whole.

The nun's freedom from family ties and responsibilities is undeniably valuable. When I met Sister Laetitia Bordes, a member of the Society of Helpers of the Holy Souls, she was about to leave for Vietnam to work with Vietnamese-American orphans there, in an order where twelve sisters were looking after hundreds of children. "It's our responsibility to do something. We are all part of that war; we paid taxes that went to maim those children. And I'm free. I see my celibate commitment as freedom. How many people are free to answer this need?"

Another argument put forward by those who advocate celibacy is that the nun's dedication is a constant reminder of the love of God. But the majority of nuns in the world work among the poor, often in ghetto communities, where the inhabitants may well not be capable of fully understanding the meaning of celibacy. A Loretto sister working in a Chicago slum points out that the people with whom she and her sisters come into contact "are not very much aware of what nuns are, anyhow—and the concept of celibacy is not something they would have any sympathy with anyway. For them, the family is a great achievement."

110

Most nuns—like most women—admit to loving children. While a few are fairly dispassionate about them—"I never wanted children anyway"—others are more emotional. "I wouldn't have been satisfied with one set of children," says a superior whose order runs forty schools. "I want all the children in the world." But if they exercise Mary's spiritual motherhood, through which they belong not to one family but to all, the unpossessive love they feel ("the joy and anguish of the celibate," as one sister calls it) does not protect them from the loneliness which forfeiting the physical expression of sex brings. Sister Mary Agnes, the Poor Clare nun who is also a published poet, confirms this. "Everyone who has dedicated their life to celibacy does suffer from a kind of loneliness. And it is possible to feel lonely in a community where you can't talk to someone. I feel less alone in my cell than when I'm with other people."

"Last Christmas, I felt so terribly lonely, I thought, Oh, God, I still have to go up to my bed alone." This is Sister Marie Keegan of the Belgian Community of the Ladies of Mary. "It's not just me talking like this," she adds. "We all feel the same. I talk about it to my friends."

Sister Marie says, "The feeling that I'm going through life alone hits me now and again. And I'm in my thirties, which makes it worse— I've still got a chance, I can still have children, I'm still attractive enough." She has deliberately chosen community and a shared life, and she wants to do something creative that would not be done otherwise, because "I see the whole world challenging me." Procreation, she says, is always going to be looked after by others. "But there is need for people to experiment with another kind of living, besides the husband and wife relationship." She says she does not despise marriage. "I elevate it. If I could live this life and have marriage too, I would. But, in a way, to tie myself to one person would be to cut myself off, and it wouldn't satisfy me. This route does. So I won't give in; I won't give up the chance to be open to all of mankind, in a sense. There are things now that make me happy that I never dreamt of before, an inner core of being in myself that I can get at, and share. But what hits me now and again is the being lonely, the needing someone. Wanting to hold somebody's hand as you go along the street."

There is one aspect of consecrated virginity that is losing favor

111

among nuns: the idea that they are the brides of Christ. More and more nuns and sisters are no longer accepting what is essentially a masculine conception of their role. As one sister asks, "If we're the brides of Christ, what does that make male religious—homosexual?"

"We're brides of Christ," asserts another, "because the church will always want to define us in sexual terms, not as people in our own right."

"You have to be an appendage to a male," snaps a third. "But I'm an appendage to no man, thanks be to God."

"I'm not a bride of Christ," explains Marie Keegan with some acerbity. "I'm just committed to his work, just as one is committed in marriage. And while it would be terrifically flattering to say I'm married to Christ, it would not appeal to me anyway, because he's married to so many; I'd choose someone more available."

But if an increasing number agree with the American sister who urges that "we must not be hung up on this brides-of-Christ nonsense; we've got to have a broader vision," the majority are still happy with this expression. "A sister *is* a bride of Christ," confirms a contemplative nun. "It's very appropriate to put it in a married setting. You go through a courtship, an engagement, and then you're married and the love grows deeper as you go on."

Both religious ritual and literature abound in bridal, marital, and sexual imagery. The nuns of the order of the Visitation of Holy Mary in Europe in their constitutions were exhorted to "live, breathe, and pant for your celestial Spouse," but this was omitted in the 1948 version on the grounds that "the Bishop would not like that." However, they kept the wording recommended for devout mental ejaculations: "Let Him kiss me with the kisses of His Divine Mouth." And in the *Ancrene Riwle* there is much use of the Canticle of Canticles, considered in the Middle Ages to be an allegory of Christ's love for the soul: "Show your face to me, and to no other. If you would have clear sight, look at me with the eyes of your heart. I am not a bold lover, I will embrace my beloved only in a retired place: thus Our Lord speaks to his spouse."

The Benedictines, in their ceremony of Solemn Profession, tell the newly consecrated virgin that "the King has greatly desired your beauty," and the prelate prays that Jesus, "who by the bridal bond binds the hearts of consecrated virgins to himself," may "make your mind fruitful through the seed of his divine word." At the beginning of the ceremony, the chantresses intone, "Trim your lamps, wise virgins; behold, the Bridegroom comes; go forth to meet him." When the newly professed nun receives her cowl, she sings of how she has despised all the allurements of the world for the love of Christ, "whom I have seen, whom I have loved, in whom I have believed, whom I have chosen for my love." And as the silver ring is placed upon her finger, the prelate tells her it is a sign that she is wedded to Christ. "Keep perfect fidelity to your Bridegroom, that you may deserve to be admitted to the eternal marriage feast." And she replies, "I am espoused to Him whom the angels serve; whose beauty sun and moon behold with wonder."

One well-known authority believes that "the idea of the spouse may be rather unhealthy." Father Eamonn O'Doherty, the Irish priest who is professor of psychology at University College, Dublin, and a professor of philosophy of religion, feels that a nun's relationship with Christ cannot be seen in terms of a relationship between husband and wife. The former is a spiritual experience; the latter is concerned with human desire, love, and satisfaction. An English Dominican father comments that "I suspect if you make your quasi-marital relationship with God, then other people are a very poor second: they just get a pious spin-off from your primary attention."

Because the idea of a bride of Christ has begun to be questioned, religious women today are trying hard to change the image of chastity and project it as positive, not negative. "It is active, not passive," claims an American sister. "It is warfare, not peace."

One of the problems with which women in the church have to contend is the way in which that church has always treated women. Christianity, like so many other religions, has seen women as associated with evil and sin. At the root of it all is the fear of menstruation and the devils which control a woman each month. Reproduction was a fearful mystery which could have only a diabolical explanation, and a woman was not only impure herself at such times but capable of transmitting impurity to anything or anyone she touched. Hindus and Buddhists share this belief, and so do Jews, hence the insistence—now rationalized as purely hygienic—that a Jewish woman during her period must sleep in a separate bed kept for the purpose and attend the ritual baths when she is "cured." A similar procedure is adopted after child-birth, until which time she does not attend the synagogue. When Christianity adopted these ideas from Judaism, this turned into the "churching" of women. Even today, Christian women of the Orthodox church will not go to communion at such a time. (A sixth-century pope was more enlightened; when Augustine of Canterbury wrote to Gregory I, "May I baptize a pregnant woman?" he was told there was no contradiction between the gift of fertility and the gift of grace.)

Woman has been seen as Eve, the seducer of men. Canon law forbids cloistered nuns to sing in any place in the church which is in public view because they are regarded as sexual bait, and for the same reason Saint Ignatius forbade a religious man to look a woman in the eye. Many conventual practices, like the flattened breasts and the shorn heads, could well have been designed specifically to neutralize women. "And we cooperated," sighs an English teaching sister in disgust. "We built heavy walls, covered ourselves in drapery, and made ourselves some kind of middle sex."

One of the hazards against which convents took—and take—careful precautions are the passions of that middle sex. "We are," says a pretty Italian nun, "obsessed with our personal purity." The euphemism used is "particular friendships," which comes from the French *amitiés particulières*, describing friendships between the same sex and referred to in most convents as "p.f.s." All constitutions contain a phrase like "Thou shalt not allow thyself familiarities with others, still less those particular friendships which are a menace to community life." The superior may be warned to "be on watch against special friendships, the greatest pest of religious communities, and if she perceive any beginning, she shall hasten to apply a remedy." If she does not, she is warned, such friendships "always tend to have unhappy effects."

The interpretation different orders put on p.f.s varies. "Special friendships meant exclusivity," explains an Irish sister, "which was contrary to the idea of community, because two people could become possessive, which could destroy not only yourselves but the community." Others see it as far more direct. "When we were novices, we knew it meant sensual friendships; we didn't think it meant just having friends sensibly."

The Carmelite *Manual for Novices on the Cultivation of Chastity* advises, "Touch no one, and do not allow yourself to be touched by anyone without necessity or evident reason, however innocent. Repress and fly from as a mortal plague, even though spiritual in their origin, particular friendships and familiar conversations arising from an attractive appearance, pleasing manner, or an agreeable disposition."

Most orders stress that nuns "must not touch each other even in play," much less "enter the cell of another sister unless she is ill and they have express permission to enter, and if they are alone in a room with another sister, the door must never be closed."

"In my youth," remembers one middle-aged Sacred Heart sister, "friendship was absolutely off the map. The old nuns said to us novices, 'My dear, when you go in twos, the devil makes a third.'" And another woman in the same order, in her mid-twenties, remembers that "we even had to go out for walks in threes—one postulant and two novices." The rule that one sister could not sit beside the same person at recreation more than once had the double-edged reason that it encouraged mixing and discouraged intimacy.

"Friendships within the community," says one novice mistress of an Episcopalian community, Sister Elspeth, "have come to be regarded with a great deal less apprehension than in recent years. Emphasis is laid on the value and necessity of being able to have a natural loving relationship without having to sublimate it into some sort of spiritual competition."

Even so, she admits the danger of a friendship's developing into what she calls an "emotional crush" which has to be worked through. The problem, she believes, is that within religious communities "we are often a bit afraid of these things, and feel a certain distaste for anyone wrapped up in such a relationship."

Some women have bad memories of how the system worked in practice. Anita Caspary, of the Immaculate Heart of Mary community in California, remembers how, as a young novice sharing a cell with another, "I once went to late mass and came home to find all my belongings put into another cell. The superior felt we were 'too attached to each other.' Only, of course, she didn't explain that she was afraid of homosexual behavior. She just said my room was changed. So we didn't have a chance to say how ridiculous it was, because we were such casual acquaintances. And I was furious—it just reduced me to a child."

115

Certainly there are cases of lesbian affections among religious women, consummated or not. But these are the exceptions; as an American says, "Almost all of the nuns I knew were dedicated individuals, and they hadn't chosen religious life on a whim. Chastity was a rule of the life they had chosen, they believed in its glory—and they lived it."

Sister Eileen Gielty says, "I never knew a lesbian relationship in any order with which I have had any contact." The American sister Anne Hyzy feels that "we live so closely together, we could recognize lesbianism right away. When you spend a lot of your life with women, that's one thing you'd be able to spot immediately." Only one woman, another American, said she had known of a few such relationships between nuns and added that, though she did not realize it at the time, there was more of a "problem" with women practicing masturbation than was generally supposed.

Nuns display an amazing degree of innocence about the nature of lesbian relationships. "We have to be very nice with each other," explained one superior to me. "Very friendly. But not familiar. We don't touch each other or hold hands, or you'd get lesbianism."

The danger in outlawing close friendships, of course, is that the emotions are repressed and smothered, resulting in what one priest has called "an irreproachable vacuum." As one Anglican father points out, "*Any* real and mature relationship with another person *must* be a 'particular friendship.'" Rita Hannon claims that, because friendship was very much frowned upon as a potential threat to chastity, "It's all too easy to meet sisters whose spiritual lives were crippled by such negative attitudes." To live in chastity, after all, does not mean to live without a heart. "It is extremely unlikely," believes one novice mistress, "that a person will go through religious life without feeling for one or more persons, within or without the community, of one sex or the other, emotions of the strongest and tenderest love. And invariably that person will then feel the ground has gone from under her commitment to God." She believes, too, that while a deep human love may lead a woman away from religious life, "that is far better than to remain stunted or stoical within sexual solitude."

Attitudes to friendship vary among communities. A middle-aged English sister sees "much more friendliness in community life now" but

116

adds carefully, "I wouldn't say there's actual *friendship* yet." On the other hand, another Englishwoman from a more enlightened group says, "We used to call it particular friendship and it was frowned upon. Now we call it personal relationships and it's all right."

Because the celibate cannot cease being sexual, she tries to diffuse her sexuality in many relationships. And of course many religious have had deep and tender relationships within the bonds of their vows. Diana d'Andolo, who struggled so hard to become a nun, and the second master general of the Dominicans, Blessed Jordan of Saxony, had a total union of hearts, as his letters to her show. And Saint Francis de Sales wrote to Baronne de Chantal, who founded The Visitation of Holy Mary, "Know then that I hold myself closely bound to you and seek to know no more, save that this bond is not incompatible with any other, whether of vow or of marriage."

Convents were always far more worried about the nuns' behavior with men, which is what custody of the eyes is all about: "An unchaste eye is partner to an unchaste heart." Relationships with all men were banned—and more particularly if they were religious. Yet an American nun eighteen years in religion says that in all that time she knew of no overt relationships between nuns and priests *or* men in the world. In 1279 the Archbishop of Canterbury, after visiting Godstow convent, where he questioned the superior and nuns about the state of affairs there, sent them a list of injunctions rectifying matters. One of these was, "Nuns are not to converse with the neighbouring students at Oxford unless they have permission to do so from the abbess, and shall knit no bonds of friendship with them because such affection brings harmful thoughts."

To surround nuns with restrictive legislation and absurd physical barriers, such as grilles in the parlor and padlocked enclosure doors, is considered by many nuns today to be "an utterly wretched indignity." (And as Saint Augustine wrote, "No one protects the virginal blessing except God who bestowed it and 'God is love.' Therefore the protector of virginity is love.")

The majority of nuns do consider that when they enter religious life they join a single-sex community. Most do so with fortitude. This is how a young Anglican sister feels about it: "We do have some priests who come here and have one or two quiet days with us, and the other day a young man was here, a student. It's nice to hear a man's voice, a masculine point of view. But it's something you give up willingly, and God somehow gives the strength to channel your love and use it in other ways. You do miss these things. But you can live without them."

The idea that nuns are not interested in men is one which they themselves consider to be very dangerous. Sister Morag Michael thinks that "it gives an impression of imperviousness, the ice-maiden touch. And this is a travesty of what one is really meant to be doing." She stresses that "we're no less women because we live here. We still have the capacity for homemaking, for receiving and giving love, and the desire to do these things that a woman normally has. But we do believe we are called to fulfill our womanhood in other ways than through marriage; if I can't learn to love in this life, it would be much better if I wasn't in it."

Just because their company is predominantly feminine, it is by no means without men. They do not usually meet them in any direct social way but, in some of the houses, as part of their work. Other nuns teach in schools where there are many men on the staff and attend conferences and meetings. "Sisters have said they miss the stimulation of the male mind in conversation, and this can be so; I think it's important as far as we can to meet and talk to men and women outside. And this does happen far more than it used to." There are several men on convent staffs doing the heavy work: picking the apples, fixing the boiler. "I think," says Sister Morag Michael dryly, "that we can probably mend a fuse." In 1971 her order appointed a male steward as community treasurer, a post formerly held by a sister, because the business affairs of the community had increased to the point where an accountant was needed. This community, at Wantage in Berkshire, is still run on highly conventional lines.

Many sisters whose lives have now become much freer expect to lead normal social lives. One recent night, for instance, an English nun went with another woman and two men to see a performance by Susanna Anders in London. They had drinks and went to a restaurant for spaghetti Bolognese. By then it was too late for their trains home, "so I had to take them all back to the convent and find beds for them. Then they wanted to play Mozart and drink coffee till three in the morning." This woman now feels that, for the first time in her life, she is actually living out her vow of chastity.

There is no doubt that strict observance of the celibate life protected the nun from temptation. At the same time it was a restraint exercised from outside herself, imposed upon her willy-nilly, and to that extent it was artificial. As Dr. Charlotte Klein of Our Lady of Sion says, "Until a few years ago, there was no alternative to exercising your vow of chastity, because you never saw a man anyway." She feels that in these last few years she has been very much happier. She enjoys her freedom and cannot be immediately identified as a nun because normally she does not wear the cross but merely a wedding band. The evening I met her she was getting ready for a dinner party. "I lead a very active social life, but I would not dance, for instance." She has a lot of men friends—"not boyfriends, people with whom you can exchange ideas"—all over the world. "I think this is true and honest friendship. But if there was danger of anything else developing, I hope I'd have the strength of character to nip it in the bud. One would like to talk to people in the community and look to them for support."

Another woman sees this sort of relationship as a good thing for sisters. "We're less protected, we're mixing more with the opposite sex; it's bound to happen to some people at least that they find themselves relating to these men as adults, and they might find the relationship deepening. Maybe they've never had this experience before, but it's not a bad thing that a lot of religious in the last few years have had to go through this delayed adolescence."

Sister Madeleine of the Augustinian Sisters of Meaux finds that since she is out of the habit many of the old protections have disappeared, and she is aware that all sorts of relationships are open to her now which were closed to a habited nun. In the course of her work she mixes with a great many people. "It's a fact that a lot of chaps put an arm round me, and I wonder what onlookers think of seeing me being embraced by a crowd of young men. It's possible to have loving relationships with men—loving and tender—and, strangely enough, that is when you *don't* have sexual problems. I mean, I'm not leading them down the garden path because there's no garden at the end of it."

She finds it a strength to know that she can have such relationships, but admits difficulties. "When you enter a relationship, you use

119

a language of words, touches, telling the other what kind of availability you are offering. I know perfectly well what language I am speaking. But there is one older man at college who is hearing something I'm not saying, and when he hugged me, it was quite different. So, very politely, I avoid this situation with him."

What does become increasingly apparent is that being a nun now does not preclude, for many women, the possibility of love affairs. "I didn't," says one, "take a vow not to love." And as an Anglican girl in her twenties, Sister Christine, points out, "We make the mistake of polarizing sexuality in our genitals, whereas it permeates the whole of our experience. So people can have a satisfactory relationship without going to bed."

"Even if you're a nun," says a French sister, "there is obviously in all relationships with other people a sexual element." Liz Thoman, an American Sister of Humility, says, "It's very hard. I've had relationships with men, and they love me, and I love them. We've got very affectionate, but we don't jump into bed—we want to, but we don't." When she entered religious life, "I was caught up in idealism, and I believe in achieving my independence as a person, as a woman. I've had ten years of thinking my religious commitment through, and eventually choosing it. Now I'm not saying I've had terrific sexual experience, but, to me, a really fulfilling sexual relationship grows. I know what would be involved in settling down with someone, and I'm not willing to give that kind of time, energy, and commitment. So the passion of the moment remains the passion of the moment."

An American sister in her early thirties, a striking woman with an assured manner, is very conscious of her vow of celibacy—"I don't call it chastity." She meets people constantly. "I have some dear friends. I do find myself making a decision between a commitment and another person. I'm not saying I decide about an engagement ring, but a decision whether you let this develop or carry on with your life. Every time, I have decided to keep it strictly friendship. I love having friends, and I get telephone calls all the time from men I am involved with, and most of them are priests. They make no demands on me, and I make no demands on them. I have to decide for myself whether something will happen or not."

The relationships this woman has are "close and affectionate. I've done my share of kissing and hugging; I won't deny that to myself or the people I'm close to. But as far as starting to live with someone and developing a marriage relationship—I can't do that. I find that unfair to my own work." This is a young American who, like many others, is reluctant to make her final vows because she feels she would be promising herself to something about which her feelings may eventually change. "At the moment, living in community is important for me, trying to love and relate to other people, and celibacy is part of it. Though I don't go to bed with men, I have close relationships with men for whom I have a very deep love and strong feelings. But that could change—though it wouldn't necessarily be a formal church marriage if it ever happened."

So the attitude of many nuns toward the vow of celibacy is changing. It was bound to, the minute the habit and the walls went.

On the whole, though, they are very relaxed about the change. Pat Drydyk, a Franciscan sister, says that, for her, celibacy is "a day-to-day decision. I very much want to do what I'm doing now, to be where I am now, but there's always that desire for more personal support." She has been through college, has worked at the Franciscan Communications Center in Los Angeles, where religious films are made, and enjoys an active social life. "People take me out to supper every night. I don't call it dating, but getting to know someone better. And it's so natural I just don't think about it. It's part of the evolution."

Others see the open choice as a strengthening. One English Catholic sister in her late forties says, "I recently had the opportunity to lead another kind of life." She received a marriage proposal. "I could have taken it but I didn't, and I don't regret it. I dance along the streets when I think I haven't done it. I would have been bored in two weeks, anyway. And I have never wanted children."

There is, of course, the risk that as the religious life becomes increasingly open, as nuns and sisters work with more and more people, more will transfer their energies to personal relationships in marriage. In fact, numbers have done this already in recent years. "But that," says one young woman, "is the risk of loving."

"The chastity business is a bore to me really. It's not something I see any virtue in doing." The nun who said that is highly intelligent, in her early thirties, and a fully professed member of an established order, the Belgian Ladies of Mary. She is no extremist in her views. But there

121

is a growing feeling that celibacy in a religious community is of diminishing importance, and its validity to the life is being strongly questioned.

Many nuns have said they do not want to give up sexual fulfillment ("I don't believe in giving up anything unless you have to") but are prepared to since it is the only way at present in which they can live the religious life. "But if there was a way for me to do both," says one, "then I would."

Some of the younger sisters who have not yet taken final vows go even further. In America I talked to three—and there must be many more throughout the country—who admitted candidly that they were on the pill. One took it on the advice of her doctor as part of her medical treatment. Another did so because she was a caseworker in a hard-core slum area and was genuinely concerned lest she be raped—as one sister in her community recently was. The third said merely that she "felt safer."

The American theologian Maryellen Muckenhirn, formerly Sister Charles Borromeo of the Holy Cross at Notre Dame, has questioned whether celibacy can even be justified within the traditional convent structure. "The convent," she says, "was too seldom a place of warmth and love. It tended, rather, to be a place of scheduled chapel service, silence, and generalized charity toward all. And celibate love *cannot* always be formal, organized, and rule-regulated." She—like so many others—finds it doubtful that anyone could grow into serious maturity without living among a small, loving group. Celibate love, she believes, must be "truly reaching toward the persons in one's life." Without this, celibacy is meaningless, "since personal love is the measure of Christian existence."

There will always be those who defend the celibate state "for the sake of the Kingdom" and who claim, as one sister says, that "you are celibate for the love of God and people, so all your resources and energy can be channeled into being available to other people and into prayer. So the religious way of life is centrally bound up with celibacy." But there is also a feeling that the belief in the superiority of the single over the married state came about largely from a lack of understanding of the significance of sexuality.

One area where there is already much change is in the celibate priesthood of the Catholic church. Christianity developed a celibate priesthood out of the Judaic belief in the basic "impurity" of women; only men who avoided the act of sex with them were thought fit to serve God. There seems little doubt that it is this insistence on the pure priest—and the underlying fear of women behind it—that influences the attitude of the church and its male hierarchy to woman and the insistence laid on their subservient role.

There is increasing realization, particularly in America, that ordination need not be a bar to marriage. While priests are not free to wed officially, they are not only doing so but those who do receive permission from the Vatican to marry—as opposed to those who resign their posts—are not being reduced automatically to the status of laymen. And for every priest who marries, a dozen are dating. Father Eugene Kennedy, a best-selling and much-quoted author, advocates optional celibacy not only to preserve the rights of priests to marry but to preserve the right to celibacy as "a healthy choice" for them.

The majority of priests who marry seem to choose former nuns as their partners. Father Philip Berrigan, brother of the poet Daniel, who spent thirty-nine months in prison for burning military draft records, has always held strong views of celibacy, which he saw as "an excuse to flee from the complexities of human love." In May 1972 he formalized his three-year union with Elizabeth McAlister, who used to be a sister of the Sacred Heart of Mary; they were married in New York by a former Benedictine monk. Father Philip, at fifty, is ostracized from his community of Josephites but is not formally excommunicated. He still considers himself a priest.

It may well be that this will act as the thin end of the wedge to alter the male view of women's role within the hierarchical structure. As one sister puts it, change is possible "if only we get a healthy way of looking at sex."

Perhaps the most fascinating development on the question of celibacy is not that there are nuns who leave their orders to marry but that there are those who see no reason why married people should not be part of religious communities. The Vatican's Sacred Congregation for Religious and Secular Institutes, the Roman overbody for all orders, has even spoken of the possibility of a religious order in Tuscany where married couples, free from the ties of their families, can enter together to live a fairly traditional religious life while doing pastoral work. The vow of chastity in such a case would mean marital fidelity, though a vow of "absolute purity" could be taken.

One American women's community, the Sisters of Loretto at the Foot of the Cross, was the first American order to update itself, beginning even before the impetus of Vatican II. The radicalism of the eight hundred sisters made some difficulties with the hierarchy: "We had a lot of opposition in the beginning when we were really rocking the boat." They now have about thirty co-members. These people—former sisters who felt they had to leave but wanted to stay related to the order, non-Catholics, men, divorced people—take no vows, but share ideas and work. They are not officially members of the congregation and therefore do not come under canonical jurisdiction.

Another American community already has associate members—about a dozen people who keep their jobs but spend a lot of time with the community—whom they are talking about admitting to full membership. "There is so little difference between us," explains a sister, "except for the vows. And even there, we know they are living the idea of the vows: a simplicity of life, a real search for the will of God in their lives. So obviously the only difference between them and us was celibacy. And all of a sudden, in the light of all these other values and shared experiences, the need for celibacy in a religious community diminished greatly." If they do bring in their associate members, then it will be the spirit—not the vows—which unites the community. They believe that if enough groups begin to think and act in this way, "the official Church in Rome will sooner or later have to deal with the emergence of noncanonical communities and create some new room for them."

The Immaculate Heart of Mary Community in Los Angeles is already a noncanonical community. Members are no longer nuns, and the community defines itself as a group of religious people. Celibacy has been made voluntary. "We are not," they say, "responsible for the personal life-style of our community members." Married couples have been brought into the group as full members—a step which at first caused "great anguish" and in many ways was seen as a threat, the end of religious life. It was the older and younger people who worried most—the older because it was such a break from tradition, the younger because they had not confirmed their commitment to celibacy. Among those who have since left to marry are some who protested most strongly against married couples. Finally, the decision was taken that if a couple was willing to give as much as the single woman in service, if they believed as much as the rest, they should be allowed to become full members. The decision was strengthened when one of their single women members, dispensed from her vows (as all are), said she was marrying and wanted to remain in the community. She is now on their twelve-woman board of directors.

But the option does not in any way mean that all members of the group are renouncing chastity. One of them, Mary Bowler, has the sleek elegance and narrow waist of a model. As she sits on a heap of cushions in the apartment she shares with a sister from another community, wearing a frothy white negligee, it is quite surprising to hear her say, "I fully believe there is a place for celibacy and chastity." She entered at nineteen and, without experience, found the commitment hard to make. She dates, now, but thinks she would not leave the community for anyone. Her worst time was the novitiate. "I missed the guys; it was hard for me."

Frances and Nelson Small are both full members of the community. Sitting by the pool at the conference center in Santa Barbara, a bundle of small children shrieking in the water, they talk about their group commitment. Frances is happily pregnant yet again, and it is hard to believe that she entered the Immaculate Heart Convent at sixteen and left "reluctantly" in 1959. After marriage, she found she missed the feeling of community—"being able to talk about God on a personal level." So she returned to the convent for a short retreat and afterward visited again with her husband. Both found the experience so satisfactory that they decided they would like to become more closely involved with the group. Now the couple and their children spend most of their free time with the IHMs, attending prayer groups and discussions, helping to raise funds and look after the property. They value the spiritual and emotional gains from the association—and there is no doubt that the IHMs consider themselves enriched by the presence of a large and happy family of children.

Of course this group, because it is noncanonical and not subject to the dictates of Rome, can behave in a way which may be regarded as extreme. There are, however, several orthodox religious communities which are experimenting with mixed-sex groups. This is not, surprisingly, a new idea; it is the wheel come full circle. Double monasteries were a feature of medieval monastic life, existing from the fourth century in France, Spain, and Ireland and appearing in England half a century after the arrival of Saint Augustine. They grew up largely because of the needs of the communities; the agricultural work could not be done by women alone, so lay brothers were brought in. Gradually, canons joined as well, but it was a mainly feminine community, with a woman invariably at the head.

The sexes were restricted to their separate quarters, and even the churches were firmly divided into two sections. None of these communities belonged to any order recognizable today, except that founded by Saint Bridget of Sweden in the fourteenth century. Hers was a double order interested in charity, education, and the collecting of books. The brothers acted as priests and confessors to the nuns. Their chapels were built with separate stalls and a grille dividing the sexes which, though it did not hide them from each other, was kept locked. The nuns lived in the inner precinct, and the men of religion—of whom there were thirteen priests, four deacons, and eight laymen—lived around the outer court of the monastery.

Today's double community is very different. Because it is informal and relaxed, because there are no gates and grilles, it is far more difficult to keep cool and separate than when a rigid framework enforced distance.

One woman who has experienced this way of life is Marie Keegan of the Ladies of Mary. A social worker, she spent a year living in an old factory in London's Highgate which served as a welfare base for Irish adolescents away from home. She shared the upstairs living quarters with two other sisters and three Servite brothers, and while such an arrangement is usual among lay social workers, for her "it was the best experience I ever had in community." She believes that living and working as they did brings out the best in both sexes. "We gave each other a lot because we have a different mentality, a different way of looking at things."

There were problems. "I wouldn't like to romanticize about mixed community. It's got terrific dangers. I think we avoided them, but I

126

don't know if we could have continued to do so." She is conscious that she has no rigid disciplinary codes about herself. "Although I'm professed, that doesn't protect me from a man. If something is good and beautiful, then I go out to it immediately." She found that in living such a close community life, "people's loveliness came out. We had no 'particular friendships,' because you've got to accept that if you belong to the community you can't have an exclusive relationship. You must leave or give it up." At one stage, though, the group did experience emotional difficulties. There was great tension; everyone became depressed. "But we recognized the problem; we did face it. We had a meeting and said, 'What's wrong with everybody?' And then people began to speak out: 'I depend too much on you; I never do a thing unless I think you're going to like it.'" There were other things. "People admitted jealousy, and we were able to talk about being attracted to each other. And talking about it was our salvation; the problem was worked out. That we could sit down and talk about something so very personal was hard to the people involved, but it was fantastic growth No one was hurt or embittered."

They all, she feels, achieved greater emotional maturity and self-knowledge than they could have in their own communities. When she returned to the comfortable detached suburban house where she lives with four other sisters, "Everything was beautiful, but I miss this element most. I realize now that a single-sex community is very much lacking in something. It's basically not true."

While this group was totally experimental, the Royal Foundation of Saint Katharine is a permanent mixed-sex religious community, the only one in Britain. Based on the community of the same name founded nine centuries ago in 1148, it lies in the heart of London's East End, down grubby Commercial Road, past the White Swan public house on Cable Street.

Through a parking lot, there is a little door in the wall. Inside is a garden where creamy magnolias flower and early roses twine around a white-barred gate. The long house with its Georgian façade is the home of eight men from the Community of the Resurrection, known as the Mirfield Fathers—the eldest of whom is eighty-five—and six sisters of the Deaconess Community of Saint Andrew, where the youngest is twenty-seven.

These two Anglican orders came here in 1968 at the invitation of the Queen Mother, who was anxious to reestablish it as the monastic community it had been in the day of Queen Matilda. It used to be a city within the city, with three thousand inhabitants and its own ecclesiastical and civil law and it has always been patronized by the queens of England. It was written in the constitutions that there should always be a women's community involved, so the Deaconess community was asked to join the Mirfield Fathers. "We started it very hesitantly," says Sister Verity, a plump woman who is one of the three original sisters to live in the house. "I don't know who was the more nervous, them or us. We didn't know what to expect, either from within the community or from our work in the area."

Sister Verity admits they all, men and women, felt shy at first. "I'd worked as one of two or three women among many men in the forces. But I'd lived in an all-female home for many years. And we found we took a long time to get used to each other. We really needed time to talk about things that mattered. So every Sunday evening we get together and talk."

The two orders preserve their own individual "family life," with quarters in different portions of the house. The sisters have a small and cozy community room; the fathers chose an imposing apartment in the original Georgian wing, where the day's papers are ranged upon a period table at the long window. They breakfast together but lunch separately because of different community habits; the sisters observe silence, while the fathers regard the meal as recreation time. Sister Christine is the kitchen steward and plans all the meals, though a lay person does the cooking. At night they have dinner together in the refectory, wash up together, then lay breakfast and have coffee.

They were determined to keep the two communities reasonably separate because they felt the groups must be strong enough to withstand the change of individuals receiving different assignments and moving on. "We had," says Sister Verity, "to balance how far our commitment was to this place, how much to our community." In fact, the sisters did find that every religious person who came to visit them said, "I suppose you're looking after the fathers?" To which they replied, "God forbid." They were glad they had independent jobs and found they had to stand up for themselves much more than is usual in a women's community. "We didn't do everything we were asked to do.

We had to resist the temptation of being nice and kind and compliant. We had to be quite firm about sharing our responsibilities." On one occasion a group of sisters came to Saint Katharine's for one of the regular retreat weekends. Sister Verity reports with amusement how one sister actually "curtsied to the fathers. When they'd gone, the fathers said, 'We couldn't have lived with any of them.' "

After five years, the whole community feels that, despite problems, they have learned a good deal by living together. "The men," says a sister, "are less hidebound by tradition than women. Women are very much more liable to hang on to their traditions for security, and this is where it's so good for us. The changes don't threaten the men so much." The Mirfield Fathers agree. Father Mark, who organizes much of the work of the community—the youth clubs, musical sessions, and poetry meetings—says that "undeniably we gain in richness of life. Men and women are meant to live together. The balance creates the atmosphere."

All the sisters feel that, since sharing their lives with the fathers, "we've all become bolder. We have the nerve to do things we wouldn't have done before. We're not shy about things. You have more courage of your own convictions because you don't mind making a fool of yourself." Another sister particularly values the intellectual stimulus. "I've found more acceptance between brethren and sister here than from my sisters elsewhere." Sister Verity says the nice thing is that "they're not shy of showing affection. The other day I felt ill, and when I went to get my breakfast in the refectory, no one said anything. But then Father Reginald poured my tea, and at lunchtime one of the fathers asked if I was feeling better and another brought my coffee over."

Father Jack Guinness holds the post of Master of the Court of Saint Katharine's and oversees the work of the house, which is mainly conducting retreats and acting as chaplains to groups and individuals. The sisters have more outside work: Sister Denzil is assistant chaplain at Queen Mary's College in the East End of London, helping with problems among the students, and Sister Verity handles local social work, with play groups and pensioners. As she sits in the warm community room, busily sewing a rag doll for her children, it is she who best sums up the advantages of this now revitalized form of religious life. "I have enormously valued being treated like a woman. It's the sort of odd things that women don't do for each other, the little courtesies. It's a subconscious thing, and I suppose I'm flattered by it. I feel valuable as a person."

These groups, whether extreme like the Immaculate Heart of Mary in California or orthodox like the Anglicans of Saint Katharine's, are giving other religious much food for thought—and, perhaps, action —about the hitherto rigid concept of the celibate single-sex community.

But none of them would claim it is an easy thing to give up the satisfactions of the heart. "There is no substitute for fully sexual love," says one nun. For her, the absence of a loving relationship with one man in her life is "a loneliness that no amount of fraternal or apostolic love can overcome.

"But then, you don't want it to be overcome, if this is your place to be."

Nuns are just ecclesiastical chars.
—ENGLISH TEACHING SISTER

5

The Male
Chauvinist Church

The church is the most exclusive male club in the world.

"What time we get up in the morning, what time we eat, and what we wear—all this is still enforced by men." A brisk woman in her early thirties settles her belt more comfortably around the waist of her gray business suit and adjusts a short black veil. "Surely," she says, "nuns themselves are more qualified to handle these matters?"

Her companion, whose delicate face hardly matches the string of degrees that trail her name, adds, "It's not that men are *stupid*. But the bishops should *not* be organizing our lives."

These women—one French, one American—are two who have battered against the stone wall of male prejudice. And they at least have made a dent—the freedom partly to abandon the habit, to acquire those degrees, and to sit in a public restaurant discussing them. But the wall still stands, almost as firm today as it was when Teresa of Ávila wrote, "The very thought that I am a woman makes my wings droop."

Teresa had good cause to feel dispirited. There is a long tradition of antifeminism in the church. That misogynist father, Tertullian, told women in the third century, "Do you not know that you are Eve? You are the devil's doorway. It was you who profaned the tree of life. It was you who disfigured the image of God which is man." A hundred years later, Saint Ambrose endorsed this: "Adam was led to sin by Eve, not Eve by Adam." In the twelfth century, Bernard of Clairvaux thought that "their face is as a burning wind, their voice the hissing of serpents." And the seventeenth-century Spanish Jesuit, Gracián, wrote, "It is clear that woman is under man's dominion and has no authority, nor can she teach, give evidence, make a contract, nor be judge."

Women were actually considered to be deformed men. In the thirteenth century, Thomas Aquinas commented that "in her particular nature woman is something defective and accidental. If a girl child is born it is due to weakness of the generative principle, or imperfection in the pre-existing matter, or to a change produced by external causes, for example by the humid winds from the south, as Aristotle says."

Even when her biological role became better understood, it was still interpreted as wholly passive. She was the object of male aggressive potency. Therefore she must also be the receptacle of male thoughts and ideas.

Despite the importance of women who figure in the Gospel, despite the reverence for the Virgin Mary, women were seen by society as the weaker sex. And the church has always been several steps again behind that. It is a sad comment on the slowness with which it moves that if Teresa of Ávila were writing in the 1970s she would have little cause to feel more cheerful than she did four centuries ago. It may be accepted by today's churchmen that women have souls—which at one time they hotly disputed—but souls, it seems, are not enough.

This applies particularly to the Catholic church because—from the nuns' point of view—it is the biggest and most hidebound. But to a greater or lesser degree, it is equally true of Protestant churches.

The power structure of the church was conceived by men for

men. The medieval lawyers who designed canon law believed that women were weak and incapable and needed protection and rigid rules to sustain them in religious life. It is true that male religious were subject to many of the same rules, but it was women who under canon law were classed with children and idiots. "The church and women," says a young nun, "is a most depressing subject. I hate to think what Freudians would say about a patriarchal church which solemnly refers to itself as 'Holy Mother Church.' And I feel intensely hurt for what women have been made to endure in the name of Christ."

Christianity has done much to keep women in their traditional role of *Kinder, Kirche, Küche*—children, church, kitchen. Even the cult of the Virgin has been used to teach them an unconscious lesson about their duty to be meek and subordinate. Women religious, particularly, have been subdued by male restrictions, conditioned to please others, not themselves. The church has used psychological power to subjugate women. It has sought domination in the intellectual, spiritual, religious, sexual, and economic spheres—and all by use of canon law, written and enforced by men.

The church may preach that there are no second-class citizens— yet an economist of international stature was refused the right to address the Second Vatican Council solely because she was a woman. For the same reason, a journalist was not allowed to receive Communion from the Pope during the council. And it is only under what one nun calls the "most patronizing circumstances" that a woman is allowed to read in church or distribute Communion.

It is a sorry tale of exclusion and suppression. From a human point of view, admits one nun, the ambition of men to monopolize and dominate is understandable, "but it is not Christian." It is nuns especially who have suffered. They are given paternal indulgences rather than rights, rules rather than freedom, dogma rather than the liberty to think.

Many men in the church, of course, see women as in need of such treatment. An American cleric wrote recently of the temptation for nuns "at all times to reduce faith to sentiment, devotion to a multiplicity of devotions, the love of God to emotional sweetness, and theology to a few narrow, one-sided notions." Even Cardinal Suenens of Brussels, a man genuinely anxious to open new perspectives for women religious,

133

refers to woman's "natural subordination which makes her content to lean on a masculine support."

Not only did woman accept her subjugation, but often she encouraged it. "Women," says one Jesuit, "compete for approval in the hierarchy structure." A Dominican priest agrees that "they expect to be exploited. It's part of being a nun. It was a conspiracy between themselves and their founders." Nuns still show a distressing tendency to accept male superiority. A French superior general, a confirmed feminist, remarked sadly, "If I tell my religious that I share a certain view, this view carries some weight. But it carries ten times more if I say that it is shared by a *père jésuite*."

"The church," says one extremely articulate and angry young nun, "has conditioned women to be subordinate to their husbands, and religious women are never allowed to forget they're living in a man's world. There's nothing liberated about that." Many of the problems, she feels, were brought about by nuns themselves. "We have surrounded ourselves with petty regulations. In the novitiate, we brought up our young sisters to be subservient. We have aped after the men in the church. We are dutiful and follow. But we should be pathfinders; we should be prophetesses." Others agree. "The role of the church," says an American nun, a sister of the Helpers of the Holy Souls, "is to be ahead of society, calling it on."

Until the mid-1960s, nuns were still treated as silent parts of the institutional system of the church, "cheap labor," as an American sister says scornfully. To a large extent they still are. Despite Vatican II's resounding call for modernization, there is no real route, no official pathway, for nuns to deal with the Holy See or even with individual bishops. The line of command continues through men: from the pope to cardinals, bishops, and priests.

It is not through lack of trying. Each country now has a body formed of the mothers general, provincials, and superiors of all the orders, who meet regularly for discussion. In 1965 the American group, the Conference of Major Superiors of Women's Institutes, sent a unanimous petition to Rome asking that it should be represented on commissions dealing with the lives of nuns. This body, after all, would be the logical one for representing sisters before the hierarchy.

The request was ignored. All the conference was allowed to do is

134

serve as a one-way channel of communication—from the Vatican down to the communities. As one American sister theologian says, "This is not enough. The superiors are democratically chosen to foster the purpose and common good of their communities. This can be done only if they speak and the hierarchy listens." She herself believes that part of the failure of the conference to become a heard voice is the average sister's "ambivalence toward power and politics—the notion that both are tainted."

Many sisters are particularly incensed that they cannot carry out the smallest change—even to modifying their headdresses—without obtaining permission from their bishop, though as one exasperated American superior has said, "Any superior who submits habit changes is foolish. She should just phone her tailor and forget about the Sacred Congregation."

The Sacred Congregation for Religious and Secular Institutes in Rome is the body governing all religious orders. But since Vatican II, more and more communities are questioning the congregation's right to dictate the details of their lives without any reference to their wishes. "How can some men in Rome say what I as an American woman can or cannot do?" asks red-haired Sister Patricia McKeough. "They're still laboring under their own culture lag."

Male domination is not something that can be tackled effectively by individuals, no matter how strong their intellectual arguments. The authorities, as one Jesuit points out, "have refused to understand the aspirations of women in the modern world and have preferred to keep to the old way of doing things, even at the expense of sacrificing these intelligent women." Dr. Charlotte Klein tried public debate with churchmen to question their attitudes on deep theological and philosophical grounds. The response? There is indeed a great role for women to play in the church—as priests' housekeepers. This is a view well in accordance with that of Pope Paul, who, in a speech about the eagerness of the church to promote the advancement of women in society, said that women had a role to play in full equal rights with men—but mainly in an area encompassed by the family.)

Another example of discrimination occurred in Louisiana in 1972 when two sisters, Lydia Champagne and Stephanie Bourgeois, were dismissed from their jobs in the office of religious education without

135

the formalities required by the diocese. Bishop Robert Tracy explained his action in a letter to his consultative bodies: "A considerable number of the clergy feel they would find it easier to deal with a fellow diocesan priest as head of the office rather than with religious sisters."

The patronizing attitude adopted toward nuns today is even more incomprehensible in the light of their work and achievements. Nuns deal with more of life's harsh realities than most lay people ever see. Alcoholics, homicides, drug addicts, deserted wives, delinquent children, prostitutes—this is the list of a hardened professional caseworker. The Daughters of Charity of Saint Vincent de Paul, for example, have operated Marillac House in Chicago for more than twenty years. From a settlement house in East Garfield Park, they have gone out day after day to serve an area with the highest crime, VD, illegitimacy, illiteracy, and poverty rates in the whole of the United States. In another Chicago slum, Woodlawn, a community of Loretto sisters works in a shabby building set among the gaping shells of houses filled with rats. Here Sister Therese Rooney, a decisive woman, heads a team deeply involved in putting the mainly black population on their feet both emotionally and financially. The community runs educational courses for those who dropped out of school and teaches office skills to women. It has also created a unique training session for people who want to set up their own small businesses. But only within the last couple of years has their work been recognized by their lay colleagues. "Professionally, we were badly treated," admits Sister Therese, "as though, in the convent, we didn't know what was happening out there; we got little pats on the head."

Even nuns who by no stretch of the imagination could be called militant feel that women are ill-used. Anne Hyzy is a tranquil girl, one of the Chicago Loretto sisters. "I don't feel I'm hemmed in by men; I don't feel I have to be liberated. My way of living isn't in conflict with men, the way women in an office might be; I'm not competing unless I want to be a priest." But she, like almost every American and European sister I talked to, believes that "there should certainly be more women in the church holding high-powered administrative jobs. It's pathetic they haven't trusted women that much. After all, there are plenty of women capable of the job who can add a dimension of femininity."

Such lack of trust is made more ridiculous by the fact that many mothers general already shoulder immense responsibilities. Some of them govern the lives of perhaps thousands of women. Mother Mary Thomas Aquinas Lee is a perfect example. For many years she has been mother general of the Good Shepherd sisters. She is a woman of wide culture who speaks several languages. She needs to; the congregation has 475 centers in five countries. She has responsibility for ten thousand sisters as well as the thousands of women—delinquent girls, unmarried mothers, state prisoners—in their care.

The problem is that after centuries of subjugation women are wary of power. They have been taught that it is evil, that those who aspire to it are victims of pride. Those who do find themselves in responsible positions fear they will display "masculine" characteristics, which is how determination and creativity have been regarded. "That woman," sighed her bishop, of Teresa of Ávila, "should have been a man."

Perhaps this attitude is more widespread among the older generation of sisters, such as Mother Gabriel, mother general of the vast Sisters of Mercy order: "Those women's-lib nuns say the authorities don't understand us—but of course they do. I think they're marvelous men, I do really. They're not affected by sentiment and temperament and jealousy and everything else." Believing that "canon law is very just," she finds it perfectly acceptable that the bishop must be consulted if the sisters wish to sell property. "After all, we might be fools. We wouldn't know anything about it. We might be had." When she was sent a questionnaire in which she had to say whether she thought women were capable of understanding finance, she answered, "No." But even Mother Gabriel does not think "they should boss us too much. There's not much logic in thinking anyone in charge of a big order could be a fool."

Many women feel that the role of the nun, by its very nature, precludes too much self-determination—like the enclosed contemplative who believes, "We can't engage in women's lib; we are not fighting for our own rights." But it was an enclosed Carmelite nun, Sister Margaret Rowe, who became one of the first to speak out publicly in Britain against the male rule of the church—and found little favor for doing so in the eyes of her community.

Sister Margaret Rowe is an articulate Australian who worked in a

Canberra science laboratory before becoming a nun twenty years ago when she joined the Carmelites at Bridell in Wales. In 1968 she wrote an article for *The New Christian* magazine in which she accused bishops and male superiors of "interference and arbitrary suppression" and pleaded that, as it was Human Rights Year, a few words should be said for the "oppressed minority" of religious women.

"There is still little recognition," she wrote, "that institutions are for persons, not persons for institutions, and it is not fitting that one man, or one woman, should suffer in order that the prestige of authority or the structure of any other thing be maintained." What chiefly worried her was that those who enter religious life forfeit no human rights, but "when are religious women going to be treated as mature, responsible adults capable of managing their own lives?" She cited as an example the three-hundred-year-old order founded to take poverty-stricken young people off the streets to educate them. This order felt it was duplicating work now done by social service agencies and wanted to move into a different field. To do so, it needed permission from men in Rome "who might not understand the conditions that exist in the East End of London."

Sister Margaret drew a reprimand from the prioress. "She has done us a disservice. Quite frankly I am aghast this should come from a nun of this order. The church protects us and helps us to lead a life of solitude and prayer. We are not aiming to seek equal rights for women."

An American sister says, in reply, "Until sisters get involved in their own liberation, they're not much use to anyone else." The speaker is Sister Ethne Kennedy. She is sitting behind a table full of what is —in religious terms—revolutionary literature. From her office on the corner of Superior and North Rush streets in Chicago, she runs NAWR, the National Assembly of Women Religious. She is the chairman of the group, which began in 1967 with one aim: to find out what effect sisters have on society, "and if they have none, why not?" She wants to release women from the "patronizing attitude" of the church, which so oppresses them that "we are not even aware of our potential." Women, she points out, "are the largest minority in the church and society, but we've been locked in this modified, monastical society in which men do the decision-making. We're taught that psychologically, theologically, and every other way, men are superior."

She herself is a member of the Helpers of the Holy Souls. She chose this order mainly because of its liberalism. But she found that in practice it was not so liberal that Vatican II did not mean profound changes. And the members of other orders suffered more. "Sisters were in little piddling groups—you were a Sister of Mary or a Sister of Charity. I felt they wouldn't get any further till I did something about it."

At that time the major superiors of various orders would meet at conferences where perhaps 170 women made decisions that involved 176,000 more. NAWR encouraged Sister Councils at which the sisters in each diocese, whatever their order, could meet for discussion. Sister Ethne organized one meeting where four hundred sisters talked to major superiors with the apostolic delegate present. The result? "Flack from the bishops." Bishops, she claims, do not on the whole like the idea of their sisters banding together and finding a unanimous voice. Their reasons range from the belief that sisters have enough to do already to the conviction that keeping them divided is the best way to ensure their own continued rule. At present, about a third of the American dioceses are not allowed to have a Sister Council.

Nor do all sisters approve the idea. A woman who wanted to join NAWR was told by her superior she could not, because "one sister per convent is enough." Another problem is finance. Ethne Kennedy found that NAWR simply could not survive on a yearly subscription of $3 and raised it to $5. They lost two thousand members. "Nuns just don't have the money."

Even so, almost two thousand sisters from all over America attended a recent conference to talk about work, renewal—and equality. "That's the question most raised," says Sister Ethne. "It's a question of how you see yourself. Basically, society is having a terrible struggle for power between men and women. As our role changes, so does theirs. And it changes at the most profound level, the level of personality." She does believe, though, that the traumatic period—certainly for American religious—is over. "I think we've had a real breakthrough with mass communications. I think sensitive men realize that men and women are complementary, creating a new society. And I think a lot of things are going to drop by the wayside."

But the battle is not won yet, and she thinks, too, that the place to seek the greatest upset is in the basic structures of the hierarchical church. "Because the structures are perpetually oppressive, and the power system of the church is pretty obsolete."

Be that as it may, the power of the bishops is still very real. Almost all the European nuns to whom I talked were in close contact with one bishop or more. To enter the Carmelite monastery in Llandovery, I had to seek formal permission from the bishop of the diocese and the Abbot of Caldey. Possibly this was due to the fact that normally no outsider may enter an enclosed community—but the invitation had been extended by the mother prioress herself.

There are communities which seem to like operating in this way. The Anglican Deaconess Community of Saint Andrew, for instance, is visited weekly by the Bishop of Kensington, and the Bishop of London comes to the convent for professions and life vows. "We can't make major decisions without consulting them," says Mother Joanna. Even though neither bishop would query any minor decision made in chapter, they are still informed by letter of what has to be done. The sisters admit they "would be very bereft if we didn't have this interest." Nonetheless I find it hard to accept what one superior general claims is true: that "women religious need a man and, deprived of the continued interest of a priest, their natural tendencies to sadism and masochism wreak havoc in the community." Yet this Frenchwoman was a practicing psychiatrist before becoming a nun.

At one time there was a reason for the bishop's visits, which had to be made at least once a year: to ensure that no nun was detained against her will or mistreated. Today such visits are unnecessary—"After all, we aren't holding parties till five in the morning with men." Some sisters find them an irritating hangover from the past. Even though the visits are now made on a purely friendly basis, and conducted with the utmost goodwill, they hate what they see as interference. "The hierarchy of England and Wales," snapped one sister, "tries one's patience to the utmost."

The trouble is that the church has no constitutional safeguard against tyrants, benevolent or otherwise. In Rome there is absolute monarchy, and power is almost exclusively male. There are some hopeful signs. Late in the 1960s, four nuns were named to the Roman Curia, the central government of the church, hitherto made up largely of men in their seventies. It was hoped that the four women—American,

140

English, Spanish, and French—would influence the Curia to liberalize rules, but so far their influence would seem to be slight. Canon lawyers are only now revising canon law on the principle that women can no longer be treated as minors.

The rights of women in the Vatican have not improved much, despite Vatican II. It is of course true that the people closest to the pope are women: his own community of attendant nuns. But they are housekeepers, getting into the news only upon the occasion of the pontiff's birthday when they bake him a cake. Although there are now a number of nuns and laywomen holding jobs in various departments, including the Congregation of the Faithful and two pontifical commissions, the tradition still stands that even ranking diplomatic representatives accredited to the Holy See must be men. When, in 1970, the West German government nominated a woman as second secretary there, she was turned down.

As Letitia Brennan, an Ursuline from New Rochelle taking her doctorate in psychology, points out, "Equality is not about to be offered to women. To be recognized, they must take the initiative themselves." Others agree. "They must insist on assuming their own responsibilities," says another. "They must insist on being treated as adult members of the Church."

In the early days of religious life, women in religion wielded enormous influence, both in their monasteries and far beyond them. Indeed, it was accepted that few communities could vie in intellectual and social significance with the foremost communities of women. The eleventh-century princess, Sophie, abbess of the German settlement of Gandersheim, even mastered common law so she could enter disputes with learned men and successfully oppose them.

Well before that, in the seventh century, one of the most influential women in Britain was Abbess Hilda of Whitby, "Mother of All." The Venerable Bede wrote that "her prudence was so great that not only did ordinary persons, but even sometimes kings and princes, seek and receive counsel of her in their necessities." She was visited constantly by church dignitaries "on account of her innate wisdom," and during her thirty years as abbess, first in Hartlepool, then Whitby, no less than five men who studied under her became bishops. Her suc-

141

cessor, Aelflaed, was equally impressive. Given into religious life by her father as a tiny baby, she was only twenty-five when she became abbess, and shortly afterward she was the chief speaker at the Synod of Nidd; yet after the Council of Trent it was 1971 before a woman—the internationally renowned economist Barbara Ward—was again allowed to address a world synod of bishops.

The power of the abbess was at one time absolute; she was spoken of as "Sovereign" and "Majesty." She ruled her own lands, held her own courts, decreed punishment and penance, and sent her own knights into battle for her king. Many religious settlements were founded by royal or imperial families, whose daughters then became abbesses as of right—often while they were still only children. In the tenth and eleventh centuries, abbesses of the chief houses in German lands had numerous privileges; those of Quedlinburg and Gandersheim were even able, under Otto I, to strike their own coins bearing their portraits. Abbesses were in close touch with the royal courts and affairs of state, partly because of their family connections and partly because monasteries were used as hotels by well-to-do travelers, including members of the ruling families. So worldly were these abbesses that Abbess Mathilda of the Saxon settlement of Quedlinburg virtually ruled the country as guardian of the baby Otto II when his father was killed in Italy in 983—and was praised for the determined measures by which she fought off invaders.

The abbesses of these two royal houses, Quedlinburg and Gandersheim, had both the privileges and duties of a baron. When war was declared, they issued summonses for their contingents of armed knights. They were summoned to the Imperial Diet and went in person until the sixteenth century. These women held, as did heads of women's orders in other European countries and some abbots, the powers of a bishop within their own territories. They bore emblems of their episcopal power, the pallium and the crosier. They wore the miter and cope, and even the episcopal ring. They conducted all their own church services except the Eucharist, for which they were not ordained. And on one occasion the Abbess of Hradschin in Prague—who was also an archduchess—even performed the crowning of the new Queen of Bohemia in a magnificent ceremony in Vienna's Chapel of Saint Wenceslas.

142

In England, abbesses were among those to whom the king looked when he needed help in defending the country. In the reign of Henry I, the Abbess of Shaftesbury found seven knights for the king's service and regularly received writs asking that she send her quota of soldiers into the field. In March 1282, when an insurrection started in Wales against King Edward, the bishops, nineteen abbots, four abbesses, and the Prior of Coventry all received such writs. Heads of major religious houses, bishops, and the archbishops of York and Canterbury were all summoned when Parliament sat—and this extended to abbesses; in 1306, for instance, fifteen abbots and four abbesses were called to Westminster.

The power of these women was well-founded in goods and lands. The oldest were the richest, and the Benedictines were richest of all; it was said that if the Abbot of Glastonbury were to marry the Abbess of Shaftesbury, their heir would have more land than the king of England. Nor was their spiritual power confined to the women beneath them. In the double monasteries of medieval times, when men and women inhabited the same religious houses, it was always under the rule of an abbess. There were priests who ministered to the nuns spiritually, and lay brothers who did the hard manual work.

Gradually their influence waned. As a result of social change, the possession of property shifted from the hands of women. They ceased to found nunneries, and where men—abbots and local landowners— did so, they gave the nuns little power. Only the abbesses of the older orders retained their influence.

It was the Council of Trent in 1545 that really curtailed the women's power. It did so in two ways. Bishops, who formerly had no right to enter the houses of abbesses with episcopal jurisdiction, were now able to do so as delegates of the Holy See. Even more damaging, however, was the curtailing of their movements: Nuns were forbidden to leave their enclosures. It was this that took the privilege of attending the Imperial Diet away from the aristocrats who ruled the German foundations. And it was this that kept abbesses of the oldest and richest religious houses in England from answering a summons to Parliament. By 1874, the episcopal role of the abbess was over.

The rule of enclosure is still rigid. Any enclosed nun leaving her house without permission risks exclaustration, which means she is no longer in any way a member of her order. Or, if she is under solemn vows and there is some scandal attached to her going, the penalty may be excommunication from the church. Though in earlier days the walls were used to keep the world out, they gradually became part of religion itself, so that a religious became by definition an enclosed person taking solemn vows. And the protective measures that developed were sometimes almost unbelievable; in Assisi, at Saint Damian's, it is still possible to see the ordinary door of the convent high up in the wall where it can be reached only by a ladder drawn up at night.

When, in 1609, Mary Ward founded the Institute of the Blessed Virgin Mary in England, she and her sisters were known as the Galloping Girls because of their refusal to have enclosure. "Show yourself as you are," she told them, "and be as you show yourself." Although the pope supported her, churchmen were horrified; she was imprisoned and a decree of suppression issued on her sisters. A century later, when Saint Vincent de Paul was scheming to keep his order uncloistered and active in France, he warned them that they must always tell the local bishop that they were not in religion. "Should some muddleheaded person appear among you and say, 'We ought to be religious; it would be much nicer,' then, my dear sisters, the company is ripe for Extreme Unction, for who says 'religious' says 'enclosed.' "

Enclosure was carried to great extremes. In the nineteenth century, when an English branch of the Carmelites founded a house in another town, they traveled in a coach with all the windows painted black. This order had originally arrived from France, to be met at Victoria Station by friends who insisted they see a little of London —much against their wishes. A young sister who asked another what she had seen received an indignant answer. "We saw nothing, of course. We are enclosed nuns."

Churchmen wielding power frequently use it to enforce what seem to be undue restrictions. As late as the 1960s, the eminent prelate of a large American diocese ordered that no sister venture outside the convent after six in the evening, and several other bishops followed his lead. But now, thanks largely to Vatican II, a sister from that same diocese says that "even appearances on late-night television are considered part of the apostolate." In the late 1960s, Cardinal Antoniutti wrote to the School Sisters of Saint Francis in America that he felt their new freedom was leading to practices that are not only dangerous but a source of scandal, such as "late hours, indiscriminate visiting . . . and worse."

The attitude toward contemplatives has always been even more strict. At about the same time, Cardinal John Carberry wrote to the four thousand contemplative nuns in America, saying that he understood that contemplatives had been seen at religious meetings and workshops. "This," he wrote, "may have serious effects on their contemplative vocation," and he "respectfully requested" that they abstain from attending such gatherings while the question of their renewal was under study.

One nun publicly and furiously contested Cardinal Carberry's moral right to tell four thousand women what to do—"moral" because there was no question but that he had the right canonically. In 1969 this woman, Sister Margaret Ellen Traxler, formed the liberal National Coalition of American Nuns to prevent the oppression of women in religion. One of her first acts was to tell men to keep their hands off the running of religious orders of women—though it was couched in more formal terms: "We protest any domination of our institutes by priests, no matter what their hierarchical status. We uphold as inviolable rights of self-determination for religious women."

The impact this had was reflected in a headline in the *Chicago Daily News*: MILITANT NUN'S FIGHT FOR SEXUAL EQUALITY ROCKING THE CHURCH. Today, Sister Margaret runs an influential organization from an office on South Wabash Avenue in the heart of Chicago. One in fifty of all American nuns are NCAN members, and those who join are active and vocal; together they are capable of making a considerable impact on the system. NCAN set out to be a conscience for the Catholic church in America. They have campaigned for good teachers for Negro colleges in the southern states, and their organization, CHOICE, sent the first whites to these campuses. They have supported civil-rights marchers and picketing farm workers, Jews in Russia and American Indian dropouts. They are fighting to get the Equal Rights Amendment to the American Constitution ratified, since they believe there is little point in fighting for equality within the church as long as women outside do not have it.

Probably the most militant feminist to remain in the ranks of any religious order, Sister Margaret would never dream of leaving the church. "I really see my life as a commitment to God, and I'm not going to go back on that." She is a member of the School Sisters of Notre Dame, but far from representing their views she is totally opposed by many of her fellow nuns. (At a conference at the motherhouse in Rome, a group of Austrian sisters asked recently that she be denied a vote at the meeting because of her stand on priestly interference.)

Some of NCAN's criticisms are undeniably justified. There are no women at all in decision-making positions in the church—and yet women represent well over half the membership. In the autumn of 1972, the American synod of bishops met to talk about justice, and not a single woman representative was present. "Imagine!" exclaims Sister Margaret. "They're talking about justice, and half their membership is denied a presence, much less a vote."

But if Margaret Traxler refuses to see herself as a daughter of a male bureaucracy, if she advises that it is better to ignore canon law than try to fight it, if she sees the hierarchy as an anachronism, she also sees the reality. The Sacred Congregation for Religious can dissolve any order at any time and acquire its houses and property. "Women have to understand this before they can link arms and fight against it."

There is yet another area where the church is tied to centuries of tradition: women are also excluded from the priesthood. A woman is one of the two classes of persons absolutely barred from ordination, the other being those who are not baptized. Yet an exclusively male priesthood is of human, not divine, devising. There is no theological justification for excluding women, only an emotional one. (One bishop has said with a shudder, "Priestesses would be a shift to pagan creeds.") A lecturer in psychiatry at the University of London suggests that woman is seen as imperfect "just as a man who is a eunuch or has severe corporeal deformity is held incapable of receiving Holy Orders." He points out that passionate reactions against the idea—*disgusting, repugnant, shameful*—show there are "powerful unadmitted or unconscious motives at work."

146

There are currently moves toward ordination for women in many churches, mainly in the form of qualified and consecrated deaconesses, of whom there are seventy in the Church of England. By 1971 the United Presbyterian Church in America had ordained eighty women and the American Baptists had appointed a woman president; in Sweden the first ordination of women took place in 1960 (although it is true this was considered so shocking an innovation that many male candidates immediately resigned).

In 1973, the body of Catholic bishops in America set in motion a study ostensibly to decide whether women should be ordained—a step which militant nuns regarded as no more than an empty gesture. Meanwhile, eleven women were ordained to the priesthood in the Episcopal church in Philadelphia, only to be told their ordination was invalid because the bishops who performed the ceremony were not authorized.

Curiously, nuns are not much interested one way or another. There are, of course, those like Sister Honor Basset of the Society of the Sacred Heart who feel that "women who are religious-minded would love to have been priests." She considers that since being a nun is the only opening for the girl, "it's got muddled in people's thinking."

But almost all the nuns I talked to seemed unconcerned beyond the point that they would like to see the possibility open and felt sure that eventually it would be. When they do discuss it, even aggressively modern women tend to do so on the most superficial level. Typical is the English sister who liked the idea of women as priests but said that personally she only regretted it now and again, as when "at Easter we couldn't pass the chalice one from the other; it was passed over to us by the priest from the bishop."

It seems a shortsighted attitude. The question of ordination for women is one which could vitally affect all nuns and sisters. The hierarchy of the Catholic church is particularly complex and deeply rooted. The nuns' chances of changing this system in order to acquire greater self-determination is minute. But it is not the principle of the hierarchy to which nuns object. Obviously there will always be a power pyramid, as there must be in any organization as massive as the Catholic church. It is the fact that it is a wholly *male* hierarchy which is the problem. Women do not object to being answerable to

147

a bishop as such; they simply resent the fact that it is a man who arbitrates so much of their lives.

It is surprising that nuns do not put more thought and effort into trying to break the emotional barrier and get women priests accepted. For tomorrow's woman priest might be the next year's female bishop—and by 1999 a woman cardinal!

The question of women priests does raise one issue which concerns nuns, and that is the teaching of theology. In the past, nuns tended to receive what teaching there was secondhand, and that at the most rudimentary level; after all, they were not expected to be interested in such a complex subject. But as the education of nuns improved, so did the need for better theological training. "You can't expect intelligent young women with trained minds to sit and listen to the little vision of Sister So-and-so," exclaims a highly qualified French sister.

The importance of training in theology and philosophy becomes even greater as nuns and sisters move farther out into the world. As an American sister, Bertrande Meyers, says, "When a nun is asked for advice, she can't just say, 'We'll make a novena to Saint Jude for this,' or, 'Just keep up your prayers and everything will be all right.' Certainly no one wants to confuse being a nun with being a theologian, but one woman who has a good working knowledge of all the different orders says that the ideal situation would be if 'at *least* two or three nuns in every convent had theological training.'"

Regina Mundi, founded in the mid-1960s, is the only European theological college provided solely for women. Its course in theology, however, is simply a massively abbreviated and simplified version of that given to men at nearby universities. It is no wonder that nuns who have taken the course describe it as "hopeless"; at least one is now rereading theology at King's College, University of London.

In 1965, John Cardinal Heenan founded the Corpus Christi theological college in Bayswater, intending that it should become a center for renewing religious education after the Second Vatican Council. Out of every 1,000 students, 750 were nuns. Then, early in 1972, the entire academic staff resigned over disputes with Cardinal Heenan, chairman of the governing body. There were several points of contention, one of the most revealing being Cardinal Heenan's objection to the policy of giving the same course in speculative theology to priests with years of study behind them as to "untrained nuns and laymen." It is useless to suppose that women can achieve any kind of voice as long as "untrained nuns and laymen" are still lumped together in the minds of the men of the church. Even promises of equal status turn out to be empty.

In 1966, the Holy See published the decree of the council, Perfectae Caritatis, which said that the institutes themselves were responsible for renewal and adaptation by means of general chapters. This was a revolutionary move since, for the first time, instead of the Roman Curia rigidly controlling all discipline, the Holy See had recognized that each order could formulate its own constitutions. But when orders tried to put this into practice, it became apparent that the bishops had no intention of relinquishing the reins of power.

There was one attempt at renewal and self-expression by the Immaculate Heart of Mary sisters in Los Angeles. The resulting clash with the hierarchy rocked the Catholic church in America, as the sisters defied their cardinal by refusing to retract any of the reforms on which they had embarked in response to Vatican II. "All we were trying to do," they claim, "was to search for new ways. We sincerely serve the church—but we objected to being dehumanized." The outcome was unprecedented: They are now, under canon law, "defectors."

The story of how what one religious sociologist has called "the battered remnants" of the Sisters of the Immaculate Heart left the religious life and became a lay community is extraordinary. It is also peculiarly American, in that no European community has experienced a similar upheaval at this point, even though renewal and adaptation have brought difficulties to many of them. Even in America, however, the Immaculate Heart sisters were not the first to give up their religious status; these were the Glenmary sisters (who now serve as secular members of their "communities of service" because the restrictions laid upon them by religious life interfered too much, they felt, with their work). Nor will they be the last. They will, however, undoubtedly remain the most famous.

The Sisters of the Most Holy and Immaculate Heart of the Virgin Mary was founded in Spain in 1848 as a semicloistered community, and twenty years later ten sisters were sent to California as missionaries.

Scarcely pausing to learn English, the community opened two schools and became the first teaching order in southern California. In 1924, with a fair number of American sisters, it broke with the Spanish foundation, but this made little difference; even when, in previous years, the sisters from America had returned to Spain, the rules were so strictly observed that they were not allowed to join the Spanish community behind the grille.

As early as the 1940s, the California community was becoming increasingly progressive, to the point where it was criticized by churchmen for giving courses philosophically ahead of Catholic teaching. The members, however, did not consider themselves at all radical; "we just answered the needs of people more immediately than most orders." The sisters ran the college and high school built by the community, nursed in their modern hospital, or worked in their conference center. Then, in 1962, the community received a canonical visitation—a rare event—from His Eminence James Francis Cardinal McIntyre, of California, a man of conformist views. "If you're going to be a nun with your motherhouse in his diocese," commented a sister about him, "he's going to see you do it his way." The visit was not a friendly one. At this time, women throughout the world were beginning to leave religious life, and every order was suffering. His Eminence, however, chose to attribute the number of dispensations being requested by IHM sisters to the inadequate training they received. He questioned the community's theological training, pointing out that it should be following not the thinking of recognized contemporary theologians, but his own. Unless the sisters conformed, he told them, they would "pay" for their views. Later that year he returned to tell them that experimentation was "dangerous" and that the changes the community had adopted—which allowed more freedom in the observance of silence and manner of prayer—were contrary to orthodox religious life. He gave the sisters sixty days to conform to traditional religious practices.

But these changes had been legislated by the order's general chapter in 1963. The IHM community is a pontifical institute, able to make changes in the internal life of the community unless Rome disapproves. Only the work of the diocese and public worship comes under the head of the diocese; his approval is not necessary for general chapter decisions. The mother superior, Mother Mary Humiliata, was so worried by the implications of Cardinal McIntyre's dictum that she went to the ultimate authority in Rome, the Sacred Congregation for Religious and Secular Institutes, and as a result Cardinal McIntyre modified his criticisms. The matter seemed closed.

It was reopened when the IHM general chapter, in accordance with the directions of Vatican II, met to discuss renewal of religious life. The changes the community wanted this time included allowing the sisters to resume their own names and handle a small personal allowance. The sisters also wanted to be allowed to choose work other than teaching and nursing and to experiment with suitable lay clothing. They wanted, in short, to be allowed to dress and regulate their lives like normal women. The sisters anticipated the objections of Cardinal McIntyre and consulted eminent theologians and canon lawyers as to the soundness of the proposals, but it made no difference; the cardinal took the new decrees as a statement of defiance. He refused to accept the arguments of the IHM sisters that the traditional habits, fixed hours, and firm government which he considered indispensable to "religious" life were a hindrance to women working in modern schools and hospitals, and insisted that if the decrees were not dropped the sisters must withdraw from the schools in the archdiocese.

The response of other religious to this was widespread. Superiors of major orders defended the IHMs, and there was a nationwide petition of support. Some theologians considered the decrees a splendid response to the call for renewal, while others rebuked the sisters for disobedience and labeled them "Hollywood types." Nuns and sisters accused them of trying to kill off the religious life. In the midst of all this, Mother Mary Humiliata—or Anita Caspary, as she had become known—went again to Rome for advice. Her answer came when Cardinal Antoniutti spoke to the major superiors of women's orders in Italy in January 1968. He said Vatican II did not authorize experiments which would obscure the meaning of religious life, create confusion, or provoke scandal. Changes affecting the nature of the institute were forbidden and, as to clothing, "in the army no one is allowed to choose his own uniform." Thus, with a heavy curial foot, did he help stamp out the IHM attempt at renewal.

The Sacred Congregation, "conscious of conflict," as Anita Caspary dryly puts it, now took a hand and presented the IHMs with directives with which they must comply: The first was the retention of the habit; the second was a set prayer schedule, with all sisters meeting at least once a day for prayer; the third concerned the importance of spiritual works over apostolic ones; and the fourth was that they must cooperate with the local bishop. When Anita Caspary protested these directives, a pontifical commission was set up to study the case, and four American bishops arrived to question the sisters. The advice they gave the community was, "Pay lip service—have a habit, keep it in your closet, and wear it once a year on feast days." Says Anita Caspary, "We didn't want that kind of hypocrisy."

So the community split. A group of fifty of the older sisters accepted the four points and continued as always, under a new superior. Some left religious life altogether. Four hundred sisters remained with Anita Caspary, when it became evident they would have to sign their dispensations and be reduced to the status of laywomen again. "When you make a decision in common sense," says Anita Caspary, "and are told to reverse it for obedience, your whole being is torn apart."

The first sister to hand in her dispensation was Sister Anna, who made her first vows in 1905. At ninety-nine, she signed the mimeographed document with a firm hand and announced, "I am now going to the chapel to make my vows to Jesus." Until her death two years later, she continued to wear the full habit of the order. Anita Caspary herself found it hard to leave religious life. "I'd have made a terrible divorcée. To find that church people seemed to disregard completely a lifetime of service and dedication, to find the church didn't give a hoot what happened to your whole life." She did not even have the satisfaction of knowing why the IHM sisters were singled out. As the Catholic press pointed out, what was being done in Los Angeles by the IHMs was being done throughout the United States by all kinds of orders. Indeed, much of their support came from religious who were putting similar programs into action. The affair ended officially in 1970, but it is very far from finished in the eyes of the religious world. Anita Caspary still spends a good part of her time traveling and taking part in television programs about her community all over the world; CBS and the BBC have both made documentaries. (In Germany, no sister of any order would consent to appear on a television discussion show with her.)

It is worth looking at what has happened to the women who stayed in Anita Caspary's group. In what direction have they moved, now they are no longer under the direction of the cardinal or the Vatican? Have they become as radical as Cardinal McIntyre feared they would?

In many ways they are extreme. They no longer live as a closed group—but then neither do many other members of religious orders. On the other hand, they still retain the feel of a religious community. They call themselves "a community of religious persons," because if they became a secular institute they would be right back under the jurisdiction of the Sacred Congregation for Religious and Secular Institutes. The members live where they choose in "a community without walls," just off Hollywood Boulevard, between the hills and the smog, in a large white-painted apartment house. Behind the wrought-iron gate, a Madonna smiles. Inside, balconied rooms rise around a courtyard set with café tables and chairs. A fountain plays, and the blue of a swimming pool glimmers in the distance. This is the hub of the IHM community.

In an upstairs apartment lives Ms. Anita Caspary, IHM. She is an elegant woman with upswept hair and an expensive dress, sitting in a cool room furnished with antiques, a bowl of glass grapes at her side, pink flowers in pots nearby. It is hard to realize that she was once Mother Mary Humiliata in long purple robes, her hair hidden away. Now she is president of the Immaculate Heart Community, whose roughly 250 members include a cellist with the Los Angeles Philharmonic Orchestra, a department-store china and glass manager, two psychologists, an electronics assembler, and three men. Some of them live here, perhaps with dependent relatives—Anita Caspary has her mother with her. Others have apartments, shared possibly with a member of a different community. One sister lives alone above a garage. The idea is that communal life is created by the members by participating in the life of the whole community. "We're talking about a network of people with the same ideas living different life-styles."

The pattern of life is relaxed—no bells, no fixed hours for rising or sleeping, no formal recreation. But it is in their membership that they have made their biggest break with tradition. In 1970, married couples were admitted to full membership in the IHM community, which members feel adds a dimension of which they could not previously have dreamed.

153

Anita Caspary seems justified when she claims that "anything that is happening in religious life with regard to vigor and vitality is happening through women." Whatever happens to the IHM community, however successfully they resolve their problems, the church will not profit by their example. The only way to change the structure is to stay and reform it from within, and the IHMs had little choice but to leave. Anita Caspary believes that in the church at this moment "the situation couldn't get much worse—and something drastic has to happen soon."

But the men of the church must change their way of thinking about women. From the parish priest to the bishops and cardinals pacing in purple through their celibate days, there must be an acceptance of the ability of women to govern their own lives, to accept responsibility, to make valuable contributions.

"If the church is going to be saved," says Anita Caspary, "it's got to make use of its womanpower."

*I don't know what we're going toward—but it's
something new.*
—SISTER PEARL MC GIVNEY

6

The Nun in the World

Sister Pearl McGivney is an example of the sister who believes, in the broadest sense, that the nun's place is among those who need her. While the nuns of Carmel pray for the world's salvation, Sister Pearl, a continent away, is fighting for human rights.

The Coachella Valley is a hard drive of five and a half hours from Los Angeles, between the luxurious pools of Palm Springs and the arid Mexican border. It is not yet four in the morning, and already the temperature is soaring into the 90s. In the darkness, the Mexican farm workers are out in the fields, picking grapes for an annual income of less than half the national poverty level.

The picket lines are out too, and Sister Pearl in her brief red skirt is with them, tramping the dirt roads around the fields, crunching underfoot the dry shells of locusts, and carrying banners with the black thunderbird, the ancient Aztec eagle with square-edged wings that

Cesar Chavez has taken as a symbol in his fight for the equality of Mexican workers.

All summer, the Coachella has been the scene of America's most prolonged and bloody interunion battle, between Chavez's tiny United Farm Workers union and the huge, rich, and ruthless International Brotherhood of Teamsters. The Chavez pickets want the farm workers to strike with them for realistic wages and decent conditions. "Strike!" they shout into the dark fields. "*¡Huelga! ¡Venganza, señores! ¡Para su respecto y dignidad! ¡Huelga, compañeros, huelga!*" Sister Pearl and the strikers start singing "We Shall Overcome," and the Teamsters retaliate by turning up their loudspeakers to drown out their voices, playing "Bye Bye, Blackbird" full blast.

Sister Pearl, with her heavy coils of dark hair, her gentle face, and her anxious eyes, looks like the last person to be involved in this struggle. Yet two years earlier she went to California for three weeks from her New York convent of the Sisters of Saint Joseph of Brentwood, to see what Cesar Chavez was doing for the Mexican farm workers, and she never returned to her community.

It is a strange life for a nun. The violence in the valley is terrifying. The Teamsters want to finish off the UFW *and* Chavez—they call him El Perro, the dog—and keep the farm workers subservient and poorly paid, as they always have been. The threats on Chavez's life come daily, and he has a squat bodyguard and two Alsatians for protection. The day before I arrived in the Coachella, six Teamsters were arrested for throwing rocks at the car in which he was traveling. While I was there, a Mexican was dragged from his vehicle and stabbed six times with an icepick before the Teamsters realized he was not the man they wanted. And the following day, one of Chavez's aides, a Catholic priest, was sitting in a restaurant when a Teamster standing 6 feet 4 inches tall came over to the table, broke the priest's nose with one blow, and walked off. A month after this incident, a picketer at another town was shot dead from a passing car.

Sister Pearl has seen much of the violence. Everyone knows she is a nun—she often wears her habit on the picket lines deliberately to show that the church is on the side of the farm workers—and the Teamsters resent her. "I've never been called a broad until now," she says. "They shout, 'Sexy—you ought to be ashamed.' Not long ago there were a thousand people picketing in ten lines of a hundred each, and I was with a nurse. We got split up and found ourselves caught between two Teamsters' cars with marchers behind us. One car came alongside and a man asked, 'When's the last time you worked in a field, Sister? How do you know what it's like?' Then he grabbed the flag on the car and scraped the wooden stake up my arm."

Sister Pearl, who is in her early thirties, became interested in the movement when she was studying theology. "Some migrants came in to talk about their situation and ask for our support. And I knew I had to do something."

Before Sister Pearl had even heard of Chavez, she went to New York's Long Island, where the potatoes are picked by Puerto Ricans and blacks from Florida and Georgia, and lived in the camps there with two Dominican nursing sisters. "The thing that struck me was that they were broken men and we were treating them like children. We were putting bandages on the wounds, and giving them aspirin, but not changing anything at all. It was work of social concern, but it didn't change the system."

Migrant farm workers are vital to the American farm system. They move around the country, from state to state, harvesting crop after crop as fruits and vegetables ripen. The majority, like Chavez, are Mexican-Americans. Some, the Chicanos, are American-born, while others are Mexicans allowed over the border. They are open to exploitation by the growers who run the vast foodbowl that is California in a situation that has not changed essentially since John Steinbeck wrote *The Grapes of Wrath*. In those days, it was poor whites who did the work; now it is the Mexicans, who suffer even more. A poverty-stricken minority only now becoming articulate, they have no place in the American dream. Often illiterate, their children receive minimal education because of the constant traveling, so they cannot better themselves. They have neither Social Security nor old-age pensions. They live in primitive shacks provided by the growers and pay inflated prices in grower-owned food stores. And the work itself is backbreaking: stooping and bending in that blinding heat—it is impossible to continue beyond midday—usually without even the most primitive sanitary arrangements.

It is the passion which Chavez brings to this cause that made

Pearl McGivney join him. "When I first met him, I thought, He's a good man and he does his job. It's when you talk to him that you realize what a great man he is. And religion is at the heart of everything he does. I wanted work with something that was hitting at the worst problems, and the migrant workers were in the most horrible situation. I guess that's why I chose the union, because it helps people control their own lives; it gives them dignity as human beings."

Pearl told Chavez she wanted to work for him. "He said, 'What are you going to do for the people? They need medical care.'" There are many accidents in the fields, not least from the dangerous pesticides the Mexicans have to use, for which protective clothing is almost never provided. But no doctor will treat a Mexican without prior payment. Over five hundred accidents each year happen to children who work illegally in the fields. California law allows twelve-year-olds to work during holidays, but an estimated 800,000—a quarter of the labor force —are under that age: seven-year-old girls picking strawberries, nine-year-olds spending ten hours a day in the lettuce fields.

With Chavez, Pearl developed a medical insurance plan, and her job is to open clinics to serve the workers. These have to be organized and staffed, and she is also in charge of the necessary recruitment, much of which is done through personal contacts. "We're trying to find professionals with a social consciousness. And we've got great people; I never met such people in my life." There are four permanent workers' clinics in California, with full staffs providing total care in the busiest areas. Pearl is developing the clinic system so that mobile units can follow the farm workers as they move. She spends weeks at a time traveling from clinic to clinic, "and I've learned how to fix a flat tire." When she arrived, "I didn't know one person. Now I go any place in the state and find farm workers, people on the staff, sisters. I always have a home. That's the exciting part about living fluidly. There's always somebody there."

But "home" really means La Paz, the mountain headquarters of the United Farm Workers, where 250 people live, both families and single volunteers, as well as the five nuns who, with Pearl, are now permanent members. There are other sisters working with Chavez— the Maryknolls from New York help the women learn child care and basic hygiene—and many nuns and priests march regularly on the picket lines and frequently get arrested for doing so. But none of the others actually live as part of the Chavez group.

The six nuns have made two rooms in an abandoned hospital—La Paz used to be a sanatorium—into a living room and a bedroom with three mattresses on the floor and white-painted walls. They went together to buy a freezer for $15 out of the $5 a week each gets as a volunteer. Pearl was so delighted with this bargain she never thought to ask if the freezer worked. Luckily, it did.

When Sister Pearl decided to join Chavez, she knew two things: "I knew that I would do it, and I knew that I wouldn't leave community." At that time she was the only sister involved, but now, apart from those with her, there are letters and phone calls constantly from sisters who want to join them. "It's *the* form of living the religious life right now." At La Paz, there are also two brothers, one of them a Xaverian. "Every day we all try to have prayers, and we talk. We even sing. It's very informal. And it's very real."

Sister Pearl's own community is supporting her both morally and emotionally. "We're all open to the possibility of a new community of the Sisters of Saint Joseph out here. But the great possibility is that something completely new will emerge from this." What she would really like is to develop a new community, of both brothers and sisters, all from different orders. "I don't think individual communities, as one distinct from the other, is a very balanced concept today. The idea of sisters in free movement is completely new; it's something I dreamed about and hoped for from the beginning." Although her community can ill spare her, she knows they will continue to back her: "When we discussed it, the community said, 'If this is of the Spirit, it won't fail. If it is of man, it'll fail by itself.' "

One of the other sisters in Coachella is Mary Jean Friel, who joined Chavez six months after Pearl herself. A devastating girl with long brown legs under her blue denim dress, she wears tiny silver peace-dove earrings half hidden by her streaky blonde hair. She does Chavez's secretarial work and, more importantly, helps him coordinate his program. She is with him almost always, taking notes at meetings, answering phones, helping him meet people, fending off those he does not want to see.

Chavez is a man who seems to inspire maternal feelings in his

159

helpers; small and quiet, for "La Causa" he has sacrificed his energy (and some say his health) for the last twelve years. He has given up much of his family life—his wife had all but two of their eight children in his absence.

Mary Jean decided to join him after considerable experience of the problems of migrant workers. She is a Sister of Loretto at the Foot of the Cross, a community founded in Kentucky in 1812 by a French priest. She became a sister because "I realized I had some kind of responsibility for being so happy all my life." Her community was asked to work with migrants in Colorado, and her job was in a labor camp looking after the welfare of the families. In 1969 she became involved in a strike with the carnation nurseries there. "A Mexican family taught us what it meant to be nonviolent, what it meant to be a striker. I didn't know really what it was all about; it just meant people I like suffered an awful lot." The evening before that strike ended, Mary Jean told the twenty-two sisters in her convent that there was a bad day ahead. "Not all the sisters were for me, and some were very much against the workers. But I learned a beautiful thing. People support you even if they don't approve of what you do. I had to get up at five thirty that morning, and when I came downstairs a sister who had argued with me the day before had hot oatmeal waiting. She insisted that I eat it, and she told me she'd pray for me the whole day."

Mary Jean and Pearl share an office in Coachella, on the corner of Highway 86 and 6th Street, where a huddle of empty shops faces a gas station and, beyond, the massive range of mountains that encloses the valley in a heat that reaches 120 degrees. The office is a large whitewashed room full of odd desks and chairs; every surface is cluttered with posters and papers, banners and badges. Twelve people are sweating away despite the air conditioning—typing, telephoning, talking. There is a knock on the door; when it is opened, a short man holding his hat mutters nervously in Spanish. Sister Pearl goes out with him and unlocks the room next door; piled inside are sacks of provisions, boxes, parcels. She fills his arms, and he beams and backs out. He is a striker. This food supplements the wage the union is paying him.

Sister Pearl's first thought when she joined Chavez was to become a transient teacher, moving with the children from place to place to get them above the fourth grade, which is as far as the average migrant child goes in school. Experiments are planned with education centers for both children and adults among the workers at Delano, but, for the moment, "It's more urgent to change radically the whole migrant situation. Cesar wants to end migrancy. Not today or tomorrow. But in the end."

Chavez himself sees the sisters as a moral asset to his people, and he believes they are safer than anyone else. "No one is going to run over a nun, you know. You'll run over a priest maybe, but not a nun." He mimes a fierce nun: "I dare you. Run over me." Pearl and Mary Jean are marginally less confident of their imperviousness. Both have sat in the back of open trucks while Teamsters threw rocks at them. They were asked by Chavez to lead eight hundred people in a march for farm workers in one of the nearby shanty towns, where many were known to be against him. "We walked around with our banners, shouting '*Huelga*, boycott, viva Chavez!' It's terrifying not knowing what's going to happen—Mary Jean grabbed me by the hand."

Both sisters are appalled by the squalid conditions under which the large families live. They enjoy talking to the women; Pearl went to Puerto Rico especially to learn Spanish before joining the UFW, for which the Brooklyn diocese gave her a scholarship. But if they are shocked by the way the Mexicans have to live, they are prepared to share it. "Some places we live adequately. In others, it's at subsistence level. We moved into a migrant house infested with roaches and rats, and from April to May we slept on the floors. There was a toilet but it didn't have a door. Very few houses have water. We try hard to enforce sanitary regulations."

Their Coachella apartment is three small rooms shared by eight women—five sisters, three volunteers—in a block a short walk from their headquarters. By late afternoon the heat of the day has subsided a little, and the temperature is down to 110 degrees. The apartment has one fan, which Pearl hastily switches on. Her community has contributed the only decoration, a green and white felt poster which reads, I SHALL BE WITH YOU BECAUSE I LOVE YOU.

Most evenings, the sisters eat late, perhaps at nine thirty, taking turns cooking while the others bathe. Mary Jean, eating her bananas and yoghurt, observes, "It takes mature people to be able to live like this." She gets the milk out of the refrigerator and giggles. "Even though we're all beautiful, we do have a few thorns here and there. You have to know your own limitations and work within those."

They are strict—not rigid—about their formal religious life. There it is a resident chaplain at La Paz, and two priests in Coachella. But it is hard to regulate times for prayer when you get up at two thirty to join the picket lines every morning. For Pearl, "Faith in God is my reason for living." Yet despire that, she sees that "the price of religious life is loneliness. You have yourself and God. I'm convinced it's not possible unless you have a real prayer life, so you're strengthened and refreshed; it makes me more alive." Her apparently haphazard life seems to her closer to the original concept of religious life than today's usual convent system. "The founders had the mobility to follow the Spirit where it led." And in this last year, she says that she has become much more aware of her vocation. "I guess it's because I have to review every day who I am and what I am. And I keep saying yes."

Sister Pearl is convinced that she could neither live as she does nor do the job she wants to do if she were not a nun. She jumps to her feet, ties a big apron around her waist, and attacks the dishwashing. "It frees me for responding with love."

Women like Sister Pearl and Sister Mary Jean are rare, even in the United States. But they are not unknown. Nuns are becoming concerned with politics in a way that would have been impossible before the Second Vatican Council. Until then, the church hierarchy said categorically that politics was not the concern of any religious. A great many people still feel that way, but more and more men and women in the States are beginning to feel that they cannot stand on one side and watch injustice continue.

This does not seem to be true in Europe, where the only active political participation I came across was one lone sister in London who donned her habit to protest outside Parliament at Westminster against the hedging that was going on over the bill concerning discrimination against women. In countries like Holland, where religious are in many ways liberated—I saw not a single habit there—the idea of a nun involved in political activity was greeted with blank stares.

It remains very much an American phenomenon. The militant nuns of America are into everything, from going to jail for a month to study the penal system and write a report, to issuing a statement on the unnecessary brutality of Black Panther Bobby Seale's sentence for contempt. When, during a 1965 civil rights march in Mississippi, state troopers moved in with guns, tear gas, and dogs, fifty-two nuns in full habits stood between the state troopers and the marchers. "The troopers were afraid to club us."

In 1971, nuns made a concerted effort to get justice for the natives of Alaska, who were being forced to sell their land to the government for oil speculation at absurdly low prices. As a result, the Justice for Alaska Natives bill was pushed through Congress. The following year, five Sisters of Charity were charged in a Louisville court with "disorderly conduct" after demolishing a derelict house there. It was a desperate attempt to get the city to realize the dangers of "rat-infested firetraps" in an already deprived urban area. Although the house was condemned and abandoned, the city had no plans to remove it, or similar houses surrounding it. The Sisters of Charity ended up with $10 fines—and the support of the president of the Senate of Religious in the diocese, who called it "a courageous moral act."

And, in 1973, it was a nun who went to Wounded Knee following the uprising as part of a task force to study every aspect of the Indian situation there—from the problems of children forced to attend distant boarding schools to the appalling housing conditions in the area.

One order deeply involved in politics is the Sisters of the Humility of Mary, a group founded in France in the mid-nineteenth century to work with the poor. They came to America as missionaries, teaching and nursing, and their range has widened to take in experimental scientists and public-relations consultants. One sister is a law student in Washington who plans to educate the poor to make the law work for them instead of against them. Two sisters have served as delegates in county conventions in Davenport; another was one of the key people working to get a candidate into the Iowa legislature, doing full-time recruiting and research. They feel that such involvement is totally justified, since it concerns social issues. "We get reforms to state and national power through the county conventions."

Another of their sisters, Eleanor Anstey, became the first nun to run for the Iowa Senate. Asked in 1972 by the citizens of Muscatine to enter the Democratic primary for state senator, she won the nomination and then spent the next three months learning about the Iowa Senate, the major issues, the needs of the district, and the whole process of elections. A colleague from her order researched her campaign, and there were press releases, stickers, and media advertising —all on a budget of $1,000. She found the experience extraordinary. "It was a strange feeling to be driving down the highway and hear your own radio spots." Although in the end she lost (by only 4,000 votes) to the Republican candidate, she intends to continue in state politics. "So many decisions, affecting the lives of thousands of people, are made in the legislature." She sees a real need for more women, particularly sisters who are free from political pressure and have no vested interests, to be there when decisions are made about criminal justice, the care of the elderly, prison reform, the environment, revenue sharing. "I saw so much apathy in government. I think we've got to have more people who care."

Sister Mary Anne Guthrie agrees with her. She is a forty-seven-year-old member of the Dominicans in Memphis, Tennessee, who ran for Congress in August 1974, the first nun ever to do so. A Democrat, she faced four men in the primary. She wants to bring women to the forefront of government because "I do not think woman, herself, has recognized her own potential. I would like to see more women in leadership positions." She sees no conflict between her religious profession and being a member of Congress.

If more and more sisters are concerned with social reform through participating in the established political and legal systems, there are also increasing numbers who see no mileage in such peaceful methods. Of all political issues, American religious have reacted most strongly to those where war is involved. It was in protest against the war in Vietnam that twelve Anglican nuns in New York received Communion in Saint Patrick's Cathedral and then lay down in the aisles wearing white sheets bearing the words, ANOTHER PERSON DEAD IN INDOCHINA. It was in protest against American troops being sent to Guatemala in 1966 and 1967 that Marjorie Melville, a half-Spanish Maryknoll nun, and others doused draft cards with homemade napalm and ignited them. Thus, along with the Berrigan brothers, America's rebel priests, she became one of the Catonsville Nine.

In the Baltimore courtroom, she spoke of American terrorism in Vietnam: the dropping of napalm, planes missing their targets, the

164

bombing of peasant villages. "I know these people," she said. "They are not statistics to me. They are just looking for a piece of land to support their children. They are not trying to overthrow the United States. That is the last thing in their minds. I wanted to make as effective a protest as possible to U.S. military intervention across the world, not only in Vietnam but in Guatemala where I had seen it." Marjorie Melville was imprisoned for two years in March 1970.

If such behavior appears unlikely for a woman who has vowed her life to God, who is concerned more with things of the spirit than the body, more with the next life than with this, it is worth remembering that nuns have a radical historical tradition.

Nuns were the first "professional" women. From the earliest times until almost the present day, a Catholic woman had only two honorable choices open to her, "a husband or a wall." She could either marry, produce children, and run a home for her family, subject to her husband, or she could enter a convent.

In the first days of Christianity, religious houses for women were centers of learning and provided the only education available to girls; they learned to read and write, to spin and weave their own clothes, and to nurse the sick.

The religious houses of northern France were famous for the quality of their education. They were the finishing schools of the French aristocracy, and young women were sent there from England as well. One English nun, Lioba, was educated at Wimborne in Dorset and left England around 748 to settle in Germany. She did so at the request of Boniface, who wrote that "her reputation for holiness and virtuous teaching has penetrated across wide lands and filled the hearts of many with praise of her." We know from the biography written of her by the monk Rudolf of Fulda that "she never laid aside her books except to pray and strengthen her slight frame with food and sleep—Old and New Testaments, grammar, liberal arts, writings of holy fathers, canonical decrees, laws of the Church." Her learning brought her a busy social life. "Princes loved her, noblemen received her and bishops gladly entertained her and conversed with her on the scriptures and the institutions of religion, for she was familiar with many writings and careful in giving advice."

The convents of the German lands of Saxony also achieved enormous intellectual and social importance, as the ruling families realized there were advantages in a union between religion and state and vied to found religious settlements. Then they sent their daughters there to be educated. Those who did not marry were thus assured of powerful positions, while those who left to wed often returned in later life. Herford in Westphalia was renowned for its learning; Gandersheim in Eastphalia, Quedlinburg, and Essen were all important until the Reformation.

It is quite obvious why girls were so eager to enter; the boredom of life in a damp medieval castle must have been excruciating. When their fathers and brothers were away fighting, attending court, or running their estates, there would have been little for the women to do. There was almost no communication with the outside world. Books were rare and precious, and not found in private houses. It must have been a relief to be sent away to a convent, usually between seven and perhaps fourteen years, then considered a marriageable age. It was not until the fourteenth century that convents began to lose their importance as educational centers.

Nuns did not go out to teach until 1535, when Angela Merici founded the Ursulines in Italy—Saint Ursula was the traditional patroness of girls—to teach girls and the common people; no one else had considered such work necessary. She received papal approval, but twenty years later the Holy See ordered the suppression of all female congregations not in enclosure and subject to common vows. To survive, the Ursulines acquiesced and donned the habit for the first time. It was nuns, too, who became the first professional nurses.

Within the convents themselves there was a considerable amount of medical knowledge, as the twelfth-century writings of a German superior, Hildegard, show. Known as the "Sybil of the Rhine," she was a wellborn woman, put into the care of the nuns at Disibodenburg at seven and professed at fourteen. She was taken very seriously; her work was submitted to the Pope, with whom she corresponded. Archbishops, emperors, princes, and dignitaries all wrote to her, often seeking advice on the most personal matters. She seems to have been a medieval sob sister. Two of her books are on medicine and are quite remarkable for their day. One of them, *Physica*, on the nature of man and the various elements of creatures and plants, is an amalgam of sensible advice and primitive superstition. She wrote about plants and fish, animals and birds, stones and metals. Many of her remedies were for indigestion, coughs, fever, delusions, and leprosy. She recommends bathing in various concoctions of leaves, which differs scarcely at all from current knowledge of the curative properties of herbs.

Convents already had formal rules for caring for the sick. The nuns of Syon had a document which advises:

> Often change their beds and clothes. Give them medicines, lay to them plaisters and minister to them meat and drink, fire and water, and all other necessaries night and day, as need requires after the counsel of the physicians, and precept of the sovereign; do not be squeamish in washing and wiping them by avoiding them. Be not angry nor hasty nor impatient though one have the vomit, another the flux, another the frenzy and now sings, now cries, now laughs, now weeps, now chides, now is frightened, now is wroth, for there be some sickness vexing the sick so greatly and provoking them to ire that the matter drawn up to the brain alienates the mind. And therefore those in attendance should have much patience with them, that thereby they may secure an everlasting crown.

All this, of course, referred to nursing their own sick; nuns were still forbidden to leave their enclosures. The first order able to undertake public nursing, to go to people's homes and look after them, was Vincent de Paul's Daughters of Charity. The peasant priest was horrified by the conditions of the underprivileged in seventeenth-century France. There was work to be done founding hospitals, sheltering abandoned children, and feeding the starving.

Early in the seventeenth century, Saint Francis de Sales, the Bishop of Geneva, and the Baronne de Chantal, a rich widow, wanted to start a congregation to do similar work, visiting the poor in their homes—hence their name, The Visitation of Holy Mary. But the bishop in Lyons, where they began, was a conservative man who argued that the presence of unenclosed nuns in his town would lead to scandal and all kinds of difficulties. Solemn vows and enclosure were the inevitable result. But Vincent de Paul, with much the same ambitions, exercised "holy cunning" and won the battle. He avoided the rigors of canon law by sheer diplomacy. He called the institute a "company" and the novitiate a "seminary." Their residence was not a convent but a "house," and he appointed not a superior but a "sister servant," while the sisters were not called religious but "daughters of the parish," and dressed in gray serge like the common people.

Vincent de Paul and his Daughters of Charity made the breakthrough from enclosure to a life in the world, an active apostolate. By the nineteenth century, ten Catholic Sisters of Mercy from Bermondsey, and eight Anglicans from Lydia Sellon's Park Village Sisterhood, as well as five nuns of the Company of the Faithful Virgin, went to Constantinople with Florence Nightingale at a time when no decent woman would nurse because of the reputation nurses had for being both drunk and dirty. Yet these nuns not only braved the sea journey but also tended British troops suffering terrible wounds from the battlefields of Balaclava, living in poor conditions to do so. Florence Nightingale, though she reckoned them among the best of her nurses, did not find them easy to get on with. The conduct of one, she wrote, "has been neither that of a Christian, a gentlewoman, nor even a woman."

It is interesting that the area of medicine in which religious women today are particularly successful is not conventional nursing at all but coping with the ills of our time: addiction to alcohol and other drugs.

The Maryknoll Sisters in New York started helping hard-core heroin addicts in the 1960s, when three sisters moved into a small apartment in Greenwich Village. They were available at all hours of the day and night, and their phone rang constantly. Between them, they had over a thousand addicts in treatment within two years, under the supervision of an expert.

The Anglican Community of Saint Mary the Virgin in Berkshire started working with addicts even earlier. Spelthorne Saint Mary in Surrey is a three-storyed Georgian manor house set in a landscaped park. The box hedges are neatly trimmed, the azaleas flourish, and swans decorate the willow-fringed lake. The parlor has watercolors on the walls and tulips in the vases. Creamy carpets cover the highly polished floors. The whole house radiates calm, which is undoubtedly one of the reasons for its success: Spelthorne Saint Mary is rated Britain's most successful unit for "drying out" women alcoholics.

When it was opened in 1879, nothing was being done to help such women; no sympathy was given to alcoholics. The sisters of Saint Mary the Virgin recognized the need and responded to it; their work was revolutionary. Soon, they started admitting drug addicts. In those days, addiction was often to opium preparations which had been prescribed for medical relief. Addicts to morphine and heroin purely for sensation did not appear in number until between the two World Wars; when synthetic drugs began proliferating in the 1950s, Spelthorne Saint Mary found the number of drug-addicted patients increasing. It continues to increase, while the average age of the patients falls.

If the sisters' work is less revolutionary now, it is no less successful. Their high cure rate is owing partly to the length of time for which they continue to supply help—the ideal length of time is a year, and they hope people will stay at least six months—and partly to the warm atmosphere and family feeling which the sisters themselves provide. This, they feel, is vital for the recovery of their patients. It is not just the budgerigars singing in the windows, or the names on the doors of the sisters' rooms—STANDFAST, WELCOME, HOPE—but something the patients feel. "The sisters," says a bleached-out blonde, "really give you a lot of themselves."

Two thirds of the patients there at any one time are alcoholics, mainly middle-aged, middle-class women whose marriages went wrong and who found themselves drinking too much sherry. The other third, the drug addicts, are largely middle-class too: the hospital nurse who under stress started taking the patients' barbiturates, the twenty-year-old girl whose parents live abroad and who needed "help to grow up"; the eighteen-year-old who got involved with a drug group.

At lunch, taken at long tables, the patients sit quietly in their skirts and baggy cardigans, chatting about the bus outing for the afternoon. One younger woman has a fixed stare and an aggressive manner. A pretty girl in a pink flowered minidress shows dimpled knees. Next to her a fragile, tousle-haired girl in tight cords remains aloof and silent. Later, in the corner of the large sitting room, she shouts to herself—desperate, shrill cries.

A dark woman wearing pink earrings was once a nurse herself. "I've been to six places before this. At first I found it very hard to get through to the sisters. I found the habit a barrier. But possibly I didn't want to be helped at the beginning. Then I found they wait for you to talk to them. So when I got the craving, I could tell them because I *wanted* to tell them. Before, nobody could make me talk."

She is particularly conscious that in a hospital "you're just a case number. And the case is more important than the person. Here, they really want to establish you as a person." She believes she has a much better chance here than in the special unit of any hospital. "Some places they don't give you any dignity, but here they build you up again. They give you self-pride."

"They treat you," confirmed another woman, "as an adult human being; they don't talk down to you." Women who arrive at Spelthorne invariably need this more than anything. Quite a few come direct from Holloway, the women's prison in London, on probation, in which case the Home Office pays for their stay. Often they have stolen to pay for the alcohol or other drugs they could not afford to buy. These patients will usually have been withdrawn from drugs already—or detoxicated, if they drank. But those who come on the recommendation of a doctor may not necessarily have gone through the period of withdrawal and may face a difficult time. Withdrawal can be very serious. They will be automatically given a period of bed rest in the infirmary, for days or weeks if necessary, and an intensive course of vitamin B to repair damaged nerve tissue.

As soon as possible, the newcomers join the life of the house. Their time is filled up by the sisters. This is vital because, as the sister-matron points out, "We meet with a lot of apathy; that's why many of these people have got into this state." Partly for this reason, partly because patients must be protected from access to alcohol and other drugs, the regime is strict. For the first month, no one goes out except in the company of a sister. After that, patients can go home for weekends if they are progressing well.

Patients start with an eight-o'clock breakfast, after which they collect prescriptions from the dispensary. Then the house sister organizes housework—helping in the kitchen or garden—before going to occupational therapy for an hour. After lunch and a cup of tea everyone washes dishes together, patients and sisters. In the afternoon there is recreation, when they are encouraged to take classes in pottery, singing, or flower arranging. In the craft room, they paint or sew or weave raffia baskets. They can go shopping with the sisters, use the library or the game room, play darts or watch TV.

There are usually twelve sisters at Spelthorne. Some are state-regis-

170

tered nurses; one is a doctor. Others have perhaps forty years' experience as club leaders. They are all considered suitable for the work they do by Dr. Max Glatt of Saint Bernard's Hospital, Southall, one of Britain's leading authorities on the problems of addiction, and consultant at Spelthorne. Under him are the psychiatrists and other specialists who visit regularly. There are also secular nurses and a full domestic staff.

The main goal of everyone at Spelthorne is to rehabilitate the "whole person," to find a place for her again in society. The sisters believe that the whole personality is damaged by alcoholic and other drug excess, and that treatment must therefore be physical and mental, spiritual and social. Rehabilitation is going on all the time; the housework and the basket weaving are all part of it. But there are more basic and concentrated efforts. The sisters give personal counseling to those who want it. "It's really a question of getting to know them, so they feel they can really open up for us. We need this specific knowledge to know how to link them on when they leave us." As one patient puts it, "You might go on an outing and find you're sitting with one sister, and somehow words come out."

Another important feature of the rehabilitation process is that relatives can come and stay for a night or two in the guesthouse, which is a tremendous help in rebuilding family relationships. "Reconciliations can take place far more easily," says one of the sisters, "in comfortable and neutral surroundings than in the emotion-charged atmosphere of the home—or even in Spelthorne, with all its associations of illness and treatment."

Each afternoon after tea there is group therapy. Some of the groups are taken by the doctor and the infirmarian, others by the sisters. It is an encounter, getting to know each other, getting to know oneself, getting to know people as a group, getting to coalesce as a group. The sisters generate all the gaiety they can. There are parties for every occasion. They have a large wardrobe of costumes and do a pantomime every Christmas and, occasionally, a Victorian melodrama, with one elderly sister famous for her roles as gay young blades. They book a year ahead for films to show in the evenings. They do everything possible to get the patients through the day without despair: "Depression is what may have started them off on an addiction." And as

171

soon as they are well enough, the sisters encourage them to take jobs in the nearby town of Staines, so they can meet testing situations while still under care. Some work in department stores, others learn shorthand and typing for office work. The sisters are anxious that the women be able to keep away from the "dangerous" places of their past. But this comes during the last part of their stay at Spelthorne.

Leaving is probably the hardest part of the cure. "A lot of people start producing symptoms when it's time to go because they're afraid of facing life outside." The older ones are most difficult to place when they leave. One middle-aged woman on drugs had a stroke and was severely paralyzed; it took over a year to get her into a rehabilitation center. This partly explains why the sisters take only women under sixty-five; after this age they feel it is not really possible to help. Many of their patients are private, but the fees are extremely realistic; there is no profit margin for the community.

Spelthorne Saint Mary could not be anything but a religious institution. It has the same soothing quality as the order's motherhouse in Wantage, Berkshire. There is no hint of the impersonal bustle of a hospital. But though the sisters "try to get to the problem and sort it out," they "don't in any sense thrust religion at people. We make no discrimination about a person's faith. We have Anglicans, Catholics, Methodists, Jews. They're completely free."

There is, obviously, a formal religious side to the life, but only if the patients wish to take advantage of it. "Unless you ask," says one woman, "the subject isn't brought up." Patients can go to mass at seven thirty each morning, joining the sisters who have started with lauds at seven, and sometimes there are modern hymns accompanied by one of the sisters with a guitar. There are prayers again after breakfast for anyone who wants to attend. Sometimes, say the sisters, the patients "become aware of a lack in their lives." They do find that quite a few "take up" religion again as a result of their experiences at Spelthorne.

But perhaps the most vital part of the sisters' work is that they are a stable community to which patients can always return and know they will be welcomed. An effort is made to keep in touch with former patients by letter, and quarterly meetings are held for those who have left. "We're always glad to see them for a meal or a short stay." Both the alcoholic and the ex-drug addict have to make a new start in a new environment, and they often find themselves very lonely until they make new friends. "It is," says a sister, "of the greatest value to them to know that they *can* come back, that they *matter* to us."

The work of this community concerns those who have fallen victim to the stresses of our society. But other orders work for those whom the law considers to be the aggressor. The Sisters of the Good Shepherd was founded in seventeenth-century France and specializes in social work with delinquent girls (who are brought "back into the fold"—hence the order's name). They run hostels for unmarried mothers; they also staff women's prisons in several countries. In Portugal, for example, they run the only prison for women, in the Estoril area, where few male guards are seen in the whitewashed buildings with their red-tiled roofs. Discipline is left mainly to the nuns, who have few problems in this devoutly Catholic country. When the nuns enter one of the workrooms, the women rise and kiss their hands as a sign of devotion.

They have good cause. Thanks to the work of the Good Shepherd sisters, their lives are not wasted even though they are behind bars. The nuns train them to weave exquisite wool rugs, which they make so successfully that the prison has a three-year backlog of orders. The women earn good money, some of which supports their families outside and some of which they save. One prisoner recently left with $1,500 from her work.

Another French order was founded two centuries later, specifically for prison work. In 1841 the Frenchwoman Anne Quinin began the order of the Sisters of Marie Joseph to combat the dreadful conditions in prisons. So desperately needed were her sisters that the government provided free accommodation for them, and before long they worked in Lyons, Montpellier, and the ancient prison of Saint-Lazare in Paris. They moved into the Central prison and La Roquette, and by 1927 they were established in Fresnes, to which it has now become customary for the French government to send women from any other prison who are in need of special care and medical treatment.

From central Paris it takes a train and a bus to reach the prison of Fresnes, whose high gray walls loom forbiddingly over the Avenue de la Division Leclerc. Along the unpaved avenue, behind the heavy iron gates, beyond the gendarmerie and its armed inhabitants, squat the apartment blocks which house the warders and their families. Among them, directly beneath the prison walls, is an ugly oblong house: the convent of the Sisters of Marie Joseph.

Sister Kathleen Mulvany is the superior of this house. Her face is ravaged by fatigue; there are dark shadows under eyes that are astonishingly, serenely blue. Sister Mulvany is obviously Irish, and the traces are still present in her voice. But she has lived in France so long now that she has trouble with her English. She gestures with her hands, searching for the words she wants, and ends up with Franglais.

Sister Mulvany did not intend to work in Europe. She wanted to go on a mission, "but my brother wouldn't hear of it." One of five children, she eventually entered the order's English house, paying the cost of not only her dowry but of the voyage from Ireland to do so. She transferred to Paris a very naïve twenty-two-year-old. "Well, you know, I didn't understand a lot about life." It was not long before that changed, and she chuckles at the thought. "I often think of my mother. She didn't want me to go to the Good Shepherd order; she thought the nuns weren't nice. If she only knew what I know now. I hear more confessions in here than any of the priests in the churches."

Sister Mulvany looks after women who are awaiting trial and those who are serving sentences. "We have women here who've got twenty years. They've done horrible things. But we don't ask what they've done. Our duty is to care for them and try to get them well. They've been judged. You can't judge them again." She brings to her work complete compassion. "They don't need pity. They need to be respected, to be treated as human beings." Nothing shocks or horrifies her; those tired eyes have seen women at the very end of their tether. "I see women in passion, and they're not themselves. Sometimes it is discouraging, trying to help people who don't want to be helped. I say to myself, You must always sow. Perhaps we'll reap in years to come."

Sister Mulvany's work starts when she receives women into Fresnes. She waits in a little anteroom for them to be taken through the freezing formalities of entering: the fingerprinting, the body search, the shower. When they reach her, they see in the sister "something else. They begin to cry. You let them cry a little and then ask, 'Can I help you?' Little by little it all tumbles out. I have to spend a lot of time with people who arrive. It's one of the most dramatic moments in their lives—when they arrive and when they're judged."

She attaches enormous importance to the care she can give at such a time. "When they come into prison, they're not themselves. By the time of their trial, they're not the same. They've had time to see the calamity they've brought into their lives and the lives of their children. They only realize that little by little."

Because of the time this realization takes, Sister Mulvany will spend hours comforting and listening to them. "I think our perseverance, being near them at this time, is something they never forget. They must never feel they're being judged by me. They talk, they say words; I understand without having the details. I comfort them and make them see they have a possibility to do otherwise, to re-evaluate their lives. I'm not here to convert. You can't force yourself on anybody from the religious point of view."

One woman she particularly remembers was condemned to death for the murder of one of her lovers. "I was working in the linen room and all the time I used to talk to her." The woman went, finally, to the Central prison for eighteen years. "One day she rang at the door and threw herself into my arms. Her first visit on coming out was to see us."

Sister Mulvany's understanding of the women's problems has a practical value above the immediate help she can give. She regularly goes before a board at Fresnes to discuss the prisoners with the social assistants and doctors. The board's comments are listened to and acted on by the director of Fresnes and the commissioners who hear the applications for parole. Sister Mulvany's great strength is that she can see past the horror of a crime to the emotion which caused it. "There was one lady who killed her husband. He was not a nice man at all; he had two other women. She loved him very much, and she couldn't see him with these other women, so she made her choice and she killed." She shrugs her shoulders and holds out her hands palm up. "And he is hers now in death."

That a nun should be involved in such work totally demolishes the idea that nuns are otherworldly. "We can't be dead to the world,"

175

Sister Mulvany exclaims, horror-struck at the very idea. "We live in the world. We're all human. We're all women."

Out of a prison holding over two thousand people, Sister Mulvany and her sisters care for at least fifty women and for any men who are sick. "They have asthma, tuberculosis, skin troubles, eczema. The women cry, but the men keep it inside and suffer from stress conditions." The sisters are all trained nurses and there is also a midwife for the births; there are always about a dozen women with babies. Most of them are single and often they are very young. The sisters help them through the pregnancy and the birth and teach them how to look after the child. These women have very much more freedom than other inmates, and usually a better time than they would have had outside, abandoned without public assistance.

The sisters treat them with great affection and understanding. "We have one girl, twenty-six, with a lovely little baby. This woman had a friend, *un amant*—we know all about that, you know. She was abandoned by her mother and brought up by a grandmother. Now, that explains a lot about her behavior." Some of them, says Sister Mulvany, have to be taught how to be mothers. And she laughs. "I don't regret not having babies—I have so many." In the beige-tiled rooms, with cream walls and turquoise bedspreads and a cot in the corner, the mothers stay for eighteen months with their children. They have full medical care and do most of the work for the children themselves: cleaning the rooms, washing the diapers, doing their own ironing. There is a modern nursery, and they have the use of a private yard, full of flowers and trees and birds. Of course the women are subject to security regulations, but their doors are only locked at certain times, during the day, and at night. Security is a matter of which the sisters are very conscious. They each give their number—Sister Mulvany's is 647—on entering, and have their own keys to the maternity wing. To enter the men's section, they ring a bell and a guard opens the door.

Apart from the medical and welfare work, and visiting both men and women, Sister Mulvany is also responsible for such odd duties as picking up the morning letters and arranging with the accountant if a woman wants to buy anything. "They're allowed makeup and presents for the family. You must always remind them that inside they must save for when they leave. Then we check that they have the money and arrange for it to be stopped until something is paid for."

To get everything done, the sisters rise at six. Their bedrooms in the convent are cool and pleasant. Beside every bed stands a little plastic bottle of Lourdes water. After meditation, they sing lauds; then there is mass. After breakfast, which like all their meals they prepare themselves, they go straight into the prison. Others meals are not taken by the community together because of the demands of the work, and dinner is eaten in rotation. The sisters all work far too hard, seven days a week. The order simply does not have enough sisters to sustain its workload. They have four days' holiday in a year—not counting the time for the voyage home. Sister Mulvany accumulated three years' holiday; "that was fourteen days. But time flies, you know." There is, she admits, "physical despair from overwork, and sometimes spiritual despair from your own heart. But that might also be a trial from God. There is much misery around us, so we have to acquire, little by little, self-control. We must never be too cold or too warm. Each has to find his own measure."

The women in Fresnes come to the sisters with all their troubles: "*Ma soeur, ma soeur, aidez-moi.*" The problems might be small—a row, a depression—or they might be big. "Sometimes a woman receives a letter that tells her everything is finished. That is terrible, in prison. Just imagine their state of mind. But, you know, the women get over it better. A man let down in prison won't get over it."

Sister Mulvany has done a stint in La Roquette, the Paris prison which deals with special cases such as professional lesbians who even in prison try to collect girls for the street. "One told me all about her life; it was something terrible. She had been born neither male nor female. I had terrible work with that girl. She turned one girl wild, so that when she was released she immediately got herself back inside so they could be together. But we visited her in hospital and, do you know, she still writes to me? She has great strength."

Many of the women she deals with now are prostitutes. "They are very humble in themselves. They know no one has respect for them, and they have none for themselves. There is something very touching about them." How does Sister Mulvany help these women? "Well, you try to convince them they can do something else; you do social work with them. Several have left after prison and buy themselves out. But others say, 'I have no profession. Do you want me to earn a hundred francs a week when I can earn that in an hour?' But I say,

'You earn so much but you're maltreating your body, drinking a lot, and you haven't put any money aside.'" The prostitutes generally put their children in nurseries outside Paris. "And for nothing in their life would they want their children to know. So I say, 'It's necessary your children should be proud of you.' Several have told me they feel real horror at doing it every day, horror of themselves. And I say, 'You must not think like that. You have a body and a soul that are God's all the same, and you can recover all that you were.'"

Many of the women prisoners are drug addicts. One of the Marie Joseph sisters became particularly interested in the case of a girl who, as a result of her addiction, was having trouble with coordination and had virtually lost the use of her hands. The sister made her follow a course to educate her hands and literally forced her to type. When the girl was sent to the Central prison, a letter followed her to the sisters there to encourage her. "Now," says Sister Mulvany with pardonable pride, "she has a secretarial diploma and a job, a very good position."

Sister Mulvany becomes most emotional when she hears from former inmates. "At Christmas we receive a lot of letters from those who have gone. We have people who have been very ungrateful and never sent a word. Some write a few times; others never forget. Others write, and you're really astonished to get a letter from them with thanks for such a word on such a day. And you expected nothing."

They lead strange lives, the Sisters of Marie Joseph, in the gray shadow of Fresnes, hearing daily of crimes brought about by passions they have never known. "The prison," says Sister Mulvany, "it is an inward world."

Speaking of religious life, she says that it is not surprising a lot of people are afraid to enter, "because they don't know how they're going to end up." She pauses and hunts for the right words. "But for me—I'm full of hope."

We're glad that you did what you did—even if
you sisters made a bad job of it.
—AFRICAN BISHOP TO WHITE SISTERS

7

Missionaries and Martyrs

The woman who joins a missionary order is of a special breed: tough enough to live the life of a sailor in Hong Kong and dedicated enough to "show our religion to be perfectly lovable before showing it to be perfectly true," tenacious enough to travel thirty-six hours by motorbike to reach a remote village in central Borneo and gentle enough to win the confidence of the inhabitants when she gets there.

There is among missionary sisters a spirit reminiscent of the last century. They are the only group of people I have met who still refer to "Palestine" and talk wistfully of "rejoining the Home Front." When they do go home, it's "on furlough." They survive alarming hazards with a mixture of prayer and practicality, like the sister who, caught in the middle of a terrible African storm, prayed diligently for de-

179

liverance and then put the feet of her metal bed into two pairs of rubber-soled Wellingtons, for protection from lightning, and went to sleep.

Spending years at a time in remote corners of the world hundreds of miles from medical help, they must be the only women who not only consider it a positive advantage to be minus their appendixes but see it as "an asset rather than a handicap if one has the kind of teeth that come out at night." It is the three Hs they value: Humor, Health, and Holiness. The American Maryknoll Sisters consider the first so important that "any girl without a sense of humor should be discouraged from considering our congregation. If she cannot laugh at herself, cannot see the funny side of life's ups and downs, she will not be able to bear even the better times of missionary life."

For the majority of missionary sisters, the life is rugged. They have to be adaptable and accessible, able to adjust to the most unlikely circumstances and acquire at least an inkling of the most difficult languages. They need a sense of responsibility and considerable emotional stability, for they often find themselves in dangerous situations. They need every skill they can acquire, from growing vegetables to carpentry. They must have initiative to face the emergencies, and something more with which to combat the loneliness.

If this is true now, it was even more true sixty years ago. Then, missionaries set out expecting to remain away for life; their communities had no money to bring them back for holidays, or even to die. Long before World War I, the Missionary Sisters of the Society of Mary in Massachusetts were going to the southeast Pacific. Of two Marist sisters sent to Fiji at that time, the first died within a year. The second, a small and frail woman, founded a native sisterhood which had a hundred members at the time of her diamond jubilee. She remained active to the end of her life, proud that she had only two possessions: her one tooth and her umbrella.

Incredibly enough, even strictly enclosed sisters did their part on the missions, though without ever infringing the rules of enclosure. When communities of teaching orders were established in foreign countries, the sisters would arrive draped in heavy veils, go into the convent, and never step outside again except to leave the country. Elizabeth D'Arcy, a sister of the Society of the Sacred Heart now well into her seventies, taught in Peru, high in the mountains of Lima. "In eleven years, I never went out of the house." Today, though, another member of the order has just spent two months traveling throughout the country.

It was a long time before this work was open to women. The first great missionaries were all men—Martin of Tours in central Gaul, Patrick the Apostle in Ireland, Augustine in Canterbury—sent out on the wave of Christianity after Constantine first granted toleration to Christians in Rome. When, under his successors, Christianity became the state religion, it was paganism that had to be suppressed.

With the voyages of discovery between 1500 and 1750 that showed a new world to Europeans, Catholicism became a world religion. Spain, Portugal, and France had the responsibility of starting and continuing missions and of building churches in lands they ruled. Central and South America, the Congo, India and Ceylon, Japan, China, and Indonesia were all affected, and the Vatican set up the Sacred Congregation for the Propagation of the Faith in 1622 to centralize the work and take responsibility and control over it. From Rome, territories were assigned and work was directed and supported. Even so, missionary interest declined, until by 1815 it had almost ceased. Wars disrupted the home bases of many orders; the Portuguese and Spanish empires were disintegrating.

The Protestant church did little missionary work until, in Germany, the new Pietism movement began to spark interest. Some organizations had continued to act as missionaries—the Dutch East India Company, for instance, considered that its chaplains were obligated to baptize and confirm the people of southeast Asia. But little was being done for the pastoral care of Christians living in pagan countries —emigrants, soldiers, merchants, and officials on government business. It was to print religious literature for use at home and abroad—chiefly in America—that the Society for Promoting Church Knowledge was founded in 1698 and a Society for the Propagation of the Gospel in Foreign Parts opened later in London.

In the late eighteenth century, missionary societies were founded in London and the Netherlands, but it was the nineteenth century which really saw great Christian expansion. As the Protestant powers of Europe acquired greater territories, out went missionaries to them, filled with zeal and charity. They were strongly backed at home; every village in England at that time had its weekly sewing party, with one woman reading aloud while the rest sewed Mother Hubbards for the heathen. Armed with these, the missionaries set off to conquer the ignorance, illiteracy, and physical suffering which they knew belonged to Satan and must be stamped out rigorously. With their Bibles, schoolbooks, and medicine bags, they did their best. But it was not enough. For all their selfless ideals and genuine concern, they made a lot of mistakes; they did not realize that it was Christianity, not the potential converts, which had to adapt. "The whole experience of Christianity we brought," says a White Sister, "was a Western experience. It's the only experience we knew. If we'd known more of Africa, we'd have done it differently."

The nuns, like the lay missionaries, set out knowing virtually nothing of the countries where they would work. For many, such ignorance proved fatal. The Anglican sisters who first went out to Uganda in 1860 thought mosquito nets were unnecessary fussiness—and died needlessly from malaria, three of them in one year, all under thirty. The Sisters of Charity fared no better. They sent out five sisters in the 1890s, and all died—the last just as she arrived back home.

As their ignorance hurt the nuns, it also hurt those they were trying to help. They had no understanding at all of native cultures and they imposed their own ideas and beliefs willy-nilly on people whose own cultures and rituals they thus helped destroy. The Presentation Sisters of South Dakota, for example, formed to work (as they still do) with American Indians, admit now that when the Indians were forced to drop their "pagan" beliefs they lost much of their heritage that could well have been preserved. Sister Carol Quinn says, "The Indian spirit of Thunderbird is our Holy Spirit. And they believe that to give is the most important thing. We didn't integrate with their beliefs; we made them give up their ways. And now among the South Dakota urban Indians, who are almost all Christianized, there is a movement by the more radical to go back to their native religion and give up Christianity."

Much of what the nuns taught must have given their "pupils" a feeling of inferiority. The orders took with them their European art forms—and their white Christ child in a winter crib. "We don't do

182

that any more," admits a missionary sister with some relief. "Now he's black." They took, too, European church music to which they added the native language, thereby helping to obliterate the native musical heritage in Africa, India, and Indonesia. It is only now that the nuns encourage the creation of hymns by people in their own language, with their own instruments and rhythms. At the Carmelite convent in Kigali, Rwanda, where over half the community is African under a Belgian prioress, the office is sung to African instruments while novices dance the Magnificat at vespers. And at the Poor Clare monastery in Likuni, the service is in Chichewa and the choir accompanied by African instruments, while even the boldly colored vestments are African. This came as a great relief to people who found the European prayer pattern quite unacceptable. "We like to use drums," says an Ashanti bishop, "to sing and pray together. The idea of someone standing up and preaching while all the others are silent is totally foreign."

Some of the innovations brought by the missionaries were deadly. Natives bundled into Western clothes to hide their unseemly nakedness did not know how to keep them clean—and suffered from infection. Nor did they realize the material must be dried when wet—and they became ill and even died as a result of unaccustomed sickness.

But the nuns were only daughters of their time, and missionary work was seen as part and parcel of the great task of empire building and expansion. Gradually, the world influenced the cloister, and now, as a Maryknoll Sister says, "We don't believe in the melting-pot concept, but in a stew where each ingredient retains its own identity." Whereas, in the past, nuns related to people in formal roles—teacher, religious, nurse—now they are involved in leisure situations. They go to family celebrations, to weddings and fiestas. They are expert in the most esoteric languages—Celine Durnan, a Franciscan Missionary for Africa, even speaks Xhosa, the curious "click" dialect of the Lusikisiki district of South Africa.

Missionary nuns have not only become more broad-minded (when two Medical Mission sisters recently left a leprosarium in Ghana, they were given a farewell party at which the fetish priestess poured libations for them) but more honest. They confess that they have more failures than successes. They are well aware that now they are tolerated in many countries only for the free welfare services and education they provide. And while they do not separate education and Christianization ("You inculcate Christianity through whatever you do"), they see now that, of the girls they educate, many wish to become Christian because to do so confers a higher social status. And others who genuinely seem to accept Christianity often, says one Belgian sister, "end up as third wives."

For a long time, those in the missionary field operated as enthusiastic amateurs. They moved into areas where they could help, but not sufficiently. They were faced by malaria and cholera, smallpox and dysentery, TB and leprosy. They saw children dying of malnutrition and disease which swept through shanty towns, and they could not really change the situation. "Unenlightened heroism," as Pius XI said, when he reviewed the medical section of the Missionary Exposition in the Vatican in 1925, "is not enough."

At the turn of the century, four sisters of the Franciscan Missionaries of Mary went to India to nurse at Rawalpindi but had to engage a laywoman as doctor, since priests and sisters with public vows at that time were forbidden to do surgical or obstetrical work, however desperate the need. The laywoman was a seventy-two-year-old Seventh-Day Adventist, Dr. Agnes McLaren, who returned from India convinced that a religious community must be created of sisters trained to fulfill all medical and surgical functions. Five times she went to Rome to seek sanction for her plans—with little success.

It was another woman doctor, Anna Dengel from the Austrian Tyrol, who was finally to fulfill Dr. McLaren's dream. She visited India, realized the need for qualified women workers, and in 1924 toured the United States to explain that need. Within a year another woman doctor and two RNs had joined her. At first they did not take vows but made "promises." They lived as though they had made the normal vows but continued to work as doctors and nurses, to prove to Rome that the two vocations were compatible. In India they staffed hospitals, opened health centers, and trained local midwives and nun nurses. In one jungle area, the verandas of their new hospital were thronged with the sick before any medical supplies had arrived. "What did you do before there was a hospital?" the sisters asked the head of the village. He replied, "We died."

184

The sisters had much to learn about the ways of the people they were serving. When a child was born in another new hospital, relatives rushed to the astrologer to tell the exact hour of its birth. Later, the mother was found in tears, the baby pushed aside; it had been born at an unlucky hour. One of the sisters had the sense to say the hospital clock was fast, and the child was retrieved.

By 1932 the sisters had permission to take private vows; two years later they adopted their gray and blue habit. And in 1936 Dr. McLaren was vindicated when the Vatican issued a decree urging that congregations start special units for health work in the missions and asking that, because proper technical and spiritual preparation was needed, "the sisters should obtain certificates as doctors or nurses." The Medical Mission Sisters now spread fast. They ran hospitals for black miners in South Africa; they moved into Ghana. Four missions were opened in Indonesia, and the first South American house was established in Venezuela. They went to the Mexican Indians and the Spanish Americans of Santa Fe, as well as to the blacks of Georgia.

Already, other orders had moved into the medical field on a professional level. It is almost impossible to overstress the heroism of these women. They were the first people to treat leprosy at a time when such work demanded real courage, years before medicine recognized the nature and manner of contracting the disease. Even then, they were prepared to share living quarters with their patients. Much of the Anglican Sisters of the Community of the Sacred Passion, for instance, founded by the Bishop of Zanzibar in 1911, has been to make leprosy an "acceptable" disease—to the extent that sufferers will admit having it in time for effective treatment. They now also staff one of the two leprosy hospitals in Britain (there are usually about 350 cases in the country at a time, mostly immigrants or English people who have been living abroad).

Some of the hospitals founded by nuns in the early twentieth century now enjoy international reputations; the Leprosy Control Headquarters in Buluba, East Africa, for example, opened in 1934 by Mother Kevin, founder of the Franciscan Missionaries for Africa, is now the biggest and most modern leprosarium in Uganda.

Those women went to the new territories quite literally for life, knowing the outward journey would never be retraced. And formidable journeys they were. By truck and train, foot and caravan, they forged their way across Asia and Africa. The Franciscan Missionaries of the Divine Motherhood, traveling to Kasaba on the Bangweulu swamps in Zambia to take over a leper hospital on the death of a woman doctor from blackwater fever, traveled by truck for two hundred miles. Then, when the road ended, they journeyed by bicycle, following narrow paths across half-destroyed bridges until the swamp became so watery they had to use canoes. They completed the entire journey in full-length white habits with pith helmets stuck jauntily on top of their headdresses. The women who went to Africa traveled like this until 1930; though the East African railway was built at the beginning of the century, they had to get to their missions from the railway on foot. It was the 1920s before any supplies were sent from home—and then they arrived once a year. At one time the only way of reaching parts of Zambia was on the sawmills train on the bush track, which was said by missionaries to possess square wheels. Passengers paid no fare but were required to sign a declaration that they traveled entirely at their own risk.

Today, sophisticated transport has made it possible for nuns to reach areas previously beyond them. (A Franciscan missionary who lives in New Guinea and teaches medicine in pidgin English remembers that when her plane first landed at Aitape the people there, who live and dress in leaves and feathers as their Stone Age forebears did, rushed out to feed the plane bananas.) And with the coming of better and cheaper transport, they started to go home after twenty-five years' service. Now orders give, on an average, three months' leave every five years, and the motherhouses of the bigger orders are constantly greeting returning workers. The minibus of the Franciscan Missionaries of the Divine Motherhood may shuttle all day between London's Heathrow Airport and the convent as sisters arrive from all over the world—Rhodesia, Zambia, Singapore, and Australia. Sisters now are able, as they never were before, to return home for refresher courses in their fields, which is particularly important for those involved in medicine.

It is the medical skill of the missionary sisters that is their greatest contribution to those they want to help. Often they are not merely dealing with sickness and casualties—which might be anything from

186

gunshot wounds to crocodile bites—but actually uncovering illness. It was the Sacred Passion sisters, an Anglican community in Tanzania, who discovered that children with polio were hidden in the villages. No one had realized the number who could not walk. The sisters started visiting them, got them into braces, and trained them to use their limbs again; now there is a special hostel for them, and local Africans are taught to make the braces themselves.

The missionary nuns, though, do not confine themselves to medical and educational problems. They are increasingly anxious to improve the living conditions of the people they are helping. Mother Mary Martha of the Franciscan Missionaries of the Divine Motherhood works in a hospital in Zambia three hundred miles from the nearest town. Horrified by the lack of resistance to disease, she decided something had to be done about the chronic food shortage. Although soil near the mission was sandy and unsuitable, she discovered that a few miles away it was good enough to farm wheat. One July morning she set out with a group of villagers to start work on this land. "I noticed," she said, "that the men got into the Land Rover armed to the teeth with bows and arrows, axes and knives. I discreetly inquired as to their use, and the men very politely informed me that the villagers near where we planned to start our farm objected very strongly to our going there and were waiting to kill us."

Another nun working in Africa, White Sister Monique Vien, watched women walking miles for every drop of water for cooking, washing, and drinking. With her none too fluent Dagarti, she took an intensive course in well-digging methods, traveling on her Honda to talk to experts. The local headmaster became her project manager, but it was she who collected the equipment to build wells in ten villages. At the first site, they found water only forty feet below the surface. After this proof that the task was possible, fifteen men worked on each well with hoes and hatchets, once the site had been chosen by the local bishop, who was conveniently skilled in water divining. In three months, each village had a well.

Other nuns teach people trades at which they can earn a living for the first time. In Kenya, in a densely populated squatters' slum near Nairobi, a Maryknoll Sister, Edith Fragola, runs tailoring and block-printing workshops, where cloth is printed with local designs before being made up. And in Sri Lanka the Sisters of the Good Shepherd, whose missionary work is mainly in schools, brought in subsidiary industry when the Provincial Mother of Good Counsel sent sisters to Italy to learn silk weaving to teach to the native fisherwomen.

Sometimes a more basic change is needed. The Maryknoll Sisters in Peru, for instance, have been forming groups of women, making them aware of their rights and opening their eyes to the way they have been exploited. Male "machismo" there dictates that women be kept pregnant, if possible, and since 1965 the Maryknollers have been teaching that until this attitude is overcome the children are doomed to poverty and semistarvation. Recently a group even picketed a new hotel in Lima where a beauty contest was being held.

But if most of the changes in the lives of the natives are for the better—greater hygiene and improved eating habits, for instance, which means more children survive—the arrival of the nuns with their schools and their Western values has also created problems. "By coming into Africa and giving the people an education," says Sister Marguerite of the White Sisters, "we created needs for them which they didn't have before—better homes, a watch, a bicycle. And to get these things, they have to change their way of life. They can't just live simply in the field. They want to go to the city and make money." Although she herself approves, "as long as they are not deformed needs, as long as they live a better life," she does admit that "we improved their education and therefore changed the whole system, which is from birth to the grave. And that system, even if different, was very valid." As a result of the breakdown in this system, the White Sisters, who have so far dealt mainly with bush people in country areas, are now moving sisters into the cities. They see their educated country girls going there for jobs and getting into trouble, and they hope that by having nuns working with students and office workers there, as they do now in hostels in Mombasa, many of their difficulties will be more easily resolved. This calamity, claims the Bishop of Kumasi, an Ashanti called Peter Sarpong, "has been caused by the Christian condemnation of puberty rites. It was almost impossible for girls to have sex before the puberty rites, and usually, when they had completed them, they were earmarked for marriage." The missionaries condemned out of hand this "mechanism of social culture," with the result that some

Christian schoolgirls become pregnant and abort, all because the church has not worked through what already existed in the culture.

Nonetheless, missionary sisters do take on work which no one else will tackle—including the government of the country involved. In Jordan, for instance, Franciscan sisters run clinics for the poor around Amman. These people are the refugees from border areas involved in the last three wars with Israel. No medical help is provided for them by any Arab government, and water supplies are so bad that babies suffer during the summer months from dehydration. The sisters themselves have found the money to open a rehydration center.

Lack of money is a constant problem for missionaries. As countries have received independence, particularly in Africa, the missionary orders have found themselves faced with financial crises. While colonial governments had once helped subsidize buildings and salaries, independent governments do not have the money. The Zambians, for instance, allow about 50 cents a day for the sixty-four maternity beds and thirty-two TB beds of the Franciscan Missionaries of the Divine Motherhood. Out of this come food, hospital clothing, dressings, and drugs, as well as domestic staff. So the aid of the charities—CARITAS, OXFAM, and CAFOD—has become increasingly important. Even so, the nuns attempt to raise vast sums of money themselves to build and run hospitals. They not only use the traditional method, and beg, they also put on film and fashion shows, stage plays and operas; one order recently held a mock "slave market" in the center of Hamilton, New Zealand, and "auctioned" the sisters.

Missionary sisters are invariably overworked to the point of exhaustion. Mother Mary Luke is a Franciscan of the Divine Motherhood, and the only doctor in a bush territory in the Zambezi valley, which contains twenty thousand people. She is responsible for the hospital in the town center and for the rural health centers staffed by medical assistants throughout the area. She travels on foot through forest and scrublands, and in summer goes by barge through the floodplains of the Zambezi.

Pamela Reynolds is a Medical Mission Sister who works as a midwife in Kalimantan, Indonesia, where it takes her three days by motor scooter to get through the forests to the most distant of her patients. En route, she stops overnight with the people she is treating, sleeping

189

in one room with the entire family. For the benefit of the sisters back home in Osterley, Middlesex, she keeps a racy diary; describing a trek to see a woman who had just given birth, she explains she had to travel over a *djalan tickus,* or mouse path, which could only be negotiated on foot. "For three quarters of an hour I followed the man up and down hills, over streams and rivers, on two bamboo poles. I thought if people could see me in slacks and a blouse following a man dressed only in briefs and a dagger farther and farther into the heart of the forest, they would never believe it."

Many nuns work as part of a mobile group. In August 1972, two special teams of workers were established for a two-year period in the Amazon area of Brazil. Each consisted of a priest, a nun, and a development specialist, traveling up and down by boat to the twenty small communities in the interior, spending a week with each. The nun cared for the women and children, giving advice on cooking, hygiene, and child care. In the evenings they held group meetings on religious matters and the problems of developing the area. As soon as this group finished its work stint, two Franciscans, Sister Regina Wachowski, a medical technologist and nurse, and Father Luke Tupper, a missionary, started traveling up and down the Amazon on a two-deck ferryboat renamed *Esperança,* Portuguese for "hope," and fitted up with an operating room, two dental clinics, and a pharmacy, to reach people in isolated villages, immunize them against illness, and thus raise the survival rate—particularly of children.

Nuns and sisters far outnumber anyone else working in the mission field. In Africa in the early seventies there were nearly 28,000 sisters, from about ninety orders, as against 15,000 priests and 5,000 lay missionaries. In Asia, there were over 47,000 nuns and sisters, while the numbers of priests and lay missionaries remained the same as in Africa. Many of these women were accounted for by the increasing number of native religious. As early as 1858, a congregation of African religious women was founded in West Africa by Mother Anne Marie Javouhey, founder of the Sisters of Saint Joseph of Cluny, who did all her work among slaves. That was at Dakar in Senegal, but it was half a century before there was any sign of religious life on the rest of the continent. In 1899 the White Sisters arrived to staff one of the first missions in Uganda, and eleven years later a group of girls were clothed as Bannabikira, or Daughters of Mary. Recent surveys showed more than seven hundred professed Bannabikira, fifty novices, and forty postulants. Their forty-seven convents run schools and dispensaries and are one of the major orders for African sisters.

The White Sisters—a nickname for the Missionary Sisters of Our Lady of Africa—find the name "not too good, actually, because people think it's racial." (It is, in fact, a reference to their all-white habit.) They originally started in North Africa in 1869 with just five sisters. They are now in fourteen African countries, and while the majority of the three thousand African sisters they have trained remain in Africa, they can if they wish join the main congregation. But the White Sisters see their task as training Africans to take over the work of the European sisters, concentrating on preventive medicine in remote areas.

Originally, little effort was made to adapt the way of life in black communities to suit the African sisters. Everything was done according to the instructions for canonical institutes from Rome. There might be an adapted habit, but it was certainly not African, and the daily customs in the convents were very Western. It is only now that they are realizing that native sisters have different rhythms of life, different needs. So the Anglican sisters of the Community of the Sacred Passion, whose black community in Tanganyika, the Community of Saint Mary, was founded in 1946, now have a different routine for their forty native sisters and fifteen novices: the European sisters have longer hours for prayer while the native sisters do much of the heavy work, which the whites simply cannot handle in that climate. And the White Sisters now encourage their native communities to sit on the floor instead of on chairs in the European manner, while the convents themselves are built and furnished along African lines. But it will be a long time before they "invent" a religious life which is absolutely African.

Any African girl who does want to enter religion is usually bitterly opposed by her family. Parents who are not Christian themselves cannot understand such a life for their daughters. Many put their girls into missionary schools because the education they receive there will ensure a better bride-price when they are married. This money is lost to the family if a girl enters a convent. But more than that, they expect the custom of centuries to be followed, and their daughter to produce children for the clan. As a Zambian sister says, "Something of me seemed to die. I saw that, for my father, it was as if his own life had been diminished, and my mother felt as though she were doomed to misfortune because I would not bear children." She was ritually cursed by her father before his ancestors: "Your companions will mock you; the hens, the goats will make fun of you. You are cursed wherever you go. All the village curses you. You no longer have any father or mother. We no longer think of you as our child. We shall perform the funeral rites for you as if you were dead."

In the majority of African countries, the role of woman is to do most of the work and defer to the man, and this presents a major difficulty for African nuns who achieve any kind of authority. Sister Jacinta is a Tanzanian, a decisive and striking woman who is head of the motherhouse of the ninety Tanzanian Sisters of Saint Therese, on the banana-covered hills above Lake Victoria. She finds she is regarded with deep suspicion by men of her own race, not least because of the innovations she is making in the area; the nuns, all peasant women, are developing their hundred acres of land with a tractor and implements to grow crops never seen before in the area. Beans and bananas, maize and coffee were all cultivated by primitive methods, but now Sister Jacinta and her sisters work side by side with the local women, teaching them how to grow more nourishing foods.

Black sisterhoods are not confined to Africa. The Franciscan Handmaids of Mary was founded in 1917 in Savannah, Georgia, by Mother Mary Theodore, because no white religious community would accept Negro girls—a situation that did not change until the 1940s. She was forced to do so when a law was considered that would forbid white sisters to teach black children. "We serve all God's people," says Mother Miriam, the quiet-voiced mother general. "But we were founded to serve our own." They do so now from Saint Mary's Convent on West 124th Street, New York, in the depths of Harlem. The convent is a square building facing a dusty park. In the inner courtyard, shaded by high walls, a fat old woman talks and talks, while a sister in full habit holds her hand and listens sympathetically.

Ironically enough, a lot of the sisters, according to Mother Miriam, are afraid to go out at night. This is partly because they fear addicts desperate for money to buy drugs, but especially because of attacks by Black Nationalists. In an area where everything Afro is cultivated, where dance halls give lessons in ethnic music and black really is beautiful, the sisters are scorned for following the "white" religion, windows have been broken, and they have been jeered in the streets. Even now, setting off for a nearby school in broad daylight, they walk in pairs. The sisters themselves have never been involved in black power. "When the black movement started," confides Mother Miriam, "I couldn't get particularly interested in it." There is a group of militant black sisters—including Sister Louise Marie Bryan who, arriving in Melbourne for the Eucharistic Congress in 1973, was photographed by all the newspapers making the clenched-fist salute and quoted as declaring, "If the only way oppressed people can be freed is by violence, then the need for violence is justified." But Mother Miriam does not agree with this at all. "They got in touch with us and said they wanted to organize because black sisters in white convents are frustrated. We didn't join—we're not frustrated. We're all black in this order." What particularly incensed her was that white women are excluded from the black sisters' group. Yet she herself regularly attends workshops and conferences with other major superiors "and I have never been segregated."

The Franciscan Handmaids of Mary not only do much of their work with whites—in the Depression, the soup kitchen they ran served more Irishmen than anyone else—but have had several white sisters. Even in the American South, integration is now to some extent a reality: "The church is really Catholic, black and white running it together." But in countries where apartheid is practiced, mixed congregations have faced severe difficulties. In Rhodesia, five black nuns, members of the Congregation of the Little Children of Our Blessed Lady, went to the house of the Archbishop of Salisbury to take over domestic duties which had previously been carried out by white sisters. The house was in the city's white area—and the African Affairs Committee of the city council forbade them to live there.

One missionary order that manages to avoid the difficulties of apartheid is the Little Sisters of Jesus. In one country where the laws of apartheid are enforced (they do not want it named in case it hinders their work), the white sisters live in the black quarter, which is absolutely forbidden. "But we're so poor and so few, they don't think we can do anything." This order is the inspiration of a woman who in 1939 went to the Sahara to start, in Muslim surroundings, a sister-hood to the Little Brothers of Jesus founded by Charles de Foucauld. The community is so new that their constitutions were only fully recognized during Vatican II, but they have expanded in the thirty-odd years of their existence to become a completely international order, many of whose sisters come from Italy and Vietnam. There are now over a thousand of them in more than fifty different countries. The founder, Little Sister Magdeleine of Jesus, was for many years mother general of the order; now in her seventies, she has retired. "I chose to be a Little Sister to *follow* Jesus. I don't want to be the one in charge."

The Little Sisters work as no other community does: by trying to become part of the group of people with whom they live. They are not allowed to own property, and since they cannot bring money into the community—no dowries are allowed—they have no capital to do so. There are no convents—even their motherhouse in Rome is a collection of little prefabs hurriedly erected on land lent them by Trappist monks, while their chapel is in a cave—instead, their homes are those of the poor they want to reach. In the bay of Hong Kong, three of them live on a sampan among hundreds of others in the fish-scented floating village of the boat people. At Saintes Maries-de-la-Mer, in the French Camargue, they have a trailer in which they follow the caravans of the gypsies from place to place. Two more sisters travel with a circus through Switzerland, Greece, and Turkey to provide help for the im-migrant workers the circus attracts. And in the Sahara they usually live in a tent lent by the Arabs.

They live simply "because we feel that's the way Jesus lived at Nazareth, so that's sufficient," and they do not rely on others. When they move in, one or two of the sisters will go out and look for a job to keep them all, and most of the work they do is manual: "We want to be of the working class." At the Tai Po market in Hong Kong, where they have a house, there are eight nuns living to-gether from Canada, China, Vietnam, and France. One works in a glove factory, the others have jobs in building construction. This work is usually done by the women of the Hakka tribe, who support them-selves by hard physical labor, carrying a long bamboo pole across their shoulders with, suspended at each end, a heavy wicker basket in which they carry rocks and dirt. Like the Hakka women, the Little Sisters wear loose black jackets and baggy black pants—with the addition of a veil. Some have more skilled jobs. Two sisters from another Hong Kong house work in a plastics factory; forty miles away, in the Portuguese colony of Macao, one sister is a nurse in a hospital for the handicapped while another works in a large fireworks factory. They generally take the jobs immediately available. In Leeds, one sister works in a clothing factory and another cleans offices.

The Little Sisters believe that "it's possible to break down barriers by being little and approachable," and to prove it they work among the half-caste Indians of Canada's Hudson Bay and in the fields of Kenya. They keep a flock of goats in the blinding heat of the Sahara and live among the aborigines near Alice Springs in Australia. They are invited into countries where other missionaries are forbidden; three of them were asked to work in the government hospital in Afghanistan. But when after three years the government asked for twenty more like them, they could not supply that number and asked the Medical Missionary sisters to help.

They are not concerned with proselytizing—"If a person becomes a better Muslim through having known us, that's fine"—but they do manage to improve conditions for many of the people they reach. They are the only women's order to be with the pygmies of Central Africa. When they arrived, the sisters found that the pygmies were regarded by local villagers with real fear. "They were hardly believed to be human. When they wanted to sell skins for food, they left them in a heap outside the village. We went off into the bush as we always do, with nothing. We were dependent on the pygmies to help us. One of the sisters actually learned to write the language, and now they bring their children into the village to school."

The Little Sisters of Jesus believe there is missionary work to be done everywhere, which is why they are also in London's Hammersmith. Ninety-eight Brook Green is a tiny house, with a creaky front gate and a cross on the door. Sister Constance, the superior, is a little over thirty, her heavy, quiet face exposed by the blue denim cap that pulls back her hair, her feet bare and sandaled even in March. When she visits the order's other houses in Britain, she hitchhikes. The Hammersmith house is as simple and unadorned as she: rush mats on linoleum, cane stools, and a little gas fire. "We're really contemplatives," she says, sipping Nescafé out of a mug. "We're just not enclosed."

The order recently started a foundation in Dublin, to work with itinerants there. "We'd known about them for years, but we didn't have any idea where to start," says Sister Constance. "We just got permission from the archbishop to go there, and two of us went with a couple of pounds and stayed with friends." Hoping to get a flat in the industrial area, they spent their time talking to the people in the streets and praying. Then they asked city authorities for a prefab, one of a group meant for itinerants. "No one thought we stood a chance. But we got it." Someone rented them a trailer which they use for a chapel, and soon afterward the sisters arrived with mattresses and haversacks on their backs. "The people saw we had nothing to offer except friendship. They're very proud. We asked for their help, while most people give them handouts. They watched us making our own furniture, and when they saw we hadn't a table they brought us one."

Now they are well settled there. Of the four sisters, one is in a printing factory and another a part-time cleaner in a hospital. In Dublin, as elsewhere, they "do what any other neighbors would do. We aren't trained for counseling, but we can listen and talk to people, and pray with them. There's so much poverty and misery and distress that we know we can't do anything to alleviate it, but we hope in times of trouble that we can influence people, maybe just to get in touch with a social worker."

Perhaps their value lies simply in this lack of professional qualifications. "Sometimes," as Sister Constance says, "people don't want to go to officials. Then we're someone to talk to."

Until World War I, America was a magnet for foreign missionaries. In particular, Italian and Spanish orders flocked in to work with their own nation's immigrants. The first American citizen to be canonized was an Italian nun, Mother Cabrini, who founded her Missionaries of the Sacred Heart in 1880 and nine years later took the advice of Pope Leo XIII to "go west, not east." Her work was with neglected Italian immigrants; by the time she died she had established sixty-seven houses, one for every year of her life. By the time the war ended, every major missionary order had a branch in America. But there were many new ones which had been started by Americans.

The largest and most famous of these is the Foreign Mission Sisters of Saint Dominic, popularly known as Maryknoll. Their headquarters is near Ossining, a couple of hours from New York City. Their motherhouse, also called Maryknoll, is a huge and rambling building set in landscaped gardens near the center of the Maryknoll Fathers. The only other building approaching its size in Ossining is, as they like to point out, Sing Sing prison.

At the very beginning of the twentieth century, a plump Irish-American redhead named Mollie Rogers was asked by her faculty at Smith College in New England to start a mission study class. She wrote for advice to Father James Anthony Walsh, then director for the Society of the Propagation for the Faith in Boston. He was working toward establishing a seminary to train young men for foreign work, and Mollie joined him. She worked as one of a small group of secretaries, and gradually they all adopted his name for her: Mary Joseph. He asked them to draw their hair back in a simple style and wear a gray uniform, and by 1914 they were starting to live a community life. At the end of 1921 there were over a hundred of them under the leadership of Mollie Rogers, now Mother Mary Joseph, and by the middle 1920s girls were entering not in fives and sixes but in groups of thirty and forty. By 1940 there were forty-nine houses throughout the United States, as well as in China, Korea, Manchuria, the Hawaiian islands, and the Philippines.

When Japan attacked China in 1937, the sisters watched the Chinese retreat, buried the dead, and sheltered women and children refugees. They became used to running for refuge from bombs; they looked after the maimed; they distributed food and clothing and ran food kitchens and clinics. The United States advised its nationals to leave, but Mother Mary Joseph followed the general policy of the church, and her sisters stayed on. On December 8, 1941, a few hours after Pearl Harbor, the Japanese attacked the Philippines, where fifty-three Maryknoll Sisters worked. Japanese police and soldiers arrived at the doors of all Maryknoll missions throughout Korea and Manchuria. They came to intern, imprison, interrogate. In Hong Kong and Manila, sisters were treated as enemy aliens. Two, suspected of passing messages, were tortured constantly.

Nine years later, it was the Chinese who were the oppressors. The

197

superior of a hospital in Toishan, South China, was picked up by the police and charged with failing to provide someone to clean the public streets or pay business taxes—though the hospital treated all patients free of charge. The convent in Kowloon was taken over. Sisters in Lao-fuheo and Wu-chou were accused of possessing opium and imprisoned, while others were put under house arrest. Bishop Francis Ford, a Mary-knoll Father, and Sister Joan Marie, who did his secretarial work, were seized in Kaying and imprisoned. After two years Sister Joan Marie was expelled from the country, but Bishop Ford died in prison.

Other missionary sisters were attacked. In 1966 the last remaining nuns were expelled from the country. Eight British Franciscans were taken from their convent in Peking, made to trample on the cross, and sent to Hong Kong; thirteen Chinese nuns of the order were detained.

If other congregations can afford to be "unworldly," the missionary orders cannot. They need to follow international politics closely if only, as one Maryknoll Sister puts it wryly, "to know who is going to throw us out or lock us up next." At Ossining, there is a specialized research department to monitor political and economic information.

Internal political changes in a country can have sudden and dramatic effects: Many missionaries, for instance, left Uganda after General Idi Amin came to power. Today, almost a third of the world is closed to missionaries. Burma is completely sealed. Work permits are necessary for those who want to go to India, Sabah, and parts of the Caribbean.

Countries which already have their own religious orders but no longer find religion acceptable to their ideology either close all convents and churches or pass laws to ensure that orders will not survive once their current members are dead. In Romania, for instance, nuns under forty and lay sisters under fifty were told to leave the cloisters and devote themselves to "a more socially useful activity." The same system is adopted in Russia; the Pokrovsky convent in Kiev, which was said to have three hundred nuns in 1967, including fifty young women, has apparently been forbidden novices since 1958. The nuns, who survived on sewing, icon work, and bookbinding, were finally dispersed two years later when the Ukrainian authorities announced the closing of the convent. In 1962 the Mikhailovsky convent in Odessa, where the nuns had earned their meager income from making vestments and altar cloths, was turned into a military hospital. But in other convents the nuns go out to work as ordinary citizens during the day and return at night to continue their religious life. This happened at the Ovruch convent in the Ukraine, said to be one of the oldest in the Greek Orthodox church. It was reopened in 1947 after forty years of closure; 140 nuns lived there. In 1961 they were ordered by the local town council to abandon the premises and work in the brick factory. They had no right to a pension because they had not been engaged in productive work.

The World Council of Churches at present estimates there are ten convents and five monasteries still in Russia, but there seem to be others working secretly. In 1963, for example, ten nuns were "unearthed" working in local hospitals in L'vov. And where convents are closed, even the Russian authorities seem to feel the need to qualify their actions. When, in 1967, the Kuremyae monastery, the only convent for women in Estonia, was closed, life there was presented as gloomy and harmful, and the nuns were charged with feuding, amoral behavior, and mercenariness, which would be a harmful influence upon local people and pilgrims. Some of the religious are merely dismissed; others are sent to forced-labor camps. In 1973 a Russian giving details of his ten-year imprisonment to a Washington security committee spoke of hundreds of thousands of people, including Russian Orthodox nuns, having been committed to concentration camps for their religious beliefs.

In 1950, over ten thousand Czechoslovakian nuns were turned out of their convents; half of them died in prisons or camps. Others had been shipped out of the country, like the 365 members of the Sisters of the Holy Cross who were either German-speaking or of German origin, and who were taken in by their order in Bavaria. About eight thousand nuns were allowed to pursue their vocations only in homes for the old, forbidden either to nurse or teach. But during the Dubček regime there was a thaw in church-state relations, and many nuns quietly returned to parish work in the cities. The government was even said to be raising $250 million to compensate men and women in orders for their unjust loss of freedom and property. But in 1972 all nuns were removed by force from their parishes and taken to work, out of sight, in mental hospitals and on farms. Some are on state farms, others in "concentration convents," as the factories where they work under forced-labor conditions are known. One of these women furnished a description of the life:

> Our nuns are being physically destroyed by the irregular meals and disturbed rest at night. The first shift leaves for work at four in the morning and returns at three in the afternoon. The second shift works from one in the morning and returns at six. They return pale and exhausted, famished, drenched with dirty water, especially those working in the wool-washing department. For the most part their health is ruined. Some have grown deaf through the din of the machines. Many are suffering from TB owing to undernourishment and lack of exercise and fresh air. Others show symptoms of nervous disease. Even the communist press has admitted half of them are tubercular. Of course they do not mention this is the result of inhuman labour conditions but blame convent life which, they say, "is bad for the health."

In other countries, bizarre charges are brought against religious. In Yugoslavia, Sister Slavka Nada Malic was sentenced to three months' imprisonment for spreading lies; she was heard to say, "When the old disappear, the young take their place," and this was interpreted as a forecast that the present Yugoslav government would soon be dissolved.

Nuns in South America have had a worse time. In Brazil, the world's largest nominally Catholic country, priests and nuns suspected of "leftist sympathizing" have been arrested and tortured. Brazilian bishops tamed by the government claim that the church is being "persecuted" by such people. In 1970, Mother Maurina Borges da Silveira, superior of an orphanage in southern Brazil, was flown to Mexico City in exchange for a Japanese diplomat. She had been arrested on the charge of allowing an opposition group to meet in her convent. Stripped and locked into a cell with a man, she was beaten up savagely and subjected to electric shocks. Her interrogators, both Catholics, were later excommunicated. Religious in Bolivia have been accused by the state of playing "war games" and aiding members of the National Liberation Army there, an accusation admitted by the Archbishop of La Paz, who agreed that individual nuns and priests have indeed aided guerrilla members. "You must consider, however, how many times this is done in the fervent desire to aid their people." In 1972, one mother superior, Carolina Betancourt, was actually expelled from Bolivia with three of her nuns, after a clash between troops and members of the National Liberation Army, who were found hiding in their convent sixty miles from La Paz. In Paraguay, too, nuns and priests have recently been beaten up by police dispersing a student demonstration—for which the chief of police was excommunicated.

In Albania, all religious ceremonies have been prohibited since 1967 and all churches, monasteries, and convents either destroyed, closed, or converted for "profane" purposes. In view of this, it is a fitting irony that perhaps the best known and loved nun of our time should be an Albanian: Mother Teresa of Calcutta.

Calcutta is a city where the rich wrest fortunes from industry. But it belongs to the derelict and hopeless who inhabit its streets; it is the poorest city in the world. It holds over eight million people and the estimate of those destitute—not official, for they are uncountable— is as many as four million. At night every shop doorway, every veranda, is covered with sleepers. Huddled in their thin wrappings against the cold, coughing quietly, they lie on the strips of matting that are their homes.

Lower Circular Road is long and rambling. Trams rattle past the little workshops and thin cows, crows scavenge in the gutter. Number 54A is the sparsely furnished home of Mother Teresa. She is acclaimed a modern saint, and with good reason, for she has chosen to work in the slums of this city and others like it, giving her life to those who keep so little of life itself: to the dying and leprous, to the tiny abandoned babies her sisters find daily in the dustbins. In return, the poor revere her. They kiss her passing feet and the hem of her sari, made of the cheap white cotton edged with blue which all her sisters, throughout the world, wear. It is with the poor that Mother Teresa and her Missionaries of Charity identify. The sisters live as the poor live, eat as they eat, suffer as they suffer. For, says Mother Teresa in her softly accented voice, "without our suffering, our work would be just social work, very good and helpful, but it would not be the work of Jesus Christ, not part of the Redemption."

She has taught high-caste Indian women, who only a few years ago would have considered themselves corrupted even to pass near

201

an Untouchable, that they must look on these people as being Christ. She teaches that the innocent are paying for the sins of the world, and that is why suffering exists. Pope Paul has called her "a symbol of the discovery in which lies the secret of peace on earth which we are all seeking—the discovery that every man is our brother." It is one of her greatest achievements that she has brought people of different religions together. Few of those with whom she works are Christian, the majority being Hindus, Moslems, and Parsees.

Agnes Gonxha Bojaxhiu, Mother Teresa, was born more than sixty years ago to an Albanian peasant family in Skopje, Yugoslavia. By the time she was twelve, she knew she had a vocation to the poor. Wanting to do missionary work, she joined the Loreto nuns and went with them to India, where she took her final vows in 1937. Nine years later she received what she refers to as "a call within a call" and realized that God wanted her to work in the slums, so she started teaching illiterate children, working in the compound of a slum family. Five came that first day; the numbers grew, and women started to join her, the first being the same girls she had taught at the Loreto convent.

Within three years the first home for dying destitutes was opened. It came about one morning when Mother Teresa found a woman lying in the drainpipe of an open sewer, her body eaten by rats and ants. She took the woman to a hospital, where she was received only because of her rescuer's persistence. Later, Mother Teresa found the same woman's dead body in the street, put out to make room for those not yet dead, so she asked the municipality for a place where she could bring these people to die a decent death. The health officer suggested she use the empty temple of Kali, the Hindu goddess, and within twenty-four hours the Missionaries of Charity had started their work.

"I take people with leprosy and TB, but it is their internal suffering that I try to cure," says Mother Teresa. "I want to make them accept dying with peace of mind. That means they die beautifully, sure of the love of God." But the care and love they receive means that many do not die, and these people are helped back to life and then given training if they are capable. When she recently received the Pope John XXIII Peace Prize of $25,000, she spent it on building a rehabilitation village for lepers on land given by the Indian government. When Pope Paul

202

visited her, he gave his white ceremonial car to be raffled for the same purpose. Receiving the $85,000 Templeton Prize for Progress in Religion in 1973, Mother Teresa, the woman who started her community with five rupees, said, "Money is not enough. Don't just give me money or things I can get for the asking. My people need you to love them."

All the sisters ascribe the success of the community completely to God. "The Lord provides," they say. "The secret is in the surrender to God and Providence." It may well be so, but Mother Teresa's personality cannot be overlooked; she has genuine charisma in an age in which the word has been devalued. She is tiny and seemingly frail, but the black eyes burn in her wrinkled face, and the energy that mobilizes her is inexhaustible. Her nights are broken by the need to do her own clerical work, but still she meets all demands made on her: the needs of her sisters for money or medicine, the meetings with officials. She does so much that often she is actually days rather than hours late for appointments. Her order is not large: seven hundred sisters in fifty houses. The majority are in India; others are established in Venezuela, Sri Lanka, and Tanzania. She has sent Missionaries of Charity into Gaza and the Yemen. Recently, they were given a convent in New York's black Harlem, where they concentrate on trying to reach children between nine and thirteen before they form criminal habits. And in Fitzroy, one of the poorest areas of Melbourne, Australia, they work among neglected aborigines. Most recently, Pope Paul invited her to open a home in Rome for the people of Baracchi, the shantytown outside the walls where the poor from the south squat in tin shacks. There, the Missionaries of Charity acquired a similar shack where they look after young children while their mothers work in the houses of the wealthy.

It is, above all, the rejected and the desperate who interest Mother Teresa, and the brief 1971 Indo-Pakistani war left both in its wake. The Missionaries of Charity moved in to live with the stateless Bihari Muslims under appalling conditions, and Mother Teresa played the major role in transferring tons of food from warehouses across the border in India. She moved to Dacca two days after it was liberated by the Indian Army and went to the aid of three thousand East Bengal women who had been left in the Pakistani bunkers. Abducted by the troops, used for months as servants and whores, the majority were heavily pregnant and abandoned by their families because they had been violated. The Pakistanis had taken their honor and their saris, lest they hang themselves. (When they were given saris, that is just what many of them did.) Mother Teresa's first actions were to find houses where these women could live and to offer them training in craft work and typing so they could support themselves.

It seems surprising that the Missionaries of Charity, who work with the poorest of the poor, should find it necessary to open houses in England, home of the welfare state, National Assistance, and the pension book. It was when Mother Teresa went with the Simon Community around the bomb sites and railway stations of London and saw all the drug addicts that she decided a house was needed. "I have walked your streets at night and gone into your homes and found people dying unloved. Here you have a different kind of poverty. A poverty of spirit, of loneliness and being unwanted. And that is the worst disease in the world today, not tuberculosis or leprosy." Each night, two sisters go out on the soup round with the Saint Mungo community, a nonreligious group which serves the itinerants of the capital, the forlorn people who sleep on benches and in churchyards. Some of these women will be housed by the missionaries in Saint Stephens Gardens, one of a mostly derelict block in Paddington, ugly as bad teeth, where the smell of rotting wood penetrates the boarded-up doors and windows. Despite the bleakness, the house is quiet. In the front room, close beside the oil stove which makes the air humid, a fat woman slumps in a chair, snoring loudly under a portrait of Mother Teresa done entirely in white rice grains. There are not many women here at a time, usually about seven. Mother Teresa is not, after all, interested in big institutions; it is the individual who concerns her. The sisters wait until the women have a chance to recover themselves, then accompany them to the labor exchange. They can stay at the house afterward until they are financially able to make a fresh start.

Not even Mother Teresa is successful in everything she undertakes. Against all advice, she took her Missionaries of Charity to Northern Ireland, where she believed by their example the sisters could remind the Irish Catholics and Protestants of God—and thus unite them. They worked with families there, looking after children, teaching the women to type and knit. But in the face of constant criticism—that her presence

204

was a reflection on the many religious communities of Ireland, that the Indian sisters were insufficiently qualified for the work they undertook—she left after a year, without a word of explanation from her or from the church hierarchy.

Just as Mother Teresa never asks for money, so she never needs to ask for novices. In India 120 join each year; in the London house there are currently twelve novices.

Several superiors from other orders, who appear to regard Mother Teresa with less than total admiration, have pointed out that the Missionaries of Charity do in fact lose more entrants—and faster—than other orders. Certainly the process of selecting applicants is less stringent than that adopted by Western religious orders, and they are less concerned with training. The order has some highly qualified women—seven doctors, a lawyer—but it does not regard any professional qualifications as essential. Nor do the brothers Mother Teresa admitted in 1963, to take care of men in the houses of the dying, to look after young boys, and to work in the docks and other areas where even the Missionaries of Charity cannot go. Their superior is a former Jesuit, Father Andrew, and under him the hundred-odd brothers live a life identical to that of the sisters.

Like the sisters, the brothers have taken a fourth vow in addition to those of poverty, chastity, and obedience: to give service, wholehearted and free to the poor. Nowhere is this better illustrated than in the chapels of the Missionaries of Charity. Throughout the world they are the same: simply a room of whatever house the sisters occupy, without seating, so that the sisters crouch on the floor Indian-fashion. There is rush matting in warmer countries, and in Europe carpet—when it is donated. The altar is bare and wooden, the hymn numbers marked on a little board. Often, there are small colored pictures of the saints on the walls. And always, dominating the chapel, there is a crucified Christ with the words *I thirst* written beneath.

Mother Teresa was first introduced to the West by Malcolm Muggeridge, who made a television film, shown both in Europe and America, about her first house in Lower Circular Road, Calcutta. She is, he believes, "one of the most remarkable people alive today, one of those figures born into the church perhaps once a century, especially at times of great confusion, who go back to the pure heart of Christianity."

She is named not after Teresa of Ávila ("I am not big enough for the big Teresa"), but for the little Carmelite, Thérèse of Lisieux, who is the saint of missionaries—though never for a moment, in her short life, did she leave the cloister. It is perfect that Mother Teresa should be so named, although, as she herself says, "We are not saints yet."

For above all else, Mother Teresa loves God and believes he wants his people to be happy and holy. Her religion is everything to her: "This, no one can take from me. This is something within me." And she smiles her rare and joyful smile. "I behave always as if Christ were here in front of me."

Religious have done a terrible disservice to themselves and the church by being so damned humble.

—SISTER OF HUMILITY OF MARY

8

Images, Sacred and Profane

Liz Thoman's battered white Chevrolet skids to a halt outside the Los Angeles Hilton. It is a stifling June evening, and a thin layer of smog floats over the city. Although it is Sunday, Liz has half a dozen rollers in her hair. She is wearing a flowered top and knee-length green Bermudas. Her toenails are painted, she wears pretty rings, and she drives much too fast.

Liz is just thirty—which she hates—and lives with a girl friend in a modern apartment block off Hollywood Boulevard, at the sleazy end, where the gay people gather in see-through blouses and sequined eyelids. She is a professed sister, a member of the Sisters of Humility of Mary at Ottumwa Heights in Iowa, but it would be hard to glean this fact from anything in her life-style. It is unusual even in the most advanced and liberal community of sisters for a member to be employed in a creative and commercial business. Liz Thoman is extraordinary in

207

that she has started her own advertising agency, The Rainbow Word and Picture Company, of which she is both creative director and chief photographer. She has been on television several times and is constantly flying to conferences and meetings. She has a great many men friends, says she falls in love at least once a year, and has had several marriage proposals.

Last year she won the Lulu, the award given by Los Angeles advertising women for the best campaign. It was presented for what must be the most stunning piece of public relations put out by any religious order. A glossy white folder proclaims in black: WOMEN IN LOVE . . . WITH LIFE. With words and photographs, Liz has pictured the lives and aims of the sisters of her own order in a series of booklets: "Life-style," "Spirit and Goals," "Health Care." She has designed, photographed, and edited it with, as she points out, a little help and a lot of support from her friends.

Liz Thoman got her training when she asked her community to let her work in a Minneapolis publishing house on a religious magazine. She became their director of advertising and sales promotion, in charge of ideas. "I turned up at junior advertising clubs in a minidress and eye shadow and they didn't know what to think. Few of them were Catholics, and they had a very bad image of sisters. I spent all the meetings counseling people. I'd say, 'I'm Sister Elizabeth,' and they'd say, '*Sister?*'" Her first television appearance came when she went, complete with earrings and makeup, to photograph Steve Allen. "He got me on the show, trying to find out what it was like to be a sister in a miniskirt."

Liz represents the first sign of the hard sell for the religious life. In Europe, public relations is confined to a couple of sisters visiting a school to speak or a community placing ads in a Catholic newspaper. But Liz Thoman is something else again. Rainbow Word and Picture is the first company of its kind set up to handle public relations for religious communities alone. In the past, several communities have employed professional public-relations consultants, although few can afford to do so. As Liz says, "The sisters have no money to pay a professional—and even if they had, how could he or she capture whatever it is that makes a religious without turning them into freaks?"

She cites a women's order which hired an agency to handle press relations and internal and external information, which cost them over

$10,000 a year. This, to Liz Thoman, is not doing the important part of the job. "What matters is image building. It's not just for the girls with vocations but for the public; you don't want them to say, 'Oh, you're a sister,' but, 'Hey, you guys are doing some really neat stuff.'" To that end, she thinks one of the first tasks is to stop religious communities from using what she calls "wall-to-wall type" in their brochures. Liz also admits her way is smoothed by the fact that "every nun I know who's talented ends up as a sculptor or something—but never in commercial work. People just flip when they see a nun in advertising."

It is too soon yet to measure how effective her methods are in terms of attracting people into the communities: The Rainbow Word and Picture Company began late in 1973. But what is certain is that, for the first time, the communities that hire Liz Thoman to represent them are being aggressive and sophisticated—and these are amazing qualities in terms of women's religious life. Liz believes that many of the problems orders face today—particularly when it comes to recruitment— stem from traditional attitudes toward any kind of publicity. "They won't talk about themselves; they just pray for years and years to someone like Saint Joseph to come and help, instead of telling the public just who they are and what they're all about. And this applies whether they want money or just psychological support." Nothing, she says, annoys her more than communities which regard public relations a "kind of a nasty thing. I get very provoked with them. Very few communities will in fact have anything to do with it, and I just don't know how they expect people to fathom what they're about if they won't tell."

We talked in her apartment, with its great pile of brightly colored floor cushions, green carpet, and a glass dining table which was once a shop door. She cooked a delicious spaghetti dinner and spent much of the evening making a dress for a conference she was flying to attend the next day. When I left after midnight, she was only halfway through and spent most of the night working on the sewing machine in her bedroom. After all the bleak, white-painted cells each with a holy water stoup and a crucifix, Liz Thoman's room, full of odds and ends, books, and bottles of nail polish, is refreshing.

Liz Thoman is far from typical. But there is no doubt that she is right: The image of the nun needs burnishing. To the majority of people, nuns all seem to be middle-aged, rather prissy, unworldly women who are in convents because they never got asked. They get placed in two categories. Either they are considered incapable of a successful career, human love, or making a home, or they are seen as superhuman "saints" endowed with every virtue. This is part of the pious odor that hangs over religious life. A great many women's communities mix the really superb work they do with an unfortunate attitude toward those whom they are helping. It is sometimes hard not to side with the woman who said angrily, of her experience with nuns, that she had never before come across so much "sanctimonious smugness."

The fact is that nuns and sisters all too often fail to see themselves as they appear to others and do not bother to adapt their ways to the climate of the times. The convent of the Irish-founded Sisters of Mercy in London's East End is a typical example of women doing a superb job while presenting themselves badly. These sisters show their devotion to the more helpless part of humanity in a wide range of activities. Apart from their work in schools and hospitals, they provide low-cost accommodations for students and businesswomen—teachers and civil servants. There is a home for women who are unable to cope with living alone, where some inhabitants have been since they were girls. And there are flats where homeless families can live rent free until they get onto their feet again.

There are several unmarried mothers, harassed girls who need time to plan their lives. And there are refugees. The first ones taken in by the Sisters of Mercy arrived after the Hungarian uprising in 1956. Now there are families who have left their homes and fled from the bombs and threats of Ulster. These people arrive in London only to find that the borough councils have no room for them even in condemned "halfway" houses. The sisters claim never to turn away a family. But the major part of the East End work is the Night Refuge for down-and-outs, the destitute men and women whose only alternative accommodation is the street. Each year, twenty thousand of them turn up at Crispin Street for a night's lodging and food which costs them nothing.

By late afternoon, two lines have already formed outside the black and somber building. Inside the doorway of the men's entrance, a man at a desk signs in each name while a habited sister watches. Each comes in silently, cap in hand. Each is asked if he has work. If not, has he tried to find any? What happened? Will he try again tomorrow?

For the Sisters of Mercy help only those who show they want to help themselves. If a man continually fails to find work, he will no longer be able to use the shelter. The sisters who never turn away a family in need have no place for a lonely failure. "After all," says the superior, "we're refusing men every day; we haven't got the space." The men (the "out of works," the sisters call them) eat in a dining room downstairs, sitting in silence at neat tables, all facing the front like recalcitrant schoolchildren. Soup, meat, mashed potatoes; it is the same food as the women receive in the room upstairs. But the women's room at least has a bird chirruping, and plants, though the occupants scarcely look more cheerful. Carefully made up, they sit quietly, each isolated from the other by her troubles, before going up to the pink-painted dormitory, where rows of black iron beds stand in tight rows.

The Sisters of Mercy do not expect the women to get jobs. "The majority of them are beyond redemption." The sisters find working on the men's side more satisfying. "They do get on their feet and come back and say thank you and give some little donation." While the sisters do not encourage people to come regularly, because "We want to help everyone," they do give those who reach them very real assistance. Those with a drinking problem will be recommended to Alcoholics Anonymous, and one sister was particularly delighted because she helped a man to save shillings until he had £100 to make a new start.

But all the time the sisters are trying, earnestly and conscientiously, to improve those who come to them in desperation. No one can stay in the Night Refuge during the day, and they have to be up and out painfully early. A shabby man stops on his way out and presses two shillings into a sister's hand.

"Will you buy a candle for me, Mother? It's me birthday, see."

"Well," she says, "happy birthday. But don't take drink, will you?"

Intellectually, the image of the nun has suffered through enclosure. There, she was unable to read freely, to look at a newspaper or listen to a radio or—until relatively recently—receive higher education at a university. What one nun describes as her "cultural deprivation" was a real barrier in her relations outside the convent. There are a great many orders which still do not allow indiscriminate reading material into their houses, such as the English contemplatives who take only *L'Osservatore Romano*, the official Vatican newspaper. But others regard magazines and books as a useful window on the world. The well-stocked library of one small convent contains Agatha Christie, Georgette Heyer, Victoria Holt, and Hammond Innes as well as John Steinbeck, Gore Vidal, Evelyn Waugh, and Iris Murdoch. They also boast Sartre, *The Last Days of Hitler*, and *More Murder in the Nunnery*.

But if religious communities have changed their ways, the public does not always realize this. Recently, American teenagers were asked why they were attracted or repelled by the religious life. A high percentage were repelled because they felt the sisters knew nothing of what was going on in the world.

They said this at a time when the educational level of nuns has never been higher and when sisters are tackling every field open to women. There are Ph.D.s working in the mountains of Peru. Sisters are made Members of the British Empire by the Queen for their services to science and education; they sit on consultative bodies and the boards of insurance companies. One sister is a lieutenant in the U.S. Air Force, and another is an attorney general. One works for Ralph Nader and his consumer group; another designs hospital theaters in Melbourne.

In one year, the Maryknoll Sisters in New York earned sixty-five university and college awards, including twenty-nine bachelor's degrees, twenty-five master's degrees, one Ph.D., and ten special diplomas. Five more won civic or church awards, one from the World Health Organization. Eleven more had articles or books published, and one sister had an art exhibition in Geneva.

Against this background it seems ridiculous that, as one nun says, "People tend to think you're kind of frozen into an attitude. They think of you as having a certain innocence, a certain protectedness. They never think of you as still going on, as any normal woman would, developing psychologically and emotionally." And an Anglican sister feels, "There's a certain image people have got of the religious life, and the way sisters behave, and you're a bit conditioned by this. They think you're different—they think you're *better*. And a certain kind of status has been assumed by religious who have accepted this." Recently this voluble woman, who is university educated and has a busy job working with students, was buying the drinks for a party her community was giving to thank a group of London dockers for their work in raising money for charity. "I went to the pub for the drinks and the barmaid said, 'Fancy seeing you here.' And the dockers couldn't believe it. 'You didn't go into the White Swan by yourself, did you?' "

Because they are seen as remote from life, it often takes longer for the nun to get through to the people she wants to help. A fifteen-year-old girl, in a home for delinquent children where she had been sent following an offense, says that she did not know the facts of life "and I didn't want to talk about things like that to a sister; I thought they were just holy." So it was months before a sister got her to talk about the sexual misunderstandings which proved to be the basis of her adolescent problems. "I never knew," the girl said later, "that sisters knew things like that. But they do, because it's important in their lives, too."

At various times in their history, convents have been the scene of many a juicy scandal. It would be odd if this were not so; standards of behavior and morality which were perfectly acceptable to society in the twelfth century are quite untenable today. And religious were only people of their times. But it is undoubtedly true that at no time have monasteries and convents been so free of corruption as they are now. For one thing, they are no longer places where people unsuited for any sort of life can be housed.

Many of the facts on which "antipapists" and pornographers seized with equal delight centuries later were not at all extraordinary in their day. It was said, for example, that Robert d'Arbrissel, the hermit who established the double order of Fontevrault in 1101 at Maine-et-Loire in France, used to sleep in the same bed with his nuns. But such methods of mortifying the flesh by exposure to temptation were common at the time, and the order enjoyed a high reputation.

Some of the early scandals came about because religious houses were much involved with politics, owing to the kingly links between many of the occupants. One such story is that of Chrodield, daughter of King Charibert, who was a nun of the Holy Cross, the order founded late in the sixth century by Radegund of Poitiers in France. When another woman was appointed abbess in 589, Chrodield complained, "Not as daughters of kings are we treated but as though we were lowly born." She and forty other nuns went to her royal relatives "to inform them of the contumely we have experienced." They went to Tours to

Bishop Gregory and left most of the nuns there, while Chrodield went to her uncle at Orléans; when she returned, many had disappeared and married. But, she said, "We are queens and we shall not return to the monastery until the abbess is deposed," and she took the remnants to Poitiers, where, says Bishop Gregory, they were joined by murderers, adulterers, lawbreakers, and other wrongdoers. A body of bishops urged the nuns to obey, under pain of excommunication. But they continued to "dwell in open revolt" and raided the Holy Cross convent at night with swords and lances, carrying off the abbess, firing and plundering the monastery. Finally, armed bands attacked the women and their followers, causing "some to be beaten down, others struck down by spears, and those who made most strenuous opposition to be cut cut down by the sword." The revolt continued for two years before Chrodield was sent, after a long inquiry, to live in a house provided for her. The next year there was a similar outbreak at Tours, where another woman felt herself cheated of becoming abbess.

As time went on, the quality of religious life did not improve, and the Black Death, which began in 1348 and raged throughout Europe, struck particularly at the closed communities. The numbers of religious were so reduced—only about a third survived—that discipline almost disappeared and religion was treated with indifference.

A poem usually attributed to William Langland, "The Vision of Piers Plowman," written about this time, declares that in one convent

> Dame Johane was a bastard
> and Dame Clarice a knight's daughter, a cuckold
> was her sire,
> and Dame Purnell a priest's concubine, she will
> never become prioress,
> for she had a child in cherry time, all our chapter
> it wist.

The Black Death also brought poverty, though it would seem that mismanaging superiors aggravated it. In 1404, Prioress Juliana of Bromhall in Berkshire was found to have "injured the convent and her own character in that she had converted to her nefarious use, alienated and wasted chalices, books, jewelry, the income and possessions of the priory."

Such behavior did not go unremarked. *The Land of Cockeyne*, a satire on monastic life published in 1430, described a monastery built of food and sweetmeats with a crystal cloister, and a nearby "fair nunnery" where the nuns wore silk and bathed in a river of milk, disporting themselves together with the monks, throwing off all restraint. A poem called "Why I Cannot Be a Nun" had characters called Dame Hypocrite, Dame Sloth, Dame Lust, and Dame Wanton, and said that, while some nuns were devout and holy, others were "lewd and forward."

Gradually, churchmen began to take over poverty-stricken convents and turn them into schools for religious education. The nunnery at Bromhall in Berkshire, for instance, was accused of enormities, misgovernance, and slanderous living and was granted to Saint John's College, Cambridge. The way was paved for the dissolution of the monasteries, and twelve years later Henry VIII decided to suppress all religious houses with an income of less than £200 annually—which meant all but the fifteen largest and richest. Their goods and lands, their houses and farms, their granaries and ornaments were all to be "enjoyed by the king and his heirs."

As the dissolution progressed, there were more and more charges of immoral behavior among nuns. Such accusations of impropriety rendered it possible for Henry's men to acquire their land and goods "lawfully," and would have been hard even for totally innocent women to disprove against the word of the king's men. Then, too, much of the loose behavior might well have been true of inmates of the convents who were not necessarily nuns; it was normal practice at the time for women of the upper classes to take themselves off to convents temporarily as penance for past behavior. It was all too easy to accuse a woman of immorality. Even churchmen did so to gain their own ends.

Some behavior, however, was due to the state of the religious houses. The nunnery at Lillichurch in Kent became so poor that numbers had dropped by 1521 to three or four nuns, notorious for neglect of their duties. The prioress was dead and the house frequented by clerics. Finally, a public inquiry was made. Asked how this had happened, one of the sisters admitted yielding to temptation but added sadly, "And had I been happy I might have caused this thing to be unknown and hidden."

As the dissolution got further under way, Thomas Cromwell, vice regent in ecclesiastical matters, conferred power on laymen to visit convents and monasteries. One common practice was to forbid the inhabitants ever to leave their enclosures, thus bringing certain ruin on houses which relied on farming for their living. All those under twenty-four were dismissed from convent life, even if they were solemnly professed. The richer convents attempted bribery, and payments into the royal exchequer usually guaranteed a measure of peace. Alice Fitzherbert, whose convent of Polesworth in Warwickshire had an excellent reputation, bought a reprieve for £50.

The agents were usually ruthless men, eager for the spoils. Vestments were seized, furniture and utensils sold, lead torn off churches and choirs, steeples and cloisters. Money, jewels, and silver were reserved for the king's use, usually to be broken up and melted. Relics and pictures were burned.

What has primarily determined the image of the nun is the social climate and the regard in which religion was held at the time. On the continent and in England, the idea that virginity was pleasing to God was very much in the foreground until the sixteenth century. But when the Protestant reformers found their voice, they declared celibacy odious, in open antagonism to monastic principles and the Church of Rome. It was, they said, foolish and presumptuous to make a vow of chastity. It was marriage, now, which was considered to be the most acceptable state before God. The nun was either attacked for her way of life or regarded with complete indifference. One attacker was the Dutch philosopher Desiderius Erasmus, who wrote of the lack of purpose in convent life and the need to cultivate domestic qualities. In *The Penitent Virgin*, he describes a seventeen-year-old who wishes to become a nun. The man arguing with her points out that if she wants to keep her maidenhood she can live with her parents and not turn herself from a free woman into a slave. "If you have a mind to read, pray, or sing you can go into your chamber as much and as often as you please. When you have enough of retirement you can go to church, hear anthems, prayers, and sermons and if you see any matron or virgin remarkable for piety . . . or any man who is endowed with singular probity . . . you can have their conversation. Once you are in the cloister," he warns, "all these things, which are of great assistance in

216

promoting piety, you lose at once." The girl goes into the convent, though—and after six days she comes out, claiming she would rather die than remain. Erasmus, while claiming to be "by no means against the monastic life," adds that he "would undoubtedly caution all young women, especially those of a generous temper, not to precipitate themselves unadvisedly into that state from which there is no getting out afterwards, and the more so because their chastity is more in danger in the cloister than out of it, and you may do whatever is done there as well at home."

As it turned out, the Protestant reformation completed what the Black Death, the Hundred Years War, and the Renaissance had begun: It swept away the monasteries of England, Scotland, and Ireland, as well as those of Holland and Scandinavia. Most of those in Switzerland and Germany also vanished.

In Germany in the fourteenth century, monasteries had drifted from being indifferent to being positively evil—partly because of the scattered provinces—and by the fifteenth century abuse of convent life was said to be far greater there than in England. The teachings of Martin Luther, who himself married a former nun, helped kill the convent system; of the many nuns who left the cloister, some married while others continued as Lutherans.

Many other convents disappeared during the reform, some dissolved by the pope because of their evil ways, others on the pretext of such lax behavior as continually dining out. One Benedictine abbess, trying to reform her convent in Urspring, found her nuns—mainly of the nobility—so opposed to her plan that they barricaded themselves into the infirmary and soldiers had to be called in. The soldiers were not much use, however, because "religious dread" rendered them helpless, and finally the nuns had to be starved out.

It was not this kind of behavior, however, that in later years was to do the image of religious life the greatest harm. Far more riveting were the stories about the much-maligned "double communities" which provided such a wealth of salacious ideas for early pornographers.

> Tho some are Barren Does, yet others
> By Fryars help prove teeming Mothers.
> When all to such Lewdness run
> All's cover'd under Name of Nun.

Th'Abbess, in Honour as She excells,
Her Belly, too, more often swells,
If any She proves Barren still,
Age is in fault, and not her will.

This ditty refers to the Gilbertines, one of the most famous and austere of the double orders, and it was written by Gabriel d'Emilliane, who discussed them in *A Short History of Monastical Orders*. Here he claims that "this Hermaphrodite order, made up of both Sexes, did very soon bring forth fruits worthy of itself; there holy virgins have got almost all of them big Bellies." He did not allow the fact that he was writing in 1592 about an order which was founded in 1148, and had disappeared sixty years previously, to hinder his flow of information in any way. "These nuns," he went on, "to conceal from their world their infamous practices, made away secretly with their children, and this was the Reason why at the time of the Reformation so many Bones of Young Children were found buried in their Cloisters." As a result, he claimed, the nuns would frequently undertake a retirement for six months, during which time they would not come to the grate "in order to hide the results of their behaviour."

These stories were merely salacious. But the nun is a figure also found in pornography. "The nun," says one British psychiatrist, "is the woman above sex. She represents the virgin mother, the mother who is asexual. So from the point of view of someone being sadistic, and getting a kick out of forbidden objects in sexual fantasies, she could come to represent someone who could be used. And it's really a form of blasphemy, this link between private fantasy and religious practice. Swear words used privately in church, for instance, or thinking of a nun while masturbating—these things deride religion."

Perhaps this explains why so much of the pornography of the repressed Victorians refers to nuns. A curious document called *Les Vestales de l'Eglise* describes the abbess administering the discipline with *"un air lugubre,"* while poems with titles like "The Pious Nun" describe flagellation in convents with great enthusiasm. *Nunnery Dialogues* and *The Monk and the Nuns, a Funny Tale* are fairly typical of English and German literature of the time on the subject of convents, both much concerned with the problems of young monks unable to satisfy the demands made upon them.

Undoubtedly, though, plenty of the shocking tales of convent life were rooted in truth. In France, in 1611, a Franciscan priest, a Provençal mystic named Louis Gauffridi, was burned alive on the charge of seducing two nuns from an Ursuline convent to which he was confessor, in Sainte-Baume.

This was a period when the decline in moral standards of some religious houses combined with the ignorance of the age to produce dreadful results. Just after the Reformation, both Catholic and Protestant countries were much concerned with mysticism and magic. In Europe, women presumed to be witches were assiduously hounded throughout the sixteenth century, and many thousands of men and women were tried—and invariably found guilty, thus meriting terrible deaths. By the end of the seventeenth century, the American colonies were in the grip of the same hysteria; the most famous witch trials, at Salem, Massachusetts, condemned nineteen to death. Possession of humans by evil demons and influence on them by the Devil were completely acceptable ideas, remnants of the incubi and succubi of ancient European mythology; a succubus was a female demon, an incubus the male demon who preyed upon sleeping women. Nuns appear to have been much troubled by their attentions during the Middle Ages.

Of all the stories of demonic possession, none is more horrifying than that of the nuns of the ancient Ursuline convent of Loudun. The prioress there in the middle of the seventeenth century, Jeanne des Anges, was an intelligent but misplaced woman with a deformed back and a vivid imagination. She heard of Urbain Grandier, the new parish priest, and invited him as chaplain to the convent. As the months went by, she began to retail her sexual dreams of him to the sisters. Many of the nuns developed obsessions and began to experience nocturnal visitations. What today would be seen as self-induced hysteria, an outlet for the pent-up sexual energies of women who should not have been in religious life at all, was to prove fatal for Grandier.

Sister Jeanne des Anges herself described how she "tore off all my veils and those of any of my sisters I could lay hands on. . . . I trampled them and cursed the hour when I took my vows . . . when I received the host at communion, when I had half wet it between my lips, the Devil took it and flung it back into the priest's face." She was said to speak in seven different diabolic voices, and she described how the Devil arched her body and shouted obscenities out of her mouth which it shocked her to hear. Before long, almost all in the convent were "possessed," and the public flocked to Loudun by the thousands to witness the shouting and excitement. Finally, Grandier was sent to the stake and Sister Jeanne was exorcised by a Jesuit.

The public has always relished scandals about nuns and convents, whether real or imagined. They have been the subject matter of a plethora of books, often far from flattering. Among the most delightful is the *Decameron* by the fourteenth-century Neapolitan writer Boccaccio, whose nuns and monks pursue their unholy ends with bawdy charm. And Balzac's nuns and novices in *Droll Tales from the Abbeys of Touraine* were equally wanton—and equally winning. This was social satire but done with great good humor, which cannot be said of one of the best-known books about convent life, *La Religieuse*, a scathing attack by the eighteenth-century French satirical writer Denis Diderot.

The image of religious life was not helped by books which purported to have been written by nuns. One of the most famous of these is the seventeenth-century *Letters of a Portuguese Nun*, supposedly five letters from a cloistered nun to the French officer who had seduced and deserted her. They are now usually ascribed to a French author and diplomat, Gabriel de LaVergne, Vicomte de Guilleragues.

But of all the fabrications concerning convents, *The Awful Disclosures of Maria Monk*, regarding a nunnery in Montreal, occasioned the loudest uproar; in nineteenth-century Canada and America there was bitter controversy over the case, and in England the House of Lords attempted to bring monastic establishments under closer surveillance.

The story broke in 1836 with the publication of a book which immediately sold 250,000 copies. It claimed to be "a narrative of her suffering during a residence of five years as a novice and two years as a black nun in the Hotel Dieu Nunnery at Montreal," to which was added "Notes, Affidavits, Confirmations and Facts of the present day, wherein Maria Monk's disclosures are fully proved and the hideous nature of the conventual system exposed."

The frontispiece was a picture of Miss Monk holding a baby, which she claimed was fathered by one Father Phelan, priest of a parish church in Montreal. When she entered, she had been told by the superior that "one of my greatest duties was to obey the priests in all things; and this I soon learnt, to my utter astonishment and horror, was to live in the practice of criminal intercourse with them." That very afternoon, she claimed, she was taken to a private apartment by one of the fathers. "I feared what was his intention but I dared not disobey. He treated me in a brutal manner." The priests, she averred, had total control over the nuns. "To name all the works of shame of which they are guilty in that retreat would require much time and space."

The story grew more dramatic. "The superior of the seminary would sometimes come and inform us that he had received orders from the Pope to request that those nuns who possessed the greatest devotion and faith should be requested to perform some particular deed, which he named or described in our presence, but of which no decent or moral person would ever endure to speak." She described in horrid detail the murder of twin babies, "the children of Sister Catherine," smothered by one of the old nuns with the greatest indifference and then thrown in a cellar and covered with lime. The accusations continued with descriptions of underground passages between the convent and the priests' seminary next door.

Published in periodicals as well as in book form, *The Awful Disclosures* was discussed at public meetings. And Maria Monk—who "escaped" from the convent in 1833—seems to have been received by society in New York for her curiosity value. Reading her book now, it is hard to believe how seriously its absurdities were taken. The inaccuracies—five years as a novice, for instance—did not seem to render it any less believable to a lot of people. Even when Maria was unmasked as a prostitute from Montreal, popular ignorance about religious life at the time was so complete that the story was still believed. It was a tasty morsel of anti-Catholic propaganda, and even the assertions of many Protestants that the whole thing was a fake failed to silence it. *Refutations* was published—to be followed by further *Disclosures* in reply. Maria Monk offered to go before a court of justice to swear to the truth of the accusations. She asked to be taken through the convent with spectators, so her account of the building could be compared with the place itself. And the very fact that she was not taken up on these offers added fuel to the fire.

By the end of the nineteenth century, there was a good deal

of doubtful literature published about nuns, some by former religious and others quite clearly by women with severe mental problems. One former religious was Margaret Cusack, "the Nun of Kenmare," an Irish Poor Clare at the turn of the century who had originally entered an Anglican community on the sudden death of her fiancé. After publishing over twenty books of pious fiction, she wrote a famous attack on the revival of Anglican communities in Britain, *Five Years in a Protestant Sisterhood and Ten Years in a Catholic Convent.* Ten years later she was lecturing in America and England on the "twin evils of Romanism and Ritualism."

A similar writer was Edith O'Gorman, who claimed to have been a Sister of Charity in New Jersey and who wrote *The Escaped and Converted Nun,* published in 1871 in New York. This tract is now in its forty-second printing. And the Maria Monk book is still in print, published by the Protestant Truth Society, a rabidly anti-Catholic organization. *The Escaped and Converted Nun* is full of the old myths. Edith O'Gorman says she was forced to hold her hands in lime because she was too proud of them; the orphans in the charge of the nuns were verminous and half-starved; she herself was made to bite off the head of a live mouse at which she had screamed. It must have been quite a community: Miss O'Gorman became superior less than five years after entering, when she was only twenty-five. She reported the treatment meted out to nuns who refused the advances of priests; they were thrown into rat-infested dungeons until they went mad. She herself left after similar advances. "I fled in mid-winter out into the world, without shelter, without protection; but better that than the abode of vipers and a life of sin." Amazing events were to follow: "Suspicion that I had been ensnared to a maison d'infamie crossed my mind and paralysed my senses with unspeakable horror," but finally our heroine decided to lecture on her past. "I was amazed at my own words. Lecture! Impossible. I, a weak, timid woman and naturally retiring, could never face assembled multitudes in order to teach the world the bitter lesson Rome had taught me." She did, though, choosing as her subject "the Romish priesthood," and at well over eighty she was still delivering two lectures a day—all over the world. She married, also: one William Auffray. "All the unspeakable delights of newly wedded love are up to the present realized by us."

222

When, in the latter half of the nineteenth century, Catholic nuns began quietly to reappear in Britain, these stories of persecutions had an unfortunate effect. Communities sometimes found it politic to buy houses in the name of an individual, since owners often would not sell if nuns were buying. The Sisters of the Cross and Passion, arriving in Lochgelly, Scotland, to staff a primary school, found a large crowd gathered outside the convent one evening shouting, "Release the sister," and, "Sister Mary Anne." It developed that the white lamp swinging on the church porch looked like a nun in a guimpe hanging from a rope, and the people were eager to believe the worst.

When Anglican communities first appeared in England, they too were regarded with great alarm and were attacked in tracts with such titles as "Sisters of Mercy, Sisters of Misery." The feeling in Wales was particularly strong, the Welsh being in the main Nonconformists. One man from a village near Swansea swears that as a child he was drawn indoors by his grandmother, who with trembling fingers locked all the doors and windows. "What's wrong, mamgu?" he asked. "They're coming," she replied, her voice shaking. "The nuns!"

In the United States there were similar reactions. When, in the 1800s, communities arrived from Poland, Yugoslavia, and Italy, they went mostly to New York and Detroit. For a long time, Maryland was the only Catholic province in America. People were suspicious of Catholics, who lived in isolated communities and educated their children in their own schools, staffed by their own nuns, habited and segregated.

Nineteenth-century writings leaned heavily for their effect on the misinterpretation of certain monastic practices. This is just as true today; "nuns" are favorite roles in strip clubs, particularly in London and Berlin. For some curious reason, they are usually portrayed as menacing bored and prostrate "schoolgirls" with whips. And publications such as Die perverse Nonnen, which sells for $10 on the porno black market, show "nuns" in various stages of undress (but complete with crucifixes), whipping a tied and naked man.

Religious penitential practices have always held a morbid fascination for the public. Most of this pornographic material is based on garbled half-knowledge. It also has to be admitted that self-torture, though undertaken for religious reasons, frequently did produce sexual pleasure—although the nuns themselves did not recognize it for what it was. Extreme physical penance is now rare, and it is certainly no longer obligatory. But individual nuns do still inflict considerable pain on themselves. It has been a real enough part of religious life to have developed its own terrifying gadgetry.

Women in religious orders justify penance very much as did Bernard of Clairvaux, ascetic abbot of that most ascetic of orders, the Cistercians: "The body of Christ is crushed, let us learn how to subdue our bodies . . . our bodies must be confirmed to the likeness of Our Lord's wounded body." Until recently, the Cistercians continued to take the discipline daily; now it is whenever the individual feels it necessary, perhaps once a month. Even so, plenty of women consider such mitigation of the rule a mistake. A Cistercian abbess told me, "I'm a traditionalist. I don't like any change, and if I had my way the discipline would continue to be used regularly."

It is with the discipline, the traditional thrashing cord of the monastery, that the religious wage war upon the natural desires and inclinations of the body. As Christ was scourged, so generations of men and women have submitted to the twelve-inch-long whip of thin waxed cord with five or six knotted tails. Another instrument is formed of a small metal ring with five chains suspended from it, each chain ending in a hook. The discipline is used on specified days, perhaps Wednesdays and Fridays, for a period of time laid down in the regulations, and only on certain parts of the body—back, legs, and buttocks —while the nun recites prayers. The pain suffered is offered up for the sins of the nun and the world. "It was a method," says a young American, "of disciplining the imagination and the memory, and thus constantly keeping out of touch with certain feelings." As an English Sacred Heart sister explains, "We felt that we were really following Our Lord, who had himself had a painful life. That helps you."

As the novice continues in the life, so the number of permitted strokes is increased—though at no time should it draw blood. But the pain inflicted is considerable, and that caused by the metal discipline, with its snakelike tails, even more so. When not in use, the discipline is kept in the cell in a black cover sewn by the owner. For many, that in itself is painful: "The anticipation is the worst part." Many women,

224

indeed, have found it almost too much for them. "The first time I used it," a Carmelite told me, "I almost went off my head in the cell."

The connection between sexual pleasure and pain is particularly close for women. This is true even when the pain is self-inflicted. One elderly sister of the Society of the Sacred Heart remembers that the discipline became "one of my major troubles. Not because of the pain, but for some people such pain can give trouble in the sexual line. It upset me in that way. I knew it was arousing me in that direction as nothing else had done. It even got into my dreams."

It was, she says, "sheer fervor" which made her continue. That and the fact that "we girls were incredibly ignorant, and it was so difficult to find out. It was a long time before I got to know what those physical emotions were." Things were not helped by the mistress of novices, who herself could not understand it. "We went to Rome—and not one of *those* women understood it either."

Nuns are less innocent now. "We aren't as naïve as we were," remarks one superior. "We can see the correlation between the discipline and sexuality."

There are other instruments of penance. The hair shirt is one. Made out of horsehair, roughly knotted with as many ends as possible left loose to prickle the wearer, it can be worn either as a long sleeveless tunic or as a wide belt around the loins. Or there are linked metal bands to go around arms or legs, designed so that the points with which they are studded press into the flesh on sudden movement. Chain girdles can be used with the same effect, although, like the discipline, they are not intended to draw blood.

Another penitential object is a small wooden cross studded with blunt nails, worn under the clothes against the skin. Pressed on the shoulder beneath a heavy mantle, this produces almost excruciating pain. Hedgehog skins serve the same purpose.

The penances fulfilled a real function in the context of religious life. "When wisely practised they produced remarkable results," says Monica Baldwin, the English ex-nun, in her book *I Jump Over the Wall*. "They do a very great deal to bring about the subjection of the body to the spirit without which the highest adventures in the spiritual life can never be achieved."

It was very much part of the formalized tradition of religious life, but even so, physical penance has lost favor. Younger and more sophisticated superiors, the teachings of Freud, and the impact of Vatican II have had their effect. But if physical penance is not obligatory to the individual in most orders, it is certainly not forbidden. The extent to which it is still practiced will depend largely upon the attitude of the country. In Spain today, where ordinary men and women make pilgrimages on their knees, extreme physical penance is still usual for those in religious orders. And at one time the Carmelites derived much of their income from making their own instruments of penance. In Paris this was "quite profitable," but when they arrived in London at the beginning of the twentieth century, they decided that "this was not likely to be so in England" and turned to baking altar breads instead.

At particularly penitential times, such as Lent, most nuns and monks probably adopt some form of self-torture. Few, though, would go as far as Saint Rose of Lima, a South American nun who, out of "love for the crucified Saviour," wore a spiked iron band around her head and carried a heavy cross for hours on shoulders already bleeding from the discipline. She was also given to sleeping on a bed of pointed stones and is said to have spent whole nights suspended on a cross.

Another penitent was seventeenth-century Sister Margaret Mary, who was so determined to make a complete gift of herself to the sacred heart that she carved "Jesus" in her breast with a knife. Not satisfied with that, she burned the letters in with a lighted candle.

These cases are clearly extreme—not to say pathological—but some religious women still regularly stay up all night, arms outstretched for hours. There are other ways, too, of practicing physical penance. A Carmelite nun now in England, who used to live in the French convent at Meaux, recalls the sacristan, a woman who did beautiful silverwork. One day she fell off a ladder and twisted her neck. She never did anything about it, despite constant pain. When asked why she did not see the doctor she replied, *"Pourquoi?* The good God has sent me this."

The public image of the nun as a submissive spinster is so strong that the Franciscan Communications Center in Los Angeles, a public-relations organization for religion, does not ever use nuns in their films or advertising because they are regarded as so off-putting.

At best they are seen as meek and docile, encased in wimples and innocence. Some are not averse to exploiting this fact, like Belgian Sister Luc-Gabrielle, who topped the record charts in 1963 with a shrewd combination of the monastic habit and a bouncy tune called "Dominique." But most nuns and sisters are becoming increasingly irate at the way in which they consider they are being inaccurately portrayed by the media. Current films and plays, claims one American sister, "perpetuate the medieval myths and present a distorted image." Nuns are shown in one of two ways: either as loveless authoritarians, such as the novice mistress in *The Song of Bernadette*, or as highly romanticized, unreal women—Ingrid Bergman playing opposite Bing Crosby in *The Bells of Saint Mary's*. Even more unlikely is the central figure in one of the most successful ABC comedy series of recent years: *The Flying Nun*, in which a round-faced Sally Field zooms around the sky in full habit and a huge white cornet headdress, while the schmaltzy situations include a Jewish wedding in the convent garden and raising money for the neighborhood kids.

A 1970 gem of the cinema is *A Change of Habit*, which stars Mary Tyler Moore and Elvis Presley. A young doctor working with a young lady out of her habit in a city clinic does not realize that she is a nun. He buys her ice cream and tries to hold her hand but never gets really rebuffed, which leads to the exquisite dialogue when she finally appears before him coiffed and starched and says, "You know I have a vow of chastity?" To which he asks, "Wouldn't a vow of honesty be better?" The whole thing ends with Mary Tyler Moore on her knees in the chapel trying to decide between religious life and Presley.

The Weekend Nun is an American offering which has already appeared twice on British television. Starring a pained Joanna Pettet, it is based on the autobiography of a former nun, Joyce Duco. The film opens with Sister Damian leaving her New Orleans convent to buy her first dress for her new job as a probation officer, then returning to the convent and the habit each night. Her superior warns her not to let the job interfere with her religious life and cautions her against working on reports late at night. She is given the case of a fifteen-year-old prostitute and establishes enough rapport with the girl

227

for her to turn up at the convent for help. But Sister Damian has been ordered to a retreat by the superior, and the girl, rushing to find her, is knocked down and killed. Forced to choose between her life as a nun and her "other" work, Sister Damian leaves the convent.

It would be an understatement to say that when this film was first shown in the States, in 1972, nuns did not like what they saw. Members of the National Assembly of Women Religious "just couldn't believe it." They objected particularly to the suggestion that religious life could not integrate with a woman's work. "When the mother superior says, 'Remember that the convent is a spiritual sanctuary,' we just about hit the roof. We don't see it that way." Nuns, no less than other people, can be overly sensitive about the difference between the way they see themselves and the way others present them. In this case, they did perhaps overreact.

The NAWR sisters immediately launched a storm of protest to the president of the American Broadcasting Company and all the show-business magazines, pointing out that the film, with its insistence on the dominance of the mother superior, its naïve belief that resort to prayer was a panacea to all problems, and its supposition that religious life does not allow initiative, hinders the struggle of "the contemporary American sister for recognition as a competent professional." They got a front-page story in *Variety*, a radio interview, and fifteen minutes on Ralph Story's West Coast morning TV show, *AM*. Since then, Liz Thoman has started a campaign offering NAWR members as consultants on religious life to the entire American entertainment industry.

There are currently numerous films and plays about nuns—quite apart from such offerings as *Sex Life in a Convent* and *Le Couvent des Femmes*. Two major films, a West End play, and an opera appeared in Britain alone in 1973. Franco Zeffirelli made *Brother Sun, Sister Moon* about the young Francis of Assisi and Sister Clare, founder of the Poor Clares. There was a film about Pope Joan, with the Scandinavian actress Liv Ullman playing the woman who is supposed to have occupied the Holy See in the mid-ninth century for a short time, between Leo IV and Benedict III. She was a nun who is said to have died when the crowd trampled her to death in indignation after she gave birth on the steps of Saint Peter's.

In London's West End, there was the premiere of John Kerr's play, *Mistress of Novices*, about Bernadette of Lourdes, and the Paris Opéra staged a new production of Francis Poulenc's *Dialogues des Carmelites*, inspired by the deaths of the entire household of Carmelites at Compiègne, who were sent to the guillotine during the French Revolution.

Much of the literature about life in convents is written by nuns themselves, invariably *after* they have left their orders. Titles like *Out of the Curtained World* and *The Buried Life* abound, but the pictures they present are as biased as a divorcée talking about marriage. Outsiders manage to invoke the women and their world far more vividly, as author Rumer Godden does in her book about the peaceful Benedictines, *In This House of Brede*. Showing a less attractive aspect of the dedicated life is *The Nun's Story* by Kathryn Hulme. A bestseller, which was filmed with Audrey Hepburn and Peter Finch, it tells of the Belgian Sister Luke who leaves her missionary nursing order because the strictness of the rule demands that she put the bells calling her to prayer before the needs of her patients. Antonia White's novel, *Frost in May*, is also about conformity in convent life, describing Fernanda Gray's education at the Convent of the Five Wounds, where the girls are subjected to discipline only a little less rigid than are the nuns themselves.

Much of the poetry inspired by the religious life is exquisite, like that of the Jesuit priest Gerard Manley Hopkins. He described the cloistered life in "The Habit of Perfection":

> Elected Silence, sing to me
> And beat upon my whorlèd ear,
> Pipe me to pastures still and be
> The music that I care to hear.
>
> Shape nothing, lips; be lovely-dumb:
> It is the shut, the curfew sent
> From there where all surrenders come
> Which only makes you eloquent.

Most poetry idealized religious women, like Wordsworth's nuns who "fret not at their convent's narrow room." Alexander Pope, the eighteenth-century Catholic, wrote "Eloisa to Abelard" when England was rabidly anti-Catholic. He describes the blameless vestal and her

Desires compos'd, affections ever ev'n;
Tears that delight, and sighs that waft to heav'n.
Grace shines around her with serenest beams,
And whisp'ring Angels prompt her golden dreams.
For her th'unfading rose of Eden blooms,
And wings of Seraphs shed divine perfumes,
For her the Spouse prepares the bridal ring,
For her white virgins Hymenaeals sing;
To sounds of heav'nly harps she dies away,
And melts in visions of eternal day.

Other poets took a more worldly view, like James Henry Leigh Hunt in "The Nun":

If you become a nun, dear,
A friar I will be,
In any cell you run, dear,
Pray look behind for me.

One of the oddest poems is anonymous. Entitled "I'm the Daddy of a Nun," it was given to me by a Catholic sister whose father—like many others—carries it around with a photograph of his daughter on the back. Published in Italy but sounding faintly Irish, it is illustrated with the Pope's hand raised in a blessing:

Sure my daughter has been vested
    And my joy I cannot hide,
For I've watched her from the cradle
    With a father's honest pride.

Since to err is only human
    There's a whole lot on the slate
That I'll have to make account for
    When I reach the golden gate.

But then I'm not a-worrying
    About the deeds I've done,
I'l just whisper to Saint Peter:
    "I'm the daddy of a nun."

It is partly the traditional view of the nun's role—held not only by the public but by some of those within religious life—which explains the furious reaction to the work of Sister Corita Kent. An American sister of the Immaculate Heart of Mary order in California, she is a tiny, graceful woman whose work shocked the religious es-

230

tablishment. Hating the simpering plaster statues that lurk in the corners of Catholic convents, she produced work completely against the grain of conventional "religious" art. Her asymmetrical Christs and elongated Madonnas were at first greeted with floods of letters, many anonymous and abusive—the more so because she was a nun. Within the convent, reaction to her work was divided, and she was blamed when some of the young sisters she had taught left the order.

Corita Kent is now recognized as one of the great contemporary printmakers. Her serigraphs—streaks of brilliant color accompanied by quotations from e.e. cummings, Ugo Betti, and Bertolt Brecht—hang in New York's Museum of Modern Art and London's Victoria and Albert. She is one of the few artists of real stature to emerge from the chrysalis of the convent to worldwide acclaim.

That she has done so is a hopeful sign. In the past, superiors would have considered it their duty to suppress any particular gift, to humble the person "lest it take away from God." It is an attitude that Saint Benedict summed up in his rule, saying, "If there be craftsmen in the monastery, let them practice their craft with all humility, providing the abbot give permission, but if one of them be puffed up because of his skill in his craft, supposing that he is conferring a benefit on the monastery, let him be removed from his work and not returned to it, unless he have humbled himself and the abbot entrust it to him again."

Even under such a rule, there were nuns whose talent could not be stifled. Mother Genevieve was one. A French Benedictine, she produced drawings, engravings, and painted glass windows, and a recent sale of her work in Paris received wide publicity. She drew priests on bicycles and old women walking in the rain, and the power and vigor with which she did so caused critics to liken her to Daumier and Toulouse-Lautrec. She saw the world with a mixture of pity and biting wit; one of her drawings is called "Le Feu à la Communauté" and shows a nun poking a fire above a caption reading, *The more you poke the better it burns and shines: You see, O my soul, you need just that.* But it needed a woman of determination, as well as extraordinary skills, to retain and develop her art in the convent.

There must have been many more—admittedly slighter—talents which were lost forever under the system. Since the softening of the rules following Vatican II, enough women of genuine artistic merit have appeared within religious orders to demonstrate that they must always have been there. It is only in the last few years, for example, that the poems of Sister Mary Agnes, an enclosed Poor Clare nun, have been published; they have been likened to those of Emily Brontë. The Goanese Sister Teresa d'Cruz of the Ladies of Mary has exhibited her batiks—pictures made on silk with dyes and hot wax—in both London and Paris. Her order permits her to wear secular dress and live in a Left Bank apartment.

Nothing is better calculated to change the image of the nun than the emergence of such women. But a convent is by its very nature not an easy place in which to foster individual talent. Corita Kent has left the religious life. It remains to be seen whether orders can, in the future, contain her successors.

*A lot of things need changing in the religious
life. Unless they are thought out and not swept
under the carpet, the religious life is done for—
and justifiably so.*

—YOUNG ANGLICAN SISTER

9

The Slowly Changing
Cloister

Until ten years ago, the pattern of life in religious communities of
women had not changed noticeably in fifteen centuries. The nun was
not so much preserved in amber as pickled in formaldehyde.

Change is coming now. For a few orders it is a radical rethinking.
For others it takes the form of cautious reappraisal. And for some it
is still only a rumor. Yet there can be no doubt that, without change,
many orders will not survive this century. Increasingly seen as irrelevant and anachronistic, their novitiates will continue to dwindle.

Peter Hebblethwaite, who left the English Jesuits and the editor-
ship of the prestigious Catholic review *The Month*, comments, "We
are not keepers in an ecclesiastical museum but guardians of the human
future and mankind." But it is purely as ecclesiastical museums that
many orders totter on. Their behavior, way of life, and attitude toward

authority, their clothes, ideas, and rules, have changed little since the time of their foundations.

For many nuns, life has been too detached, physically and emotionally, from the world. Within their walls they became isolated, their perspectives distorted. They were the last strongholds of the studied manners of the middle-class woman of the nineteenth century; they became, says Cardinal Suenens of Malines-Brussels, "like a fortress whose drawbridge is only furtively and fearfully lowered."

Segregation from the world has left nuns and laity facing each other across a gulf of incomprehension. That trouble has intensified over the last few years, because convent life has taken little note of the emancipation of women outside its walls. Often, rules and regulations for nuns are still those laid down for young women who were totally dependent on their parents until marriage—when they would become dependent on their husbands. They were not expected to earn their own living outside the home; they were not even expected to venture outside the house unaccompanied. For such women, religious life could not have come as much of a surprise. But for today's women it must be stifling to be suddenly encased in the rigid corset of the convent.

Convents are governed by regulations, as all organizations must be. But these are so numerous and so ancient that, in observing them, religious communities are forced into long outdated behavior patterns and quite literally held back from modern life. This was never intended by the founders, who would surely be horrified to learn that regulations made for practical reasons should have become sacrosanct in themselves with the passage of time.

Some of these regulations are laid down in the founder's rule, which concentrates on the charism or spirit of the order and is meant to be a statement of the direction and task of the community. Too often, brought into line with canon law, the rule has become merely a legalistic document dictating duties and obligations, a petty god directing each detail of life; novices in some orders still learn it verbatim and recite it on their knees before the novice mistress. Even in a relatively young congregation, the rule may be centuries old. Many orders, for instance, adopt that of Saint Benedict and use it as the pattern for their lives. Yet Saint Benedict wrote in A.D. 540 for his monastery of Monte Cassino.

Then there are the constitutions and customs, which vary from order to order. These set out information on the government of the community: details of each stage of the life, strictures regarding votes for officials, even minute directions regarding such niceties as skirt lengths.

The regulations may have been written to suit the situation in one specific part of the world. Teresa of Ávila, for instance, writing in Spain, laid down instructions about buildings which were suitable for that climate. Thus when the Carmelites first came to England and planned their great stone house in Notting Hill Gate, the architect was horrified that it was to include no heating at all. It took the insistence of a cardinal to persuade them to put in a furnace, and then he had to declare that it would not constitute diminution of the Primitive Observance, since Teresa herself would have supported him wholeheartedly if she had ever experienced the English climate. He used to write them notes every autumn pointing out that it was no luxury but only plain common sense to light the boiler now they had it.

Every detail of convent life was dictated with equal firmness. Being dressed in a particular way, walking always in icy cloisters, eating at scrubbed tables—all these things came to constitute the very identity of nuns themselves. Although a founder might have been a woman of quite staggering courage and independence in her time, her modes of thought and behavior were bound to lose their pioneering flavor with the passing of centuries. But her community continued to cling to the old observances. So the original spirit of her order—the fearless innovation and the brave initiative—was lost, drowned in a welter of archaic absurdities: refectory regulations patterned on the eating habits of eighteenth-century French peasants, stilted recreational practices of a Victorian household, clothes of sixteenth-century Belgian widows.

At present, regulations vary not only from country to country but from convent to convent. There are orders, like the contemplative Cistercians, where there has been no discernible change since they were founded in the eleventh century; they live in total silence, without any common recreation, sleeping fully dressed on pallets of straw in a shared dormitory. Others, like the Society of the Sacred Heart, have recently come out of strict enclosure and are now allowed such freedoms as speaking at meals and traveling alone. (Although they were teaching sisters, adult women had to be accompanied if they were forced to so much as step outside the convent door. One sister remembers how she once found waiting for her a seven-year-old boy who announced, "Me mum's ill but I'm here to look after you instead." She recounted it in a London restaurant as an amusing anecdote, but she was talking about just five years earlier.) And there are orders where the change from an overly regulated life has been carried to extremes. This is most obvious in convents in America's Midwest. The Sisters of Loretto at the Foot of the Cross, for instance, was one of the first orders to give up the habit, and their sisters, like Mary Jean Friel of the sixth chapter, are free to work where and as they wish, as unconfined and liberated as any Western career woman.

The communities having the hardest time with the problems of change appear to be those which realize the need for adaptation but are uncertain in which direction to go. The more involved a community or an individual becomes with modern life and the problems of its people, the more absurd become the rules and regulations designed to protect the nun from being contaminated by the world. If a woman has spent her day coping with aggressive adolescents in a slum school, it is clearly ridiculous that she should have to miss a meeting with their parents because the convent rule insists she be inside by 6:00 P.M. The reason for this was, quite simply, that "timing used to be geared to before the invention of electric light," as an American sister explains. Less than ten years ago, her order rescinded the rule that had every member of the convent inside by 8:00 P.M. in summer and 6:00 P.M. in winter and safe in bed by 10:00. Another order's ill-considered "modernization" allowed the sisters to stay up late for reasons of work —but insisted they still rise at 5:15 next morning. "We tried to live modern nights and medieval mornings."

The result of hanging on to such obsolescent regulations was that nuns and sisters often simply defied them. "Parents would come to see me at night," recalls a young American, "and I'd learn later they'd been turned away because it was my time for prayer. I wasn't supposed to talk to people on the street, yet that was my best place to get to know them. I felt my belief in the gospel message was very simple and beyond a rule—so I ignored or broke the rules."

Nuns were trying to do modern jobs under medieval systems. It was part of their obedience that they were never consulted about the tasks allotted to them but simply expected to carry them out to the best of their ability. In active communities, sisters would be sent where they were most "needed," regardless of their inclinations or talents. At one time this was a perfectly acceptable part of religious life, but the system began to break down when nuns moved into more specialized work for which thorough training was required. The woman who labored for a degree in English and then spent a decade teaching Latin felt understandably unhappy, as did the American sister who "entered for the poor—and then I was dismayed when they sent me to Rome for theology." One sister taught mathematics in an American parish. It was a subject she hated, and for more than four years she grew increasingly depressed. Her superiors knew that she had entered to work with the sick, and she had been assured that after her training she would do so. But when the time came, she was told to deposit her personal judgment in the hands of her superior. God, she was repeatedly told, wanted her for other work. After several requests were ignored, she left the order. Another sister spent six years doing accounts and secretarial work "which horrified me. I can't type, and I can't add two and two. It couldn't have been more repugnant." Even so, she found unexpected advantages. "I learnt that the way you did the job transformed it."

Sisters used to be put through university by their orders quite often as an obedience, whether they wanted to go or not. Sister Honor Basset of the Society of the Sacred Heart was sent to Oxford, much against her wishes. "It didn't seem to be in tune with my vocation; I'd entered for the religious life, not higher education. The order wanted me to get a degree but I didn't want to become a bluestocking. But it was an obedience. So I went." She found "a lot of the life excessively hard, and I went through a very bad time." Part of the problem was psychological. The sisters had been taught that interest in the world was wrong, yet they were expected to get the best out of the life. They had to obtain special permissions to attend lectures; they had to be chaperoned everywhere by another sister. "I remember waiting around for two hours in the cold for my chaperone's lecture to finish so we could go home." At the end of her three years, Sister Honor did in fact fail. "I talked it over with the mistress of studies and Reverend Mother. And they said, 'You know, we want you to get a degree.' So I started again."

A nun in the same order's house at Leamington Spa entered at the turn of the century and studied for her degree from inside the convent. Under university rules she had to appear in person for the final examination. The problem was discussed, and the order felt she should not go dressed as a nun. At that time, hair was always cropped. So she was given street clothes and a wig. Because the exams were from seven to nine at night, and Greater Silence would be in force when she returned, she promised that if she had done well she would leave the wig on top of a box.

After university, it was common practice for a sister to return to the convent with her degree, only to be given some job, such as working in the kitchen, which in no way used her newfound knowledge. "The greatest sin," according to a woman who experienced this, "would be intellectual pride."

While the sister was at university, her schedule was supposed to follow as closely as possible that of her order. The rigid "pattern of day" was exactly that—a day divided neatly by bells into half-hour intervals. For a contemplative, this worked perfectly. For a busy university student or a teaching sister, it imposed an extra strain to which the brevity of the allowed recreation time merely added. The average sister in a teaching order started her day at five with chapel; then came meditation for twenty minutes, the office of Our Lady for fifteen, and mass, which took an hour. This would be followed by breakfast and a full day of school with fifteen minutes of prayer at midday, half an hour during the afternoon in chapel for Adoration, and another twenty-five minutes of office in the evening.

"And you had to get in your rosary for a quarter of an hour, and then night prayers. When the children's dormitories were closed, we used to go to bed at nine o'clock; it was marvelous." In all that time, recreation was half an hour of spiritual reading in the community room or listening to a book read while doing needlework.

For a great number of congregations of women, these practices —or similar ones—are still current. So a twentieth-century girl who decides to enter a convent may well find herself experiencing what amounts to culture shock.

Sister Madeleine of the Augustinian Sisters of Meaux says, "In the convent you're suddenly brought into a cultural situation that is not really Victorian but positively feudal. And this causes tremendous conflict inside yourself." It is laid down that the entrant must allow herself to be molded by the rule into the pattern of the order. She must give up her opinions and her tastes, "reveal her repugnances to her superior," and obey. She must respond with deference toward those in authority, move on the instant when a bell rings. "And when," says Sister Madeleine, "you go to the chapel or lunch, you may be told very sternly to bow down low somewhere and whisper your apologies to the superior before carrying on."

In the past, those entering accepted such authoritarianism stoically. "You took it just as you had at home," explains an American, "where you conformed to your parents' wishes." The discipline was applied as rigidly to a woman responsible for teaching college as it was to the youngest novice. "I once returned home feeling terrible," remembers an American history teacher. "I said to the superior, 'I think I have a temperature. May I go to bed?' She said, 'Yes, but go to the chapel first and say all your prayers privately.' So after a full day at school, feeling really ill, I stood for an hour in the chapel."

This extended to all aspects of life. In one enclosed order, the nuns wore heavy cloaks in choir, a custom retained from the time of the eighteenth-century founder, when the stone-floored choir in winter would have been freezing. A nun remembers asking her superior why they continued to wear the cloaks despite the too-efficient central heating. "All these things," she was told, "are part of the life of penance and mortification which we embraced when we made our vows."

A nun in her eighties, living in a far more relaxed atmosphere in her updated convent than when she entered sixty years ago, commented on the system: "All I can say in its defense, it certainly made a dead set at self-will." It did even more than that. By such minute ordering of detail, the convent implied that its nuns were incapable of decision. But there was a reason: community. "The important thing was always the community," says a sister who believes she would have left if her order had not begun to change at the first possible moment. "The individual sisters were only important insofar as they made up the whole."

Uniformity of life and habit did indeed attempt to obliterate all personal differences between nuns. Eileen Gielty, an immensely talkative Irishwoman, says that when she replaced the portress during the school holidays and took over the door and telephone duties, "People would ring and say, 'What's your name?' And I would say, 'I'm one of the sisters.' It wasn't false humility; it just didn't seem relevant to say what your name was, because you weren't expected to come across as a person."

Such diminution of personality, combined with the strict rule, had the effect of making many nuns feel remote from each other. "We felt deprived of relationships," confesses one elderly woman, "lonely for sheer companionship." And if the nuns were isolated within the community, different orders were as little known to them as foreign countries. "Nuns in convents down the road didn't have anything to do with each other. It's only in the last five years that I've met members of any community other than my own."

Before the changes of Vatican II, when Mother Turnbull, the great musician of the Sacred Heart order, went to teach Gregorian chant to a community of Carmelites, she was not allowed to enter the enclosure but had to do as best she could through the parlor grille. Even when nuns went to another house in the same order, strict segregation was observed. "They had rooms separate from the rest of us," remembers one sister, "and they didn't even eat with us but in a little parlor. Now there's much wider hospitality among nuns—they can even come and share our meals."

Until recently, there were no holidays. As the enclosed still do today, everyone lived the same pattern, day in, day out, year after year. Communities would follow the contemplative practice of observing "Lot," or cell days, when rules were relaxed and they might talk more than usual, stay in their cells and read, or go into the garden. "Lot" derives from the custom in medieval monasteries of letting blood three times a year, after which the nuns spent four days getting their strength back.

Only five years ago, even active orders did not allow their sisters to go home for emergencies. Now, even the majority of contemplatives would permit this. Many of the sisters to whom I talked still feel bitterness over the deprivation their parents suffered as a result of this restriction. "After I entered," says one, "I never saw my parents except in the convent parlor. My father died alone during the war. That wasn't Holy God."

Some orders were lucky enough to own or share "holiday" houses, convents by the sea, perhaps, where sisters could go for a week. "Then you could get up at half past six because you were on holiday. You still had your duties to prayer, and the morning prayer had to be made before nine o'clock, and there were certain strictures with regard to time. But on the whole you were free to go for walks or generally lie around." Even there, a certain code had to be observed. "You couldn't lie out flat on the grass; it wouldn't be religious."

Gradually, sisters were allowed away from their convents. "We considered it a holiday to go into retreat, or perhaps your superior would send you on a course." Then, in 1950, an international Congress of Religious was held in Rome. This august assembly decided that the real purpose of recreation was to restore soul and body. Sitting around the superior in conversation was not recommended; useful and agreeable pastimes, such as light manual work or the playing of games, were preferred. Nor did it like the idea of religious being allowed breaks. "One should beware of vacations and furloughs, lest in giving recreation to the body, harm be done to the soul." Even less did they like the idea of religious going home. "The constant and prolonged contact with worldly persons—it makes little difference that they are relatives, friends, or acquaintances—puts the soul in the frequent occasion of failing in its duty and of assimilating, little by little, the spirit of the world."

It was 1960 before Cardinal Suenens urged that a sister be allowed home, "for contact with the realities of life will give her more understanding of others." He deplored the fact that many religious were lucky if they got one day's holiday a year. Many sisters expected to go home for seven days once every nine years. Then this was revised—to seven days every six years. "You felt," remarked a sister in such an order, "very much out of things when you went home for the first time." Once home, the sister was expected to "endeavor to give edification by her deportment"—scarcely an incitement to relaxation.

Only within the last few years has the rule of enclosure been relaxed sufficiently to allow nuns who need medical treatment to enter the hospital. Previously, they had to be treated within the convent. Members of some orders, such as the Sacred Heart, did not even leave for operations; the surgeon came to the house. But doctors will not operate under those conditions now, and it would be hard to find a dentist prepared to bring a foot drill. (Though at least one contemplative community has an old-fashioned drill kept on the premises, and their dentist comes in to give them treatment. The elderly nun who showed it to me commented with some acerbity, when asked if they would not prefer the new painless water drill, that "we would not go out of our way to avoid discomfort.")

When long-established European communities started branches in the United States, new problems arose. In America, where in many places a car is the only practical form of transport, even sisters in car-dominated Los Angeles used to rely on kindly disposed lay people to drive them around, since driving was considered "unmonastic." In Europe, this particular barrier has taken a lot longer to break down.

It was the same stern approach that kept many religious communities from modernizing their domestic arrangements. "Monastic simplicity," in the minds of many religious, means nuns on their knees polishing floors to a fine finish by hand, rather than using floor polishers. They were often told they would only get to heaven on their knees —be it praying or scrubbing. That many still believe this is evidenced by the rows of white-habited novices I saw crouched in the hallway of a large Sussex convent, rubbing away in sweating silence.

Much of the more primitive labor has vanished. Most convents now have, for example, washing machines instead of tubs. There are photographs of Saint Thérèse, the consumptive "little flower" of the Carmelites, working away with her sisters at the washing, on her knees by a large pool, kneading linen by hand. This usually took place every six weeks or so and explains why each sister had to have a trousseau of several complete changes when she entered. It was not unknown for novices to have their hands badly skinned and bleeding after a full day's washing, from the pure ammonia poured into the water.

The Anglican community of Saint Mary the Virgin has in its huge washing room at Wantage, Berkshire, great copper vats, real Victoriana, in which the wash is boiled. Until recently, the ironing was done with heavy old-fashioned steam irons; convents must be the only places in the world still using such beautiful and antiquated machinery. Sensibly—but sadly—this community has just changed to conventional electric irons.

For some, following the old ways is a matter of asceticism, such as the Spanish nuns who made it perfectly clear they think American sisters lax and soft for their use of electric machinery. Others simply cannot afford modern conveniences. In one old Benedictine monastery in Britain, for example, there are just three bathrooms: one in the infirmary, one in the novice quarters, and one reserved for the abbess. The rest of the nuns wash in bowls on the floor of their cells in true monastic fashion, standing upon bath mats of sacking.

It is the emphasis in the rule on decorum, on modesty and purity, that above everything else has dictated the behavior of communities of nuns. "We were always living many years behind the manners of the country, and ladylike behavior was demanded of us." This caused, thinks Sister Madeleine, "a terrible strain between your inner beliefs and aspirations and the things you do spontaneously as a person of twenty —rushing downstairs, putting your feet over the arm of a chair, relating to men in the way of our time."

The Rules of Modesty ordain how the nun must behave. In many orders they are still followed to the letter, while in others they have given way to behavior more natural to women of today. These rules insist that hands must be joined in a special position, clasped together at waist level. It is a breach of discipline to hurry, much less run; their walk must be measured except in a case of pressing necessity, and even then they must "as far as possible have regard to religious propriety." Then there is "custody of the eyes," which have for the most part to be cast down, while care has to be taken lest they wander from side to side. "Men," states the rule of one order, "should not be looked at indiscreetly." Nor should anything else; curiosity is to be avoided at all costs, and it is stressed that if the sister looks at the person to whom she is talking, she is creating a dangerous situation fraught with temptation.

Some prohibitions are obvious, if a trifle pathetic. Looking in shop windows, for instance, is worldly and could be a distraction. And if a sister is talking to someone in an office, she must on no account allow her eyes to stray to the papers on the other's desk, for fear of curiosity. It is, indeed, a minor breach of rule to raise the eyes unnecessarily— even for a moment, in choir or refectory. This is to avoid distracting the thoughts, which should be applied to God. "Vain, perverse, and

243

wandering thoughts" are to be guarded against. So carefully were they guarded against that a lively girl in her late twenties says that in her novitiate, "After two and a half years we'd never been allowed to look at the pictures in the corridors." The rule also insists that the head should not be turned to the side unless there is need. It is to be held straight and inclined forward, without leaning to either side.

The sisters are exhorted at all times to "show joyousness in their countenances rather than sadness or other less regulated feelings." The lowered voice is also an essential part of seemly behavior; nuns are expected to maintain "calm composure" and avoid "vehemence." Equally important is treating everyone with perfect consideration. The rule expects that in conversation nuns will wait "with perfect patience" until the speaker has finished.

Behavior in the refectory is also rigorously controlled. Meals are not to be thought about in advance because such gross and sensual thoughts would be unmonastic. The convent is no place for gluttony. "You feed your body just enough to get a certain amount of work out of it." The sister should never retire from the table without having mortified herself in some slight way—not having a glass of water, perhaps, when she wanted one—though she must not scruple to eat and drink what is provided, "accepting from the hand of God indifferently what one liked or did not like." It is possible to be reprimanded, as one nun was, for "eating her soup in a worldly way," while saying something was "nice" would bring the retort that it was a worldly attitude to be a gourmet.

Many of the more curious mealtime customs began when orders from one country started houses in another and, in the name of simplicity, retained the rule with regard to meals. The Sisters of the Institute of Notre Dame of Namur, a French order, had one plate which had to be wiped free of grease with a piece of bread. There would be no cups, just a handleless bowl for water. They had both knives and forks—but everything had to be cut at the start of the meal, then eaten with the fork. "We were absolutely never allowed to use the knife during the meal—but it had nothing to do with religious life. It was part of the French and Belgian customs, when a poor family shared the only knife."

Throughout the meal, silence is observed. "If you drop something, you get down and kiss the floor for offending against the silence of the house." There are gestures to be learned to express different wants: the index finger and thumb closed for bread in some orders, in others put flat upon the table. For salt, a circle is drawn with a knife, for butter the knife is pointed, while water is requested by rapping the goblet on the table. And since eating is so gross an occupation, the mind is occupied with listening attentively to reading. In the United States, communities have started to tape these for convenience.

The rule of silence in the house is observed so that nuns can listen better for the voice of God. The shadows of silence, the spaces of recollection, have always been considered indispensable to the religious life. As one eighty-year-old says, "There's a lot of talk about abolishing silence, but that's rubbish. You can't have peace if you don't have silence." And it does, says a superior of the Deaconess Community of Saint Andrew, "help you focus on God rather than on one's busyness." There are other advantages in silence. "When you didn't have to talk," says a sister, "you could get away with murder—you didn't have to express an opinion." If there were times when silence, as the Poor Clare poet Sister Mary Agnes has written, seemed to be "pressing steel plates about my ears," there were times too when it was a protection from irritation and gave some measure of privacy. In some orders, if speech was absolutely essential, permission to speak would be asked with a bow and two fingers to the lips. The nun so approached would answer "Benedicite," to which the answer was "Dominus," before anything else was said. Another order might use "Ave Maria," to which response was "Gracia plena." But like so much else, the rule of silence became obsessive, so that even the accidental slamming of a door was an infringement. Lapses had to be reported to the superior. "You had to kneel and she would give you a penance and you'd kiss the ground."

There are official times for admitting faults. Among the Benedictines, for example, when the Chapter of Faults takes place, the abbess calls on six nuns to make full and clean confession of any fault, any wrong done. On their knees, they confess to every unkind thought or careless action, and the community shares each nun's shortcomings and sinfulness. Some communities call this process the "culp," a corruption of "mea culpa." Marie Keegan of the Belgian Ladies of Mary recalls, "It was usually in the dining room. Six or seven of us lined up

245

at a time, back to back; then you lay down on the carpet, face down with your arms at your sides, and said, 'I confess to you, dear mother, and to you, dear sisters'—and then you read it off a bit of paper. A typical culp would be, 'I thought uncharitable thoughts; I spilt milk and didn't say anything about it.' A great one if I was really stuck for something was, 'I broke the night silence.' Then you got a penance." In addition, there were all sorts of extra penances. Any sister who wished could prostrate herself in the refectory for five minutes to show she was a sinner and that everyone might trample on her. Another penance, carried out weekly in many houses, was the kissing by the novices of the feet of the entire community in a gesture of humility.

Women's communities have always been stricter than men's about sharing information. "The idea of passing news of any sort in a convent was anathema ten years ago," says a French sister. "If you even missed something someone said in conversation, you couldn't ask what it was." One nun remembers that when she entered only one daily paper came into the house, and the community was allowed to read only the one middle page of news. When the Duke of Windsor abdicated, the news was considered so unsuitable that delivery of the paper was stopped for a week. "I only heard the scandalous story years later." A woman who entered just before the invasion of Belgium, in 1914, never saw or heard a single war news item throughout World War I. Occasionally a nun would hear from the superior about a relative's being killed or wounded. Then, after four years, the bells were rung and the superior announced that the war was over.

For many communities, even reproductions of sacred art were considered unfit for contemplation, and the pages of illustrated books were glued firmly together. Statues were clothed neatly in white flannel petticoats. At the other extreme, a Sussex convent in 1963, in all innocence, commissioned frescoes by a curious and talented painter known as Frantz Salieri; they caused a scandal in the Church of Rome. A few years later, he emerged as the director and designer who helped make transvestism acceptable.

Even information that seemed useful to the nun in her work might be withheld. A nun who became infirmarian after World War II knew nothing of medicine. Her family sent her a modern encyclopedia of nursing which was immediately confiscated, containing as it did so

246

much which it was quite unnecessary for her to know. Although such censorship may appear extreme, it can be justified in monastic terms; superfluous knowledge clouds the mind which should be filled with thoughts of God.

The reason so many of these medieval practices survived lies in the history of the religious orders themselves. For long periods of time they virtually disappeared in various countries, and when they returned they looked to the past for inspiration. In Britain during the reign of Henry VIII, for instance, and in France at the time of the revolution, religious life all but died out, while in America it had not begun. When it was once more acceptable, it merely started up again where it had left off. When the Anglican sisterhoods were developing in the nineteenth-century England, they were very much a restoration rather than a renewal: Gothic architecture and romantic novels were fashionable, and this was mirrored in a burst of nostalgia for medieval Christianity. Equally old-fashioned in many ways were the native American communities which, in the nineteenth century, appeared in the wake of the established European missionary orders already there.

Yet rigorous as the regulations were—and are—it would be wrong to assume that all nuns suffered under them. As Sister Margaret Moran of the Good Shepherd points out, "I have the theory that, in fact, the more people conformed to such a set of regulations, the more individual some of them became. They came through as fantastic characters, lovely to meet." But a docile character might well be broken; many nuns have had nervous breakdowns. "Mind you, they weren't always recognized, and one in my order never really got over it." Most nuns would agree with the English member of a teaching order who feels that "because you had this very basic idea of committing your life to Christ, you would put up with a lot of things. When you went into the convent you knew a certain kind of behavior was expected of you and you just conformed to that. But there were other things in your life which were meaningful and which compensated."

Even so, admits a mother superior, "Only now are we learning how many older sisters suffered an almost constant frustration which they accepted willingly—but not always cheerfully—as part of the cross they bargained to carry in following Our Lord." Sister Russell, a superior in the Society of the Sacred Heart, remembers, "I went in very uncritically and accepted anything they said must be done; I think even in that state I loved it. But I can see now that we stopped questioning and thinking. People thought it was possible to be a good religious without thinking."

The regulations encouraged the nuns to be passive and childlike. A Mirfield Father recently visited an Anglican women's community, where he asked for a glass of water. "I'll just ask Mother," was the response. Even today, "firm yet motherly" is the phrase used by a congregation formed in the 1960s to describe the qualities needed by a superior. This, too, is a harking back. Most communities started as small families, with rules and regulations which suited such a structure and the omnipotent figure at its head. No training was considered necessary for the post. A superior received the grace of her office; her inadequacies and shortcomings were divinely overcome. It did not always work. One enclosed nun I talked to was elected superior, though she felt from the first she could not undertake the office. Within weeks she had a nervous breakdown and actually ran away from her convent without telling anyone—for which the penalty, waived in her case, is exclaustration. She was, of course, penniless but took the money from a collection box, promising herself to return it. She ended up sitting in Westminster Abbey without a clue as to what to do next.

Although many women are capable of filling the role superbly, the very structure of convents encourages autocrats. "Harassed superiors have been known to treat their subordinates as if they were unwilling conscripts," observed one priest. "A convent," snapped one American sister, "should not be run like an asylum—or an army."

Sister Audrey Kopp, an American nun and a professor of theology, observes that "although canon law states that any decision that affects the whole must be made by the whole, it doesn't always work out quite so democratically." She points out that the superior can, if she so wishes, manipulate the ideas of the sisters. She is the person who controls radio and television and censors newspapers and letters.

Enlightened superiors have always worried about the question of obedience, well aware that an overly rigid "mother" may use the rules unjustly to make her own life easy but that of her nuns intolerable. Teresa of Ávila, who had a particular devotion to this virtue, retails with horror what happened when "to another prioress came a

248

nun and showed her a very large worm, saying, 'Look how beautiful it is.' The prioress in jest replied, 'Then go and eat it.' She went and fried it. The cook asked her why she fried a worm and she answered, 'To eat it,' and would have done so. Thus through the great carelessness of the prioress that nun might have done herself much harm."

This does show how little justification superiors need give for their commands. It is, for instance, quite possible for a superior to forbid a younger sister "imprudent behavior"—movie visits, or accepting invitations to people's homes—without having to define what "prudent" behavior actually is.

There are many nuns—some still inside, some outside an order—who have talked to me about what, to an outsider, sound like cruel and unnecessary restrictions: the Brazilian nun who was told never on any account to touch the small children in her care, even to hold a hand; the contemplative forbidden to write poetry in her cell, since it was "self-indulgent." Some stories have more dangerous overtones. There are women who have known themselves to be in need of help for psychological problems which elderly superiors were quite unable to comprehend. One sister, unable to sleep in a tiny room because she was beginning to suffer from claustrophobia, was asked if she expected hotel accommodations and advised that this was her cross and she must bear it. Another woman, who at a time of considerable anxiety had walked in her sleep onto the roof of the convent, was accused of "attention seeking" and had to "speak her fault" before the entire community.

It must be stressed that all too often it seems not to have been a lack of sympathy but of understanding which led to such situations. This fact, however, can have given little comfort to the American sister who went to her superior for spiritual help—only to be handed the keys of the community car and told to go to a drive-in movie and have a hamburger.

The major safeguard against abuse of the role of superior has always been the process of election. A religious cannot usually be considered for the post of superior until she is over forty. Elections are held every three years in most orders, and reelection is usually possible only once. It was not until the eleventh century that heads of many religious houses were actually elected. Before that, the rule generally passed from mother to daughter, since a woman of royal blood would often found a religious settlement with her marriage portion and retire there on the death of her husband. This system meant that many heads of religious houses were little more than children themselves.

The ceremony of electing the head of a monastic community is full of dignified ritual. Today, among the Benedictines, the abbot president, head of the congregation, arrives at the monastery on the appointed day with two monks, who are the scrutators. The voting is held in the locked choir, under oath. A list of all those eligible is handed to each nun, who cuts out the name she chooses. This process is repeated until one name achieves the necessary number of votes. It is a serious business. "Conspiring to be abbess" is forbidden by the order.

When the choice is made, the abbot president confirms the new abbess in the name of the Holy See and hands her the pectoral cross, ring, seal, and keys of the monastery. Then the choir is unlocked, the whole community enters, and the abbess is taken to the abbatial chair, where, one by one, all her nuns kneel before her and put their hands between hers in the age-old gesture of homage and obedience, and to each she gives the pax, the kiss of peace.

Until now, the religious community has been very much a two-tiered society: While uniformity was considered desirable, the social patterns of monastic life were positively class-ridden. Not for nothing was the head called "superior," and not until Vatican II was the word "inferior" for her subjects outlawed. Any woman who entered took with her the status she had in the world outside. And although in the religious life nuns were discouraged—to the point of being forbidden—to discuss their backgrounds in order to avoid jealousies and comparisons, their role in the convent was decided by who they were and what they brought with them.

The choir nuns were educated women who entered with an often handsome dowry. They could speak Latin, follow the prayers, and read and make music—hence the term "choir." A large number of early convents, indeed, accepted only those who were nobly born—so much so that in the fourteenth century the pope had to intervene before the Order of Franciscan Minoresses would take members of the new landed gentry. (Apart from daughters of dukes and barons and the Lord Mayor of London, there were later included daughters of a skinner, a draper, and an ironmonger, and two whose fathers were fishmongers. Presumably their financial status was acceptable.)

Women who entered without benefit of education or dowries were the lay sisters, sometimes known as claustral or coadjutrix sisters. Working women who wanted to dedicate their lives to God, they lived largely separate from the choir nuns. Their prayers were different, being simpler—they did not say Divine Office—and they often had their own chapel. Their clothes were less elaborate; they took their recreation separately and sat in the refectory at special tables; they even had their own mother assistant. On them, the smooth running of the monastery depended. They scrubbed and polished, washed the floors, and cooked, thus freeing the choir nuns for study and writing, the fine art of music, and illuminating religious manuscripts. Then, too, medieval nuns had both male and female servants, not only to work the vast tracts of land and keep the herds of cattle and sheep but often to serve indoors. In a document written about A.D. 1400, the nunnery at Barking recorded that the clerk to the abbess was paid thirteen shillings and fourpence, her yeoman cook twenty-six shillings and eighteenpence, while her groom cook and pudding wife got a gown a year worth two shillings. And the abbess and cellaress both had double portions of food—presumably to feed these servants.

While the lay sisters were exhorted to "look in a spirit of true humility upon all members of the community as above them," the choir sisters were told to look upon their lowly and obscure duties "with a secret appreciation and a certain kind of envy." Gradually, attitudes changed. It became common for choir nuns in most communities to do their share of heavy work, usually under the supervision of the lay sisters. "When I was young," remembers a Sister of Mercy superior, "we washed the convent walls ourselves. I get a man in now. I wouldn't let my girls do it."

In enclosed communities, the lay sisters are of course still essential; they are the inmates' hands and feet to the world outside. And no one is more staunchly defensive of the old caste system than the lay sisters themselves. At the Carmel in London's Notting Hill, where the lay sister is still outside the enclosure, she is fiercely proud of her role and dislikes intensely the new freedom beginning to creep into enclosed orders. "My vocation is looking after cloistered nuns. I can't do with them running out all over the place."

This class system is one of the factors making change both slow and painful. Another is the very nature of a religious community: It is not a commercial, industrial, or professional organization, based on self-interest, but a state of perfection, founded because each member seeks her own sanctity—and that of others.

For most communities, it is not the young sisters who find the idea of change difficult, or the older ones, who accept it philosophically. It is the sisters in their middle years, the forties and fifties, who find change a painful ordeal. It is hard for them to view practices to which they are accustomed as suddenly militating against the good of the community. And in this age group are found the superiors and mothers general of the various orders. "The mothers general are scared," comments one American sister. "They don't understand how deep the changes will be." It is certainly true. Talking to me about renewal, one superior sighed heavily and said, "They want dinner when they feel like it, that sort of thing."

It is ironic that while the male establishment of the church neither eagerly seeks nor really welcomes change ("Like a mighty tortoise moves the Church of God; Brethren, we're treading where we've always trod"), by 1948 even Pius XII was telling religious superiors to adapt or perish. Yet when, in the mid-1960s, Cardinal Suenens published his revolutionary *The Nun in the World*, advocating change for orders of women, it was a mother general who, it is said, asked Pope Paul for his head on a plate, and she was not altogether joking.

She was too late; the tide had already turned against the old ways. By 1956 the Holy See had established the Conference of Major Superiors for women, of mothers general and provincials who met to discuss all sorts of problems, including education. The Holy See had wanted a priest as president, but the women refused and elected instead the mother general of the Adrian Dominicans. The Sister Formation Conference devised a curriculum of study for religious to encourage communities to train their women to professional standards.

Religious women were beginning to speak out. "The totally regulated life," declared Maryellen Muckenhirn, the best-known woman

252

theologian in America, "is not human, especially under the pressures built into modern life." And a French nun insisted, "I want to live a religious life, but not in a medieval way." Even some of the men of the church—though not the more hidebound—were beginning to speak out on the side of change. A French bishop declared that his nuns were tied by their rule and hampered by the habit. "Religious life seems like a cage—they cannot go out and fight the enemy where he is, outside." An Italian bishop accused his sisters of "proceeding at the same old sedate trot," with no idea of the rapidly changing conditions outside. "They are sleeping through the time for action."

When the Second Vatican Council opened in 1962, 2,600 cardinals, archbishops, and bishops assembled under Pope John XXIII. "We are going to shake off the dust that has collected on the throne of Saint Peter since the time of Constantine and let in some fresh air," he said. Pope John did not last out the council, but under the Curia—the cardinals who govern beneath the pope—the council continued as Pope Paul was elected.

Then, in accordance with their instructions to return to their sources, religious orders looked to the pioneering spirit of their founders. Behind the convent walls there was much prayer and heart-searching about the future. Hundreds of different orders considered how they could remodel their way of life to fit more usefully into the world. They saw Vatican II as a green light and responded eagerly. There were renewal workshops and community discussions. Professors of canon law and moral theology were invited to give lectures. The rules and the books of customs were rewritten.

One of the first orders to start modernization was the American Sisters of Loretto at the Foot of the Cross, whose mother general, Sister Luke Tobin, was the only American nun to attend Vatican II. She, more than any other single woman, inspired much of the most thoughtful change within religious orders in America. "I'm regarded," she says wryly, "as someone who has been a lot more forward than I should have been." Her order gave up the habit and moved into work it considered more relevant than the original teaching, nursing, and orphanage jobs. Nuns began to work with drug addicts and the Job Corps; they made themselves part of the community in a new way.

For others, change was harder. Not every community made the

jump to more modern life so successfully: members of one Anglican community now express some regret over their decision to close down their embroidery school and send the sisters out as chiropodists.

Italian and Spanish orders in particular face a two-fold problem. First, the women of those countries are, as one Spanish sister carefully puts it, "not advanced." And second, they feel, in the words of an Italian nun, that "here, there are always the regulations. We would not be the first in Italy, we would not lead the way. We have to be so quiet all around the pope." In these countries the nuns are still heavily veiled, the grilles still firmly in place.

Some orders are quite simply reluctant to change. "Religious life," remarked a French nun sadly, "used to be a sort of pinnacle." A middle-aged sister regretfully agrees with her. "It was a very rigid life, but clear as daylight what you should and should not do. Now it isn't so clear; there's continual flux and adjustment. You have to learn to interpret independence in the right way, freedom in the right way, liberty in the right proportion."

That women have always found it hard to interpret the rules is confirmed by Father Gilbert Volery, who is secretary to the Conference of Major Religious Superiors in Britain. "Women religious know the laws better than men, often enough. But they cannot reason with them—they take them en bloc." He ascribes this to their lack of training in philosophy and theology.

This difficulty is exacerbated by the fact that, in many convents, the decision-making machinery is beginning to change. The role of superior is being looked at and found wanting. Many communities have decided to replace her with an elected president or an executive officer. In American convents there are even "chairnuns." The superior's position is no longer one of unquestioned power; she is expected to be not a policy maker but an implementer, carrying out decisions taken by the councils and cooperating with other people. "I've never made an individual decision," says Sister Barbara, who heads the large American Maryknoll order. And superiors are getting younger: Sister Barbara herself is forty-seven, while the average age of her sisters is fifty-one.

In some places, the superior has vanished in both name and role. Indeed, her image has become so tarnished that many orders have dropped the term "motherhouse" altogether and now refer to their "house of formation" or "head office." Orders which had no particular plans for abolishing the role of superior found they did so perforce —like the Sisters of Charity of Nazareth, founded in Kentucky. They decided to renew by forming several small communities and discovered that no one would accept responsibility for such a group lest she be misinterpreted as assuming the role of superior. Other orders deliberately decided to have a team instead of the superior. When this happened to the mother general of the English Congregation of Our Lady of Sion, she was absolutely delighted. It proved, she said, that she had been doing the work of four people.

In very small groups, the need for a superior disappeared automatically. "We're missing it," says a nun living in a house of five. "It was nice in a way that the superior spoke for everybody. You have to pay for liberty."

Even where the mother superior does exist in a more or less unchanged situation, attitudes toward her have undergone a transformation. "Mother," said a pretty Anglican. "She's the peg on which we can hang things."

Change is also hindered by the generation conflict. "We're more open to ideas now," says a forty-year-old sister in an Episcopalian community, "but we've got a long way to go in certain pockets of resistance. At a recent chapter I was very conscious that the young group weren't looking to the mother to suggest ideas. They wanted independence of thought and action, and they were genuinely suffering because they were being denied it. And the older group, I could tell, were thinking, Why should they have it all their own way?"

There is no doubt that many older sisters are afraid of stepping out of line. They have a certain conception of obedience which does not question accepted customs. Of such women, Cardinal Suenens gently observed, "Seen in this light, any innovation seems doomed in advance."

In such congregations, the young occasionally attempt blockbuster tactics. A thirty-year-old American Sister of Charity says, "There were enough of us in the order to say, 'Look, we have to go where we want to go, because the church and the order are not relating to social needs.' Twenty-four of us formed a committee on renewal and experimentation, and we hashed out a policy to present to the general chapter meeting, demanding progress and change. The majority were still conservative, but they weren't organized into a power group."

Along with the total authority of superiors, the absolute obedience they once demanded has vanished too. The pattern of day has become more relaxed, and the rule amended to fit with differing timetables. Sisters are encouraged to go out to clubs or lectures or extramural classes. They are able to catch up on sleep they miss and make their private prayers when they choose, as long as they fulfill a certain amount in a week. "The accent now is on personal responsibility," explains a sister two years away from her final profession. "Each person works out what she needs in time of prayer."

For many convents, formal recreation has also been relaxed. I have been at recreation in one Catholic community where a whole roomful of elderly sisters sat upright on hard chairs happily watching a children's puppet show on color television. Not all have softened, though. Some orders still make it obligatory to take recreation as a community exercise, and in numerous houses a book is read aloud to sewing sisters.

One change that met with mixed feelings is the relaxation of silence. Several houses I visited, having found that living in community is far more difficult where free speech is permitted ("Now we have to cope with a lot of people's problems and difficulties"), plan to reintroduce at least a partial return to the rule of silence.

Other changes are so slight as to seem to outsiders scarcely worth mentioning. It is hard, for example, to realize the difference a telephone makes to an isolated community. Other freedoms struck many sisters themselves as outrageous when they were first introduced—the possibility of going to a movie, for instance, or smoking a cigarette.

Some changes are undoubtedly for the better; others have probably been made too hastily. Too many communities have heedlessly flung away centuries of tradition in a desperate attempt to adapt rapidly, and it has recently become apparent to many orders that the more they strive to modernize, the fewer entrants they get. Figures published in Britain show quite clearly that the moment habits were modified and nuns made themselves hideous by cutting off the bottoms of their skirts, vocations dropped. Oddly enough, the reaction to such

256

modernization for at least some women in America is just as traditional as for those in Europe. "I would have joined the Maryknollers," said a cheerful American girl to me, her face framed in a monastic wimple, "only I wanted to wear a habit."

The habit remains the most potent symbol of religious life. "The bridge that takes you over into convent life," says one Belgian sister, talking of her time as a novice, "is a sort of romanticism. Particularly about the habit." The nun's clothes are important. If she wears a habit she has chosen to be "a sign of God in the world." She is announcing exactly what she is.

It is, however, an announcement that increasingly large numbers of sisters are flatly refusing to make. "I don't believe," says Marie Keegan of the Belgian Ladies of Mary, "that when I walk down the street in a black habit, people will say, 'There goes a visible witness of God.' Hell, no." And in the United States, Liz Thoman, with long hair turned up at the ends, blue eye shadow, pink lipstick, and fingers full of rings, sees no reason not to wear attractive clothes. "I will not hide behind a false front in order to be 'not available.' The biggest thing is your own response, and your availability from your response. In California, no matter what you wear, people are going to stare at you. I can't keep from being who I am."

This attitude is a dramatic break with tradition, for distinctive clothing has always been part of the religious life. In the old monastic orders, men and women wore virtually the same clothes: robe, scapular, and sandals, with the addition of a veil for women and a hood for men. These garments have a beauty of their own, a quality of timelessness and simplicity. They were also highly suitable for the life for which they were designed: nothing could be more practical than full-length serge for cold cloisters and stone-floored cells in November. These clothes came to be seen, by both nuns and lay people, as religious in themselves. So identified were they with the essence of a vowed life that "taking the veil" became another term for entering.

Many nuns and sisters today are finding clothes an increasing problem, as attitudes change within the orders. When, for instance, Mother Mary Joseph founded her English Vocation Sisters, she put her sisters in calf-length skirts, much to the chagrin of the orders with whom she was working. "They said we lowered the dignity of religion by the length of our skirts. Now some of them are shorter than ours." But even if Mother Mary Joseph is prepared to shorten skirts, she is determined to stick by her dark green habit. "The Vatican Council said the nun must be a sign in the world. How can she be, if the world doesn't see she's a nun?" She also sees the habit in purely practical terms. "We have made a vow of chastity, and I do think when a religious sits down, you shouldn't be able to see up her skirt."

There are other positive advantages to the habit. "You say to yourself, Well, thank God I don't have to worry what I'll put on tomorrow. It's the same tomorrow as it'll be in another hundred years' time." Another nun finds the habit a safeguard against herself. "Scratch the surface and I'm just as open as any other woman to the distraction of wanting this kind of hairdo, this color dress." It is a small sacrifice, they consider, in exchange for so much. One nun remembers that four months before she entered she bought a scarlet suit. "I love scarlet. It costs you to give that up for black and white. And it should cost —that was being a woman."

The habit is also seen as a badge of authority, which would otherwise be lost. "Would you take so much notice of a plainclothes policeman?" A sister working with disturbed adolescents felt that "the boys needed someone to look up to, and the habit proved I was genuine. They could understand me doing this work for God. What they hated was the idea of someone doing it for them. So they accepted me more readily than the social workers." The same feeling was expressed by the young lay social worker working with girls who had been through the police courts on drug offenses and were sent to her on probation. "Those girls were impossible—I couldn't get a word out of them. Then I started taking them, two at a time, down to the sisters. The results were fantastic. The girls knew the nuns weren't being paid to be interested, that they really cared." By the same token, the habit can provide protection. One of the Little Sisters of Jesus, the feminine branch of the order founded by Charles de Foucauld, says, "We couldn't go to some of the places we do if we didn't wear it. If you're living in a slum among Muslims in Algeria, working in local jobs, they'd think it very odd if they couldn't see what you are. And although it's true that sometimes people are hostile to religion, we want to go in as religious—and break down those barriers."

There is a protective aspect to the habit, though this would seem to be failing a little at present; several American nuns wearing it have been mugged and had their handbags snatched. It remains, to a degree, an extra safeguard for the nuns themselves. "I saw those sisters," said one superior of a highly conventional order, "laughing out loud, uncontrolled. Now you couldn't do that in a habit. You know all the time who you are."

One nun advanced a practical reason for traveling in a habit: In the United States, nuns can fly at clergy rates if they wait for standby seats. "If you're not in a habit, it's hard to be identified." The same applies in parts of South America, where religious are allowed a 10 percent reduction in fares, though there, claims a sister, "it's to get you on the plane so it doesn't go down."

Older sisters, in particular, cling to the habit. They have neither the means of dressing themselves properly nor the figures to get any sort of pleasure out of current fashion. "At seventy-five, I don't have enough hair to go without a veil." An Anglican superior finds the habit the most comfortable garment she has ever worn. "It's made to fit and it's not too tight. Having been in the forces with a hard hat and a collar, and a belt tied to give you as much waist as you could manage, I'm much happier in this." The majority of her age group does not even want to shorten their ankle-length hemlines. "At the moment we can get away without stockings." And they are very conscious that the habit is a great disguiser of age. One ex-convent schoolgirl says she was amazed when she made a return visit not long after leaving to find a lot of aging women in baggy skirts instead of the gracious nuns she remembered.

There are increasing advantages in the habit, now that nuns are more and more invited to social occasions. The head of one training college whose order was half into secular clothes was invited to attend a civic dinner on behalf of the college. "I felt it ridiculous to buy an evening dress for one occasion. I was far better off in the habit." Then, too, it gives quite a lot of immediate information about the sister who wears it. From her habit it is possible to tell a woman's order, the type of work she probably does, and often even her nationality. Some habits are quite explicit about the allegiance of the order they represent; the Bridgettine nuns, in their muted gray, wear a white linen wimple, veiled in black, with the crown of white linen bearing a cross with five red drops of blood.

Some feel the advantages the habit gives them are unfair. "When you're wearing it, you've got instant, easy respect. It would take me *years* to earn the respect I get just by having a veil on my head." This is confirmed by the superior whose argument for preserving the habit is, "You lose prestige in a poor house if you put on secular clothes. I can ring the bell in any poor home and I'm let in at once; you're one of the sisters, you're accepted."

Yet often the work a sister is doing might be hampered by religious clothing. One Anglican sister who accompanied a group of chaplains to the Munich Olympics with the British team says that at first the habit really erected a barrier. "If I hadn't worn it, an awful lot of time would have been saved."

"It's kind of spooky," claims an American, "to be dressed as a nun when people don't care what nuns are." This is something missionary sisters often discover. In Nigeria, for instance, even native sisters now wear short dresses and bright headscarves because the people, often Muslim, would immediately reject them in the habit. And "children and dogs," says an Anglican sister, "are put off by black." That the majority of nuns and sisters still have black habits is another relic of former beliefs. For although black was the color of mourning, again symbolizing the death of the religious to the world, it was also worn because of the ancient belief that, cloaked and veiled in black, human beings were invisible to the spirits and therefore free from evil molestation.

Clothes are important to women as a way of expressing individual personality and taste, as well as background, and a woman in uniform is denied all three possibilities. Clothes also provide a psychological lift at times, which is why one of the worst things about the old convent habit was not being able to change it. A nun might start her day at six in the morning, do a hard day's work, and then go to a meeting in the evening; all she could do was wash her face and put on a fresh linen band. "It felt very nice to have secular dress," says one American Loretto sister. "You feel much more feminine and clean." Then, too, the more open and varied a sister's life became, the more she needed change. "To have just one dress for classroom, sports,

Eucharist, cooking, shopping, travel, formal dinner, and public concert may seal off for many women a good exhaust valve," feels another American.

On the whole, the more sophisticated the work of the sister, the more eager she is for change. Nuns attending secular universities, for instance, had a hard time. "It was a bitter experience, getting used to the students in my habit. You were supposed to conform; you felt caged in. I wanted to say, 'Oh, for God's sake, I'm a real person.' " Another sister was the only nun on the mathematics faculty. "I was the center of attention, and they were extremely nice. But all the same, you are different." Sometimes they even came across active objections. "Why," asked a lecturer in philosophy of an American sister, "must you shout at me that you're a sacred person?"

The voluminous clothes do have an unfortunate effect on the beholder. "They suggest," claims a nun who is also a psychiatrist, "smugness and self-righteousness. They enclose the nun from the touch of others." Another sister feels that "the habit cuts me off from society. I hate the fact that people make assumptions about us—such as that we're not allowed to talk to men."

But the clothes of a woman in religion were never intended to have this effect. *Ancrene Riwle*, the early-thirteenth-century directive for anchoresses, was quite explicit about the role of the habit and quoted Saint Paul: "Keeping oneself unspotted from this world . . . in this lies religion: not in a wide hood or a black cape, not in a white rochet or a grey cowl."

The founders—of whatever period—followed this teaching, and when they began their orders they merely wore the clothes of their day, choosing for their convents what was available and commonly worn; this was true until the nineteenth century and the Gothic revival. They never anticipated that such clothes would come to be considered part of the rule itself, so that any change would be unthinkable. As a result, nuns may still walk around dressed exactly like widows in the 1840s, bonnet, cape, and all. "It's very dignified and beautiful," comments a young sister now in secular dress, "but it looks like a theatrical costume."

Until very recently, the Notre Dame sisters, an early nineteenth-

261

century order, wore virtually unchanged the peasant dress of their French founder, which looked "incongruous" in their Lancashire house, one sister said. It had a crossover bodice and a gathered skirt in black serge, and the bodice was pinned with the nineteenth-century equivalent of a safety pin, a long steel pin which not only became increasingly difficult to purchase but was also dangerous to use. "You had to learn how to put them in without jabbing yourself." Snap fasteners would have been easier, cheaper, and more comfortable—but the founder did not mention them. Equally bizarre were the buttons of the society of the Sacred Heart. This order was founded in France just after the revolution, and the habit was finished with many tiny engraved buttons, the exact design and size of which was laid down by the founder. In England these became increasingly difficult to obtain, and eventually they had to be ordered specially from France at enormous cost, "hardly," comments a superior, "in line with religious poverty."

Some of the odder dress styles had been curious even when they were first worn, reflecting as they did the ideas of suitable fashion held by male advisers to the various orders. The Sisters of the Cross and Passion, for example, founded to help working girls in the industrial areas of Manchester and Bolton, were enlightened enough to wear secular dress when going to teach in the schools. But they wore, in the mid-nineteenth century, a long black mantle, a large black straw bonnet, and voluminous black crepe veiling. This costume caused so much attention, even then, that they had to abandon it.

With clothes, as with convent rules, eccentricities began to creep in as religious orders spread from the country of their foundation. Uniformity of habit was seen as a means of binding together the different houses. Every nun of a particular order, no matter where, wore the same habit, kept the same hours, lived in all respects the same life. Climate was allowed to make no difference. The Immaculate Heart sisters, arriving in San Francisco from Spain, dressed as if the Californian climate did not exist: a violet-blue habit and scapular covered with a heavy mantle for chapel and feast days; stiffened coifs ("They would be just soaked with perspiration"), square band, a soft transparent veil and a heavy black one over it. When the Sacred Heart nuns founded houses in South Africa and the Congo early in the twentieth century, they went out in the same hot black robes they had needed for European winters.

"Finally it was realized to be a limitation, not an advantage," says Sister Honor Basset. "We were allowing local needs to be dictated from Rome." And the American Maryknoll Sisters remember all too well how it felt working in some of the world's hottest climates in the full habit, "the veil fitting tightly against your head, then all those layers down your back, the scapular and the cape." Just one concession was made to the heat—the habit was white.

By far the most elaborate parts of the habit were the collars and headdresses. "We had to have twelve enormous fichus, feet and feet long, of a beautiful lawn. These had to be hemmed by hand, because you were never allowed to do machine work." Then there were the caps. "Ours had a thing on the top to give fullness, called a caterpillar and held together with incredibly little stitches. Then there was the frill. It was the length of a room, of fine gauze that was virtually impossible to sew. It had to have a centimeter hem and be whipped on a very flat needle with a cord. As you went through it, you pulled every fifth frill until this huge length of material was the length of your face. Then this had to be sewn onto the cap, and if each side wasn't exactly even it would be bulgy and couldn't be properly goffered on the goffering machine."

These massive confections were totally impractical. "You could never go out in the rain; the pie crust just lay down and died." And they had to be specially cared for by a woman who was employed by the convent to do nothing else. Each one took an hour and a half to starch, and she did sixty every fortnight. "We knew it was totally unrealistic. But we didn't get nylon frills until 1966."

The headdresses of many orders were bonnets with long sidepieces, which were actually designed to act as blinkers, so that the nun could look only straight ahead toward God. These continued to be worn even when nuns began to drive cars. One Sacred Heart sister, deputed to be driver, took the test endlessly until she discovered the instructor had no intention of passing her while she continued to wear her headdress, since he was convinced she could not see a thing. And the American Immaculate Heart sisters were officially asked by the authorities to adopt a driving veil.

Headdresses came in so many layers—eight was normal—that nuns developed a system of securing each layer to the next and simply lifted the whole thing off at night and kept it on a hat stand or a

263

broom handle in their cell. They would then don a bonnet or a soft night coif. Dr. Charlotte Klein remembers going at the end of the 1960s to an international conference held in an expensive Wiesbaden hotel. She got back to her room after a convivial dinner to find her bed turned back, with her nightdress and bonnet carefully laid out by the maid.

By this time, cropped and shaven heads were recognized as being culturally odd. The elaborate headdresses with which they were covered, like the complicated habits, were making nonsense of one of the major reasons advanced for keeping the habit: that it was simpler and cheaper than normal women's clothing. This may once have been true—but not in today's world of permanent-press fabrics and simple hairstyles.

When nuns began changing to secular clothes, their hair presented a problem. After years and years under confining headdresses, what hair they had left was in a poor state. "Thin and ratty" is how one woman described hers, "and odd lengths where I'd cut it short." Others had deep indentations above the eyebrows where, for years, the tight headband had rested continuously. Even going to the hairdresser was an embarrassing experience. "I didn't know what they'd think of me or what I should ask for. I'd entered at eighteen, and I don't think I'd ever had a proper hairdo. I said to my superior, 'I haven't got the courage to go in there. I feel such a fool.' In the end, she had to take me in, and explain it was an experiment, and ask them to make me look presentable."

The vanguard of those orders who have modernized started around 1967. The first extravagance to go was the pie frill around the face. Then simple dresses were adopted, still with a scapular and belt. The first nuns to publicly abandon the habit were the Sisters of Loretto at the Foot of the Cross, who were in suits by the spring of 1966. Soon afterward, the Congregation of Humility of Mary of Ottumwa, Iowa, received amazed press coverage when Sister Jean Reidy, taking her degree in philosophy at the University of Notre Dame, appeared in nothing more radical than black and white store-bought clothes. It was, she says, only then that people invited her to their homes. By 1970, an American sister returning after a missionary stint of ten years found a profound change. "I went to a leadership conference of major superiors, and out of six hundred and fifty women, seventy-five percent were in lay clothes: modern, professional-looking people."

By this time, the majority of orders which wanted to had at least one sister with permission to experiment with different types of suitable clothing. Currently, many European orders have several different sets of clothes being worn by different members of the community. One order I visited had four variations. The superior wore the full-length black habit, veil and all, the only compromise being that the fabrics were synthetic. A teaching sister had a black, long-sleeved, mid-calf-length dress with a back-of-the-head veil. A university chaplain was in a dark gray suit with a white blouse and no veil. And a fourth sister, setting off on holiday, wore slacks and a sweater.

But in September 1972 the Sacred Congregation for Religious issued a warning. The traditional habit might be modified to accord with practical requirements or hygiene, but it might not be abolished altogether or left to the judgment of individual sisters. Although the nun must be recognizable as a religious, she would be allowed to wear purely secular clothes if the nature of her work demanded it, though "even in this case the dress of religious women should always be in some way different from the forms that are clearly secular." This letter was sent to papal diplomats around the world with a request that they ensure that the dress rules were kept in their areas. The directive was sent by Cardinal Antoniutti, showing once again that men are more determined to retain the habit than women. Abandoning the habit was one of the four points over which American Immaculate Heart of Mary sisters broke with the church establishment. They had been given permission for one sister per house to experiment, if this was done with "a terminal end in view"—which meant, they discovered, "if we promised to stop."

The churchmen who want their daughters in religion to be veiled and robed insist they do so to protect them, to preserve their modesty and chastity as much as to make them a sign of God in the world. But it is surely significant that in other societies where women are so treated, covered up and hidden from sight, it is not done out of any kind of respect but because they are scarcely seen as people in their own right. They are the property of men, and in a masculine society they are second-class citizens. No wonder the overwhelming reaction of nuns who have abandoned the habit has been that for the first time they feel they have achieved liberty.

There are, however, some persuasive arguments advanced against change. It is becoming increasingly obvious that attempts to update a habit dating, perhaps, from the sixteenth century frequently result in women who look as if they were dressed exclusively at jumble sales. Habits, with their billows and belts, full sleeves and fichus, simply do not lend themselves to shortening or narrowing. The worst possible advertisements for religious life are the sisters who hack three inches off their hemlines, shorten their veils into headscarves, and wear thick cotton stockings and plastic shoes. They look underpaid and under-privileged—depressed drudges in dusty black. That they are aesthetically displeasing is not, perhaps, important except insofar as, like it or not, our society is a material one, and people are judged for better or worse by their appearances. But what such unsuccessful updating does show is a terrible timidity. They are making a token gesture which is failing, and such compromise simply points up their inability to adapt to current needs. They would do better to scrap what so clearly is not working and start again.

It is this possibility, of course, which really frightens churchmen. It is true that, fashion being what it is, almost any contemporary fashion chosen by an order today will in ten years look scarcely less archaic than the original. But it is men, not women, who shudder at "the thought of a mother superior with the latest copy of *Vogue* under her arm." It is men, not women, who growl, "If you're not careful, the sisters will all end up by looking like nurses or air hostesses." And it was a man, not a woman, who commented after talking to "liberated" sisters in Paris, as they sat in their lay clothes smoking and drinking aperitifs, that "it was as if I had encountered for the first time a maiden aunt in hot pants."

It is not difficult to find styles that will look neither flashy nor forlorn, that will not date quickly, and that will suit most wearers; the Little Sisters of Jesus in London, in their blue denim dresses with matching veils, perfectly accord to the council decree that habits should be "simple and modest, at once poor and becoming. They should meet the requirements of health and be suitable to the circumstances of time and place as well as to the service required by those who wear them."

But there does seem to be a strong case for suggesting that nuns should either stick to their original clothes, where circumstances permit, or abandon them totally. There is no obvious reason why enclosed contemplatives should, as American Carmelites have done, adopt a skirt and sweater. On the other hand, it is clearly ridiculous for nursing sisters to dress, as the Poor Servants of the Mother of God did until the beginning of the seventies, in heavy black serge, with a blue scapular and huge buttoned-on oversleeves, heavy petticoats underneath, a black veil and blinkered headdress on top, and the whole thing finished off with heavy black shoes.

Some women, having modernized to a degree, would not dream of going further. Sister Hilda Mason, a Sacred Heart nun, "couldn't go out of black and white. So much has happened to me, walking round with the veil on. People come up and ask for prayers. Sometimes I have coins pressed into my hand for the poorbox. I'm asked to put mentally deficient people off the bus at a certain street. And in Lancashire the conductors pay your fare."

Others are not interested in modernizing at all; they want to get out of the habit entirely. An English nun who abandoned it five years ago did so after thirteen years in the convent. One morning she was walking in a park when she saw a young couple embracing on a bench. As she approached, they tore themselves apart and sat with their eyes cast down in guilt. "I realized that what my clothes were saying to them was that I was a representative of God, of Christianity, and therefore had a hatred of things like this. I felt so terrible, I wanted the crocuses to go back into the ground. I—or at least my clothing—was saying that life, vitality, sexuality were dangerous and possibly dirty. That's what my *clothes* were saying, despite my personal beliefs." Her community was already discussing change. "I returned to the convent and said, 'I won't wear the habit for a minute longer.' I had a very understanding superior, who gave me a blank check. I couldn't go to the shops in my habit, so I put on some very odd old clothes which I found, and went out looking extremely queer." She took herself straight to Oxford Street, to the first shop she saw, which happened to be a department store, Bourne and Hollingsworth. "I bought a pinafore dress, an ill-fitting coat, and even worse shoes. I wanted to look inconspicuous, and ended up looking strange."

Abandoning the habit is an emotional experience. "Can you imagine

267

what I felt like," asks one sister, "when I took off all those voluminous garments? I felt so vulnerable, like some little creature that had been skinned." Others found it a relief. "It was a great revelation when I changed into ordinary clothes and people met *me* instead of a cardboard image." And "I can walk into an airport terminal," claims an American, "and not have everyone within five hundred yards know I'm a nun." Still others find it hard to remove the habit totally—like the German sister who opened the door to me wearing dungarees, a sweatshirt—and a veil.

Most nuns have encountered considerable difficulty in buying clothes, not least because of the cost. "When I saw how prices of dresses had gone up since I entered, I wouldn't touch them with a barge pole." The dilemma between the vow of poverty and the cost of maintaining a semirespectable wardrobe is solved in many cases by home dressmaking and buying at sales. The smartest-looking sister I met, an American Maryknoller in a navy and white dress with matching two-tone shoes, said the dress came from her sister and the handbag from her mother as a birthday present; the shoes were the only new item.

Individual taste provides unexpected hazards—"We're discovering now," said one superior dryly, "that some people have no taste at all" —but the majority appreciates that certain clothes are unsuitable. "I could never wear a low neckline because I'm a consecrated woman," says Eileen Gielty of Notre Dame. "And what would people say if they saw a sister in red? It's a sexy color, it does have this image. And we're not trying to attract people." Another woman, who admitted red was her favorite color, says she compromises by always having a maroon jumper.

Of course, the minute modern clothes are acceptable, that is still not the end of it. In Western society the woman who does not make use of such basic "cosmetics" as deodorants is regarded as an eccentric oddity. "If we're going to appear as ordinary women," insists Eileen Gielty, "we should at least look decent." Communities are moving toward the attitude defined by the young English Sacred Heart nun who says, "We can use discreet makeup as long as it's not to please other people but to look like everyone else." They are still very much aware of the reactions this provokes. "People throw up their hands in horror," comments a pretty young sister, "at the very idea of nuns wearing makeup. But I don't think we should live as if we were behind bars." So far, Americans are the only religious I have met who wear more than a soft lipstick and a lick of mascara; they use eyeshadow, nail polish, and perfume. They also wear jewelry and fairly dressy clothes, but with restraint. Earrings, for instance, would be worn as a "luxury" at a public event or other formal occasion.

The superior of one European order which has just decided to go into secular clothes—"I'm glad to get out of that veil, it caused so many migraines in the past"—says that at first they thought a habit would be suitable for formal occasions, like jubilees or funerals. "But then we decided that really we couldn't find anything that constituted so formal an occasion that a suit couldn't be worn." Other orders have dropped a formal habit because, like the Little Sisters, they felt it an unwarranted expense to have a white habit worn perhaps twice a year.

The real revolution is that young women entering religious life now simply do not regard the habit as essential, and they refuse to hide behind it. "They want to be entirely genuine," remarks a novice mistress, "and to them, any sort of habit is dressing up." An American in dungarees and a patchwork poncho confirms this: "You're no longer yourself. You just become 'a nun,' an artificial thing."

Many conventionally habited nuns see the new easiness of dress as unfair. "They have the best of both worlds," is the view of one woman in her fifties, "the freedom of the world and the security of the convent to return to." Others consider abandoning the habit to be nothing less than the thin end of the wedge. "When you put on secular clothes, that's one foot out straight off."

While most of the changes in religious life are greeted with relief —"We were too much of a hothouse before, too artificial"—there are women for whom they are too much, and in the wrong direction. These women see freedom to eat in public and wear pretty clothes as petty. They interpret lack of rules and irregular hours as instability. Father Edward L. Heston, Secretary-General of the Sacred Congregation for Religious and Secular Institutes, says, "You should see the stacks of mail we have from very good religious who are complaining about the excesses of renewal programs."

In the United States, a group called Consortium Perfectae Caritatis

("Association of Perfect Love") dedicates itself to trying to defend religious life against the "false ideas" of freedom which have developed. These nuns, who number about a hundred, think Vatican II has been wrongly interpreted and seek to follow the directives "more accurately." They believe that nuns should continue to wear the habit, and respect the authority of the male, and consider that too many have replaced a life of prayer with a life of action.

If Vatican II went too far for them, for others it did not go far enough. Father Andrew Greeley, an outspoken Chicago sociologist, speaks of the "tragic mistakes" that have been made in the American church since the Vatican council. This he says, "released tremendous social and intellectual forces. If these forces had been properly understood and properly channeled, there could have been tremendous creative growth."

For some orders, the new way of life has arrived with a vengeance, like the American house where, at breakfast—a meal provided by a catering company—the superior arrives in curlers to say grace: "Good food, good meat, good God; let's eat." Yet others are still suffering from uncertainty about which way they are going. One community, the Ladies of Mary, which started advocating renewal as early as 1956 from their motherhouse in Brussels, feels that "as a congregation, we're going through the doldrums. The ground has been taken from under us. There's something to replace it, but as yet it's not crystalized under people's feet."

"There is so much discouragement, so much frustration, so much despair in the American church at the present time," believes Father Andrew Greeley. Yet he believes, too, that somehow there will be a renewed religious life. "An institution which has served human needs for fifteen hundred years is not likely to vanish completely, but a heavy price will have to be paid, in terms of both wasted energy and personal suffering."

Many nuns are not sure even of that and use harsh words of themselves: "of *paralyzing* mediocrity" was the way one young sister described women's communities today. Intelligent women feel hampered by restrictions a masculine church still imposes upon them. "They don't understand," explodes Maryellen Muckenhirn, "that we have to get out of ourselves. We can't sit forever and listen to our

270

arteries harden; we have to get out of our little nunny world." Such women feel passionately that nuns should be providing a blueprint, discovering new paths, attempting to live out the kind of life other people are not free to risk. Religious orders all too often see virtue in doing what they did well in the past. There is inertia where circumstances demand change and social concern.

There are still a lot of discontented women in religious life. And change comes from discontent. Thinking sisters believe their future is in hazard. "What is happening to nuns now is what has happened to women in the last hundred years," says Sister Honor Basset. "The world is developing an attitude to women, and this is part of that development. Either we are going to be of use today or we are not, and if you have really got a call to serve God in today's world, you have to consider this very carefully.

"I think the feeling is that nuns must move forward or they will die out."

*The Church knows all the rules. But it doesn't
know what goes on in a single human heart.*
—GRAHAM GREENE, *The Heart of the Matter*

10

Can Convents Survive?

Religious life has enjoyed a largely one-way traffic in personnel
—into its convents and monasteries. Today the traffic is still mostly
one-way—but in the opposite direction.

The future of religious communities of women is threatened by
two facts: fewer and fewer girls are entering religious life; and, every
year, greater numbers of sisters are leaving.

It is a malaise that has been increasing noticeably over the last
thirty years, but it has reached dangerous proportions only since the beginning of the 1950s. Articles and books have appeared in the religious
press on the "vocation crisis" and the "sister shortage"; conferences
are held to discuss the problem; seminars are convened on "survival
strategy"; prayers are offered.

Throughout Europe and America the situation worsens. Convents
are closing as orders amalgamate understaffed houses. Schools are aban-

doned because there are not enough sisters to run them; convalescent homes are sold; hospitals are handed over to local government. The needs are still there, but the nuns are not. Small communities have chosen to band with others who follow a similar life-style; in England, for instance, the Sisters of Perpetual Adoration merged with the Religious of the Eucharist, and the Sisters of the Faithful Virgin with the Congregation of Our Lady of Fidelity. Many others, however, have simply closed down houses and retreated. Within the few years it took to assemble this book, several of the places I visited disappeared— including two schools, a home for mentally defective women, a home for disturbed adolescents, and a hostel for orphaned girls.

Communities with novitiates built to house fifty now consider themselves lucky to have five; even more communities have found themselves with none at all. As recently as 1967 the Sisters of Mercy, an Irish-founded order, expected to have forty novices at a time. In September 1972 they had nine, and four of these left within the year. The Augustinian Sister of Meaux in London attracted seven novices between 1965 and 1974, but only three remained. The American Maryknoll Sisters had nearly fifty entrants in 1962, in 1966 the number was down to twenty, and by the mid-1970s three or four were considered a respectable number; of those who enter, a larger proportion than ever is likely to drop out before reaching final profession.

Orders can chart the fall in entrants. The Carmelites remember a "tide of vocations" which started in 1905 and went on for thirty years. Every year there were dozens of ceremonies: Clothings, Professions, the giving of the black veil. Today, they too are amalgamating their small houses. The Dominican Sisters of Bethany is a Dutch order which runs foster homes for parentless girls. In 1901 it was strong enough to send twenty-three sisters to Chicago, where the order speedily acquired eight novices. In 1973 it made plans to give up its work. "We had to," said the superior. "There just weren't enough of us to do it. To look after eight girls only, we need two nuns—and we're down to six sisters." Now, the Sisters of Bethany are working individually in hospitals. "We might as well go home and do something there."

It is hard to believe that once there were so many new orders being formed that it was finally forbidden to found one unless it was based on a recognized rule. Yet the slogan for the religious life is superb: "Everyone who has left house, or brothers, or sisters, or father, or mother, or wife, or children, or lands, for my name's sake shall receive a hundredfold, and shall possess life everlasting." Why, then, do so few follow?

The reasons are many and complex, but one overrides all others: opportunity. There was no lack of entrants in the past because, often, there was no other life a single woman could decently lead. Until Florence Nightingale, even nursing was considered coarse and degrading. An unmarried lady could be a governess, if she had to earn her living, or a housekeeper, or even a dressmaker. But she had no vote, no chance to hold any kind of public post. She could do neither welfare nor administrative work unless her qualifications were exceptional, and this was unlikely, since the universities were closed to her. In Catholic countries, the same tradition that kept religion strong kept her down just as strongly. Even more recently, the possibilities open to a woman remained restricted, and the respectable unmarried girl became an old maid. There was just one way she could begin to free herself: by joining a religious community. There she could teach or work with prisoners, or in hospitals, or with deprived children. She could travel the world as a missionary. She had a busy life, was part of a loving community, and was sure of a home in her old age. At its very worst, it was a better fate than many.

But today, to be single is no longer considered pitiable; the woman living alone is as likely to be envied as not. She can spend her time how and as she wishes, tackling almost any job for which she is fitted, and she needs no veil to do so respectably. If she feels she needs a community, a group of people with whom to share her life, she can look around and find a growing number of alternatives to a convent. Quite apart from the trend toward communal living, there are groups of all shades and tones of religious belief, from Jesus freaks to lay communities. That is, of course, if she wishes to remain single. Today, 90 percent of the population in the United States and Britain, for example, can expect to be married by middle age, against 75 percent in the last century—another nail in the coffin of religious life. Yet another is the increased employment and financial prosperity in previously poor Catholic communities. The richer a country, the fewer its vocations. It is in times of crisis that there are plenty of recruits; during the

Depression years in America, there was a vocations boom. With money comes increased sophistication—and the spread of birth control. And with financial security, attitudes change. "There's very little emphasis on sacrifice in family life today," according to the superior of one affected order.

The falling off of vocations is not a fact in isolation but part of the general tide running throughout Europe against the church. Fewer people are baptized in church, fewer are married there. Attendances have fallen drastically, particularly in the last ten years. Even in Italy, the increased secularization of society has greatly affected vocations. Italy has about 160,000 nuns in its huge collection of different orders and convents, and many there have either closed or are on the brink of doing so through lack of recruits. Sister Maria Lorenzina Guidetti of the Daughters of Saint Paul says with some sadness that, in the past, "a vocation was always considered a blessing, especially in the southern regions and in Lombardy and Emilia." Those days are ending.

A French sister observes that "vocations don't seem to exist in France" and names several orders which have one or no postulants. She believes women's orders are suffering from the phase of *aggiornamento*, the rethinking and moving forward which followed Vatican II, and that uncertainty over the direction religious life is taking inhibits many girls from entering. At the end of the 1960s, a group of sociologists examined monastic life and found that in Austria, for example, contemplative communities of women were doomed to disappear soon, except for perhaps three or four convents, since out of nineteen houses, fourteen had had few or no entrants for many years. The sociologists found the same situation to be true in North America, Britain, and much of Europe. The experience of the Daughters of Charity of Saint Vincent de Paul confirms this. They have found a lowering of vocations in almost every country—with an exception, interestingly, in those countries where, because of the political situation, a nun can most expect to be persecuted by the state. The majority come from the Philippines and Yugoslavia, as well as Vietnam, Indonesia, and Japan. "Once sisters were sent out from Europe to these countries," observes Sister Agnes, secretary-general of her Paris house. "Now they're springing up there." Meanwhile, vocations continue to

275

decline in Great Britain, Germany, Holland, and Belgium. And in America, according to a superior there, "Religious life has such a bad name right now that the really live American girl who twenty-five years ago would have joined Maryknoll just wouldn't go there today."

Sisters do their best to understand and explain what is happening. They suggest all sorts of reasons, from the unhappy example of over-worked and harassed teaching sisters to the "debasing effects of mass media entertainment." Bertrande Meyers, an American sister, blames the "deplorable practice of steady dating begun in the too early teens" and the softness of American youth, while Pope Paul thinks the vow of obedience is too much for the modern young woman to take.

The majority of women are philosophical about the shortage. "I think we shall get through this," believes Anglican superior Sister Thomasina of the Sacred Passion sisters. "Once or twice before, we've had a bad patch. If we die out, it shows the work God has given us has come to an end." Sister Marissa of the Poor Servants of the Mother of God is not concerned about her postulants, although she has only two. "We live in hope. There's so much glamour for young people. But if they have a vocation they'll come, no matter about the glamour."

At the same time, they realize the necessity of catching the public eye, although they find this hard. One contemplative community re-cently took part in a television program. After much heart-searching, they allowed a whole film crew inside the enclosure—all men except the continuity girl. For two weeks their lives were disrupted, but they felt it was worthwhile for two reasons: They wanted to give the out-side world a chance to see just what a life of prayer meant, and they hoped it would attract girls to their life. The film was shown in Britain, Australia, and South Africa. The response was tremendous—they re-ceived letters, gifts, and a great deal of admiration—but not one girl came forward as a novice.

In the past, priests and nuns toured schools seeking young recruits for orders. They still visit, but now, as one vocational director put it, "We do so to persuade people to become Christians." The vocations industry has had to become increasingly high-powered, and many American orders now have a mediator or recruiter who does nothing but encourage vocations by publicizing community efforts to reach suitable people. Shortage of entrants is just as acute among men's orders, but none of the women's communities has yet reached the point of the American Trinitarians, who advertised for brothers and priests in *Playboy*. European communities concentrate on a softer sell. In Britain, for example, there is a full-time vocations director in almost every diocese. He will be a member of the National Conference of Diocesan Directors of Vocations, a body which meets only twice a year. Prayer is a far more popular method of encouraging entrants; the Vocation Sisters even organized a group of sixty to go to Lourdes and pray for them from there. In 1972, nuns from ninety-five convents gathered for a one-day "pray-in" for vocations. Five hundred of them, with guitars and the culinary assistance of the army catering corps, descended on a Surrey seminary to "dispel the everything-is-rotten-in-the-state-of-Denmark feeling conveyed by the press, reporting the drop in vocations."

Then there are "convent weekends" and working holidays, to which girls are invited to learn more about nuns, with conferences and discussions. And there are "vocations weeks," when a team of religious men and women spends mornings in a diocese, visiting the schools and the sick, and evenings celebrating mass in different houses in the parish, all in an effort to increase interest in religious life. Occasionally there are massive religious exhibitions, where perhaps a hundred different orders and societies will show films and staff booths to describe their work, while missionary fathers give concerts on native drums, and sisters model their modernized habits as "the most exclusive fashions in the world."

Despite all the doleful omens and convent closures, some new orders have begun in the last twenty years and survived. But as Mary Garson, an English psychologist who founded the Sisters of Our Lady of Grace and Compassion in 1954, says, "It is battling against the tide at the moment." She decided to look after old people, not because it was something she particularly wanted to do—she would rather work with children—but because she saw the need. Now fifty-one, she is energetic and youthful, always traveling between the motherhouse in Sussex, a Victorian folly which looks like a Bavarian schloss escaped from its native hills, and the nineteen smaller houses.

During the first few years, "people came and went. They served a purpose." It was not until 1959 that any stayed, and only two of her present sisters date from that time. There are thirty-three at the moment, and this can go up to forty. There are also four novices and two postulants. "But we could have many more in the community if we hadn't decided to become more exacting." Those who do enter come mainly in answer to advertisements. Sister Mary Garson was the first sister in Britain to advertise her order regularly in the Catholic press. "We had to do it—if you're new, nobody knows you." She finds that about two girls a month are sufficiently interested by the ads to come and try the life, and five actually enter each year. "One year they might all stay; the next they might all go." In 1973 she decided to make an extra effort to attract vocations and lay workers: in addition to going to churches and leaving literature, she visited schools with slides and made a filmstrip about the order. "But I don't feel that vocations are picking up, personally."

Now advertisements, hundreds of them, are used by almost all orders. "Come, give yourself to God," urge the Sisters of Saint Paul. "There is work for you to do in the ecumenical vineyard," claim the Swedish Bridgettines. "Searching for fulfillment?" ask the Handmaids of the Sacred Heart. "If you are courageous enough to accept the CHALLENGE of no geographical boundaries, of no limit to your dedication to Christ through Mary," write to the Marist Sisters. If, on the other hand, you feel that "Our Lord is calling you to consecrate your life to him in the service of souls by teaching, nursing, youth work, child care, housekeeping, catering, or secretarial work," then contact the Sisters of Providence. You can spread the Good News with the Dominicans, or work with Christ for the salvation of souls with the Sisters of the Convent of Saint Lucy.

The contemplatives advertise too, rather more gently. The Olivetan Benedictines welcome inquiries from "ladies wishing to try their vocation," and the Benedictines of Stanbrook Abbey, Worcester, promise "Prayer, Serenity, Wisdom."

What does seem to be happening is that more and more inquiries are coming from women in their forties and fifties. The Vocation Sisters, who pass on inquiries to suitable orders, say that the number of women in this age group has "greatly increased." Such entrants are described tactfully as "adult," rather than "late," vocations. But the orders are less than enthusiastic about them, for aging communities are already a problem. In many orders, nearly half the sisters are over sixty-five and only a tiny percentage under thirty, which bodes ill for the future. Then, too, older people find adjustment to convent life more difficult, so many orders do in fact refuse to accept entrants over forty-five. Even so, the median age of women in religion in America at this moment is fifty-five to sixty. The only reason that there are not convents full of elderly ladies is, simply, that the majority of nuns and sisters live in small working groups which disguise the problem of aging communities.

The sisters say, resignedly, that every age in history produces its own apostolates. And it is probably true that the high standards demanded of entrants now, both educationally and emotionally, have something to do with the small numbers entering.

Even in the early and most enthusiastic days of convent life, there seems to have been no shortage of literature designed to lure reluctant virgins. Herrad, twelfth-century abbess of the convent of Hohenburg in Alsace, was a painter, and in pictures and text she put together a work called *The Garden of Delights*, which begins, "Hail, cohort of Hohenburg Virgins, white as the lily," and goes on to tell of the pleasures she may expect from religious life: "Delights await you, riches are destined for you, the court of heaven proffers you countless joys. Christ prepares espousals wondrous in delights, and you may look for this prince if you preserve your chastity."

By the middle of the thirteenth century, there was much material written in English for nuns, mostly spiritual love songs with titles like "The Wooing of Our Lord." Another offering of the period was *Holy Maidenhood*, which shows signs of early women's lib; the unknown author, upholding the superiority of the free maiden over the one tied to family life, encourages girls to become nuns to escape the troubles of the world.

> And how, I ask, though it may seem odious, how does the wife stand who when she comes in hears her child scream, sees the cat at the flitch and the hound at the hide? Her cake is burning on the stone hearth, her calf is sucking up the milk, the earthen pot is overflowing into the fire, and the churl is scolding. Though it be an odious tale it ought, maiden, to deter thee more strongly from marriage, for it

279

does not seem easy to her who has tried it. Thou, happy maiden, who has fully removed thyself out of that servitude as a free daughter of God and as His Son's spouse, need not suffer anything of the kind.

Somewhat less subtle methods of approach were used to attract convent entrants in the 1960s. "The Scandal of the Nun-Runners" screamed the newspaper headlines, but it was churchmen themselves who spoke of "twentieth-century slave traffic" as they accused convents of "buying" young girls from the poverty-stricken southern Indian state of Kerala. So great was the worldwide publicity, so horrified the outcry, that the Vatican was forced to hold a public investigation. Sad to relate, the traffic appears to continue.

It seems to have begun early in 1960, when girls from parts of Asia began arriving in increasing numbers to enter European convents. The "trade" appeared to be a charitable effort to help the daughters of poor families to achieve a better standard of living and, at the same time, to assist the convents of Europe during their vocations crisis. As such, it received the blessing of many ecclesiastical authorities in India and Europe. The problem was that these girls' motives for entering were hardly religious. The majority came from families where food was scarce and the standard of living near poverty; the chance for the girls to escape to Europe and learn a foreign language and new ways was tempting. For others the convent was a way of continuing their studies when their families could not afford to support them. Still others entered because their families had no money for the dowry without which they could not marry.

In 1964, ugly rumors of the condition of these girls began to circulate. Many of them were minors—the youngest was only fourteen —and it was said that they were not becoming nuns at all but were being trained by the orders in the work they did, usually nursing or medical work, and used for menial tasks. Several had breakdowns. But the real scandal lay in the profit being made by a small number of Indian priests who supplied the girls to the European convents. The nuns paid up to $750 for each girl, which they believed went partly for plane fare and partly to the girl's parents. At the same time, the parents were also paying out money they could barely scrape together, believing they were contributing to the girls' upkeep. One priest was later said to have received what he called "donations" of over $75,000 from European convents alone, which he claimed were used to build a recruitment and training center.

The Vatican finally undertook a full-scale inquiry, and while it refuted allegations of "nun-running" it did admit defects in the recruiting system. The number of girls involved was said to be 1,571, although people who had been concerned over the girls put the figure at several thousand. However, no more girls were to be sent from India to foreign convents, and a committee was set up in 1972 to supervise the work of recruiting, training, and sending girls abroad for religious life.

There is no doubt that the convents took the girls in good faith, believing as they did that they had already professed to a vocation. Their mistake lay in their naïveté and the fact that they were simply not curious enough.

It is significant that it was nursing orders, desperate for vocations, which brought the Indian girls over. It is the active orders, in particular those teaching and nursing, which are suffering most from the lack of entrants. Over the past few years an odd pattern has developed: More and more young people seem drawn to the contemplative orders. In many cases it is these communities which have grown in numbers and strength, most notably since World War II. Mother Mary Joseph, who runs the Vocation Sisters, finds that girls say, "I want to go the whole way."

The Sisters of the Good Shepherd is an order with a wide appeal to the woman with a social conscience. "Get lost in God as a Good Shepherd sister by helping troubled teenagers, unsupported mothers, maladjusted children, alcoholics, and drug addicts." The order is active on four of the five continents and boasts over ten thousand sisters. They have, like some other congregations, their own contemplative branch, the Sisters of the Cross of the Good Shepherd; there are two thousand of them. The huge London convent, with room for thirty in the novitiate, has at present five novices and one postulant. The much smaller contemplative branch in Ascot, where there are just thirty-five sisters, also has five novices.

There is also an increasing tendency for sisters in active orders to move to contemplative houses. It was happening in sufficient numbers

281

by the early 1950s for religious women to start asking themselves whether it was a providential development or a romantic attitude of contemporary life—and for Rome to point out that the members of an active community have the means of sanctity just as do those in the contemplative life. "Stay where you are; you can be a saint in your own community."

Cardinal Suenens, more recently, has pointed out that despite their differences—contemplatives seek the love of God and salvation for the world, while active religious work through speech and the direct transmission of God—"the impulse of love is the same. The silence of one gives power to the words of the other; those on their knees give strength to those who march."

It is hard to forecast what will happen in the future. Superiors themselves are convinced that vocations will reappear. Individual orders point to an increasing intake after the slack period during the late 1960s and early 1970s, and the religious press insists that "there can be no question of decline when the quality of vocations is observably higher than it has ever been." But even if vocations reappear at the pre-Vatican II level, it is doubtful whether they will be sufficient to balance the numbers of those leaving.

Leaving the convent without permission used to be a crime punishable by excommunication, and this is still the theoretical penalty in an enclosed order. But the penalty does not seem always to have been applied—the Holy Cross nun who escaped from her Poitiers convent in the sixth century by climbing down a rope, and then regretted it, was permitted to return, the only condition being that she had to use the same rope to do so.

Today, literally thousands of nuns are leaving their convents every year. There are no accurate figures available, partly because it is not a tally anyone cares to keep, partly because it is hard to distinguish those who have actually left from those who have taken a year's leave of absence to consider their future or, as one superior put it, "are just dithering." But a conservative estimates suggests that from 1967 to 1974 more than thirty thousand women left American convents alone, while a more accurate one is likely to be that in just one year nearly ten thousand walked out. In 1975 the Vatican confirmed that the sharpest drop in the number of nuns had occurred in the United States and Canada. Its own estimate was that over the previous four years the number of Catholic nuns in the world had fallen by 24.6 percent to 609,369.

Even so, the general feeling among the church establishment in 1976 seemed to be that the departure rates were very much lower than they were a couple of years ago. One American bishop, whose Midwestern diocese contains around a thousand nuns in twenty-nine different communities, claims that the number leaving has dwindled to a trickle. Sister Luke Tobin, for twelve years superior general of the Sisters of Loretto at the Foot of the Cross, believes that the exodus "was the aftermath of World War Two." She saw a tide of enthusiastic and idealistic young women flood into convents in the fifties and early sixties and then recede, mainly between 1963 and 1969. "Basically they left because of disillusionment, a sort of second sight when they began to think they'd come in too soon and made too hasty a decision."

Leaving used to be the ultimate disgrace. "Changing your mind about religious life was absolutely unforgivable," remembers a former sister. "I had a terrible sense of failure," confesses another. But now, suggests an Anglican superior, "leaving is more common than it was, in exactly the same way divorce is more common. We're much more permissive, you know. We're not really so isolated. What goes on in the world goes on here, too." She believes that the attitude of people toward their religious vows has changed, just as in the world the attitude has altered toward the marriage vows. "The feeling of being bound by a vow has lessened. It doesn't mean the vow has any the less value; if you aim for the highest, you're bound to fail at times."

Other women echo this feeling. As an American sister put it, "It's ridiculous to talk about this once-and-for-all call to God—he may be calling you to something else." Evelyn Whitehead, a former member of the Glenmary sisters, remembers that "in the past the vows were formalized; we understood that vocation was a lifetime thing. God had called you, and to retract was to repudiate an invitation." This explains why the idea of leaving religious life used to be just about impossible. All the circumstances which conspired to put a woman into the convent—the lack of opportunity for single women, the prejudice against such women in the eyes of the world—conspired to keep her there. The result was that many women remained in convents who should not have done so. Monica Baldwin, who wrote *I Jump Over the Wall* in the 1940s, was the first woman to have left with so much publicity. She admits that she soon discovered it was not the life for her, but even a "dreadful, tragic mistake" hardly seemed sufficient reason for "backing out of what one had taken on," and so she remained in the convent for eighteen more years with that knowledge. Others stayed even longer. A Sacred Heart superior remembers "one person who really should have gone. She didn't, she stayed till her death; she just couldn't face the feeling that she'd disgraced herself."

Some remained because they could not face the repercussions on their families, and even now this is a very real problem. Many Catholic parents, happy to give their daughters to religious life, are often horror-struck when they leave. One Belgian nun described how her sister had left the convent for a year to try and decide about the life. "Our parents have a small farm; they struggled to give us an education. My mother prays desperately that she'll go back at the end of the year. The fact that here she is, almost thirty and not married, is a terrible worry to them—they were ashamed to tell the neighbors." Another woman says sadly, "When I left, it nearly killed my mother. It broke her heart." A former sister explains that "in Ireland, it is still considered a frightful disgrace, a terrible failure, for a daughter to return home from the convent. My mother didn't know how to show her face to the neighbors."

There are women who remain in their convents because of other fears. Says a superior, "It does so depend on a person's relationship with her superior. If she feels she will be understood, well and good. But suppose you've got the sort of superior who simply couldn't put herself in the situation. There could be difficulties." A woman now out of religious life believes that "many women would have left long ago, but the superior would say, 'I'm sure this is just a temptation; I'm sure you've got a vocation.' And if they did go, before Vatican Two, they were treated like traitors." But even if they did not leave, many considered doing so and freely admit it, like this Sacred Heart sister in her late seventies: "I've had one or two real crises, and sometimes I've known that if I'd had a home to return to, I might have given way." Mary Garson, founder and psychologist, says that "every religious has a very big problem at some time or other, when things are exceptionally difficult. Then she asks whether she should be there, and it's a test of whether she sticks it out or whether she doesn't—like marriage."

Before Vatican II, if a man or woman left religious life it was assumed that he or she could not live it any longer because of some personal inadequacy. Even today it is still sometimes considered—if not actually spelled out—that leaving is a form of faithlessness. Yet after Vatican II there was a dramatic increase in the numbers of those leaving. Women claimed that the opposite was true, that it was because they wanted a really religious life that they were going. "I had to leave the convent," says one such woman, "to do what I entered to do —live for others."

Some superiors feel that these women are merely reflecting the restlessness in society. "Individuals entering religious orders come from this unstable environment," says an Anglican superior, Mother Joanna of the Deaconess Community of Saint Andrew. "They themselves are bound to be influenced by it and will bring some of the causes of instability with them." Such people, she believes, expect a change of circumstances, and even of vocation. They expect, too, immediate and perfect fulfillment. There is also, she thinks, an inability to accept and use difficulties in a constructive way, which may result in a desire to escape from the religious life, "or in neuroticism which springs from prolonged repression."

In medieval days, depression, boredom, and despair were acknowledged enemies of the soul, and nuns were solemnly warned to be occupied "in profitable and honest travails" so that such emotions should be "scared away and eschewed," as the Franciscan minoresses' thirteenth-century rule explained. The melancholy and sadness peculiar to nuns even had its own name: "accidie," or acedia, as spiritual torpor was known. Teresa of Ávila knew about it and wrote a whole chapter on this "grave malady" in her *Book of the Foundations*. She believed this "subtle disease" was an instrument of Satan. "The matter is dangerous," she wrote, "and one sister in this state is enough to disquiet a monastery." She charged the prioresses to have recourse to penance; "if one month's imprisonment be not enough, let them be shut up for four; you cannot do their souls a greater service.

"Some," she wrote, "waste away in weeping. . . . It is very necessary at times to correct the peccant humours by the use of medicines to make them tolerable." Diet was important. "Care must be taken that they eat fish but rarely, and it is necessary also that they should not fast as much as the others." She apologized for "giving so much advice about this evil, and none about any other," but explained she did so because, whereas in other illnesses the patient either recovers or dies, in this case they do neither but "lose all sense, and that is a death which kills all others. They carry about within themselves a cruel death of sorrows, fancies, and scruples."

Psychologists find that today's equivalents of accidia are the psychosomatic troubles from which an increasing number of religious woman suffer. Mary Garson believes that in many cases it is a sign of rebellion, particularly common in young sisters. "In the early days, I used to come out in a rash, which was probably frustrated aggression, and I'm sure that's what Teresa of Ávila's illnesses were." The commonest example, suggests an American nun (another psychologist), is painful menstrual periods. A sister suffering these may well be pushing her yearnings for physical love and children back into her subconscious and will neither admit nor discuss them. But, at the same time, the pain is regular proof that her body is able to hold a baby, so in a way it is welcomed.

One woman who suffered from severe psychosomatic illness because of her unhappiness with convent life was diagnosed twice as having multiple sclerosis and at different times went blind in both eyes. "I could not see because I did not want to see." She left her community in 1966, a year when an estimated thirty-six hundred nuns left convents in the United States alone.

This nun, Midge Turk, can laugh about it now, but she remembers with mixed feelings how she felt when, after eighteen years as Sister Agnes Marie of the American Immaculate Heart of Mary community, she left religious life. "I hadn't any clothes and I hadn't any small talk. People would ask me, 'Have you been in prison?' " That was in the mid-sixties. Today she is college editor of *Glamour* magazine in New York, and looks every inch the part—streaky blond hair, expensive scarlet suit, modern jewelry. But the transformation was not easy.

Agnes Turk came from a devout Catholic family, and though it was never actually said by her parents, a life given to God was considered the best one possible. After high school she attended Immaculate Heart College, staffed by nuns of the community. She had a steady boyfriend; "I was not the nun type." Yet she decided she ought to enter the IHM community while she was still at college, feeling that if she did not, "I would have to live a life of agonizing penance."

At first, the life was trying for an eighteen-year-old. "I wondered if God really cared whether or not we completely stripped and remade our beds from scratch every morning." Then she found her first taste of teaching and mission life completely fulfilling and took her first vows for a year. She hesitated—and took them for the second year. Then, "I finally stopped floundering. I would be a nun, and I would try to be a good one."

By 1964 she was experiencing periods of depression and illness. One morning in 1965, she awoke to find she was blind in her right eye. It turned out to be a nervous condition and was cured. Therapy followed, but six months later the sight went in her left eye—and again was cured. This time she heeded the warning and in 1966 was granted a dispensation from her vows. She was nearly thirty-six. "I was so secure; all my friends were there. Leaving was a terrible thing, the thought of having to go out and do it all over again." She had no job, no self-confidence. "I'd had two nervous breakdowns, I couldn't keep my health, I felt I couldn't do much of anything." She went to New York and through friends landed a job in a school theater department.

She met a man and began a hectic social life, but "I could *not* tell anyone my background. I spent the first few months without telling anyone, and my friends say now they couldn't believe how anyone could be so naïve. They'd ask, 'Are you really thirty-six?'" On one occasion she sat next to comedian Alan King, one of the most televised men in America. "I said, 'And what do you do?' He asked the man who brought me where he'd found me, and I just blushed.

"A day didn't go by when I didn't make a boo-boo. I'd say a lot of wrong things. I didn't wear makeup because I was so inept with it, and I'd wash my hair and dry it in the oven and singe it." Although she still considers herself a Catholic, she does not go to church anymore. "I honestly don't have any guilt feelings."

Midge Turk finally exorcised convent life by writing a book

about it. *The Buried Life* appeared in 1971, and "the greatest therapy for me was having to think about it." It brought her considerable fame —perhaps notoriety is a better word. There was an article about her in *Time,* and a film on NBC. She appeared twice on the Dick Cavett show and was deluged with letters saying she had no business to be out enjoying herself; she should be committed to the poor and back there working for them. But not for a moment does she regret those eighteen years. She sips her martini reflectively amid the palms of the Waldorf-Astoria Hotel and says that not only did she enjoy that time, but "I wouldn't be where I am now if I hadn't done that. I'd have been married at eighteen, have five kids, and be living in the suburbs running car pools." She does not want to marry, although she has been living with the same man for several years.

Clearly, her present way of life suits her. She says with some satisfaction, "I went to Charlotte Ford's wedding party. I know a lot of big names; I consider them my friends." There is no doubt that today she is a very different person from the uncertain woman who walked out of her convent. "But when I entered, I did what I thought I had to do."

Anita Caspary, Midge Turk's mother general toward the end of her religious life, says, "We've lost a great number of creative and talented people. It isn't that they're upset; we keep in touch and they come back, help us raise funds. Like Sister Corita Kent. She's with us in spirit, but *we've* lost." Not only does the community lose women who joined during the old days, but more recent arrivals, too, "very attractive, intelligent, independent girls who have had their own cars, their trips to Europe. They've been given privileges by the community, and many have kept up strong bonds of friendship and even continue to teach for us." Anita Caspary is sure that "we have to ask, Why did the twentieth-century woman enter the religious community, particularly the more independent, the post-post-Victorian girls, especially those who came from highly affluent backgrounds? Was it the idea of a nun, built up in the Catholic home and school, that brought them in? Whatever it was, until we get at that, we won't know why they're leaving now."

For some time, religious orders have realized that the reasons given by those leaving have not been causes but symptoms. But it is only now that an attempt is being made to discover why nuns, monks, and priests abandon their vocations. In May 1972, the Pontifical Gregorian University in Rome took an unprecedented step and began a detailed study. The man in charge is a fifty-year-old Jesuit, Father Luigi Rulla, head of the university's psychology institute. The depth-analysis methods he uses were pioneered by Freud—although as recently as 1950 Catholic clergy were officially warned against practicing or submitting to Freudian psychoanalysis.

Even before the results of the study are known, some causes have been admitted. A Jesuit priest who has worked closely with many women's communities discovered to his surprise that a major factor is loneliness. "Often they are unable to communicate with their fellows at a time or in a place that makes for fellowship. Living in proximity does not make for community."

He is not the only one who thinks this way. Several novice mistresses suggest that the development of personal relationships has been neglected for too long by religious communities. They feel that the number of nuns who have to seek professional medical help confirms this view. Not only is there an increase in mental breakdowns but also, to a lesser extent, of physical ones as well. Novice mistresses put forward a lack of communication, disintegration, and isolation as some of the causes, and an Anglican novice mistress points out that once a sister becomes isolated, "the life is no longer dynamic but a gradual decay into bitterness, with nothing but a frustrated old age and a long-delayed death at the end." This exactly echoes the emotions of the woman who left in her early thirties because, as she explained to me, "Being in a convent is great when you're young. But I looked at the older sisters and started to wonder how long it would take me to become as bitter as some of them."

The conviction inside the convent that those who wish to leave are failures has given rise to harsh treatment. This is perhaps less extreme now than it was a few years ago, but it is still true that those who leave are often regarded by their sisters as pariahs. A former missionary sister (who left because she was horrified when she was allowed, during a training course, to visit a patient dying of cancer but forbidden to do so once her course was finished and she was again under strict enclosure) says, "The minute I'd asked for my dispensation, I was taken out of the school where I'd been teaching with no chance even to say good-bye to the pupils." Nor did the sisters discuss among themselves the fact that someone was leaving. Even when novices were sent home as unsuitable, the others were never given any reasons or even told that they had gone. Even the normal good-byes were not said. Margaret McConnell describes the departure as "like a slaughter at a prisoner-of-war camp. The loss was swift and unexpected, and no explanation was ever given." The leaver's last night is often still spent in a guest room well apart from her sisters.

A sister may, of course, leave her order freely if she does so at a time when she would normally have renewed her temporary vows. If she wants to go sooner, her major superior will give the necessary dispensation. Whatever the cause of her leaving, the measures which must be taken should always be carried out with "justice, charity, and kindness."

After talking to her superior, the sister who chooses to leave normally talks to the provincial of the order, who then sends for the papers. These are signed and processed, the apostolic delegate sending them to the Holy See. If the reasons are considerd sound, a "rescript" is granted and the nun is released from her vows and the obligations to religious life and restored to her secular state. The sheer machinery of extricating themselves was complicated enough to inhibit many from going. "I couldn't face all that to-do filling in forms, endless visitations." But those who stayed for such a negative reason, comments an American novice mistress, should not have been allowed to do so. "I'm not saying they were bad nuns—they weren't as keen as they should have been, and this had repercussions on the others." It could take as long as six months before the rescript arrived: three copies— for the nun, the convent, and the papal archives—declaring her "reduced to secular state." Now, however, the answer often comes inside two weeks and carries no official stigma; the recipient of a rescript is still a full member of the church and can marry in one if she wishes.

In fact, the system has changed so much that, according to Sister Honor Basset, "All sorts of *extraordinary* things are happening, which take us by surprise. I even heard of one person who decided she didn't like the people who were responsible for governing. She wrote the papers out herself, didn't tell her superior at all, and simply announced to her friends that she was going; she did it all back to front."

Despite the changes, a woman is still apt to find a huge rift between her and those who remain behind. To a degree, this is understandable. When a nun leaves it does affect the whole convent. "It leaves a sadness, a feeling that someone who's been really dear has gone. We're a family, and what happens to one happens to everyone." But more than that, it inevitably must seem to those remaining that the departing sister has found the life they are living second-best. Perhaps that is why some religious take a degree of comfort from the difficulties of those who go. "They have their little regrets," comments an American sister. And "those who have left," says another, "write and tell us how lonely they are." But some women feel genuine anger at their going: "When people left, I felt aggrieved."

This may explain the appalling difficulties many women face as they go. This was particularly true in the 1950s, when leaving was still a very unusual event. At that time, convents seemed genuinely not to know just how difficult the transition to secular life was. And they did not trouble to find out. It was not callousness, merely ignorance, a fact which can have been of little help to the nun who slept in Grand Central Station for nine nights, existing on a can of Metrecal a day, before she found help. Things have changed to a degree. In 1975 a woman of fifty-seven, a potential provincial superior, was given, on leaving, a car and "a good deal" of money. In 1971, on the other hand, a nun from Virginia was given her ticket to New York—one way—and $5. She was sixty years old. It is only within the last three or four years that convents have allowed people to stay on until they get a job and some security before leaving.

The woman leaving convent life is faced with a question of sheer survival. As one woman said, "If I could not survive here, where would I survive?" For many, the answer is all too plain—a one-room apartment, a clockwork job, and an emotional desert. But over the years, the number of nuns—and monks and priests—leaving their orders has reached such epic proportions that organizations have mushroomed to cope with their difficulties. Most are in the United States, but there are some in Britain and even in Italy. The largest of these organizations is Bearings for Reestablishment, Inc., which operates out of a brownstone on New York's East 49th Street and has a sign in the reception room: CAUTION. HUMAN BEINGS HERE. HANDLE WITH CARE.

Bearings was started in 1965 by a former priest, Bill Restivo, who wanted to fill the void into which religious fell on leaving their orders and also to give them small loans to tide them over "while they got their bearings." In those early days, Bearings provided the men and women who came to the office with food, clothing, and a place to live while they looked for work. The organization was often the only recourse for people who found themselves without friends or money and with no wish to ask their orders for help—even if it might have been forthcoming. "People used to turn up on the doorstep with a suitcase," remembers a staff member, "and say, 'Here I am, help me.'" Some of the people who came to them had been in their community twenty or thirty years, having entered straight from high school. "Half a lifetime of chastity, poverty, and obedience is no ticket to success in a competitive consumer society." Often, these people could get no references from "previous employers" and therefore had to look for the type of jobs where none were needed.

Bearings never asks the cause of leaving. "We don't want people to cry on our shoulder." It is in no sense a clinic, but helps people through the early part of what they call the "transitional process." The organization has found that men and women respond best to group therapy. "It's a quest for identity." And, although quite a lot of religious do want therapy, it is more a problem of reorientation they face than anything else. They very rarely feel bitter. In fact, says a psychiatrist, "very few have deep-seated problems—certainly no more than anyone else."

Finding work is hard. Used only to the noncompetitive religious world, unused to handling money, these "formers," as Restivo calls them, find themselves at a great disadvantage when they try to resume normal life. Then, too, they have to contend with the public image of someone who has "failed" as a religious. Bearings warns them not to hide this fact, since many "formers" have actually lost their jobs when it eventually came to light. One sister to whom this happened said she simply could not believe it. "It was as if they'd found out I was a habitual criminal." And a former priest who held a job for four months before revealing his past was then asked to leave because he was felt to be "unstable." Bearings overcomes the question partly by tact, referring to former religious as "people who have left professional church occupations," and partly by common sense; the advice they give to job hunters is full of the most basic information, such as: Go to interviews alone, be on time, do not try to show anyone that you are a swinger yet.

Their preemployment counseling gives what is so desperately needed—an idea of the sort of work the former religious might do. Bearings can advise on anything and everything, from counseling at alcoholic clinics to working in a store, an important service for people who may never before in their lives have made such a choice for themselves. Over the years, Bearings has built up a reputation among personnel officers for "good" people who are prepared to start at low salaries just to gain experience. They are single, able to move around freely, and conscientious.

Bearings reckons to see around a hundred people a month, of whom half are women, and although it is hard to be sure without accurate statistics, thinks it probably sees less than 20 percent of all the people who leave. The organization now has offices throughout the United States. Nor is it the only such organization now operating. Contact in Philadelphia and Next Step in San Francisco both do similar work, and there is clearly a need for yet more; Bearings has letters from nuns and priests as far away as India and the Philippines.

Increasingly, Bearings has found its role changing. More recently, the need for the original emergency function has slackened slightly. People are now planning their leavetakings more carefully. Many have friends who have left before them, to whom they can turn for advice; some of those contemplating leaving contact Bearings well in advance, or are advised to by their superiors, to plan properly and lessen the transition problems.

Bearings has begun to see yet another form of transition, a sort of dropping out from within. Some religious, unsatisfied with their jobs inside communities, were leaving without seeing what alternatives might be available to them within the more worldly and general framework of religious life. So Bearings received a foundation grant to start the Manhattan Career Center to counsel such people. There was, for instance, the case of a women's order obliged to close a school which was no longer economically practical. Twenty women, who had taught there for between five and twenty-five years, were without work. The Career Center ran a special counseling group for them, and they moved into child care, drug counseling, and teaching black people.

Another need which Bearings and similar organizations fulfill is social. The typical sister who uses Bearings is thirty-four years old, with a B.S. in education, part of an M.S. or M.A., and teaching experience. She is more concerned with her social life than with her career, whereas her male counterpart is career-conscious. She may want to live on her own, particularly if she is above thirty-four, because she has lived with women for years. She is usually in desperate need of a social life, and if she is lucky enough to live in or near New York, or one of the other cities with a similar organization, she can join its social club with a $2 membership. Bearings has a social director who organizes theater-going, socials, hikes, and house parties. Those who live too far away for such activities are advised by Bearings to join "community things—we suggest political clubs, chess groups." The social-club newsletter invariably contains a list of betrothals, with an asterisk for those who met through Bearings. And this pinpoints another major motive for women leaving religious orders: attitudes toward celibacy have altered radically in the religious lifetimes of many women. They entered believing genuinely that this was the way of perfection—and found themselves trapped when current thinking put forward the view that neither men nor women can develop normally and happily cut off entirely from relationships with the other sex; that man is closer to God in contact with his fellows than he is apart from them; that a life without deep personal relationships is less than complete. So religious who leave are often anxious to marry, and while it would appear that priests often have a specific person in mind, nuns rarely do.

The majority of women who leave convents do so between the ages of thirty and thirty-eight, whereas men tend to leave a few years later. This is connected very strongly with a woman's biological role. Between eighteen and twenty-two, celibacy is acceptable to most women. Adolescence is over and energies are channeled into university or some other training to make a career. It is at this time that a girl usually enters and takes her vows. Afterward, the structure of the life involves her completely. "I didn't have time to think," says a young Italian woman. "There was so much to achieve, there were so many goals to reach." Nor was there any personal romantic involvement to hasten adult sexuality, so it was often not until her late twenties or thirties or even forties, after the sister had achieved many of these goals, that she had time to think about any dissatisfaction she might feel. In any case, a healthy woman's physical sexuality is stronger at thirty than at eighteen. To cap all this, "The menopause," according to American sister-psychologist Judith Tate, "carries a very special emotional pain for the celibate woman. Not only did she never have marital love and children—but now she never can."

There are, of course, many women who leave religious life and make a great success of subsequent marriages.

Oak Avenue, Twickenham, is a neat London suburban street, and Number 60 looks trim and secure. Inside, a man is busy painting the hallway pale blue, while in the garden a sturdy three-year-old shouts and romps, and a blond woman cuddles a fat baby on her knee.

Therese McVeigh works full-time as head of the English department at a boys' school, and relishes the holidays when she can spend more time with her family. She is thirty-nine; she started her family late. But few of her friends, and none of her colleagues, know that this is because she first spent eighteen years as a nun.

Therese effectively entered at fourteen. She and her elder sister left their secondary school in Ireland to join the Good Shepherd sisters as school postulants. When they arrived at the London convent, each was handed a black dress and a black net veil.

Even at fourteen, Therese and forty-nine other young girls began to learn the rudiments of religious life: mass every morning at six thirty, meditation for half an hour every weekend, keeping silent for two hours a week. They were not watched, but a reasonable degree of perfection was expected. "The novice mistress sat by the door, and you knelt down beside her and kissed the floor and admitted what you'd done wrong, and she would give you three Hail Marys to say." The girls were treated as mature adults. "The fact that we said we had a vocation made them assume we had that kind of maturity, but we were only well-intentioned schoolgirls. They treated us as people pre-

295

pared to sacrifice ourselves, and it knocked a lot of the courage out of us."

Looking back, she feels that the worst part of those first years in the convent was that when she and her sister entered they had been promised they would return home, "so I wasn't leaving for good." In fact, she was not allowed to go home for fourteen years. "The novice mistress said it would disturb me, and my parents accepted her judgment."

At sixteen, Therese went into the novitiate. "I wasn't, at that time, very spiritual but I was beginning to absorb the atmosphere." But once she was actually teaching and living the full convent life, "I just wasn't happy. I had no deep human relationships, because nuns are expected to live for the love of God alone." She emphasizes that "it wasn't that I needed a sexual relationship. In fact, I never did feel the need for it; I was very young for my age. It was just that I didn't feel I mattered very much to anyone." By the time she was thirty-two, she was conscious that "I was getting older and I had this unfulfilled feeling. I decided to go. It was a hard decision because I had great friends, and in the convent they emphasized night and day that we had an obligation to stay. But the long littleness of life got me down."

Her reason for leaving was given as incompatibility of temperament and bad health, and in less than a week the papers were processed through Rome and she had six months' dispensation. It would be a year before she was fully dispensed from her vows, so she could try life in the world and decide whether or not to return. "I left with dignity—none of this dressing me up in frumpish clothes. The mother superior gave me a hundred and fifty pounds and took me to the station, and my sister met me at the other end with clothes she'd bought.

"I decided I would get married within a year. I couldn't see any future for myself as a single woman teacher; I felt I'd develop mannerisms and oddities. The second vocation in life is marriage, and it never occurred to me that I'd have any difficulty." She started off by going to a cosmetician in Bond Street. "They really had a go at me —plucked my eyebrows and did me up. I'd cut my hair at my sister's and it looked desperate, because for all those years I'd worn a bonnet round my face. Then I bought some clothes and gradually got used to things—I found false eyelashes helped me. Then one day a lorry tooted three times, and I knew I'd arrived." She began going to dances as the only way to meet men. "I took great risks. Not knowing the moral standards of the day, I didn't know the kind of man that was trying to pick me up, as an ordinary girl would."

She need not have worried. She had seven proposals, "which I took entirely for granted." Looking back, she feels she led people on. "But I was protected by my own innocence—and I was trying to live all my youth in two years." She had left the convent in February. In April she met the man she later married, who was teaching at the same school as herself. "I was still a nun when we met, but I wouldn't tell him," partly because he was a complete agnostic, partly because she was still fully bound by her vows. "But I thought I could get to know him without canoodling."

Therese says she is incredibly lucky in her husband. "He's a terrific husband, he really is ideal. It took me a long time to enjoy sex after marriage. You're trained to repress any thought of it, to cast it out of your mind, and so you don't come to terms with it. But my husband was delighted I was a virgin and he was marvelous." There are still odd hang-ups from the convent, attitudes that have spilled over into her married life. Food is one of them. "If you said something was nice, you were told it was very worldly to be a gourmet. And when I came out, I never said whether anything was nice or not. But my husband says I'm the worst cook in Britain, and he once went out to buy fish and chips in the middle of one of my meals. I was amazed—I expect him to eat what I put in front of him."

They hoped for children straightaway, "so there would be more richness to life," but waited three years to begin their family. Therese adores her children but admits that "I still have tremendous admiration for the religious life, and I got great fulfillment from it. It gave me a rock certainty in the existence of God and an afterlife. I've thought if I were faced with tremendous sorrow that maybe I would come to terms with it quicker. But I still feel there are parts of religious life I'd love to have kept—that tremendous friendliness in community life. If my husband died, I'd like to go back in my old age. The children are marvelous, of course, but I could hand them over; I've kept that detachment. But my husband's happiness is in my hands."

It is an unkind irony that the most liberal and forward-moving orders have lost the most members—and were the first to do so. This explains the great numbers who left communities in America's Midwest early in the 1960s. The first nun to appear in mufti on an American university campus, the theologian whose books on renewal became standard textbooks for changing communities, Corita Kent of the startling lithographs—these are the women who have left their orders. At a time when the church has in many ways never been so exciting, never offered so many possibilities to its sisters, never been so free, so open to ideas, the women who leave are some of the best and most adventurous. Recently Bearings and Next Step, as well as Human Resource Developers—a private consultant firm that places former American priests—have noted the increasingly high caliber of those going. A growing number have left after holding positions of authority, and records show them to be even better qualified and more creative than their predecessors.

These women are leaving because they find the change too great. *Aggiornamento* brought with it uncertainty and restlessness, and this lack of clarity about the life and what it is meant to be has not yet resolved itself. In the mid-1960s, after their chapter discussed and planned change, over one hundred Italian Daughters of Saint Paul left —out of three thousand. As an American put it, "The women religious I see are adapting and adapting and adapting until there's nothing left."

It does happen that changes within a community drive out members who would otherwise not have dreamed of leaving. One young American, a former Glenmary sister, was "really happy" as a nun; "I might well have been a mother general when I was forty." But her order disagreed with the hierarchy over the increasingly restricted life they were forced to lead. First she joined their noncanonical splinter group, FOCIS, which continued to work among the poor of Appalachia and accepted married couples and non-Catholics as members; eventually, she broke away completely.

Dr. Corinne Hart was an Immaculate Heart of Mary sister in Los Angeles who went with the group which became noncanonical. After nearly three years, she decided to leave altogether. Now in her forties, she had spent most of her life in the order, but says, "What's holding us together is the past. For me, I have no sense of what the future is for this group. I don't see the vision of ours working any more; there is nothing I can do as an Immaculate Heart that I couldn't do as an individual." Dr. Hart is a businesslike, slightly brusque woman who works in Los Angeles at the Franciscan Communications Center, making religious films. She lives in one room over a garage, "and it's lovely to get home alone." Even while she feels that "it was security and not wanting to hurt the older sisters that kept me this long," she deeply regrets the final step. For her, there was real pride in being an IHM. "But now I find the freedom of life-style we're experiencing incompatible with maintaining an institution."

Others go because the changes are not enough, and they feel their communities have not taken the cultural leap that is necessary for survival. They see religious life as irrelevant to the church today, an anachronism surviving into the twentieth century by virtue of tradition and reverence rather than need. Some, like Reverend Mother Mary Clare, mother general of the Anglican order of the Sisters of the Love of God, find this not only understandable but blame the community, which they believe is responsible for the loss. She sees genuine cause for frustration in "conditions which are outdated or outmoded" and in regulations which deny nuns "right and proper channels for growth in initiative and responsibility." Women who find their ideas in conflict with those of their community very occasionally move to an order they find more congenial. But most of these seem to find it hard to adapt to their new order.

It is far more common for dissatisfied sisters to leave. One sister now planning this step has no idea where she will go or what she will do, "but it's no longer possible for me to live and work in such an intransigent structure." Another found that "it wasn't a place where I could function, so I moved on." A third insists that her leaving "wasn't a question of turning my back on Christ; I simply had to have the freedom to make mistakes." And a fourth felt, "I'd given up my freedom. I just woke up and said, I can't take any more." Some rationalize their feelings even further and admit they left because they could no longer stand living in a male-dominated society. This is true mainly of American women like Maryellen Muckenhirn. "I left because I could no longer go on with women who wanted to continue being put upon by men—and foreign men at that—who don't understand our life-style at all." Ms. Muckenhirn is in her early fifties and now teaches philosophy of religion at Chicago's Marillac College. "I was twenty when I entered and I loved it: I never had an unhappy day, and I was in the community for twenty-three years." She believes she was really suited for religious life. "I just wanted to teach and read; I wasn't interested in clothes and marriage." But over the years she became conscious that she was with "a very conservative group." For a long time this did not matter, since she was always on her own within the community because of her work; "I've never lived in convents." Finally, she became aware that "if you change and develop and alter your ideas, you suddenly find you're not acceptable." And when she left at forty-three, she realized that "I had outgrown the life."

Maryellen Muckenhirn feels neither regret nor guilt at leaving Sister Charles Borromeo so far behind her, and when she receives letters asking if she plans to start a new community, "I go up the wall. To gather together with a group of middle-aged women? I don't *want* to." What she does want is "to live like a free human being. I'm interested in trying to really shake off the convent."

Ms. Muckenhirn did so by leaving. But even those who remain are beginning to agitate for the end of dependence on the physical institutions of convents. As Sister Lillanna Kopp, the American sociologist and author, insists, "Marble motherhouses are what destroyed the old orders." The feeling now is that massive convents, as much as the way of life within them, provide artificial insulation against the harsh realities of the world.

Growing numbers of nuns, like radicals throughout the church, are highly critical of the wealth of that church. They dislike being women of property despite their vows of poverty. They see it as scandalous that they live in half-empty convents while the homeless sleep in doorways. One young English sister who raised this issue with her superiors was accused of "wanting to lower our standards" and told, "We must preserve our calm and our interior life." She sees such talk as a sign of spiritual bankruptcy and considers that the standards are middle-class rather than Christian. This woman, like so many others, sees the church caught in the grip of wealth when she believes the sisters should be "prophetesses, instigators, an advance guard calling the people on." And a young American, a Sister of Saint Joseph of Carondelet, insists "we must rekindle the church. And we won't do it by living in big houses with the rich." Another American nun has even suggested that new institutes should write "self-destruct" clauses into their constitutions so they would have to start again every twenty or thirty years, thus avoiding a "shoring up of possessions." Even the most successful of the "old" orders acknowledge now that change must come. Honor Basset, a superior in the Sacred Heart order, believes that "we are at a transition stage where many things are forcing a new type of religious out, and it hasn't come yet." She feels that "something quite new will emerge and sweep the field for a time—I can feel it coming. I can see a stage where religious orders become more like regiments in an army, each regiment with its own characteristics and its own spirit and so on, but all doing more or less the same work."

Certainly, the most interesting new communities are not growing up in the old way. In the past, a community would take on some particular task—hospitals, schools, perhaps houses in slum areas. Now there is a totally different approach. In a world of increasing knowledge the specialist is king, and as religious women are leaving their houses to follow their own interests and work while remaining part of the community, they are getting together with people of similar interests to work jointly on projects. As early as the winter of 1961 a group of nuns from Chicago decided they must coordinate their resources to meet the needs of the people. They called themselves the Urban Apostolate of Sisters, and more than eight hundred from five areas joined to work for education, communication, and action, assisting white, Spanish, and Negro communities. They were so successful that a similar inner-city venture, Caritas House, was started in Washington, concentrating more heavily on basic education for families.

Such projects have had the effect of radically changing the concept of community. "Community" used to be something ready-made into which the entrant walked; she was expected to be a sister not in any way singular or different from the others. Community was seen in geographical terms: everyone in the same place at the same time—in chapel, in the community room, in refectory. But so greatly has this sense of community lessened that it is not so much the sisters of an individual order which constitute community as a particular work or

301

cause. Sisters are realizing, as Eileen Gielty of the Sisters of Notre Dame of Namur says, that "community is the sense of belonging, doing what you do with the strength and support that comes from belonging to that group." Thus to an American sister student spending the summer with a health group for itinerant farm workers, community "is the sisters I am living with."

Nuns are now beginning to talk of members of various communities joining permanently to form centers where some particular work would be pursued. Such groups would be like enough in taste and temperament to be able to work and live together on a semipermanent basis, with no such thing as a Dominican, a Franciscan, or a Maryknoll; they would all be part of a single Christian community.

One such project is already under way: In September 1973 the World Justice and Peace office opened on North Third Street in Milwaukee, Wisconsin. "This will be a model for intercommunity action," promises Pat Drydyk, a dark and gentle girl and one of the first members. There are eight other sisters from five different communities working with her, and "when we work together," claims Pat, "there's a beautiful interaction. This is the first place I've worked where the impetus really comes from everybody."

Pat Drydyk is a Franciscan sister. Her order specializes in teaching at high school level and working with retarded children, a field in which they are pioneers. Until she started this project, Pat worked at the Franciscan Communications Center in Los Angeles, making films primarily for children. She did a series on the prophets of today, "and I interviewed Cesar Chavez of the Mexican field laborers. Until that time I had been an armchair liberal; this was the first time I had a real desire to become involved in their perseverance and their warmth. I felt it really put us to shame as religious." It was an emotion that was to change her life. Within a year she had got together with the eight other nuns, all equally anxious to do something "revolutionary." Their first move was to gather together a hundred "key" Americans, including two leading nuns, Sister Margaret Ellen Traxler of NCAN, the National Coalition of American Nuns, and Sister Luke Tobin, of the Sisters of Loretto at the Foot of the Cross, and take them in a chartered plane to the Coachella Valley, where they joined the picket lines against the Teamsters. The Justice and Peace team spend much of their time doing research into social injustice such as poverty and discrimination, and organizing their own communities to take the most effective action.

Pat long ago moved away from regular convent life and in Los Angeles shared an apartment with a Victory Knoll sister. In Milwaukee she lives with ten other sisters in a group ranging in number from twenty-five to sixty-five, but she feels this is too large and hopes soon to move into a smaller group, preferably composed of the people with whom she works. This could mean sharing a community life with sisters from different orders, with varying constitutions and life-styles. "It's not community in the sense of a structured setting," she admits, "but it's community for me." She believes it unlikely that the present convent system will be around in twenty years. "It may evolve into a more open structure that would allow for different kinds of life-style."

Like all the other women I met living away from their communities, Pat is anxious not to cut herself off in any way. When she was working in Los Angeles she telephoned regularly and exchanged long letters, just as would the member of any close family. And she does in fact worry that, as increasing numbers of young women work away from their communities—and this is happening in such numbers that many orders have now opened their own personnel offices to help the sisters find suitable jobs—the older sisters must do without the young and enthusiastic workers. What is more, it is unlikely that, having worked outside the structure, they will ever again want to take up the old ways, however softened they may be by Vatican II and progress. Pat feels that "the question is, not can convents afford to send sisters out but can they afford not to? They saw my moving out as an enriching experience for me in the community. They backed me completely in my decision. They said, If it's the right decision for you, it's right for the community." And she does feel strongly that "you can't expect people to sit in one place and still do creative work."

Many European communities for whom such moves are still unthinkable are undertaking experiments which are nevertheless radical in their terms, and which they hope will help define for them the pattern of the future.

In the polished entrance hall of a large girls' boarding school on a leafy road near Tunbridge Wells, an elderly nun, stooped in her black and white, sits in a small reception booth. A tousled girl in jeans and a baggy sweater dashes in, jangling car keys. They smile at each other. "Hello, Sister." Both women are members of the Society of the Sacred Heart. Although they live in the same house, they each have a different superior, separate living quarters, and a totally different life-style. They are involved in an experiment which they believe will help their order develop in the best way possible.

It began in the summer of 1971, when Sister Honor Basset was superior of the house. The time had come to plan renewal, but it was hard to know in which direction to go. The problem was that the community fell naturally into two halves: the younger sisters, active in teaching, with their lives before them, and the considerable number of older women.

After much discussion they decided to form two groups, divided more or less on an age basis, which meant that the younger people had both their youth and involvement in their work in common. The older community of eighteen took the name Wells ("because still waters run deep"), and Honor Basset continued as superior. Life there now goes on much as it always did. Many are still in the full habit, though others, like Sister Basset, wear the optional dark suit and white blouse, with a short veil. The formal hours of prayer—though these have been amended in recent years—continue in the tranquil chapel. Once strictly enclosed, the nuns now go out, though still not casually.

The younger group of thirteen has become Bridge ("they're the bridge to the new"), and chose as superior Sister Russell, headmistress of the school, though she insists that "we have yet to work out the role of superior." Their life-style has changed drastically.

The older sisters find the breakaway group easier to understand than do the middle-aged. Mother Stuart is in her eighties, a frail, bedridden woman. "The younger people are moving away from our form of life. Nothing we can do will stop it. I feel that something very good and new will emerge. It may not be what we knew when we were young—but I'm not frightened." On the other hand, Sister Hilda Mason, a teacher in her early forties, decided to stay with the older group. "I would hate to see religious life split into generations."

She regrets the split deeply. "We were one family and now we're torn in two." She finds that "being organized is very satisfactory. Also I like silence; I think it's strengthening." She sees good in both methods but is convinced that "if it went further and we went into little houses, I'd apply to the bishops and join an order who've kept big houses. I think a community based on compatibility is asking for the moon." But Sister Honor Basset sees no alternative. "At the moment, we let people have what they feel they need, knowing it won't be going on forever. One knows that with another generation there won't be many of the things we're used to—the living will change."

Certainly for the Bridge community, the rigidity that characterized the life of their order until so recently has gone. Sister Russell is particularly conscious that "the young lay tremendous stress on reality. Any custom that is artificial, they ask, Why keep it?" They wear the clothes they choose, putting on pants or sweaters and skirts. They can use discreet makeup and curl their hair. They play tennis and swim in the grounds, and in the summer they go hosteling with the children in their care. They do not go to the movies, not because they are not allowed to but because it costs more than they can afford. All decisions are made as a group. But perhaps the most important change in the little Bridge group is that previously the concept of community was strictly tied to the order of day—rising at 5:20, doing everything by the clock, retiring at 10:10. Work was not the prime thing; the life was. Now their work in the school is a far stronger link between them. They go to bed when they feel like it; they take walks when they choose to. In fact, they are no more restricted than most teachers in boarding schools. In the eyes of the Wells community, their greatest change is in the way they pray. Some days they join the Wells community in chapel; at other times they group in their crowded community room. Someone reads from the scriptures, and they might sing a psalm; then, after minutes of silent prayer, they will speak rather like Quakers at meeting. This, to some of the older sisters, is anathema.

Whatever the outside reaction to their community, the Bridge sisters believe that "unless we have a change in our community life, there'll be no future in the twenty-first century, because young people of caliber won't enter. You're looking for something, either in marriage or convent life, where you can continue to grow. One wants that situation which makes a more complete human being." These Sacred Heart sisters are taking what they hope will be a successful path to complete renewal.

In the United States, changes within the old community structures are seen mostly in orders like this, particularly those located in the Midwest. The traditional family-shaped convent has to accept the new urban life with its stresses and problems, its speed and facelessness. Those orders which have not adapted have either disappeared or shrunk to the point where they will soon do so. "The end of many smaller institutes is in sight," warns American psychologist Sister Annette Walters, "a chilling reminder that what God has given he could also take away."

There is, however, a countermovement: From about 1960, groups with a new concept began to spring up. They multiplied rapidly after the impetus of Vatican II, and now a regular yearly register is sent out to incorporate information about them. At least a hundred of these little experimental communities have appeared in America alone, though some disperse when their members decide they would prefer marriage or careers as secular single women. Despite this evidence of attrition, there are well over fifty flourishing at any one time, some with a membership of three hundred or so women. Most of them are not subject to the Sacred Congregation for Religious and Secular Institutes, since they are too small—some have only three members. Nor are they bound by special promises of obedience to any bishop, though most are formed with the approval of their local bishop. They are operating in quite a different way from the old communities, virtually as lay groups in a commune situation: sharing a home, dividing duties, regarding their income as common to all. There are no plans to claim for them official recognition; this would, they think, merely hamper their work. They are constantly changing and evolving, but the members are no less dedicated than the religious of the formal structures which were found so deadening. Their aim is to follow the spirit of Vatican II, and they feel that to do this they must bypass the outdated rules and antiquated customs that still govern so many sisters. Many of them, in fact, are actually women who have left religious communities after many years of devoted work.

The largest of these groups was founded in 1970 by Lillanna Kopp of Portland, Oregon, to "experiment and pioneer new forms of religious life for the twenty-first century." Sisters for a Christian Community (SFCC) covers thirty-two of the United States as well as Canada and England. There is no mother general, no motherhouse. Each sister makes her own home, which she might share with one or two other members. She chooses her own work, pays her own taxes. No formal vows are taken, but she will write her own commitment to Christ. She need wear no habit, but she will probably, like Sister Kopp, wear a crucifix. Other groups are tiny, like the Fides community of San Jose, California, where five sisters of Notre Dame of Namur decided, in 1966, that they should explore a life more suited to the needs of a contemporary church. Their work is wide-ranging, from giving theology courses at the local college to helping overworked young mothers; the parish of Saint Teresa pays them a salary. And in Nanaimo, Canada, live five former religious in a little house on Newcastle Avenue. This group is headed by Margaret Rowe, the Carmelite who spoke out from her Welsh convent against the male hierarchy and who left her order shortly afterward. She is now conducting what is really a three-year experiment in contemplative living in the modern world, trying out private and communal prayer, coresponsibility, and shared decision-making. The group earns its own living and undertakes voluntary work for the Department of Indian Affairs and the mental health organization, visiting the lonely and neglected people not reached by official charities.

Many groups are solely for former religious—the Society of Mary Immaculate in New York, for instance, which does not ask members to leave their homes to join; the Sisters of Mount Thabor in Detroit, who are contemplatives, living in a convent they leave only when necessary. Others combine lay and religious, like the Contemplatives of the Sacred Heart, founded in 1964 by Madeleine O'Connell, who went straight into a convent from high school at seventeen and left in her mid-thirties. One other member of her group is a former religious; the rest are college girls and factory workers, hospital attendants and lawyers, dancing teachers and hotel maids. The purpose of the group is to help its members live a contemplative life in the world, and while they are expected to work for at least four hours a day, beyond that they do not leave the house in Kingston, New York, except to do charitable work. They will accept people who would not qualify for other communities—those with minor nervous ailments or heart trouble, for instance—and everyone is expected to observe chastity and obedience, although the vows are "a personal affair."

What these groups are doing is blurring even further the already fine distinction between religious communities and secular institutes, whose members may observe poverty, chastity, and obedience but who remain lay people. It is the secular institutes which many see as an alternative to the traditional religious life, which, they consider, has outlived its raison d'être. Even Cardinal Suenens has conceded that there is a feeling that secular institutes are better fitted for modern life than traditional convents. As Honor Basset admits, "Many young people today feel they can do more good outside than they could in a convent," although she does feel this is because "they don't understand the wonderful experience of living closely with people who are all contemplating God."

The best known of the Protestant communes is German. Imshausen was founded in the 1930s by Vera von Trott as a shelter for orphans and refugees and has developed into a stable community of ten women and five men who live in the ancestral home of the von Trotts under the monastic vows of poverty, chastity, and obedience. From all over the world visitors come to them, not only lay people but professed religious. Some stay briefly; others spend months with the community.

That lay apostolates attract people in the numbers they do proves the need for the kind of commitment they ask. The major difference between them and religious communities does not any longer lie in the style of life they adopt: both wear secular dress, neither need live in a formal community setting, both observe chastity. But it is here that the crux of the matter lies. Nuns once past their temporary vows promise chastity for life; lay people promise celibacy only for the time they are with their group. And while with many this does indeed cover a lifetime, it need not do so.

It is beginning to look as though the attitude of the church toward chastity—that the consecrated virgin, the woman in vows, is set apart and her every act made sacred because of that consecration—might eventually change. Fewer men or women are prepared to put themselves for life into a condition of celibacy. But they may be happy to experience this state for several years, as shown by the number of those leaving the priesthood and the convent for marriage, and also by the increasing number of older married couples who seem interested in entering religious life after their children are grown. Indeed, Rome itself has spoken of the possibility of a community of such couples in Italy.

Michael and Jane are in their early thirties and teach in the theology department of a large American university. When they met she was a Glenmary sister and he a seminarian. When their dating became obvious to the authorities, Michael was asked to leave his order, Jane left hers, and they married. Both regret what they see as their forced departure from religious life and plan to form the nucleus of an experimental community. Both think that virginity should be regarded differently by the church: "A dimension of a task, rather than a lifetime decision, so that the church could ask that, to be a religious now, you be celibate for the kingdom." They see a short-term vocation as a perfectly logical and workable proposition, whereby a person could spend perhaps ten years in full-time dedication in "a work-related temporary life situation. Then at, say, thirty you could turn to something else." It is this short-term vocation that they want to see become an acceptable part of religious life.

Established religious orders, or their individual branches, are coming more and more to see that some of their communities may be made up of lay people who join them with a limited commitment—not limited emotionally but by availability. Such people would not be sisters but members of the community for as long as they choose while carrying on their own lives. It is a totally new concept of community, and one which may be the pattern of the future, as more and more adventurous groups fully accept people who are bound to them not by vows but by a moral contract.

Some of these, as we have seen, are noncanonical—the Californian IHMs, for instance, and the former Glenmary sisters whose splinter group accepts married couples and non-Catholic members. Yet conventional orders have also taken this step. The Servants of Mary in Ladysmith, Wisconsin, have made some changes to encourage the personal growth of their sisters, such as allowing them to choose their own clothes and assignments. They followed this up by reopening the community to those sisters who had left before such changes were made. At the same time, they decided to allow members of other orders to join them—and as a final touch ruled that outsiders may join the order for a limited time.

Other groups are attempting change within the church structure. In a Dominican monastery of pinkish stone at Sainte-Baume, in Provence, live several Dominican priests, a group of contemplative Dominican nuns—and five married couples with ten children between them. Father Maillard, the priest in charge, explains that the idea is that the community should "enlarge horizons" for its members. The lay people, he explains, "have come with a desire for spiritual renewal. They no longer felt at ease in the traditional forms of the church, and they saw coming here as a means of going forward."

The community decides together who they will accept. Anyone wishing to join to resolve personal problems would be rejected. "Psychological balance and a stable married life are necessary qualifications." The couples include an American dancer and his wife and their small daughter, who was born at Sainte-Baume; an engineer, who directs the retreat center with his wife; a former mechanic on a transatlantic liner, who handles all the community's maintenance work, and his family; and the former director of a metalworks, with his wife and child, who manages a guesthouse which accommodates more than 200 people. For the community maintains a cultural and spiritual center where groups come for discussions on anything from psychology and sociology to religion, and to take part in all sorts of activities—painting, Yoga, ceramics. There are retreats, weekends of reflection, handwork sessions, and amateur dramatics.

The priests, nuns, and married couples live in separate quarters, and their evenings are "family" occasions, but they all eat together at midday with any guests who might be visiting them. There is a common treasury, and all goods and decisions are shared. The whole community is present for daily mass, though other parts of the Divine Office are recited by the priests and nuns. "In this way we want to create a true community."

One experiment, which has been violently criticized by Rome, still continues in a small abbey in the rich lands of Britanny's Côtes-du-Nord. Boquen consists of a twelfth-century church, a monastic house, and a few farm buildings—the classic Cistercian setup. But the half-dozen brothers there have abandoned almost all the traditional forms of Cistercian life. They have left off their monastic robes and no longer observe monastic silence in special places or at special times, and they have opened the monastery to all who wish to enter. At the gate, a notice invites anyone who passes to share their quest for truth and unity in brotherly love, and by this they do not mean a chance to walk around or join an occasional service. These brothers of Boquen have opened their whole community life to outsiders.

The community consists of up to sixty people, men and women of all nationalities. Many are themselves religious, of different communities. Others are lay people, single and married. They go to share the heavy Breton bread of the brothers, not only in the refectory but in the Eucharist. They work in the house and garden, help with the meals, join discussions every evening, and use the primitive dormitory accommodations for visitors. Some live permanently with the brotherhood. Others are attached more loosely, living away from Boquen to carry on their professional lives but spending free time there and taking on responsibilities.

This—by Cistercian standards—incredible situation has been going on since 1966. It began with Dom Alexis Presse, an extraordinary man who felt, after being abbot of La Trappe, that a more primitive and simple monastic life should be the aim. He founded Boquen on stones razed by the French revolution, but having established a community there he felt it was not enough to return to the original austere spirit of the order. "We have either to vegetate or adapt," he told his ten brothers, and the successor he appointed, Dom Bernard Besret, created the new community. A Breton in his mid-thirties, a doctor of theology and professor of philosophy, he was involved in Vatican II as an expert on religious life. He believed the isolated monastic life was a contradiction of what Christianity should be; that everyone should be the same; that barriers of sex, age, and condition were artificial. His experiment at Boquen was regarded with deep suspicion by the superiors in Rome, and he was eventually deposed. But so many thousands of people—friends, students, Frenchmen, and foreigners—flocked to the monastery, to attend the last service he would give there and to pay tribute to his inspiration, that six months later Rome

311

was forced to acknowledge the feeling for him and allow him to return, though as monk, not prior. Boquen has shown what can be done with the most rigid of structures, and perhaps it will still become, as one sister involved puts it, "the center of a critical, lyrical, and political Christianity."

All these rethought forms of community life—the admittance of lay and married people, the mixing of orders within one group, the new double communities—are appearing as viable alternatives to the formal religious order. The only orders not affected are the established contemplatives. It is surely inconceivable that the Cistercians and the Carmelites, the Benedictines and the Poor Clares, will ever change. They are too entrenched, they have survived too much. The basic essentials of contemplative life are as relevant today as they have ever been; prayer is timeless; there will always be those enviable fanatics for whom only complete immolation is enough. Even then, contemplatives make up only 6 percent of all nuns.

The other survivors of the present orders will be those active communities which have moved into vital work and found a life-style to match. Mother Teresa and her Missionaries of Charity, the Good Shepherd sisters, the Maryknolls, the Daughters of Charity of Saint Vincent de Paul—if their intake is smaller than it was, it is still there. Their work is geared totally to present needs: poverty, delinquency, nursing, developing underprivileged areas. They deserve success.

But there are many thousands of sisters who fit into neither category. They are those who believe that formal, institutionalized religious life will cease to matter once the present generation of sisters in it disappears. The young are not interested in institutions, and anyway, as one American sister points out, "Religious institutes are means, not ends."

It is becoming increasingly difficult to define the borderline between Christian laywomen dedicating their lives to others and those sisters who, to all intents and purposes, live and behave in a similar way. These nuns do not lead a formal religious life in any sense. They pray when they want to, dress as they choose. They tend to live away from their communities and work with people who may or may not be members of religious orders.

If nuns are to survive in any large numbers, these new groups which are springing up—small, autonomous, without written constitutions or even figures of authority—must be allowed to live and work as they wish with the recognition of the church. They must be allowed to exist officially as part of the religious life.

Before that happens, there will have to be radical rethinking by the churches. How will they define a nun? Should the vow of chastity be the criterion? But celibacy is already a feature of the lay communities. What of stability, another formerly essential qualification? Surely, in our fluid society, this will have to be demoted. There will have to be an acceptance among churchmen—and churchwomen—that where the old ways do not have the strength to survive it is better to allow change than to permit decay and disappearance. This cannot be a slow process; if the churches do not move fast, they need not bother to move at all. They may count time in hundreds rather than tens of years, but the women in religious orders do not. Too many of them have been lost to religious life already. There just isn't any more time.

*We come to the monastery to seek God—and
death is the shortest route to him.*

—CISTERCIAN NUN

Requiem

The life of a nun is dedicated to God, not for reward in this
life but in the next. It is a preparation and a waiting for death, and
though the nuns know there will be purgatory, they know too that,
like life, it is part of the redemptive work of Christ. "Unless we are
helping in the redemption, there are no bigger fools than we."

It has been said that when a nun dies it is like breaking a pane of
glass: You put in another. But the knowledge of the life to come does
not preserve these women from sorrow for those they have lost, does
not in any way lessen their mourning. Yet the ceremonial is joyful,
as the early Christian burials were joyful. There is no death. Only a
change of worlds.

In the Cistercian monastery of the Holy Cross of Our Lady of
La Trappe in Dorset, when death approaches a nun, a wooden rattle
is rung in the cloister, the signal for the commencement of ritual

almost unchanged since 1098, for the Cistercians of the Strict Observance follow the most primitive form of monastic life in the Western church.

All who can, answer that call, hurrying to kneel in the infirmary for the anointing by the chaplain, for the responses and the psalms. When they have prayed for the saints to intercede for her soul, when the priest has summoned and the last prayers have been said, when the end has finally come, the body is left quiet for an hour so that the soul may go gently. At the foot of the bed the great Paschal candle, Christian symbol of eternal light, burns in its wooden holder.

Then the infirmarian washes the body and clothes the dead nun in her habit: black scapular over white cowl, rough stockings and handmade sandals. From the garden one of the nuns brings fresh flowers woven into a crown, for "this is part of life."

When the dead woman is dressed and ready, six of the nuns carry her down to where the priest with his incense burner receives the body. In procession after the juniors, and followed by the priest, she is borne into the church and placed on the white-sheeted bier facing the altar. She will not be left alone before her God. In their stalls by her side, two nuns recite psalms through the rest of the day and on through the next night without cessation, while the Paschal candle flickers at her head.

Next afternoon, the community assembles to sing the requiem mass; then she is carried through the cloister by the nuns singing a somber Gregorian chant. Through the garden of the abbey she goes for the last time, to the private walled cemetery where even in death the nuns keep their enclosure. She is laid beside the grave dug by the lay brother, and the nuns stand in two choirs on either side as the priest blesses the place and hallows it with incense.

Then the sisters, three and three, lower her carefully into the grave, supported on wide bands of linen. For Cistercians lie uncovered in the earth, buried without a coffin.

And before the last service they will perform for their sister, before two nuns start to drop soil softly onto her still body, before they return to the church to sing for her the psalms of penance, all kneel. They bow to the ground and touch it with their knuckles as only Cistercians do. And three times they beg that God may have

315

mercy on her soul, their voices rising in that most plaintive and poignant chant of the church:

Domine miserere super peccatrice.

Domine miserere super peccatrice.

Domine miserere super peccatrice.

Index

317

Gregory I, Pope, 114
Guidetti, Sister Maria Lorenzina, 66, 275
Guinness, Father Jack, 129
Guthrie, Sister Mary Anne, 164

Habits worn by nuns, 27, 93, 256–63 *passim*, 265, 266, 269, 270
Haircutting ceremony, 92–93
Handmaids of the Sacred Heart, 278
Hannon, Sister Rita, 79–80, 83, 116
Hart, Dr. Corinne, 298–99
Headdress, 263, 264
Hebblethwaite, Peter, 233
Hedwig, Saint, 106
Heenan, John Cardinal, 32, 148
Héloïse, 60
Helpers of the Holy Souls, Society of, 48, 110, 134, 139
Henry I (King of England), 143
Henry VIII (King of England), 215, 247
Herford (Germany), 166
Herrad, Abbess (convent of Hohenburg in Alsace), 279
Heston, Father Edward L., 269
Hilda, Abbess (at Hartlepool and Whitby), 58, 141
Hildegard ("Sybil of the Rhine"), 166–67
Hinduism, 113
Holy Child Jesus, Society of the, 107
Holy Cross, Sisters of the, 199, 213
Holy Cross Abbey (Dorset), 48
Holy Cross at Notre Dame, Sisters of the, 122
Holy Cross of Our Lady of La Trappe (Dorset), 314–16
Holy Family of Louisiana, Sisters of the, 86
Holy Maidenhood, 279
Holy Mary, Visitation of, Order of the, 112, 117, 167
Holy See, 20, 33, 42, 55, 64, 95, 96, 134, 141, 143, 149, 166, 228, 250, 252, 290
Hong Kong, 194, 195, 198
Hopkins, Gerard Manley, 229
Hulme, Kathryn, 229
Human Resource Developers, 298
Humiliata, Mother Mary, 115, 151, 152, 153, 154, 288
Humility of Mary, Sisters of the, 120, 163, 207, 264
Hundred Years' War, 217
Hunt, James Henry Leigh, 230

Hyzy, Sister Anne, 104, 116, 136

I Jump Over the Wall (Baldwin), 225, 284
Ignatius, Saint, 114
Image of nuns: building, 209, 210, 211, 232; distorted in films and plays, 227–28
Imelda, Mother (Carmelites), 24, 37, 38, 39, 40, 52
Immaculate Heart Community, 153, 298
Immaculate Heart of Mary (IHM), 69, 86, 115, 124, 125, 130, 149–50, 151, 152, 230, 262, 263, 265, 287, 299
Imshausen (Germany), 308
In This House of Brede (Godden), 229
India, 181, 183, 184, 198, 202, 203, 204, 205, 280, 281, 293
Indians, American, 182
Indonesia, 181, 183, 189, 275
Indo-Pakistani war (1971), 203
Initiation rites and rituals, 73–99 *passim;* and receiving new names, 75–76
Inquisition, 40
Institute of the Blessed Virgin Mary, 144
Institute of the Sisters of Notre Dame (Namur), 53, 244, 261, 301–2, 307
International Congress of Religious (1950), 241
Ireland, 52, 107, 126, 205, 217, 284
Israel, 189
Italy, 52, 60, 93, 107, 166, 188, 194, 254, 309, 375

Jacinta, Sister (Tanzanian Sisters of Saint Therese), 192
Japan, 67, 181, 197, 275
Javouhey, Mother Anne Marie, 190
Jeanne des Anges, Sister, 219, 220
Jesus Crucified, Sisters of, 67
Joan Marie, Sister (Maryknoll Sisters), 198
Joanna, Mother (Deaconess Community of Saint Andrew), 49, 56, 140, 285
John of the Cross, Saint, 23, 40, 42
John XXIII, Pope, 203, 253
Jones, David, 28
Jordan, 189
Jordan of Saxony, Blessed, 117
Joseph, Mother Mary (Vocation Sisters), 61, 62
Joseph, Saint, 22, 84, 209
Joseph, Saint, Sisters of, 156, 159, 190, 301

Reynolds, Sister Pamela, 189–90
Rhodesia, 186, 193
Rogers, Mollie (Sister Mary Joseph), 197
Romania, 198
Rome, ancient, 92, 108
Rooney, Sister Therese, 136
Rosalie, Sister (Carmelites), 20, 31
Rose of Lima, Saint, 226
Rowe, Sister Margaret, 137–38, 307
Royal Foundation of Saint Katharine, 127–30
Rudolf of Fulda, 165
Rulla, Father Luigi, 289
Russell, Sister, 247, 304, 305
Russia, 42, 58, 145, 198–99
Rwanda, 183

Sacred Congregation for Religious and Secular Institutes, 33, 123, 135, 146, 151, 153, 265, 269, 306
Sacred Congregation for the Propagation of the Faith, 181
Sacred Heart, Contemplatives of the, 307
Sacred Heart, Handmaids of the, 278
Sacred Heart, Missionaries of the, 196
Sacred Heart, Society of the, see Society of the Sacred Heart
Sacred Heart of Mary, Sisters of the, 84, 123
Sacred Passion, Sisters of the Community of, 185, 187, 191, 276
Sade, Marquis de, 60
Saint Patrick's Cathedral, 164
Sainte-Baume (France), 310
Sainte Union des Sacrés-Coeurs, La, 79, 83
Saint-Simon, Duc de, 59
Salem witch trials, 219
Salieri, Frantz, 246
San Francisco, 262, 293
Sarpong, Bishop Peter, 188
Scandals in convents, 213, 214, 215, 219, 220
School Sisters of Notre Dame, 146
School Sisters of Saint Francis, 145
Scotland, 217, 223
Seale, Bobby, 163
Second Vatican Council, 22, 65, 67, 87, 133, 135, 139, 144, 148, 149, 151, 162, 194, 226, 232, 250, 253, 270, 275, 306, 311
Sellon, Lydia, 168

Servants of Mary, 309
Sex Life in a Convent, 228
Sexuality: in women, 295; correlation between discipline and, 225
Short History of Monastical Orders, A (d'Emilliane), 218
Silence, rule of, 245, 256
Sister Councils, 139
Sister Formation Conference, 252
Sisters for a Christian Community (SFCC), 307
Small, Frances, 125
Small, Nelson, 125
Society for Promoting Church Knowledge, 181
Society for the Propagation of the Faith, 197
Society for the Propagation of the Gospel in Foreign Parts, 181
Society of Helpers of the Holy Souls, 48, 110, 134, 139
Society of Mary, Missionary Sisters of the, 180
Society of Mary Immaculate, 307
Society of the Holy Child Jesus, 107
Society of the Sacred Heart, 66, 96, 147, 225, 235, 237, 240, 241, 247, 262, 304
Song of Bernadette, The, 227
Sophia (sister of Peter the Great), 58
Sophie (Abbess of Gandersheim), 141
South Africa, 183, 185, 262, 276
South America, 181, 185, 200, 259
Southeast Asia, 181
Spain, 20, 41, 42, 107, 126, 149, 150, 181, 226, 235, 243, 254
Spelthorne Saint Mary (England), 168–72 passim
Spode House (England), 70
Sri Lanka (Ceylon), 181, 188, 203
Stanbrook Abbey, 91, 278
Steinbeck, John, 157, 212
Stock, Sister Mary Simon, 49
Story, Ralph, 228
Suenens, Cardinal, 133, 234, 241, 252, 255, 282, 308
Superior, election of, 249–50
Sweden, 106, 126, 147, 278
Switzerland, 194, 217
Syon, nuns of, 167

Tablet, The, 33
Tanganyika, 191
Tanzania, 187, 192, 203